KIMSEY RISE

A Family of Farmers

Cecilia Johansen

PAGE PUBLISHING, INC.
Conneaut Lake, PA

First originally published by Page Publishing 2020

Cover Artwork by Gray Artus
North Carolina Farmhouse

ISBN 978-1-6624-1237-0 (pbk)
ISBN 978-1-6624-1238-7 (digital)

Printed in the United States of America

To my great-aunt Nellie Fay Kimsey Middleton for her "true and accurate" memories and handwritten genealogy of our family.

We arose from the ashes of our homeland,
and we will arise from whatever will come.
You may go if it is your heart's desire.

—Benjamin Kimsey

Contents

Preface

AUNT NELL, AS we called her, gave to her nephew—my father, Charles Clark Smith—the history of our Kimsey family. Subsequent letters were written to him and my brother, Michael Clark Smith, recalling other stories of the Kimsey family stretching back to Benjamin from 1725—who may or may not have lived in Scotland. I choose to believe he did and am basing my story on that premise. There was some truth in my aunt's words and those of ancestors down through time—over 250 years—but, memories can be faulty, confused, or just plain written down wrong especially with the Scots' habit of giving the same first name to their offspring.

Kimsey Rise: A Family of Farmers is a work of fiction. I wrote the first part of this story after a trip to Scotland with my first husband, Charles Kanewa, in 1986. I caught the fire of the beauty of the country and especially the field of Culloden Moor. Aunt Nell had related that "four MacKenzie brothers had fought in that infamous battle and from there they fled to Lord Baltimore's Colony." When and where they changed their name to Kimsey will always be a mystery; however, the story pleased my father—being rather proud of his Scottish heritage—and he praised my efforts—even if he did not quite believe my hypothesis to be true! I was smitten, and I follow a mere thread of those Kimsey brothers.

Nellie Fay Kimsey was born on January 21, 1885, in Dallas, Oregon. She died on October 27, 1960, in Venice, California. Her sister was Ida Leola Kimsey Smith, my grandmother.

Acknowledgments

THANK YOU TO Charles Clark and Marguerite Ann Smith, my loving parents.

Michael Clark Smith, cherished brother, co-author of our ancestry.com page.

Janelle Smith Ozeran, cherished niece and author of our ancestry.com page.

Waimea Writers Support Group, Kamuela, Big Island, Hawaii.

Waimea Writers Guild, Kamuela, Big Island, Hawaii, without you, my friends, I could not have done it.

Susan Switzer, my dearest friend and editor.

Anthony Melita, Revolution Tours Inc., who gave me extraordinary appreciation of the war.

Buncombe County, North Carolina Genealogy Society.

Tennessee State Library and Archives, Nashville, Tennessee.

Sarah Gilbert of Cordilleran Tours, custom tour of Salem/Dallas, Oregon.

American Cruise Lines, Cumberland River Cruise from St. Louis to Nashville.

Barnwood Builders, White Sulphur Springs, West Virginia, DIY Network, who gave me extraordinary appreciation of log cabins.

A special thank you to Gary Kimsey, a gentleman I met online searching for the Lewis and Clark expedition. Gary Kimsey is a former newspaper reporter, magazine editor and public relations specialist. Retired from the corporate world since 2014, he now writes blog articles and edits literary works written by friends (and as it turned out, he is my fifth cousin once removed).

Nell Kimsey Middleton Oregon 1947

Author's Note

WE SAT IN a living room that was hardly bigger than a postage stamp—not unusual in my purview. Back in the day, my parents' home had one bathroom, and we ate in a kitchen so small that if you wanted something in a drawer, you had to move the table. Early in my life, we lived in a twenty-six-foot trailer, so size had no impact on me.

Nellie Fay Kimsey Brown Middleton lived on Louella Avenue in a small bungalow in Los Angeles, California. She was aunt to my father, Charles Clark Smith. We visited her nearly every Sunday in the mid-1950s when we moved out to the Golden State from Illinois. I was a preteen at the time, and she was a loving old lady with white hair, and it seemed to me that she was always wearing a cotton flower-print house dress. As an adult, my perception changed, however, when I saw a photograph of her in shirt and pants. She was standing with newly chopped wood in her hands.

I liked her house as the floors creaked when you walked on them. In the living room was a built-in china cabinet with all manner of appealing things to a young girl—dishes and knickknacks and collectibles from Nell's seventy-five years on this earth. It was a bright, sunny place with sheer curtains and pull-down shades. There was a small dining room, and the kitchen had a story of its own when in 1933 a magnitude 6.4 earthquake hit south of Long Beach, California, on the Newport-Inglewood fault. It impacted all of Southern California, causing enormous damage and killing over one hundred people. Aunt Nell's four-legged gas stove took a trip across the linoleum floor from one end of the kitchen to the other, and she never stopped talking about it.

Vintage doilies beckoned us toward the same couch or chair on which we sat each Sunday as if they'd had our individual names crocheted into them. I was a bit restless at that age and always had something in my hand to show Aunt Nell, or my mother made sure I had something in my hands so I was "seen and not heard." Cat's cradle string game comes to mind, as do sock puppets.

We came for dinner after twelve noon Mass, and I always remember pot roast or fricasseed chicken and vegetables, and always white bread. Joining us for the meal were Aunt Nell's ex-husband, Mid Middleton, and his love, Ollie. At the time, I did not know how they were related, and it doesn't really matter. They just lived in a small apartment attached behind the house. After our meal, my parents and Aunt Nell retired to the living room, and I was invited to watch television with Mid and Ollie. I sat with them, usually looking at an old Western movie on a circle screen. The picture was so small, you needed to sit fairly close to catch the action of cowboys and Indians racing across the plains from one side of the screen, only to disappear almost instantly on the other.

Before leaving the old house on Louella Avenue in the late afternoon, it was obligatory to stroll in the backyard where Mom and Nell would talk about the flowers and plants in her yard. I delighted in feeding the goldfish in their small pond.

The best fond memory from those visits, however, was listening to the discussion between an aunt and her nephew about "four MacKenzie brothers who fought at the Battle of Culloden Moor in Scotland in 1746 then fled to Lord Baltimore's colony, possibly as indentured servants. Once free, they moved to Bedford County, Virginia." This was her story told proudly to my dad.

When my husband and I took a trip of a lifetime to Scotland, I picked up a spark walking the moor's battleground. It was fanned into flame on paper, and forty-nine pages spilled out from the typewriter in September of 1985. While Dad really liked the story—"You write like Louis L'Amour," he said to me (both of us read all his books)—Dad didn't particularly agree with my imaginings. Research back then consisted of oral ramblings of a grandaunt or your nose stuck in the Library of Congress poring over dusty volumes or three-inch-by-five-inch pencil-written cards at The Church of Jesus Christ of Latter-day Saints Family History Library in Los Angeles. Now everything is available on computer, and I hope he would be proud of my "imaginings" now backed by memories presented in black-and-white of descendants' oral histories based on family bibles. All these are fastened firmly in the ancestors.com industries. There are copies of handwritten census takers, army paymasters keeping track of what was owed to soldiers, journals of survivors from many war campaigns, ledgers of items on a shopkeeper's shelves, records of property deeds and arrest warrants, colonial papers carrying not only news, but also advertisements of slaves for sale—ancestors' words going back to the 1600s in the history of our America.

I write apologies here to any of my Kimsey/Kinsey/Kimzey kin out there who might be offended by my thoughts in this historical novel. They are my thoughts and my novel and not meant to be detrimental. I have researched as best I can and find there are many wonderful stories about our family, and I appreciate all of them as sincere.

View of Culloden Moor looking north to Inverness left center and the Moray Firth on the right where the battle took place April 16, 1746. (Photo by author)

Introduction

AN OSPREY SOARED through the breathtaking air of the golden Scottish Highlands. With every flap of its six-foot wingspan, it climbed higher and higher then veered sharply downward, seeking its prey. The long stretch of the Loch Ness, sparkling in the deep fracture of the earth, threaded its way beneath him and spewed into the Moray Firth alongside the banks of human-inhabited Inverness. A dip of a feathered wing brought the raptor low over the water, talons extended. Hunting, his black eyes did not take in the ancient Caledonian forest or the Cairngorm Mountains off to the south, nor the MacKenzie highlands jutting northward. Food to feed its fledglings was his only business, and nothing could distract him. Suddenly, screeching whistling booms disturbed the air currents and startled the large bird. Smoke from the moor below filled his nostrils, parched his throat, and clouded his eyes, blocking the sight of the large fish breaking the surface. The Atlantic salmon dove away from its hunter, and the osprey screamed in terror, frantically flapping his wings before his feathers were scorched.

Prologue

There need be no lasting sorrow for the death of any of Nature's creation, because for every death there is always born a corresponding life. And what life shall follow the death of the glacier, what creation shall come to that sea bottom on whose cold burnished rocks not a moss of dulse ever grew! In smooth hollows crystal lakes will live, to sandy beds sedges will come. Pines and firs will feather the moraines, advancing like an army and followed by the dearest flowers and happy animals, and instead of a robe of white ice will be a robe of yellow light upon the new Edens...

—John Muir[1]

AT TEN O'CLOCK, broadswords and dirks bristled for a surprise night attack at Nairn on the camp of William Augustus, Duke of Cumberland. As two columns of Scots left the field at Inverness and advanced in the darkness, Prince Charles's line got lost over the fog-covered ground and turned back, leaving confusion for the

---

[1] John of the Mountains, The Unpublished Journals of John Muir, Edited by Linnie Marsh Wolfe p. 168.

remaining Highlanders. The twelve-mile march was aborted and doomed the Scots. The air had been let out of the pipes' skin bags, the rush of excitement collapsed.

By dawn's light on April 16, 1746, sweet clear music of the moor disguised the purpose for which the field would be used on that day. The rising sun stirred insects' chirrup, birds' song, and a brisk wind brushing over the heather's bloom, all going about the business of life without thought of the devastation that would dispel them. Sounds tuned to ears which heard them, fragrances familiar to the Scots who sniffed them revealed themselves to men waiting, waiting in clusters for orders to battle promised for the life or death of men and ideals. Hanoverian King George II was enthroned, occupying the seat that rightfully belonged to the Stuarts. The murderous horde of William Augustus was late, sleeping off the effects that rum played on their spirits celebrating the twenty-fifth birthday of Prince William, King George's third son.

The day lingered, and another sound mingled with what nature had to offer—the growling of empty bellies. Time went on, and the sounds of grumbling mixed with an urgent wind and driving rain propelled many to abandon the field that lacked sustenance. If they were fighting, then the fatigue, the hunger, the anger would be alleviated by the exhilaration of battle.

Benjamin MacKenzie and his two brothers moved off to find a sheltered spot, but only a low uncomfortable gray stone wall was available to rest their backs. A long time ago, wee bairns played around and climbed on this wall running along the boundary of Leanach's farm. The Scot wondered where the children had gone. The brothers talked in low tones, always vigilant for the call to stand and fight.

A man sat beside them. His clan[2] had left the field, he said, opening a knapsack. The aroma of bread escaped the overstuffed bag. He broke the bread and shared it, then sliced into a block of cheese—

---

[2] Clan: a Celtic group especially in the Scottish Highlands comprising a number of households whose heads claim descent from a common ancestor. A group of people tracing descent from a common ancestor (https://www.merriam-webster.com/dictionary/clan).

grand sweet milk cheese—and proffered some to the brothers on the edge of his knife. Their mouths watered.

"I'm Hugh Mercer," he said with his mouth full and sharing the last remaining morsels with others gathering around.

Between bites, Benjamin thrust his hand toward the newcomer. "I'm Benjamin MacKenzie, and these are my brothers Alexander and Charles," he said, nodding toward each.

Hugh understood why they didn't speak. Smiling eyes were all that were needed to present themselves and be grateful. The boys left to get water.

Benjamin swallowed the wonderful repast, and when clear of his throat, he said, "Thank you, my friend…Where are you from?"

"Aberdeenshire." Hugh coughed with a bit of cheese caught in his throat.

"Are you related to the esteemed Reverend William Mercer of the same shire?"

He nodded.

Hugh Mercer was a handsome lad about Benjamin's age, with curling hair cascading over his forehead and ears. His Highland garb was dirty, and the leather sporran[3] was stained with spattered blood. A white rose cockade on his bonnet was smudged, and his boot soles were worn thin. He said he fought with the prince at Falkirk in January. "We won the battle even though we were outnumbered, but Stirling Castle, still held by the English, turned out to be an impregnable fortress. We retreated in defeat which led to what will happen here today," he said sadly, letting his watery gaze travel the open moor. "We could not regain our beloved Scotland."

Benjamin spoke, "My father told us stories of the battle. Maybe you knew him—Robert MacKenzie? But today he refused to follow our clan chief's command." His eyes blazed with defiance, and the telltale vein popped out on his forehead. "But I…I love my country too much to let the English be unchallenged." He then quickly

---

[3] Sporran: a pouch usually of skin with the hair or fur on that is worn in front of the kilt with Scots Highland dress (https://www.merriam-webster.com/dictionary/sporran).

changed the subject to prevent his own tears from overflowing. "I heard your father speak at Ord Muir in '35 when I was but a wee bairn. Mother said my father's soul was saved on that day. Reverend Mercer was surely a great and powerful speaker."

"That he was. He wanted me to continue the tradition, but I chose medicine. I'm an assistant surgeon with Prince Charles's army."

Lively conversation ensued until midday when a budding friendship was cut short by the great man himself. Prince Charles Edward Stuart rode before the men gathering them like a magnet. The Redcoats marched to the field of battle in strengths far outnumbering the mighty clans. Rows of arrogant scarlet stretched before the already beleaguered Jacobites[4] whose plaids were dirty and wet but worn proudly with great flourish. They brandished weapons and targes[5] toward the enemy as their chiefly prince stood before Scotland's finest men, all ready for the first volley.

---

[4] Jacobite: a partisan of James II of England or of the Stuarts after the revolution of 1688; from Jacobus, the Latin form of James (https://www.merriam-webster.com/dictionary/Jacobite).

[5] Targe: a light shield used especially by the Scots (https://www.merriam-webster.com/dictionary/targe).

Chapter 1

End of the Battle

April 16, 1746

BENJAMIN MACKENZIE LAY wounded and unconscious on the bloody field of battle. The smell of death awoke the twenty-one-year-old, and his thoughts began converging. Why was he so cold? Was he dead? Move something—the little finger. Yes, it moved. His eyes flickered open. Was he blind? It was dark as pitch. He tried to focus. He wasn't blind. An ominous curtain of clouds hanging low in the sky and red as the fires on the moor occasionally parted.

Ah, he could see stars.

He began to move his stiff body but cried out in pain, remembering the grapeshot exploding into his leg. Moving laboriously, he finally pulled himself to a sitting position with his back against a wall—the wall which enclosed the farm of Leanach. He closed his eyes.

It had been cold in those predawn hours on Drumossie Moor[6] waiting for the battle to begin. Fear and hunger gnawed at the clansmen awaiting the arrival of the royal one. No food, no sleep, and too

---

[6] Drumossie Muir (Moor) covers a huge area which includes the site of the Battle of Culloden in 1746 (https://www.theguardian.com/environment/2011/dec/28/country-diary-drummossie-muir).

many battles with failed outcomes had caused mental and physical exhaustion. Benjamin thought this was their last chance.

All their pain and frustration had been swept away as the prince paraded before his Highlanders. He made a gallant appearance on that fine gray gelding in his tartan coat and blue bonnet with its white ribbon rose as a cockade, the sign of a Jacobite. His majestic figure inspired his loyal subjects also sporting the same decoration upon their heads. The only thing left for his men to give, however, was their deep Scottish pride as the Highlanders awaited orders that would lead them to battle. But still it was delayed until midday when their loosely arranged regiments wearing well-worn tartans were starkly contrasted to the straight, efficient lines of English Redcoats stretched before them. The fight against Hanoverian rule would end here on this field, the Scots firmly believed.

Images of the battle flooded Benjamin's mind. A strong wind had carried smoke and rain across marshy Drumossie Moor into the faces of the Highlanders. Cannon were heard for miles, their deadly balls of lead exploding into the heather-covered moor and carving large chunks out of the Highlanders' lines.

Benjamin was in the front line together with his brothers seventeen-year-old Alexander and fifteen-year-old Charles. They were fighting shoulder to shoulder with Rosses, MacLeods, MacLeans, and other clans. Some stayed out of it or fought with the English. Clan loyalties were divided despite the prince's personal appeal to the chiefs for men and arms. Four thousand Jacobites were dispatched to face nine thousand of King George's finest elite soldiers. The specter of the Redcoat lines drove fear into the Jacobites' hearts.

The Highlanders' lines were shattered by a volley of cannonball, and Benjamin saw many of his clan go down. Those who charged ahead stepped over bodies and into puddles of blood. They were fighting to the death to get the prince on the throne of Scotland, so they hacked with their swords and fought with their dirks. Wave upon wave washed the moor with blood, smoke, and whistling lead. The Highlanders' hide-covered targes were scant protection from ball and shot.

Out of the corner of his eye, Benjamin had seen a friend-turned-enemy—a clan Campbell man—slice into Charles's face. But he had no time for the concern welling up inside as another Campbell lunged at him. Benjamin's sword found its mark with the sickening sound of the blade snapping off. He grabbed his dirk, and suddenly three pairs of arms were all over him. He slashed at the man on his right and knew it rang true. Just as quickly, he thrust the blade deep into the midsection of the next. Then Benjamin twisted his targe in time to deflect another, but the heavy claymore of an enemy clansman hit broadside, slid off, and gave him a glancing blow on his shoulder, forcing him to his knees. An orphaned great sword lay in the mud, and he quickly grabbed it, switching his dirk to his left hand. Another enemy lay at his feet. A way was finally cleared in front of him, and he caught a glimpse of his brother. Undaunted by blood flowing from a four-inch cut along his left cheek and soaking his shirt, Charles was absorbed in fighting for his life. The feeling of pride in his brother was short-lived, however, when Benjamin himself was hit. As he went down in the slop of the field, he saw dead Redcoats in a pile beneath his brother's feet, and Hugh Mercer falling under the heels of the enemy. That was the last thing Benjamin remembered as he crumpled on the cold earth soaked with rain and fluids from his kinsmen, and the battle passing over him.

* * *

In the dark, propped against that same uncomfortable Leanach's wall, Benjamin heard no sounds of battle, but instead, there was moaning, crying, and angry voices on the moor. His eyes and nose stung with blood stench, gunpowder, and lead-infused dank earth, and burning thatch. Was the battle over? Who had won? Where were his brothers? He tried to straighten himself, but pain shot up his leg, and he stifled a scream as those angry voices were coming closer to him.

He tried to raise himself to see and recoiled in horror. Highlanders who were down on the field, but obviously alive, were given no quarter and shrieked as they were butchered, and the shouting, torch-carrying men were coming toward him! Frozen with fear and pain, he could not get away, and his very short twenty-one years played out before him. Tears accompanied his contrition. *Lord, forgive me.*

An English officer screamed orders, "Clear that damnable debris out of the path of those cannons." That 'debris' was bodies.

Death hovered above him as a hated English soldier's bayonet was poised for the kill.

Their eyes met. *Wait! I know this boy.* "Billy, what are you doing? We were friends once…" Benjamin thought he saw a fleeting look of compassion.

An officer yelled, "Argyll, get it over with!"

Furtively, Billy looked around and said, "I'm sorry, Ben. I don't want to kill you."

Benjamin threw his arms up protecting himself from the raised weapon. The tactical killing bayonet pierced his thick tartan fabric and woolen coat and sliced into his ribs. Ben's body could take no more, and blessed unconsciousness relieved him of all pain.

A cohort of uniformed men tossed bodies onto a peat cart and dumped them in a heap next to Benjamin by a wall—the wall by Leanach's farm.

* * *

Out of the darkness, Benjamin heard rustling sounds and a muffled voice saying, "It's no use…We've searched for hours. They must have dragged him off with the others. Oh, God, don't let him be at the bottom of the—"

"Ssh! Just keep calling softly. I won't give up…Benjamin, where are you?"

"Alex? Charles? It's me."

A hoarse whisper answered, "Where?"

"The other side of the wall."

The two boys slithered down to a break in the rocks and crawled around the mountain of bodies.

"Are you hurt?" Alex asked.

"Grapeshot broke my ankle."

"Give me your dirk."

Alex jammed a rag in his brother's mouth. "We won't be able to walk him out. Find something, Charles."

Benjamin recoiled in agony and bit the rag hard when Alex straightened out his foot and then wrapped the lower portion of his leg between the two dirks for a splint. With pride, the three boys carried those dirks, made by their father, with the hide-covered grip emblazoned with the MacKenzie clan crest.

Ignoring the pain, he blurted out, "Where have you been? What happened with the battle? What about the prince?"

Alex was sharp. "Looking for you. The battle was lost, taking all of an hour. The prince escaped and stop asking so many questions."

"What are you two doing with those red coats?" He shifted his weight and winced in pain.

"We got 'em off some bodies. They'll think we're English soldiers." Charles seemed to be enjoying himself but suddenly got very serious. "The Hanoverians are stationed all around the moor, but we have a plan to get you and us out of here. Now shut up!"

They put Benjamin on the peat cart, placed a red coat over him, and covered him with a length of dark wool Charles had plucked out of the heap of dead bodies.

"The guards will think you're English too... Isn't this fun?"

"Eejit!" Benjamin mumbled. "You think this is great sport, Charles?"

Alex whispered to them, "Be quiet! Hold your breath, Ben. We don't want to come this far and have you executed."

"Me?" Benjamin shot an annoyed glance at both of them.

Suddenly, the trio realized they could just see one another's faces illuminated by the dull red glow of the fires reflected on overhanging clouds and revealing the ghostly battlefield.

"Oh no! Come on, let's get this over with."

A small wood fire loomed in front of them, and a harsh command sent shivers up their spines. "Halt! Who is there?"

Two soldiers, who had been warming their hands, suddenly pointed their muskets at the intruders. Firelight glinted off brass buttons and red of the coats, but the men looked like headless bodies standing above the small fire. Alex grabbed the handles of the cart and pushed forward past the firelight to keep Benjamin's face hidden. The Highlanders saluted the officers.

Garish shadows crossed the landscape, the clouds pushed away by stiff breezes, and it was incredibly dark. Benjamin had lowered his chin to his chest and decided to trust in his brothers' plans.

The second soldier relaxed his aim. "They're some of ours. What are you doing here this late? All those damned Jacobites are dead."

In his mind, Alex had been rehearsing what to say, but his anger at that stinking Redcoat's statement changed to panic when he heard Charles's voice.

By some lucky happenstance, Charles had just reached into the pocket of his coat, and his fingers hit upon a folded bit of parchment. With all the swagger he could muster and swallowing his Scot's burr, he said, "We've orders to remove this man's body from the battlefield."

"Really now...And who gave those orders?"

"The Duke of Cumberland himself." He thrust the piece of paper at the man.

Of course, he was counting on the darkness to help them. Alex held his breath, and Benjamin could not believe his brother's audacity.

The soldier tipped the paper this way and that trying to read the scrawled words upon it when suddenly sparks exploded from the fire, startling the English officers. Spooked on that wretched moor, the man returned the paper to Alex and said, "Well...who is...who is this important officer?"

He began to circle the cart, and Benjamin was about to burst holding his breath.

"He's the duke's cousin, and the duke wants to give him a proper burial."

The soldier began jabbing at and lifting up the blanket from the "dead man's" chest, revealing a little of the red coat, and a brass button that caught the fire's glow. The covering began slipping off Benjamin's legs, and the glint from the dirks caught Alex's eye. He bent over quickly to cover the area.

"His lower legs have been blown away," he said.

The soldier gagged in horror. "Very well! Get out of here!"

Alex pushed the cart as hard as he could, and at a distance, Benjamin finally took in a deep breath. "That was close. What were you doing back there? That paper could have been a love letter, for all you know. You could have had us killed."

"Could have but didn't. Let's not think about that now." Charles pleaded, "I want to go home."

Benjamin warned them, "We'd better go by the fields. The Redcoats are bound to be on the road to Inverness."

The three brothers rattled and bumped along and got stuck a few times in the mud. Fear grew as they saw patrolling infantry running through the fields with torches burning everything in their wake. An awful wailing floated across the land like the old sod itself was crying, and tears came to their own eyes. They hid behind peat stacks and hillocks to give them shelter lest they get caught and shot on the spot. The boys pressed forward to their family.

* * *

Some outbuildings were scattered around their father's farm, and baled hay was stacked close to the byre.[7] As they approached the heather-thatched cottage, all was dark and quiet, and they were surprised to see it not a burned-out hovel. Dawn parted the earth from the sky under heavy clouds and began to lighten the North Sea and the low hills.

"Hurry," Charles pleaded.

"Aye, laddie," and each brother grabbed an arm, gently lifting Benjamin off the cart. Unable to support himself, he tried hobbling on his one good ankle.

Leaving his brother hanging on Charles, Alex peered around the corner of the house. The door was broken in, cocked unsteadily on one leather hinge. Quietly he crept toward the gaping hole, not daring to breathe. Nothing moved and all was silent. He motioned

---

[7]   Byre: a barn.

for his brothers to follow. A cock crowed somewhere in the wild landscape announcing the dawn and startled Alex, putting him on alert. He stepped into a jumbled mess onto the cottage's earthen floor and on top of something which snapped beneath his foot—a wooden toy.

"Put him on the bed." Alex told Charles.

"Where's the family?" Benjamin asked. Adrenaline from the long day was replaced with nausea from exhaustion, lack of food, and loss of blood.

"He's heavy," Charles complained, bearing the weight of Benjamin alone. Alex swiftly closed the door by putting the heavy latch in its place to keep the door upright in the frame. Pushing debris off the cot in the semidarkness, the pair eased Benjamin down.

"We need light if you're to tend to his injuries." The boy-turned-man today on that battlefield shuttered the windows and retrieved a piece of kindling from the woodbox to coax a flame from a small still-glowing ember in the fireplace. Charles lit a candle.

For the first time, Alex noticed Charles's face. "And yours as well. That cut is nasty."

Charles still looked like a child with tangled black ringlets sticking to his sweaty face. Scotland's blush was always about him. His ruddy cheeks bloomed in the cold air, especially when a sweet lass looked his way. He was a man as far as fighting for the sod they loved, but despite his looks and the thin brush of a mustache under his nose and whiskers sprouting along his square jaw, he was still his mother's boy. She doted on him.

To Benjamin's amazement, Charles moved to the table, bent down, and gently knocked on the dirt floor. For a breathless moment, silence, then a return knock. Charles flashed a smile to his brothers then tipped the table. A hatch in the floor nailed to the four legs was one of their father's inventions during their troubling times.

"When did you do that, Charles?" Benjamin asked mystified.

"Father did it after you and Aggie moved out. Comes in handy for safety's sake."

Jamie popped out of the floor like a cork out of a bottle squealing at the top of his lungs and rushed to Charles's arms. The six-year-old redhead, with a swath of freckles across his nose, was swept into the air laughing in delight. Behind him were their mother, Mary, and on her heels, Agnes, Benjamin's wife carrying their wee bairn.

"Mother, Aggie, look who's here!" In the light of the small flame, hugs went around, and tears washed the faces of the little family.

"Alex, Charles, I'm so glad you're safe…and Benjamin?" Mary was ecstatic and smothered them all with motherly affection at her ample bosom.

Agnes was close behind her mother-in-law. "Ben, what happened?" she said, worry lines furrowing her face. But she didn't give him time to respond and began barking orders. "Charles, bring that lamp here, and, Alex, cut away those torn hose."

Finally, Alex pleaded, "Could someone get us more light over here? Jamie, get me some water, okay. There's a good lad."

Aggie, as she was affectionately called by her new family, put three-month-old Ian in the small cradle beside the cot, then seated herself so Benjamin's head was resting in her lap. She bent over her husband and kissed his smudged forehead.

Charles lit another lantern, and Jamie dutifully brought the basin of water, sloshing it about as Mary searched a smashed chest for cloths to bind her son's wounds. Now in better light, they could see the extent of the injuries and, for the first time, the bloodstain on his side as Aggie unbuttoned her husband's waistcoat and shirt. She shuddered when she saw the wound.

Benjamin reached back and took her hand. "It's not as bad as it looks."

He told her about Billy Argyll actually saving his hide albeit nipping it. As he talked, he realized at the end of the story that two of their family members were missing.

He sat up, the motion causing a swimming in his head. "Where are Father and Duncan?"

Both women and even Jamie, who clung to his mother's skirts, began to cry.

"He's dead, son, and Duncan too," she told him softly through her tears, her head hung in despair.

The three young men who went through hell on the Culloden battlefield realized their brave women at home had suffered, too, at the hands of the English.

Benjamin, the eldest son, usually reserved like his father, with stinging anger demanded answers. "Why…Why? What happened?"

Mary collapsed in her chair and quietly recounted the story. "Robert was dispirited by the prince's retreat from Falkirk and failure to reclaim the castle. Like others of our neighbors, he was tired and had had enough of the fighting. Most of the farmers around Inverness, including your father, went on with their ploughing as usual. Some people from town even went as spectators to see the battle until the cannon roared. Most thought it a waste of time. While your father was proud of you, he would not heed the rallying cry for more Highlanders to support the cause. More fighting would not get them anywhere and would only bring hardship and despair."

Mary wiped her face with her handkerchief and, with rising anger, pounded the table with her fist. "He was murdered by the damnable Redcoats in the fields he loved. They shot Duncan, too, and thought him dead, but somehow he managed to crawl back here. Hiding with us in the cellar, he died in my arms…" She sobbed and clenched the table for support. Aggie came to her side to comfort her.

Only Ian's whimpering disquieted their grief.

Anger and rage for the wastefulness of it all exhausted Benjamin's spirit. Men fought for a purpose yesterday but died in vain! His little brother and father died in vain!

Sick at heart, he placed his hands over his eyes to shut out the horrible scene of his stricken family. But as his thoughts came into sharper focus, and his calculating mind began to work, Benjamin realized he was now head of the family. For today they would grieve the loss of husband, father, brother, and their beloved country, but he must pull his household together to strengthen them for what was to come. English patrols were already scouring the surrounds, tightening their stranglehold. He knew they would kill outright anyone who got in their way, or capture, arrest, and hang the Jacobites as examples to their countrymen. More severe, however, was banishment to the colonies which was worse than death. The MacKenzies were not safe, for they were too close to the field of battle and the town of Inverness; they must get away somehow tonight. Yes, tonight!

The warmth of his family surrounding him relaxed Benjamin's stiff, cold, and very tired body, and much-needed sleep came at last. Aggie realized her husband's body had gone limp and was about to cry out, but Charles's finger to his lips warned her to be quiet. They smiled at each other, then she slipped Benjamin's head off her lap and covered him with a blanket. Tiny Ian continued to fuss, so she picked him up and went to another corner of the room to nurse him.

Alex dozed in a rocking chair, and Charles, with a noticeable sigh, began to clean up the mess about him. His brother's injuries weren't desperate, but that ankle would need support from a crutch. He also realized the whole family needed to stay hidden and be on guard.

Shaking Alex awake and motioning for him to follow, Charles picked up Jamie. He looked into his little brother's serious brown eyes and told him to be very quiet. Then handing him back to his mother, he told Mary and Aggie, "Keep the cottage shuttered and no fire." They nodded, and the boys closed the door behind them. Aggie secured it with the latch.

The cottage was L-shaped with a main cooking/living area and a small bedroom for their parents. Open curved timbers, where birds sometimes perched, supported the roof, and the brothers slept in the loft. Projecting from their modest home was a low rock wall with rowan trees growing all around blocking the winds that came up from Moray Firth. The gray-green leaves shivered, shaking off drops of morning dew. Their buds of small white flowers were beginning to open, but the clumps of summertime red berries were yet to appear.

The boys skirted low along the rough stones to the end of the cottage. Nothing stirred except that same cock crowing nearby, and the pair, ever watchful, quickly crawled through the gate and across the yard to the byre. With the rising sun, smoke from smoldering heather-thatched rubblestone cottages mixed with ground fog covering rain-slick grasses. Black spirals from the battlefield and all the way down to the town of Inverness twisted eerily. The boys caught their breath at the sight, shivering with superstitious fear as they entered the byre.

The animals were gone, stolen by the enemy, and the gloom of the byre was relieved only by a ray of sunlight streaming through a crevice in the thatch. It illumined thousands of particles of dust raised by the brothers' footfalls in the loose straw of the byre. Evidence of their father was everywhere, for Robert spent much time there with the animals and at his small workbench. Not only had he been a farmer, but a first-rate carpenter as well. He lovingly made all of the family's furniture, and his last project had been a cradle for his first grandson. Now the boys could barely contain their tears as they fashioned a solid crutch for Benjamin. Each had his own thoughts about the father who so recently was taken from them and to whom they had not said goodbye. In all ways, the men of the family were like their father: reserved and quiet, strong and proud.

Robert, a big bear of a man, weighed easily fifteen stone.[8] His black hair, salted with gray, spread out over his broad shoulders and tossed about his face by the wind from the Firth. When it grew too long, Mary would come after him laughing, with the sheep shears in her hand, but he protested loudly. "No, woman! You will not shear my locks. Why, I'd…I'd lose my manhood just like Samson shorn by Delilah."

The sleeves of his linsey-woolsey shirt were always rolled up, displaying great hard muscles acquired through years of hard labor. He wore a waistcoat of wool to keep Scotland's chill from his chest. A MacKenzie hunting kilt, in muted blues and greens, filthy with wear, was held in place by a wide belt of leather. If the boys got into mischief, the belt would come off and his kilt would drop, leaving only the long loose shirt to cover his loins. The thought of the belt could sting, but the laughter following the dropped tartan eased a tense moment of discipline. Each boy was held aloft and scolded through the wide smile on their father's handsome face. "Do not do that again," he would say, "or the belt will chase you all the way

---

[8] One stone equals fourteen pounds.

to Inverness." His dry humor reminded them that they were Scots through and through.

Completing the crutch, Alex turned to leave, but Charles stopped him. "Let us gather together whatever we can, just in case."

He found a grain sack and began placing things inside: some of his father's tools, ropes, and the last of the crop of root vegetables—potatoes and turnips. Alex saw their father's coat hanging on a nail and snatched that too. He briefly held it to his nose, breathing in the scent of the man. With as much care as they had come, the brothers left the byre and returned to the cottage without seeing anyone.

Except for Benjamin's loud snoring, all was quiet. Charles and Alex looked at each other then at Aggie playing with Ian. "How do you put up with that?" they both asked in unison.

She laughed. "Wool balls."

The tension broke a little, and they gazed admiringly at Aggie. She was beautiful at eighteen. Born in Wales, she was petite and well-rounded. Benjamin met her on one of his merchant trips to Ireland, and as the brothers settled in for some much-needed rest and food, the pleasant story was vivid in their minds.

* * *

Benjamin had always been interested in the ships that came into the Moray Firth, and as a young lad, he preferred spending time at the waterfront rather than helping his tenant-farmer father or learning scripture at his mother's side. He was hired by a nineteen-year-old Irish merchant skipper named Paddy O'Sullivan to discharge salt that he brought from Ireland. The two became good friends, and eventually, Benjamin learned the merchant trade. They became partners, and their ship was called the *Eileen O'Rourke*, named for Paddy's onetime sweetheart. Benjamin, also nineteen, was much admired for his shrewd business sense and his fairness. A dry sense of humor also endeared him to everyone. The two merchants, with their hired crew, made many a run between the isles, and their reputation preceded them.

Their little ship hauled into Dublin one night with a load of fish and wool. As the crew began unloading, Paddy said to Benjamin, "Instead of a tavern, why don't we go up to me brother's place. There is someone he wants you to meet."

"Aye, Paddy."

James Francis O'Sullivan lived only a short distance, or so Paddy said, but that short distance was above the squalidness of the dockside and a good half-hour walk. The fog was thick and blew against their frames in icy damp waves, and even Benjamin's yards of tartan plaid could not keep out the cold. Arriving at James Francis's door, both men were chilled to the bone. As if by some flying ghost that preceded them, the heavy wooden door flew open before either laid a hand on it, and a wealth of light and warmth played upon their tired wet bodies.

"Good evening. We've been expecting you," bellowed the large voice coming from an even larger body. "Enter my home and warm yourselves."

The two men stepped across the threshold into a room obviously made especially for this man. Everything about it was massive, including the boulder fireplace. Benjamin could only imagine something comparable in a laird's castle in Scotland. Despite its enormous size, the room showed a woman's soft touch with small pots of wildflowers and lace doilies. Benjamin could only stare in disbelief until Paddy shook him from his trance.

"Stand in front of the fire and dry yourselves," James Francis commanded as he disappeared into another room. He returned uncorking a bottle, and amber liquid filled three crystal glasses. The men each took a swallow, and when O'Sullivan's rich timbre was thick with Irish whiskey, he said, "I liked you ever since Paddy first told me about you, Benjamin, and I knew the two of you would be good together." He emptied his glass.

Benjamin had just taken a sip, and while it was velvet smooth passing his tongue, halfway down his throat, it had the kick of a Scottish dray horse. He coughed. "Thank you, sir."

James Francis's laugh roared through the room. "Now, young man," he said, wiping his eyes, "let's get to the point. I'm a man who doesn't like to beat the piper. I have a few ships doing the same things as Paddy, not only between these tight little islands but the continent as well, trading salt for wool and fine wines. There is a place across the sea, however, of untold wealth, waiting for a bigger fleet of ships—Lord Baltimore's Province, and those Crown colonies of New York and Massachusetts. I realize they're small now, but I have a vision."

He became very excited as he continued, "In two months' time, I shall make the voyage myself across the Atlantic to see this place with me own eyes, and…I want you and Paddy with me in the venture!"

His eyes were shining, and instead of a big Irishman, he looked like a small boy ready to set out on a great adventure. Benjamin sat speechless. The dream of his life was to sail the wide seas, and now this. Was it real?

Paddy asked, interrupting his friend's thoughts, "Well, Benjamin, has me brother put the venture to you?"

"Yes," he said stammering. "I…I don't know how to reply, Paddy. This needs to be discussed. What say you?"

Paddy opened his mouth to speak and was left gaping by a rustle of skirts and a shy "Excuse me, gentlemen, but dinner is served."

A diminutive beauty stood before them, ablaze in a ruby red dress with a low-cut bodice covered with a white silk handkerchief. The sight of her caught Benjamin's breath. Her coal-black hair was tied up with ribbon and curled seductively over her bosom.

"Ah, my dear little Aggie," James Francis said as he stepped forward and kissed her cheek. "Come meet me family." Paddy grabbed Benjamin's arm and physically brought him to his feet.

From behind Aggie peeked two little red-haired waifs with elfish grins.

The big man held out his arms. "Come, children, come, come, come." In one sweep, they were whisked into the air and buried in his curly red beard. "Have you been minding Aggie in all that is good?"

They squirmed and wiggled until James Francis put them down, and both ran as fast as their short legs would carry them, hollering, "Uncle Paddy, Uncle Paddy!" Bending over, Paddy hugged and kissed each one, and then turned to Benjamin. "May I introduce

Master Breandan and Mistress Danielle," he said through a broad grin.

The children's faces with the bright sweet blush of the warm fire-heated room were suddenly timid as Benjamin shook each little chubby hand and the children vanished behind that ruby red skirt.

"And this is Agnes Lane, the children's governess." She stepped forward and extended her hand. Benjamin delicately kissed it then looked into the most beautiful green eyes he'd ever seen, as deep green as Scotland's Caledonian pines. Her beauty made him dizzy. At that moment, Benjamin lost his heart to the sixteen-year-old orphan girl who came to work for the big generous widower and his two motherless children. He and Aggie were married in April of 1744, and the partners of The Isles Trading Company went about their business despite the turmoil of complicated politics, religious upheaval, and day-to-day danger.

Chapter 2

The Escape

April 17, 1746

"HE'S GOING TO be hungry when he wakes up," Charles mumbled with a mouthful of oatcake.

"Aye, brother. I am famished." Benjamin came out of his deep sleep, glad to see the family gathered together.

Aggie helped him sit up. Even in his pain, her husband devoured cold golden brown oatcakes spread liberally with the last of the sweet yellow butter and drank the last of the milk squeezed from the teats of the West Highland Kyloe.

He learned the news as he ate: their shaggy-haired cows had been stolen by the Redcoats. Robert bought them at the market when he and Mary were first married in Ord Muir not far from his MacKenzie ancestral burial grounds in Beauly Priory. The couple lived along the banks of the River Beauly in the early years.

"We'll have to leave here, you know," Aggie said bluntly, her words stunning them to silence.

Alex hesitated, "Yes...I agree...and I have a plan."

More silence as they waited for him to continue. "We must collect father's body and give him and little Duncan proper burial. We'll do it tonight when there is no chance of being seen. Then Charles and I will go down to Inverness to find out what's going on. I think we can already guess part of it, but—"

"That talk frightens me," Mary interrupted. "I don't like it at all."

"Mother," Benjamin said, swallowing his last bite of oatcake, "we're all frightened, but maybe it's not as bad as it seems." Although he really didn't believe what he said, Mary was calmed by his words.

The day-long wait weighed heavily on the family. Each was worried the Redcoats would show up at their door any moment and finish the destruction of their home—and themselves. Benjamin, exasperated with doing nothing, stood and almost fell from dizziness. Shaking it off, he picked up his crutch and practiced on it, hobbling in circles around the small room to the delight of Jamie who wanted to ride it. Mostly they slept, ate, and each packed their meager belongings in an old poke—a simple bag gathered up with rope. Mary took Robert's pipe, a dried thistle sealed in a locket he gave her for their wedding, a hand-painted fan of a Scottish garden inherited from her mother, and bits of medicinal herbs. Jamie had his little carved wooden toys from his father, and his brothers their dirks, and Robert's few tools and the root vegetables.

A hazy sun finally set over a weary land, but no one wanted to venture outside as acrid smoke hung in the still spring air. Blessed night with its blanket of clouds finally arrived, and the two boys prepared to depart.

The candle on the table was extinguished, and Benjamin spoke to his brothers. "Let me go out with you." The door was closed behind them, and he shivered. "I can feel the danger in the air tonight."

"Don't worry about us," Alex said nonchalantly. "We'll be all right."

"I wish I could go with you…Now for some older brother advice. Stay away from the roads, keep low, then go straight to Inverness. Keep your ears and eyes open and talk to no one. No one must know about us. When you've found out all you can, come back and we'll be off to our freedom from the evil that has settled on our beloved Scotland."

"Sermon finished?" asked Charles jokingly. "You were always wordy."

"Listen now, you had better leave, but please be careful. As I said, the night is full of peril with the enemy all around. We wait with endurance for your return. Godspeed!" And he hugged them and slipped back into the darkened house.

Quickly Alex and Charles dug a single grave in the muddy earth, and buried the wrapped bodies of father and son into it. No mark, no cross was placed upon it, just a quick prayer accompanied by their tears. The boys began their grisly journey.

The distance by road to Inverness was not great, but the twists and turns of skirting smoldering cottages and avoiding debris—including bodies of men and beasts—made the time to town almost intolerable. Heavy rain-filled clouds hung over the moor and glowed blood red from fires still burning in distant settlements. Shouts of enemy victors grated on their nerves, and cries from wounded men and wailing women caused fear and abraded their purpose. Frequently, they plunged facedown into the mud or behind whatever protection they could find to avoid being seen by predatory bands of English Redcoats.

Arriving at the outskirts of Inverness, Charles and Alex were relieved not to be detected—but as they carefully picked their way down a small alley, they heard voices. Melting into the frame of a doorway, the brothers waited breathlessly with fearful dread.

The voices came closer, and two men stepped around the corner of the building and into the shadows. "Aye, the English are a murdering bunch. They've even been killing those not involved in the battle, including women and children." The other said, "It's not safe to be caught out in our plaids. My own brother is shackled in an English prison boat." Their anguished voices faded as the men hurried away, and Charles and Alex breathed again. But a pungent mix of excrement and cooking smells accosted their nostrils.

Glad to leave the disagreeable stench of the alleyway behind them, the brothers threaded their way through the seemingly deserted town and concealed themselves at every turn and hiding at any noise. As they came closer to the Firth, they savored the odor of the North

Sea and heard the lap of wavelets on the small pebble beach and the creak of wooden boats at the wharf. A candlelit lantern swayed in the distance throwing strange shadows on a ship's naked masts and spars. The ship looked ghostly and gaunt, and silently the boys went to investigate. They hid behind stacks of trade goods ready for loading as they slowly approached that entrancing light.

Their spirits rose when they saw it was the *Eileen O'Rourke*, the ship belonging to Benjamin and Paddy. Checking the surroundings, they moved unobserved up the plank, but Charles stopped short with Alex nearly stepping on his heels. They could hear muffled sounds when they got closer to the roundhouse. It was Paddy talking to one of the seamen. Alex motioned to Charles, and the two slipped into the room to the astonishment of the captain.

"Boys, what in the name of Saint Columba[9] are you doing here? Where's Benjamin?" asked Paddy, very much alarmed.

"Our family is in dire straits. We need to get out of Scotland. Benjamin is wounded, and our father and little brother have been killed." Their words spilled out as fast as they could speak.

Paddy turned down the oil lantern and poured two measures of whiskey for each. "Well now…well now." He turned to the seaman. "Go down below and get Michael Kelly. He and some mates came back a while ago. Let's see what they've found out."

The man left the roundhouse. Someone yelled "Redcoats," and Paddy hid the boys in the lockers. A squad was ordered to search any ship for Scottish partisans, and the Irish crew didn't take kindly to the intrusion. But Paddy was not inclined to have his men arrested nor his boat confiscated. Smiling broadly, he calmly ordered his men to stand down and told the Englishmen to search all they wanted. They pushed past him into the roundhouse.

Following them, Paddy said, "Our salt was unloaded hours ago. We simply await the morning for our new load of fish and wool sitting there on the dock." With a grandiose gesture of his arm, he said to the seamen, "Take these worthy men on a tour of our fine ship.

---

[9] Saint Columba (521–597): Irish Christian saint who evangelized Scotland.

Start at the bow and don't leave an unturned barrel." His blue eyes sparkled with the deception.

Paddy held his breath, seeing a private fingering the three empty glasses sitting on the table. Perhaps thinking nothing of it, the man followed his compatriots. Paddy ran his fingers through his thick curly black hair and whispered to Michael Kelly, "Come with me," and, entering the roundhouse, worked quickly to remove Alex and Charles from their incarceration. "Listen carefully. They're searching the ship. If you want to come with us, get your family here before dawn. Now off with you. Mike, get them over the side."

The boys silently slipped into the water and away from the Redcoats and town without incident. They needed to get out of the land that they loved. Their fate had been decided.

April 18, 1746

In the morning, the ship was in the North Sea sailing with a brisk wind toward Pentland Firth between the north of Scotland and the Orkney Islands. Benjamin thought how fine it was to be back where he belonged—tasting the sweet salt air and hearing the shrill cry of gulls and barking seals. Paddy was especially pleased to see his old friend; it had been many months since last they sailed together. Paddy shook his head as Benjamin talked about the battle and the interminable wait pressing on the Highlanders' minds breaking them down before it started. "Even the prince gave up," said Benjamin, hunched over, sighing with painful grief.

The Irishman told his passengers to keep their heads below deck until nightfall. English vessels prowled the coastline, and he wanted no confrontation. Navigating the strait in the dark of night, Benjamin could only see the rugged cliffs and sea stacks in his mind's eye as they sailed into the North Atlantic.

He remembered lifted striations of ancient lava; fissured remnants of land topped by lush green grass grazed upon by dots of red and black kyloes; the gray shades of sky broken occasionally by glints of sun sparkling on the wide sea. In an instant, it was gone. And he shed tears for the possible death of it to him.

Skirting the coast of the Outer Hebrides Islands, the MacKenzies had no thought of what lay ahead of them. One evening after supper, they lingered over a local favorite—a fine honey-flavored malt whiskey—that Paddy had been trading along the coasts of Britain. They were talking quietly of the business and how it was growing; however, Benjamin noticed his mother's sadness.

Swallowing his own sinking feeling of dread, he said, "You hardly touched your food this evening. Are you ill?"

Mary lingered over her tea, fingering the cup and tracing the small gold band around the edge. Paddy's extravagances were not lost on her.

"No, son. I'm just concerned about us. Where will we go? How shall we survive? We have only a little money and few possessions."

Benjamin noticed his mother's red hair had grayed considerably, and the fine lines on that lovely face had deepened. Knowing she was profoundly troubled, he kissed her cheek.

"God in his goodness has protected us thus far. He surely will not abandon us now…How would you feel about staying in Ireland for a while?" he blurted out without thought.

"We could stay there until all this fighting is over and then go home," she said hopefully.

"I don't think Scotland will ever be the same," Aggie started softly, color rising in her cheeks and tears welling up in those green eyes. "The chiefs of the clans will no longer have any authority, and we will all be under the thumb of King George. You Scots, who have fought so passionately against this…could you live under those conditions? We may never be able to go back!"

Paddy broke in, "Why not come with me? James Francis left for the colonies a month ago and took the children with him, and I just rattle around in that big house when I'm home. It would be a great burden off me shoulders if I knew someone was there besides the caretaker." Here at last was a temporary solution to their problem.

In a few weeks, the displaced family was living as normally as possible in Ireland. Benjamin's ankle was healing, and the boys did what they could to eke out a living. Aggie was delighted at being in her old home again, but this temporary safety was short-lived. One afternoon, Jamie came running in the house.

"Mother, Mother!" He gasped for air, and his cheeks burned with dread.

"Slow down, Jamie. Where have you been that you are all out of breath?"

He put his little clenched fists in Mary's lap. "Mother, I've run all the way from the harbor where there's a big ship, and it has men in red uniforms, and the boats were lowered over the side, and there was a red, white, and blue flag flying." He stopped to take a breath, and Mary sat frozen, looking at Aggie. The young woman was calm but quick to respond.

"Benjamin's working at Mrs. Flanagan's. Watch baby Ian." A nod, and she was off.

Ah, thought Mary, *is this what it comes down to? Driven from your home and now driven from your land of exile. When will men stop this infernal fighting?*

Infinity rolled by as Mary waited with the little ones for the rest of her family to return. When they did, panic rode over them like hell on earth. The Redcoats had swarmed off the ship and rushed into the street.

Benjamin was giving orders like a madman, but all to no avail as a sudden pounding on the heavy door made them all jump. The little ones began crying. Mary grabbed Jamie, and Aggie pressed Ian to her bosom while clinging to her husband. The door was battered down to the screams of the women, and twenty fully armed men crowded into the room.

An officer shouted, "Don't move, you traitor MacKenzie!" Backed by men with fixed bayonets, the officer held a pistol to Benjamin's temple. He flinched at the cold steel against his skin. "You are under arrest for treason against the king of England, and the sentence is banishment!"

No trial, no hearing, just banishment. Oh, God! Where?

Bound tightly with cordage, Benjamin gnashed his teeth in frustration and disbelief. "You are making a mistake, sir. We are the Kimseys from Ireland." He was trying to throw off suspicion in the

Irish brogue he had learned from Paddy and sharpened in their newly adopted home. The women furtively glanced at each other, and the boys picked up the name change. It made no difference. Unformed questions raced around his head.

Alex and Charles tried to defend their family, and for their efforts, each received the butt of a musket to the jaw, sending them sprawling, Charles's slowly healing cut leaking again. Shielding Ian in her embrace, Aggie was even thrown roughly aside trying to aid her brothers-in-law. A soldier crowded them into a tight knot.

"Now!" the officer growled and swept them forward like so much dust under a broom.

Chapter 3

Prison Ship

May 2–3, 1746

BENJAMIN'S MIND RACED, first with shock and hate for the soldiers who seized them, and second—how were they found out? Paddy was the only one who knew, and he would not betray his friends. Where was he? Then who? But his thoughts were cut short when they arrived at the ship and brutally shoved into the hold. It was the bowels of hell in that creaking hull, and when their eyes finally adjusted to it, they discovered a few familiar faces.

A MacLeod man, who had fought with the brothers at the Battle of Culloden Moor but was uninjured in the battle, spoke up. "Come over here by me, my wife, and wee bairns. There is scant room for you here."

While the Kimseys picked their way through the crowded space, MacLeod continued, "We thought you were all dead when they burned your house or maybe thrown into a hated English prison ship to rot. We were arrested right after the battle and held in Stirling Castle before they brought us here."

Mary was crying afresh remembering her husband and young son dead, and now her beloved home burned, sealing their fate forever. Aggie tried to comfort her, but no one felt comfort since their worst nightmares were realized.

There were not enough places to sit much less sleep. Women and children occupied hammocks, and men stood, taking turns sitting on bales or barrels or forced by motion sickness to recline in the filth of vomit, excrement, and rat droppings on the wooden floor. They were like sheep in a pen tossed and rolled by an incessant sea. Would the ship's timbers, groaning about them, become kindling for the fire, and they, as sacrificial lambs, be used to appease their English tormentors? The prisoners turned their fear into prayer and singing, taking sustenance from their Presbyterian faith in God and love for one another. At least they were together—among Scots.

Occasionally the traitors—only a few at a time—were allowed on deck to get fresh air, and in spite of the circumstances, Benjamin thoroughly enjoyed the barked orders and cries of the seamen at their work and the sound of the waves against the hull. He did not have to cling to the sides as the others did and walked freely about, at least as far as the armed Royal Marines would let him.

May 5, 1746

Several days out, a ship was spotted off the starboard bow, and suddenly all were shuttled below to their putrid hold. But Benjamin had wandered afar, not hearing the command. All of a sudden, he became aware his fellow Scots were not on deck and saw the reason. The ship was drawing close, and he concealed himself behind some boxes and coils of rope. It was a cruiser. Benjamin was very familiar with the English patrol ships on the coasts of Scotland, and now one was alongside.

Some words were exchanged through the captains' speaking trumpets, and a tackle was sent down from the main yard. In it a man was whipped into the air and dropped down on the deck of the prisoner ship. Benjamin stretched a little from his position to get a better view of the man. His eyes burned in their sockets, and his jaw dropped—Michael Kelly, the mate from Paddy's ship! Benjamin was at a loss. That was the last he remembered because a hardwood belaying pin stopped him cold.

When he awoke, it was to the awful stench of the hold and Jamie's eyes staring at him, his little red head bobbing over him like a lantern.

"Mother, Benjamin's awake."

Mary had no water to offer him, and he sat up removing the soiled damp cloth from his swimming head.

Life aboard the ship became a misery. They were not let out of their prison, and what little water supply remained became intolerable. Their meager supplies of oats, bread, and cheese—food they were given to survive—had long since run out, and now they relied solely on the garbage the English threw to them. Fever ran wild among the weakest, including little Ian, then Jamie, and finally Mary. She had soothed so many brows for so many days that she collapsed in complete exhaustion. All were beside themselves with worry and helped where they could and prayed when they could. *Who would survive?* they asked themselves. Death stalked the cramped quarters, choosing the most feeble of their countrymen, and bodies were hauled out by ropes to be dumped unceremoniously into a watery grave.

After sloshing about in the bowels of the English pigpen, a blessed day arrived when the hatches were opened, and the prisoners were ordered out. The weakest were helped up the ladders by others who could barely stand. All came up grateful to be allowed to see the light of day. A warm squall of rain washed over them, blessedly taking away the stench of their living hell. They drank in the fresh heavenly water.

Benjamin huddled with his family and took stock of what he saw. Alex, Charles, and Aggie were pale but okay. Baby Ian and Jamie were weak but recovering. But his mother, who had to be carried up on deck, was gravely ill. If he could just get some clean dry things to put on her.

He remembered the kindness of one of the seamen in the first few days—a young man who had a family in Liverpool. They had conversed a little until a guard rudely pushed the Scot aside, ordering him to get back with the traitors. Benjamin decided to try again. He found the seaman counting barrels of fresh water and making sure the empties were collecting their share of the rain.

"Sir," said Benjamin. The man's face lit up, but caution seized him.

"What do you want? I'll get thirty lashes if I'm caught talking to you again."

"Please, my good man," begged Benjamin. "I need a blanket for my mother who is very ill with fever. Could you spare one?"

Suddenly the seaman was violently pushed from behind and sent sprawling. Benjamin heard the sharp command given in an Irish brogue. "Get forward, man, before you're sent to the hold as well."

"It's you, Michael Kelly? I should have guessed." Benjamin despaired at the betrayal.

"Yes, it's me! I've hated you from the moment you hired on with Paddy, and then you became his partner. I wanted to run that ship. I knew I could do a better job of it. You two could have made a lot of money if you had listened to me."

"We would have paid you more," Benjamin shot back, his jaw set like iron.

"Ah, but I wanted it all, and I got it. The English have paid me well, and I'll have me own ship too. As soon as we get to the colonies, I'll run you and those stupid O'Sullivan brothers out of business."

The two men squared off, and strangely no one stopped them. *No doubt they want us to kill each other.* Michael Kelly's shock of dirty gray hair encircled his whiskey-reddened face as they glared at each other. He had aged—years of drink had not been kind. He and the O'Sullivan brothers had grown up in the streets of Dublin together. The brothers made something of themselves, but Michael, always jealous of them, only survived in bitterness by using his fists.

A sudden wind gust cracked canvas against a mast that momentarily distracted Michael. Benjamin seized the opportunity, hitting him squarely on the jaw. The man lost his balance and tumbled backward over a grate which caused cannonballs to roll, but the punch made no difference. Scrambling to his feet, he hit Benjamin like a battering ram, crumpling him to the deck. Some of the crew flinched as Kelly picked up his foe by the shirt front with one hand, and the other—a large balled fist—hammered his face unmercifully. Sailors and prisoners alike stood in a ring and watched while blood washed down Benjamin's face and soaked his ragged shirt.

With Ian cradled in her arms, Aggie screamed in terror at the sight of her husband's bloodied face. The baby's shrill cries added to the cacophony of sound. Mary stretched out her motherly arms, fingers clawing the air to save her son. Alex and Charles, desperate to help, were restrained by the crew.

Benjamin staggered to his feet, and Michael charged him with his head lowered, but this time he was repelled when Benjamin shifted and sent the Irisher headlong into the railing. He rolled over, grabbing Benjamin's leg, and sent him crashing into the capstan. Stunned, they lay on the deck a few seconds trying to focus, but that bull would not stay down. The Scot was quicker than the heavier Kelly and rebounded to his feet, the life of his family nerved him for the struggle. Quickly he swung an ill-secured block full force into his enemy's face. Michael was a bloodied mass clawing at his injuries.

"I'll get you for this, you filthy Jacobite!" Michael bellowed.

Pain ran through Benjamin's body as he stood victor over the inert Michael, but a pistol cock at the back of his head quickly changed the direction of his thought.

"Shackle the instigator in the bilges." The curse no prisoner wished to hear would be Benjamin's fate for the rest of the voyage.

In the days to follow, his family was a mirror of despair. Mary MacKenzie's frail body gave up the will to live. Before death took her, though, she clung to Aggie and said, "You have been like a daughter to me…Thank you…for our first grandchild." With her last breath, she whispered, "I love you all." She said no more and died in that blanket the seaman secreted to her. Aggie held her for a long, long while until she was harassed by a soldier with a wicked bayonet inches from her face.

"Move along! Move along, woman!"

Benjamin languished in the slime and rat-infested bilge. Arms bound to a timber, he valiantly tried keeping his shackled legs out of the knee-high water, but the weight kept pulling them down. His active mind tried every avenue to get control of his situation, but all his strength was stripped away. Never before had he felt so powerless.

Even after the defeat at Culloden Moor, he had his family to sustain him. Now he knew not the fate of his family nor the land to which they were going. Would he even survive his incarceration?

Anger welled up in him at the evilness that men do in the name of right, and that anger plus hate curiously sustained him for a while, but they eventually sapped what little was left of his constitution. In the gloom of the bilge, Benjamin was unable to tell day from night. *How long have I been here? How long…Lord?*

Was he becoming delirious? Had the ship ceased its struggles against the waves? He remembered someone saying something about the West Indies, and images of savage men with ugly painted faces appeared to him. Did he hear voices outside the hull of the ship? He could not be sure. His mind wandered in a nightmarish maze, and he lost all sense of time. He dreamed the prisoners were set adrift on a raft in the eye of a hurricane. They were moving very fast, dashing headlong into an abyss of nothingness. All were terror and screams and begging of a god who seemed not to care.

Although he was contorted in delirium and pain, Benjamin somehow negotiated with God. *Lord, in your tender mercies, spare us. Let not our sins unduly influence you for surely as we live we are but sinners. If, Lord, you choose to let me live, I will give you my life—a life of peace, love, and dedication. But not my will—yours, oh Lord.*

Chapter 4

A New Home

Baltimore, Maryland 1752

June 23, 1746

"LAND HO!" A sailor shouted from the crow's nest, which sent an excited ripple throughout the ship. Everyone strained against the railing to catch a glimpse. The headlands of Cape Henry came into view, but the bay's name of Chesapeake didn't come easily to the Scot's lips.

Aggie ignored the sight of land to go about her daily task of begging the captain to allow her husband out of the bilge. Today, to her astonishment, he said yes. She wanted this moment but feared it too. What would they find when they opened the hatch? Would he be alive or dead? Her heart beat wildly. Her breath stalled.

Running ahead of the crewmen, Aggie was belowdecks and stood there waiting. *Hurry up, hurry up*, she thought impatiently. When the hatch was raised, she was down into that hole before the men could stop her. The stench of rotted refuse would be unendurable to all but her.

"Bring a lantern," she ordered.

They obeyed not because they liked this job but for her courage. She waded in, pushing aside dead rats and debris. One man held the lantern behind her, and the other came forward to unlock the shackles and tie a rope under his arms. Both men choked on the vile scene.

Aggie shuddered and pointed to the man with the lantern. "Find someplace to hang that and get down to his legs. You...get on his left. I will do likewise on his right."

They lifted Benjamin's limp, unconscious form from his liquid grave and hauled him to the deck and into the light of day. It was no easy chore, but the seamen marveled at the small woman's strength. Alex placed Ian into Jamie's arms, then he and Charles joined her.

"Why didn't you tell us? We would have helped you" came the sharp rebuke.

"I didn't want to risk the captain's change of heart by wasting time," she snapped back. Never taking her eyes from her beloved, she cried, "He's still alive! Get me water and blankets."

He was put on the English wool, and Aggie, sitting beside him, stripped away what was left of his foul rags. Only love kept her from cringing at the sight of his emaciated body—a skeleton covered with skin. She gently cleansed him, dressed his wounds—especially his wrists torn by the shackles—then let the sun warm him as she worked. A small bundle of clothes was handed to her. She looked up to see the sailor who had given them the blanket for Benjamin's mother. No one stopped him now. She looked through her tears into his face and grasped his hand, saying, "God bless you."

Aggie sat right there in the middle of the deck holding her husband, crooning softly, and soothing his feverish forehead with a cool cloth.

The ship's company were busy at their posts preparing to enter port. Sails were lashed into position for the bow-first berthing at the quay.

Aggie recognized the pretty gray and white seagulls soaring and diving through the late-afternoon sky. They sat anywhere they chose, nodding their heads as if to say, *yes, you've arrived safely*. Suddenly, she was homesick. That feeling was short-lived, though, as her attention was pulled to the shore. Torches were being lit as evening began, and she noticed the chatter of the crowd for the first time. The Scots were ordered off the ship.

Benjamin did not notice that the movement of the rocking ship had ceased, nor the quavering legs of Alex and Charles who carried him down the gangplank onto flat dry land. He lay semiconscious on a pallet beside them. Aggie thought it catarrhal as he struggled for air with alarming fits of hoarse coughing. She was impatient to get him to safety.

Finally, all human merchandise and their buyers were gathered in the street as the contractual agreements were carried out. Names were called, and individuals came forward to collect their property. The MacLeods passed by the Kimseys with their bundles in their arms and wished them well. The Scots were to be indentured servants, sold to masters to be used in kitchen, garden, pasture, or field—wherever a hand was needed.

Alex and Charles were sold to a man who grew tobacco in some place called Virginia.

"No!" Aggie pleaded. "Not another separation." The man's stern face was illuminated by torchlight, but there was something in his eyes, and she spoke boldly to that new master.

Her tears streamed through the smeared dirt of her face. "You will take good care of them, Mister…?"

"MacCorkindale, ma'am." He removed his hat and broke into a smile. "I expect hard work and a full day out of a man, but I am fair."

"That's what I expected. I will remember your name," Aggie answered, smiling at the Scotsman. She exchanged hugs with Alex and Charles. Jamie ran crying to their arms not understanding any of it, only that he was losing his brothers.

A rasping whisper escaped from the pallet. Benjamin could barely speak.

"Take care...of...yourselves. We'll be together again... someday."

Overcome by bitter grief, the brothers stooped to hold his hands. Then they, with their new master, were swallowed by the darkness into a strange land.

Suddenly Scots and others in the crowd backed away. A repulsive smell preceded the town's butcher. He barged through the crowd. "Move aside. Move aside. Get outta ma way. Cap'n Jack, whattaya got fur me?" he sneered, pulling on his purse strings to pay for his servant.

Fear pierced Aggie's heart at his horrid manner and appearance. A filthy ragged hat covered his matted hair, and a greasy leather apron covered him from Adam's apple to knees. An ill-fitting and likewise grimy coat, that had seen better days, did not cover his rotund gut. And mud, blood, and dung caked his heavy boots. He spat a most vile wad of black matter onto the ground.

The ship's captain shoved the papers into his hand and coldly said, "Campbell, this is Benjamin MacKenzie," pointing to the man on the cot. "Give me my money."

Looking at the knot of leftovers sitting in the dust at his feet, Butcher Campbell laughed in his face. "So, this is what you bring me—an invalid who calls himself a man? How do you expect me to use him in my slaughterhouse? And what do you want me to do with two kids and a scrawny woman? Ha! What a joke!" He spat in Benjamin's face. "I wouldna give a copper farthing for the likes of a MacKenzie, let alone one who was sick. Let him die in the street." And he threw the contract back in the captain's face and pocketed his money.

Everyone left, and the English sailors either went back to their duties aboard ship or dispersed down the road to a tavern in the small settlement.

Urgently, Aggie beseeched the captain, "What will become of us?"

He turned his back and walked away, leaving her standing alone.

A racking cough from Benjamin and whimpering from her hungry and sleepy children were unbearable. She had never felt such overwhelming dread. What could she do? With no one to help them, Aggie pulled Benjamin's blanket close around him and gathered her ragged shawl around her own cold shoulders. She, Ian, and Jamie sat huddled together, weeping.

A voice came out of the darkness. "I'll pick up that contract, Captain."

"Well, MacDonald. I wondered if you were coming," he shot back in contempt.

Patiently, the Scotsman said, "We were detained. Are these the only ones?"

"Yes. Sign here."

Aggie didn't see the exchange of money. She heard her name but was too exhausted to raise her head.

"Aggie MacKenzie?"

Her dull eyes lit up in recognition. It was James Francis O'Sullivan. He picked her up out of the dirt of the road and held her affectionately. Her tears came in a great torrent, wetting his Irish plaids.

Through her agony she begged, "What are we to do?"

"Hush, child." His voice soothed her.

There were three people with James Francis whom he was introducing as "Mr. and Mrs. MacDonald and their son, Davey." Aggie could barely focus.

"Here, dear," said Mrs. MacDonald. "Let me take the wee bairn."

Then MacDonald and Davey took Benjamin's pallet, and James Francis picked up the sleeping Jamie.

The buggy ride was a blur, but when they reached the MacDonalds' home, Aggie could feel love and warmth in the dwelling. The little ones were cleaned up, fed, and put to bed. A doctor was summoned to check on each, and Aggie would not rest until her husband was examined. It was pneumonia and infected wounds. The doctor placed some stoppered bottles on a bureau and explained what each was for. She was too tired to understand the directions, but Mrs. MacDonald saw her finally relax.

"Davey, show the doctor out. I know what to do. Come, dear, I have just the thing for you."

Barely able to walk, Aggie was ushered into a room in which a servant was filling a wooden tub with steaming water. Aggie looked at herself in a full-length mirror and cried out. Her hand went to the beautiful long black hair, now a dull mass of tangles filled with lice. She then touched her cheek and peered closely at her ashen skin. Mrs. MacDonald dismissed the servant and directed Aggie to place her filth-laden, bug-ridden tattered clothes in a basket and then to climb into the tub. Noticing the thickened waist and tummy, she picked up another bucket of water. The precious cascade of warmth over Aggie's hair took away all anger, fear, and loss, and as she washed with the clean odor of lye soap about her, the two women chatted.

"I don't mean to pry, dear, but are you with child?"

"Yes, ma'am." Her tired eyes glowed. "The first of next year."

The kind woman smiled and rose to her feet. "You finish up, and I'll get you something to wear for the night."

"Thank you, Mrs. MacDonald." Aggie relaxed her head and neck against the edge of the wooden tub and thought of the growing life within her. Ireland proved to be more than a temporary exile—it was where her second child was conceived.

The next morning, summer heat slipped through the open window, and Aggie awakened to the lavender fragrance of her soft white linen shift. She stretched lazily and threw back the covers. For the first time in many months, she felt alive and happy, awakening from a horrible dream. She lay there a few minutes then felt her husband stir.

"Good morning, love. How are you feeling?" she said, placing her head on his chest and looking into his eyes.

Weakly, he took a strand of that long black mantle of hair which played out over the covers and caressed it in his fingers. "Very weak," he whispered, "but the sight of you brings me strength." She stretched toward him and kissed his lips. "Oh, that I were well, my girl."

"We'll have none of that." She laughed and moved to the window to look out on the beautiful gardens and verdant fields beyond. "Mrs. MacDonald told me we're in Lord Baltimore's colony"—and she turned to look at her man—"and your second child will be born here early next year."

A weak smile crossed his face, and with renewed hope, he knew he would get well quickly—especially when he discovered that James Francis was in the colony and Paddy knew of their whereabouts.

The following day, the little family was moved into an unused servants' quarters, and Mrs. MacDonald told Aggie to make whatever changes they needed as this would be their home for as long as they wished. Their cupboards were stocked with food, and Benjamin, with medicine and proper nutrition, began to regain his strength, although he had that painful limp from the battle.

On a particular Sunday afternoon, after Benjamin's recovery, the pair walked the dirt paths through their benefactor's abundant vegetable and flower gardens. One could taste the agreeable aromas of the hardworking farmers' hands and the bounty of God's creation.

All through their recuperation, they had not discussed any of the horrors of those shipboard weeks—weeks that forever changed their lives. Aggie was keenly aware that the feelings were just under the surface. Finally, with some gentle prodding, Benjamin began to open up. He said he mourned the loss of his mother and was filled with hate for the awful unceremonious burial at sea.

"They just dumped her body overboard like so much garbage," he cried unabashedly to his wife, guilt and anger spilling out of him, and the telltale vein popping out on his forehead. "She should have been buried with Father and Duncan in decent graves with our family at Beauly."

"It will pass, my love. It will pass. Give it time," Aggie said slowly and twined her arm under his, looking lovingly at her man, tall and handsome under the trees that framed the neat rows of corn. The Scottish strength of his profile—full black eyebrows, that resolute chin, and carven nose—was always undermined by the deep dimples of his cheeks when he smiled.

"It's very hot," Aggie said, fanning herself. "Shall we sit in the cool grass? I noticed you seem to be limping more today. Let us rest." The sun sparkled through the trees' leaves, making shadows dance across their faces.

Not able to let go the pain of loss just yet, Benjamin continued, "I miss Alex and Charles…terribly." He sighed. "I hope they are well…I wonder what Virginia is like…What was that man's name?"

"MacCorkindale. They will do well by him, I have no doubt, and I feel confident we will see them again someday soon." She noted a discernible lift of his spirits.

In the tranquility of the moment, a deep peace settled over the couple. Aggie picked some small white daisies growing between the summer blades of grass and lowered her head to smell the faint delicate fragrance. Benjamin watched the movement of the corn's stalks and silk pushed by a gentle breeze. With sudden desire, he turned to see a sunlit radiance around his wife. Not only was she a pretty woman, but also, she had an exquisite beauty of heart and soul. And then there was that rock strength beneath. Slowly, tenderly, he touched her face then reached back to untie a yellow satin ribbon holding her long locks in a cluster of curls. She was wearing her hair that same way when he first met her. He pulled the curls forward over her bosom, then kissed her lips. A long left-behind passion bloomed in them, and they made love for the first time since their union in Ireland.

Jamie was growing like a cowslip in the garden, and Ian was crawling everywhere and into everything. And Aggie was growing big with child. Benjamin had much to be thankful for and would build a new life for them. He never forgot his promise though—the promise of something special for God. Right now, it had no form, but he lived each day to the full, loving and living at peace.

* * *

The Scots banded together for the mutual benefit of their kinsmen escaping English rule or sold as indentured servants, and Mr. and Mrs. MacDonald were enthusiastic members of that community. However, they were more like parents than masters looking out after the little MacKenzie family as if they were their own children and grandchildren. Coming from Scotland in 1726 as a newly married couple, they lived in the old colony of Maryland for twenty years. Their son, Davey, was born in Baltimore, and they had a fine tobacco plantation with freed colored slaves working the fields.

Mr. MacDonald always sold his crop to a middleman and made a good profit, but he wanted more, not because he was greedy, but to help those in need. With the Scots' loss to the English at the Battle of Culloden Moor, the victors cut the connection between the chiefs and their clans. During the aftermath, the tenant farmer could no longer afford his land as his clan chief had become his avaricious landlord charging exorbitant rents. Ruthless evictions followed. By any means possible, if a clansman could get passage on a ship to America, MacDonald offered sanctuary, work, food, whatever he could to make his fellow man live better. Those were his values.

Donald found James Francis a willing partner, and when he discovered Benjamin's past, he couldn't believe his good fortune. Freedom was granted to the family as it wasn't his intention to hold them as servants for seven years, but if Benjamin was willing—Paddy was due in the harbor the following week—they could then talk of forming a larger merchant shipping company.

James Francis had spent much time in the colonies over the past few years traveling to the perimeters of the wilderness. He realized the great potential he saw and convinced his brother that his stubbornness would get him nowhere. "Open your eyes, man," he would say, and they finally brought Paddy along with their arrangement—on a trial basis, of course.

Paddy had reason to be nervous because tobacco was beginning to decline in the 1740s, and many farmers were planting wheat and grains. But in the southern backcountry, tobacco continued to be a cash crop, especially since the Scots merchants encouraged its cultivation by direct purchase.

James Francis had half a dozen ships plying their trade back and forth from the thirteen colonies to the West Indies and the Kingdom of Great Britain. With his increased wealth, he commissioned a new ship from the fine builders in Glasgow and decided to give it to his new captain, Benjamin Kimsey. He was one of the best suppliers and best contacts in Maryland, Virginia, and the Carolinas, and he knew his newest partner would do well with his backing. Their venture was extraordinarily successful.

Aggie ran the household for Mrs. MacDonald, who spent more time giving of herself through her Presbyterian kirk. But this young pregnant woman was obviously going to need more help, so when the next ship was due, the older couple was there to pick up any unclaimed contracts. From good fortune, there were two girls who had bought passage in steerage as servants—the Crowley sisters.

Mary Crowley, the little four-year-old, tried to be of help, but more often than not, she liked to chase after Jamie and devised ways to pester him. Her bobbed brown hair annoyed him no end the way it tossed about with her incessant chatter. Rebecca was a big strong girl and claimed to be sixteen, but Aggie had her doubts. Rebecca eventually confessed she was only twelve but lied for fear she and her sister would not be allowed to come to the colonies. She also struggled with another problem that was pried out of her. Rebecca had stolen the passage money. She explained that their parents had died, and the girls were sent to live with an uncle who was very mean to them. She discovered the uncle's money pouch one day while cleaning.

"Oh," she said, "I didn't take all of it. Just enough to get us here."

The two sisters became endeared to Aggie, especially since they were Welsh. Rebecca looked after Mary as well as working hard for the MacDonalds, and she saved all her earnings to pay back what she had stolen. The girl vowed to educate herself and her sister and commandeered Aggie whenever there was a free moment to teach them to read and write.

The number of Scots immigrants in the southern colonies grew rapidly. The Isles Trading Company blossomed in that environment of growth of the new land where freedoms, never before known, were becoming treasured commodities. As its merchant ships traveled the coast of the colonies, they brought back stories that some folks still longed for home, but most colonists were realizing the development of a new idea in government. Despite the variety of immigrants, many felt this virgin country was just an extension of the English kingdom, and a restless spirit began to appear. Nevertheless, news from the homelands was always eagerly awaited in the form of dispatches, letters, and gossip. There was a realization that they were still tied to the apron strings of England and not ready to make a run for independence. The new country needed to walk first.

The Kimseys ignored the rumblings of the sleeping giant, preferring to keep to their own affairs. After all, they had been through a severe political upheaval that ended in tragedy and were in no hurry to become involved again, especially Benjamin. He worked hard to forget the fighting and killing of those last years in Scotland and won the respect of his crew and admiration of his business partners in the process. But Donald MacDonald was quite outspoken and frequently invited his cronies and colleagues home to discuss the state of affairs and attempt to recruit the unwilling Scot.

* * *

On a sweltering rainy afternoon after three successive rainy days, Aggie could not stand her underfoot ship-captain-farmer-husband a moment longer. He had been home from the sea for several weeks but could not work in the fields with mud up to his knees. She was sweating from head to toe even with her apron and skirt tucked up under the strings showing her shift. Locks of hair curled around her moist neck.

"Oh, Benjamin. Dear heart. My one and only love." Her smoldering gray-green eyes gave away the irritability she was trying hard to control. He wondered why her eyes always turned gray when she was angry. "This is not your ship. You cannot go poking, prying, pestering, and ordering." All four feet, ten inches straightened up and stared him down. White knuckles clenched a menacing broom. "I am overworked, have no wage for what I do, and you keep tracking mud onto my clean-swept floor. GET OUT!" she cried.

Suddenly the kitchen door flew open and banged against the wall during the height of her tirade. It was MacDonald who swiftly crossed the floor and took her by the shoulders, saying, "Aggie, I've never seen you look lovelier," and he kissed her damp forehead.

MacDonald turned quickly, put his arm over Benjamin's shoulder, and said in a whisper, "I guess I've come in the nick of time. How about a good Irish ale?" The younger man nodded in relief, and the two went out of the kitchen door, leaving a frazzled, deflated woman standing in their wake.

The rain stopped as the men waded through the mud-swollen street, but MacDonald's words seemed to be lost in a watery haze that hung before them. Benjamin did not have much to say but breathed deeply, glad to be out of the clutches of his woman and the confines of the kitchen. The dampness felt good in his nostrils. It was the smell of the sea. But lately he began to know the longing wasn't as keen as it had been. He felt loneliness on long voyages, a loneliness that could only be quelled by his beloved Aggie and the bright faces of his growing family when he returned home.

Over those years, when he was in port, he dug and prodded the clumps of black earth in the fields alongside Jamie. But the love of the land was not in him like it was in his brother who, except for his red hair, was becoming more and more like their father, Robert, who had worked the land his whole life. *The boy is sixteen now and as tall as I am*, thought Benjamin. *Where has the time gone?*

As MacDonald opened the tavern door for him, the camaraderie of laughter and bagpipes suddenly crowded out his wife's complaints.

Benjamin looked at MacDonald and apologized, "I'm sorry I wasn't much company on the way over."

"That's all right. I could tell you were deep in thought."

Benjamin laughed. "Let's get a drink. Too much thinking makes me thirsty."

The pipes were playing a familiar Scots folk song, and everyone was singing as the two made themselves comfortable. It was a soulful hundred-year-old ballad about a colorful highwayman called Gilderoy and the bonny lass who loved him. Their love wasn't to be, however, as Gilderoy was hanged for his crimes, nevermore to "deck her hair with garlands nor kiss her sweet rosy lips." There were tears in some eyes in that room enhanced, no doubt, by fiery whiskey flowing down their throats.

Their reverie was jolted away from the old sod, however, by a wailing heard above the rest. It could only be coming from that Irish Paddy O'Sullivan who never could sing. With some of his crew, he strolled over to the table to join their old comrades. The friends' faces lit up, and they rose to their feet to clap the men firmly on the shoulders and finish the last refrain of the song, "Wi' sorrow ne'er had wat my cheek for my dear Gilderoy!" Glasses were raised, and the bottoms of tankards went dry.

"Well, you old Irish dog! Paddy, how are you, old friend? Here, sit down and tell us what you're about. How long has it been, oh… and a drink." And Benjamin motioned for the taverner.

MacDonald asked Paddy of James Francis and prodded him for news and any political gossip. Paddy recalled it had been three years since they'd last seen each other and told of their adventures and the storms they survived along the way. Paddy didn't go in for politics, so poor MacDonald was frustrated. But he had heard a rumor that the Iron Act[10] might be repealed.

---

[10] In American Colonial history, the Iron Act, short-titled the Importation, etc. Act 1750, was one of the legislative measures introduced by the British Parliament, within its system of Trade and Navigation Acts. The Act sought to increase the importation of pig and bar iron from its American colonies and to prevent the building of iron-related production facilities within these colonies, particularly in North America where these raw materials were identified. The dual purpose of the act was to increase manufacturing capacity within Great Britain itself, and to limit potential competition from the colonies possessing the raw materials (https://en.wikipedia.org/wiki/Iron_Act).

They all laughed and joked and sang the afternoon away until MacDonald noticed the time. The Irish were invited to dinner.

Abruptly, the heavy tavern door flew open, and an unseen presence blew a cold chill over the backs of the men in the warm room. Someone cursed and stood to close the door but hesitated. Everyone gaped in puzzlement at the inert body that was dropped onto the hard wooden floor. The proprietor, who had just set down a tray of mugs, stepped forward to assist, but the gravel of the dour voice of the man who dropped the body warned him away. "I look for that cur Benjamin Kimsey."

"You found him" came the reply, and a shiver ran down the spine of every patron in the place as the man's voice extinguished the cordial atmosphere.

There appeared before them not a specter but a grizzled and sodden Michael Kelly. A gray stubble was on his chin, and a black patch covered one eye. The dead white flesh of scars marked his face where the block and tackle had hit him aboard ship. He was disheveled, and his gnarled fingers curled menacingly into fists foretold mischief.

"Your wife wouldn't tell me where to find you, so I borrowed Jamie here to show me the way." Kelly dropped to one knee and grabbed the red hair of the unconscious lad on the floor, showing Benjamin how the young man had been coerced.

Benjamin cast a worried look toward his brother, but with his heart racing in anger, he stood straight up from his chair, causing it to crash to the floor and making the patrons jump in fright. He placed his hands on the table to steady himself, fighting his urge to kill.

"And my wife?" he demanded.

Michael sauntered across the floor, enjoying his control over the situation. He took someone's mug off a table and downed its contents in one gulp, savoring the heady spirits and enjoying the obvious pain he was causing.

"Oh." He lingered over the words. "She's still alive, though I'm not so sure about Jamie here."

Benjamin's fear for the life of his brother, whose body lay in a heap on the tavern's floor, competed for precedence with his desperation to get home to his pregnant wife.

One of Paddy's crew went for his pistol as the disgust for this hated man went way back, but Kelly's lead ball was quicker and dropped the Irisher right where he stood.

"Anyone else wish to make a stupid move?" The uncovered eye burned in its socket.

Everyone backed off, but Paddy moved gingerly toward the injured man under the watchful gaze of Kelly. He bent low and found his crewman was still alive. Slowly, he reached under the seaman's coat, and his fingers hit upon a knife that he knew was there. Paddy whirled onto his feet and lifted his arm to throw the blade, but Kelly produced another pistol and shot the weapon from his hand. The cold metal hit the floor with a clatter.

"Finally, I have you both under one roof. Now I can make good my promise." A thin smile spread across rotten teeth, and Kelly arched backward in diabolical laughter.

Benjamin saw Paddy was only grazed and seized the opportunity. He threw the table to one side, breaking glasses and wetting the floor with ale and whiskey. Kelly tossed the empty pistol in the corner, and the two men were at each other once more. In the throes of battle, the combatants smashed tables, broke chairs, and bounced off walls, only to come at each other again. The crowd flowed with the brawlers forward and back, punching and ducking, tasting in themselves the pull of the battle.

Benjamin's friends were dismayed as the tide turned in Kelly's favor. The Scot tripped over a broken chair and fell against the bar. Before anyone had time to react, Kelly came at him, seizing his throat, and began to squeeze. Benjamin struggled to get that awful hand away but couldn't find the strength. Everything was going black. Kelly grabbed a heavy mug ready to finish the deal. Immediately, a thought pulsed through Benjamin's mind as he was losing consciousness. *Why is this happening? I'm a man of peace...A man of peace...*

The pressure stopped, and his eyes fluttered open to a confused but surprising aspect. The heavy body of Michael Kelly lay across him with Paddy's knife in his back. Blood dripped in a pool by his side. Jamie quickly pushed Kelly's body off his brother, and three men helped Benjamin to his feet. He staggered, trying to catch his breath and calm his senses from reeling. The tavern's patrons were shaking Jamie's hands and patting his back, congratulating him on his courage in saving his brother's life. The proprietor poured whiskey for all, and the battered brothers were helped to an upright table.

Hurting from a black eye, bruises, cuts, and scrapes, Benjamin was having trouble putting the pieces together, and while trying to collect his thoughts, Davey came in with news and the county constable. He said he had gone to his father's house and found it had been hit by a hurricane. Michael Kelly had come in like a bull, Aggie told him, and started to threaten her. Jamie heard the commotion and went to the aid of his sister-in-law, but the big man was too powerful. She was struck and pushed to the kitchen floor, and Jamie got the back of Kelly's hand, flinging him across the room and hitting his head hard on the table as he went down. Aggie saw Kelly pick up Jamie as if he weighed no more than a feather and leave with him.

"I fetched the doctor then followed the trail of destruction here," Davey finished. The constable knew of Michael Kelly's reputation and did not press charges against Jamie.

Benjamin was sick at the sight of dead men and desperate to get home to his injured wife, pregnant with their fifth child. Poor Jamie was holding his splitting head. Their Irish friends, stemming the flow of blood from their own cuts and bruises, helped the stricken men to MacDonalds' home.

As they walked along, there was a heavy sky hanging over Benjamin's heart and the Baltimore wharf. The turbulence engulfed the glens of his mind, and a huckster taunted him with doubt. He loved the waves and wind of the open sea sailing the coasts of Scotland and Ireland and across the mighty Atlantic. From the colonies, they had traded salt cod in Jamaica and Barbados for sugar and molasses. Paddy, James Francis, and Benjamin had crisscrossed one another's wakes with their ships of The Isles Trading Company. It made him a wealthy man, but he was gone for long periods from his wife and children.

Those devilish doubts tried to block dear memories of Scotland, the brave land for which he fought: those flocks of sheep herded by collies along volcanic roads; rock hovels covered with growing grass turf; double rainbows over the firth; the warmth of his plaids; running barefoot over rocky crags; and the supreme joy of fishing with his father, Robert, along the River Ness. Those joyful memories were gone, blotted out by the war and English tyranny.

Abruptly, the clouds parted, and he awoke from his uncertainty to silver beams of sunlight streaming through the darkened clouds of the Maryland colony. His way was supremely clear—he would quit the sea and keep his promise of working for God in peace, love, and dedication. The how, he was sure, would be pointed out to him.

Chapter 5

The Kimsey Spring

1756

DURING THOSE YEARS of seafaring, Aggie did the churchgoing with the children, and Benjamin worshiped the Lord in his heart and always tried to live a good life.

After all that had gone on, the desire for guidance was upon him, and he turned to the only religion he knew—the Presbyterians with whom he had been raised in Scotland. But they were suffering from a schism in membership[11] and a confusion of teachings that Benjamin did not understand. There was a growing religious group which was active and successful—the Baptists. He turned to his old friend with his thoughts.

Age had crept into MacDonald's bones. He sighed and sat down next to the fire. "I am filled with sorrow to see that you want to leave the farm, Benjamin, just when we're so prosperously helping newly emigrated Scots. Paddy and James Francis will be sad to hear of your decision also, but, my young friend, you must follow your heart."

---

[11] The Old Side-New Side Controversy occurred within the Presbyterian Church in Colonial America and was part of the wider theological controversy surrounding the First Great Awakening. The Old and New Side Presbyterians existed as separate churches 1742-1758 (https://en.wikipedia.org/wiki/Old_Side%E2%80%93New_Side_Controversy).

"Sir," said Benjamin with total respect for the man who sat before him, "you know I have an obligation to fulfill, the promise I made to you years ago must be realized."

"Well, son—and you know you are a second son to me—back when I gave you your freedom, you chose to stay. I never intended to hold you and yours as servants, but one thing I wish to give to you and Jamie…" He stopped to light his pipe, and a small cloud of fragrant tobacco smoke encircled him.

"Give, sir?" questioned Benjamin. "Why, you have given our family the finest things in life—friendship, patronage, opportunity—"

MacDonald interrupted, "But, my boy, you gave us so much in return. Please allow me to do this last thing for you. I have two properties, one in North Carolina and another in Virginia. Both are fine and ripe for the plough. Talk to Jamie and decide between yourselves. Oh, and by the way, I have heard tell of a Hopewell Academy in New Jersey that's newly established by the Pennsylvania Association of Baptist Churches."

Benjamin's way was suddenly clear.

* * *

1757

Jamie chose the way of the land. He knew what he wanted, but being only seventeen, he had much work to do before his desires could be fulfilled. The deed was in his name in a place called Bedford County, Virginia, carved out from old Augusta County, and he was excited at the prospect of seeing his land and the possibility of finding his brothers Alex and Charles. But he wisely decided to work another year for Mr. MacDonald. He then would ask fifteen-year-old Mary Crowley to marry him. Yes, somewhere along those childhood annoyances, he began to fall in love with the little terror who turned into a sweet, charming woman. They would see the land together for the first time, he decided, when the year was up. The plans, unfortunately, fell apart as she was to accompany her sister Rebecca back to

Wales. "We must repay our uncle and take care of family matters," Mary explained.

"But, Mary, I shall be heartsick while you're gone."

She stood before him on the same quay where they had all disembarked and looked deep into his eyes. What she saw was not a little boy but a tall, thin handsome young man about to step into the frontier. His large brown eyes were moist with brimming tears, and his square jaw betrayed a small quiver. She raised up on tiptoe and threw her arms around his neck.

"You are so brave and fine to let me do this thing. I can only say that I shall be pleased to be your wife upon my return."

He held her at arm's length to remember everything about this girl: a blue bonnet trimmed with lace; striking violet eyes in which he lost his senses; brown ringlets framing a lovely face of creamy white and rose-red blush; a blue satin-clad wisp of a waist. He gently took her to him to kiss her lips. His heart raced between love and despair; his mind reeled between desire and loss. That tender kiss caused a raucous display, rude with laughter, applause, and whistles, and interrupted their last love message. Sweet Mary Crowley joined her sister on the ship's deck, the gangplank was withdrawn, and the ship took to the sea. Jamie had no idea how long it would be before he could reunite with his love.

* * *

The year went by quickly. Jamie worked hard, shoulder to shoulder with Mr. MacDonald and his son, Davey. He grew three inches and put on twenty pounds during that time and also learned a great deal more of the farmer's trade. His mentor was a good teacher, and Jamie matured with the wisdom only a grandfather could give. Since his parents were both dead and Alex and Charles had been torn away from him, Benjamin replaced Jamie's father, and Aggie, his sister-in-law, became his little mother. A store of knowledge had been handed him from all of them. Now was the time to use it well—but still he procrastinated. *Why?* he asked himself. His family had already left for the seminary in New Jersey.

The impetus to leave came when Davey took over his father's farm and Jamie's help was no longer needed. Many more Scots were arriving from their homeland, and MacDonald spent all his waking hours at the quay in Baltimore, waiting for Paddy's ships that would bring men who were desperate to work the land. Among them were Scots-Irish from Ulster, lured by the talk of land for the taking, who would go west into the mountains of Appalachia. They were known to be fierce fighters and were well paid by those living on the edge to protect the frontier. MacDonald helped his countrymen by any means needed.

One morning, as light from the fresh day crept through the window of Jamie's small log cabin—one among many in the line of workers quarters—a small chattering goldfinch landed on the sill. When Jamie threw back the quilt, instead of flying away, it flew into the room. He sat still watching the creature peck at crumbs on the well-worn wooden table, and when he put on his breeches and tucked in his shirt, the bird remained. Jamie talked softly to it and noticed the small black eyes watching him while the goldfinch continued to take its breakfast from the table's larder.

Jamie poured water from the pitcher into the basin and washed and dried his face. To his astonishment, the goldfinch flew past his ear and straight into the bowl, flapping its wings with such intensity the water spattered onto the floor. Then when Jamie opened the door, the little bird sped past him straight into the yard. It hovered awhile, then flew off into the rising sun. *Odd*, he thought, *like my year at the MacDonalds*. The little bird seemed to be giving him a message—it was time to go. Thoughts of how he would get to Virginia bothered him.

"Good morning, son," MacDonald said, pulling the canvas taut.

"Good morning, sir. What have you got there? May I help?"

"Yes, of course. Here, tie down this last rope of the canvas."

"It's…so big," Jamie said, mouth agape at the enormous size of the wagon.

"It's called a Conestoga. Made in Pennsylvania by the German settlers up there."

"Are you going away, Mr. MacDonald?"

"No…You are." The old man looked up at him with tears in his eyes as he tied the last knot. "It's time. The year you promised me is over, and now you must make your own way."

Jamie thought of the bird—an omen.

Breakfast awaited them in the big kitchen where Aggie had worked alongside Mrs. MacDonald and fed so many. Jamie would be the last Kimsey to leave. Nothing much was said while they ate. As Davey and his father talked briefly about the corn crop, Mrs. MacDonald went on about visiting a sick woman in the settlement and how she needed to pick flowers for the kirk's altar.

When they finished, she moved to Jamie's side and kissed his cheek. It was then he noticed a fine mesh of age lines around her kind eyes and engaging smile—she had grown old in the last ten years but wore it gracefully. She grabbed her apron and quickly left the room, wiping her eyes. Davey shook his hand and left the kitchen, following his mother. Then Mr. MacDonald walked with Jamie to the wagon.

Tethered to the wagon were six horses, each at least seventeen hands high. The teamster would ride the wheel horse, the left rear of his team, which had the saddle and stirrups.

"Mount up," MacDonald offered.

Jamie was perplexed as he stood staring up at the wagon with its six-foot-high sideboards. The canvas top was twenty-eight feet long, and the rear wheels, five feet in diameter. It looked like some of the ships he'd seen with Benjamin at dockside.

Mr. MacDonald handed him the reins, jerk line, and whip, giving him a quick lesson with each. "Haw and gee—left and right—a long pull on the jerk line to the lead horse, he'll go left. Short pull—right. The wagoner's whip is used sparingly. They understand, and you will quickly learn their ways. Along with the land, this is my other gift to you to help you get started on your new adventure. I wish I could go with you, but at my age, the time has passed for me to go traipsing around the countryside. You will do well. I know it." He extended his hand toward his "second" son. They shook, and MacDonald handed him a leather pouch. "Here are the deed, letters of introduction, and compensation for your year's work with me with the Scots' emigration. Henry Middleton, along the James River, runs a ferry out of Lynchburg and will point you in the direction of your land."

Jamie wanted to jump off the horse and hug MacDonald, but that wasn't their way. He only said, "I am proud to be your son, sir. Thank you."

"Paddy's waiting for you at the quay. His ship will take you to the mouth of the James River."

Jamie Kimsey got more than just stares as he rolled the enormous Conestoga through town. Many people knew him well from his years living in the area—the barber, tanner, cooper, blacksmith, church folks, and especially the pretty lass who flirted with him when he stopped for sweets at the dry-goods store. Jamie waved to his friends, sad to be leaving such a wonderful community, but looking forward to having his beautiful Mary with him in their new home.

Dockside was bustling with ships and flotsam moving gently on the lapping water, and families either greeted or said goodbye to loved ones. All manner of trade was in progress with their accompanying smells: hawkers selling raw fish, broiled meat, and bakery goods; cows, mules, and oxen being loaded on ships and leaving trails of dung behind them. Even the stench of the squalid dockside slums would be part of Jamie's memories of Baltimore.

Jamie's eyes finally caught sight of Paddy waving. The horses shied a little at the gangplank, but with a gentle whip to their flanks, continued onto the ship, blinders blocking their vision of the water below. The wagon and animals were secured and given feed, water, and an apple apiece, then Jamie was free to join Paddy on deck.

Once his friend was discharged at Hampton Roads, Paddy would fill out his load with more tobacco, then sail for England. He told Jamie to hail another ship going upriver, disembarking at City Point before the unnavigable falls at Richmond settlement.

Following the trail overland to Lynchburg with a stop at Henry Middleton's store for directions sounded simple enough to Jamie; however, many long miles stretched ahead of him, including another water voyage. He had better be careful, or he might regret his submission to self-satisfaction. Vigilance was the key word.

Jamie stood at the ship's rail and marveled at the sight of the harbor disappearing from his view. In twelve years, Baltimore had come a long way from being a forested countryside with streams and falls, a few wooden structures, and the wharf's small settlement. He was only six years old when he experienced war and death, banishment and loss, and going from the ship into the black night of Lord Baltimore's colony. Now, he recoiled from those dark memories. Boys playing along the banks of the Chesapeake drew his attention back to the light. Men fished from small rowboats. Ships bound for England plied the waterway from many ports, and towns stretched as far as he could see with plantations owning the riverbanks and docks. Christian crosses of many different denominations looked down somberly over the town as immigrants, leaving behind their own religions, received consolation provided at every door.

Paddy shouted as he navigated the stairs from the poop deck, "Jamie, how are you? Look at you. You're taller than I am."

"Fine, sir." They took hold of each other, both grinning from ear to ear. "How long has it been, Paddy? Have you seen Benjamin lately? And James Francis?" Jamie's smile disappeared. "Or my brothers?"

"I think the last time I saw all of you was when Ben fought Michael Kelly. That's a couple of years. I was back at sea after that. Did Ben enter the seminary?"

"Yes, he did."

"And no, I haven't seen Alex or Charles." A noisy flock of gulls interrupted the melancholy mood, and Paddy changed the subject. "Donald caught me in the nick of time as I was loading new cargo. Tobacco is a little slow right now. I'm stopping along Hampton Roads to flesh out our load, so taking you down there works well for me...and for you. I hear he gave you his land in Bedford County? He's such a generous man." Called away by a crew member, Paddy left Jamie to watch the countryside go by.

It took most of the daylight hours to reach their goal. The town of Hampton had a busy port with a long dock jutting out over the shore, and his team was alerted to its activity by a small herd of horses being discharged from a rather odd flat-bottomed barge bobbing in the water. Jamie was at the nose of his head horse, holding the bit strap and stroking the soft muzzle of the beautiful animal to calm the team. Nostrils flared at the sight of their distant cousins and the prospect of sweet earth and delectable grass soon to be under their hooves. Paddy helped Jamie get the heavy load off his ship and parked, and the friends went to the customs house to take care of the loading of his ship and the purchase of Jamie's passage for the next morning.

The men shared a drink with Josiah Lee, the proprietor, and his wife provided them with an excellent dinner of fried river catfish and just-baked potatoes out of the ashes of the fire. A small inn built on the back of the customs house would give them shelter from the cold night.

Before Jamie settled in, he went out to his team with more apples. He removed the harnesses and straps so they could pasture easily in the large secure corral provided for stock. He drew close to each one, speaking softly and patting them, concerned for their welfare on the arduous journey to come. A worrying thought brushed his mind. No, they would all make it. Walking in the dark, he moved to his wagon and checked all the ropes, but he could not sweep away the worry.

Jamie was up early. He dressed quickly and retraced the leather straps, lacing and buckling. Then he maneuvered the animals to the front of the wagon and attached the trace chains. With that accomplished, he went back in the customs house for breakfast, the scent of coffee and bacon drawing him out of the morning chill. Just as he sat with his fellow travelers, eggs fried in bacon fat in cast-iron skillets were brought sizzling to the table. Mrs. Lee couldn't get the spoons to the diners fast enough, and the yellow yolks dripped their gold onto their plates. Before they left, Mrs. Lee was at the door waiting to give each one a lunch wrapped in the old news of the *Virginia Gazette*.

Jamie stuffed the last bite of butter-and-jam-covered biscuit into his mouth and was on the wheelhorse in an instant. A swat of leather on the rumps, he drove the team toward the dock. Mr. and Mrs. Lee watched from the porch, as did Paddy. He was proud of the way Jamie handled his team and whispered a silent prayer for his success. The dockboards creaked, and Jamie held his breath as he guided the team toward the end of the pier. A wide heavy plank spanned the dock directly onto the barge. The team hesitated to move onto it, but with a gentle flick of his whip, they moved forward, and Jamie let out a sigh of relief when the craft settled in the water with the great weight. Each animal was detached, and all were secured individually. Finally, they were on the way up the James River. Jamie looked back and waved to Paddy, saddened by the thought that they might never see each other again.

The barge was propelled by rudder, oars, and a sail. Captain Connor seemed amiable, and Jamie was eager to talk with him. There were several of this type of craft made especially for heavy transport, Connor said, converted schooners with one sail removed. "Blacksmiths and millwrights among the immigrants are highly sought after by the settlers," he shared. "You seem especially talented with that rig of yours, teamster." Jamie was pleased by his new title.

In the next moment, the captain tensed. He whispered to Jamie, "You got a gun?" Jamie nodded. "Well then, get it…slowly."

Jamie turned back to his wagon, taking his time. Covered by the overhang of the canvas, he reached in to retrieve his musket then rejoined the captain.

"What's wrong?" he asked.

"There's movement along the shore…in those trees. Been hav'n a trouble with the Indians lately." He patted the weapon. "Keep it handy."

Also on board were four sailors manning the oars, a couple going to Richmond, two men headed west into the Appalachian Mountains, and a family with two small children. They were sent to hide under Jamie's wagon, and the passengers were soon well armed and ready in case of trouble. The Indians began a hair-raising barrage of wild whoops and threatening posturing. With that, Captain Conner steered the boat toward the middle of the James as a bombardment of musket balls landed harmlessly in the river. Jamie and the other men returned fire, chasing away those individuals from the shoreline attack. One shot, however, hit an oar and splintered it to bits, unnerving the oarsman. The threat was over, but their unease remained throughout the voyage.

* * *

The wharf at City Point jutted out into the river like a welcoming hand awaiting the weary passengers. The sailors helped Jamie with his load, then disappeared to a local tavern, and the captain walked the path to the customs house with Jamie driving his big wagon alongside. He said their destination was back downriver to Hampton once the boat was filled with barrels of tobacco and passengers.

"You been to City Point before? Used ta be Charles City Point before they shortened it."

His intended speech was of no interest to Jamie. The lad was just anxious to get to his destination and clucked his impatience with delay.

Captain Conner snorted at the snub. "Well, I won't leave you without direction."

He was a plain man with no distinguishing marks about him, so Jamie had no reason not to trust him.

"You can see the confluence of the James and the Appomattox rivers over that way." He pointed. "But you want to follow the shore along the Appomattox going west. Follow it until you come to McKinney Bridge and take it across to the north side of the river. Anyone can show you the trail from there." He had his hand on the doorknob, and taking a different tack, he said, "Have a drink with me before you go."

Not brought up to be rude, Jamie decided he would do well to thank the man instead of being uncivil. He parked the wagon alongside the customs house, and the minute he walked in, he perceived something was amiss. Instead of the homey atmosphere like Hampton, it smelled like a tavern with fetid odors of men soaked in the drink, stale tobacco, and grime-infested floors. Intoxicated yelling and raucous laughter accompanied suspicious eyes peering over the rims of tankards sizing him up and checking out his rig through the open window.

"Nice load ya got thar, sonny. Them horses sure do make a mighty purty piture. How much you paid for 'em, boy?" a drunk named Isaac demanded.

Jamie put a coin on the table for their drinks and quickly bid adieu to Captain Conner. He felt those eyes stabbing him in the back as he exited the place.

Outside, he ran into the two well-provisioned and heavily armed men heading toward the mountains, and with a glance over his shoulder, Jamie asked, "Would you care to accompany me in case of trouble?" They caught his inference and welcomed him with a smile.

Back inside the customs house, George Isaac oiled his way over to the captain and pounded a half-empty bottle on the table in front of him. Filling the empty glass, he sat in a drunken daze, puffing on a chewed cigar stump and coughed a large wad of spit on the floor. "Who's the tenderfoot with the big plough?" The fringe on his grimy buckskins fairly shook with greed for that rig.

Chapter 6

New Friends

TEN MILES DOWNRIVER of the Appomattox, people and wagons waited in a queue to cross a bridge. Taking his place in line, Jamie spent the time learning about the two men heading to the frontier— Robert French and Kenneth MacQuarrie. Robert, a loner, hailed from Pennsylvania. His mother was a Lenape Indian, and she told her son that his father was a sailor from a place called Nowhere—"where the sun rises," she'd said, pointing across the water. Jamie wondered if his last name presented a clue. Not accepted in the tribe, Robert was bullied from the time he was three and grew into a scrappy fighter. Living on the outskirts of civilization, he became a hardened woodsman and skilled hunter, preferring skins and fur to the frills of genteel life—not that he would be accepted in that life given he was a half-breed. He had been married to a squaw who was killed in a skirmish a few years earlier at a place called Fort Necessity[12] in the Ohio Territory. "Call me Robbie," he suggested to Jamie.

His friend Kenneth came from a long line of clan chiefs in his Scottish home on the Isle of Staffa in the Hebrides—toughness was

---

[12] The Battle of Fort Necessity (also called the Battle of the Great Meadows) took place on July 3, 1754, in what is now Farmington in Fayette County, Pennsylvania....The Battle of Fort Necessity began the French and Indian War, which later spiraled into the global conflict known as the Seven Years' War (https://en.wikipedia.org/wiki/Battle_of_Fort_Necessity).

in his sinews. Both Benjamin and Paddy had told Jamie many stories of sailing past that weather-swept island, embellishing them with ghosts and other strange creatures like dragons and witches all alive and well, at least in the minds of those who had been there. Kenneth wore his plaids—faded red and green ragged and filthy with age. Jamie laughed to himself thinking he'd probably worn them in one of the wars of the distant past. Safe to say, while they granted him his Scottish identity, they didn't grant him any quarter with the English in the colonies. Jamie figured that was probably why he chose a wayfaring life away from hatred and danger.

"His only trouble is drinking," Robbie said about Kenneth. "Started with a 'wee dram of rum,' he told me. Someday it will be his ruin." He shook his head. "Pity it is. He's a good man."

The line started to move. Jamie held his breath and hoped the bridge would take the weight of his team and heavy wagon. In the middle of the bridge the boards groaned. Once on the other side, he let out his breath. "Whew," he said to the man collecting fees and who eyed the substantial load.

His bony hand stroked the sparse hairs on his chin. Finally, he said, "That'll be three cob, mister."

"I don't have any Spanish dollars," Jamie replied. "And besides, you only charged the wagon in front of me one cob!"

"Yah but yur three times the size of that 'un."

But Jamie was a thrifty Scot. "How about a copper farthing?"

The man spat on the ground and folded his arms. "How 'bout five?"

Jamie was getting annoyed. "How about three and the directions to the trail to Lynchburg!"

That did it, and McKinney pointed west. "You'll need to pick it up at the bend thata way." He spat again.

Jamie flicked the coins to the owner of the bridge. That McKinney was surely making good money gouging the folks who needed to cross.

The bridge at the Appomattox River was disappearing from Jamie's view as was the money from his pocket. He hoped there would be no more expensive fords in the coming days.

They left the gentle breezes along the riverbank for suffocating humidity inland where the sun burned their skin, and dust from the trail got in their noses and stuck to their damp skin. Even with the river in the distance and an occasional overhanging arch of oaks and pines providing some shade, the adventurers stopped often.

Protecting his great wagon and concealing it from those who would attempt to take it by force was Jamie's main concern. Before nightfall, he hid it in a grove or wood with a dense layer of branches to cover the white canvas top. His friends helped him water the horses at the river, then they picketed them in any grass that could be found close by.

Jamie discovered early on that Mr. MacDonald had given him a good larder of food stuffs for the trip—oats, flour, bacon, sugar, coffee—and with a bit of hunting of rabbit or possum roasted over a good hot fire, they could eat well enough. The men hunkered down for the night when the only disturbance might be the hoot of an owl doing its own hunting.

Near dawn, Robbie and Kenneth were awakened by birdsong and oak cakes frying alongside the meaty deliciousness of bacon curling in the pan. Jamie was grateful he met the men along the James River. They proved to be good companions and helped with hunting and the time-consuming hitching of the six horses.

A week went by and cooler, overcast, and rainy weather allowed the team to make better mileage. On a good day, they could chew up sixteen miles. However, with dead-calm heat riding along on their backs, only eight—or ten if lucky—could be covered before the horses and men gave out. Jamie had been told by the barge captain that it was about "a hunert or so miles to Lynchburg and another thirty to Bedford or thereabouts." At the rate they were going, Jamie calculated it should only take them another two or three days to get there.

Before dawn, on what Jamie thought might be their last day out, some of his horses, all normally quiet and calm, began to snort and whinny. Their instinct for fear startled the men who were already restless in their sleep. Robbie was out of his bedroll in an instant, and Jamie and Kenneth smelled trouble too.

"What's wrong, Robbie?" Kenneth whispered, grabbing his flintlock and busily loading ball and powder.

Robbie's muzzle-loading long rifle was already poised for trouble. He put his finger to his lips then pointed to the left of the trail. Was it just travelers making an early start to beat the heat, or farmers heading to town on market day?

Swiftly, the invaders rushed into camp through the trees and lead balls from long barrels exploded with fire and smoke lighting up the still dark day. One of the troublemakers lay bleeding in the dirt, and the booms of the gunfire in the cool morning frightened a large flock of birds which fled through the treetops. Sparks from the red coals of the campfire danced in the blackness when lead balls hit tree branches and sent them crashing down, igniting fresh flames.

Jamie's pulse beat in his ears, and the ugly face of his attacker was disfigured in the glowing red of the fire as Jamie stuck him with his dirk. He pushed the heavy weight off him and quickly assessed the raging combatants. Fire-reflected faces bobbed in and out of the darkness on the trail that was now a battlefield.

Slashing at two men at once, Kenneth was causing mayhem. One robber got away from Robbie and came after Jamie, and then they did the death dance with bare hands. It was the man with the grimy buckskins from City Point, George Isaac. Boxing the man's ears, Jamie bruised his knuckles on the man's skull. They wrestled for a spell in the dust where Jamie's hand came upon his weapon. He quickly dispatched his enemy with one swift jab to Isaac's gut.

Jamie winced with the pain in his hand, not knowing if it was broken, and Robbie stopped to reload as two of the marauders ran away. But Kenneth's blood was running onto the cold earth.

"No...No...Kenny." Robbie swiftly went to his side and held his friend with much tenderness until he breathed no more.

A long, loud neighing from the horses alerted Robbie and Jamie that something else was amiss. They ran quickly to the picketed animals and angered at what they witnessed—two of Jamie's team stolen.

Three of the thieves were left to rot in a shallow rocky depression among trees and bushes where they were thrown. Kenneth was carried up a grassy knoll overlooking the beautiful flowing river and buried in a decent grave in his beloved plaids. Jamie recited some prayers his mother had taught him as a little boy in Scotland, and Robbie made a makeshift cross to record the passing of his dear friend.

It was midday before the pair finally left the camp, the sun fully upon them. Only four of the magnificent animals were left, straining to pull the heavily loaded wagon as they limped into the small settlement that was Lynchburg.

"Do you want a wee dram to take away the pain, Robbie?"

"No..." was all he said, hunched over in the depths of loss. Robbie would not be consoled.

Plodding through the main street, Jamie yelled at a blacksmith at his anvil, "Could you tell me where Henry Middleton's Ferry is located?"

"Straight through town you come to a fork in the road. Take the right hand."

Jamie waved and slapped the horses' rumps—twice—to get their attention. Their heads were lowered in pure exhaustion, and sweat streaked their hides.

Middleton's place was only a short way out of town. He was just hauling the ferry across the expanse of the river and looked at Jamie. "Do you want to cross?" he yelled.

"No. I look for Henry Middleton."

"All right, park your rig around back. I'll be there in a minute."

He came around the large log two-storey building in a flurry. "Let me help with those horses. You can put them in the corral and stay the night. You looked whooped." Depleted in body and spirit, Jamie and Robbie were grateful for his kindness. The animals delighted in fresh hay and large tubs of water. "I'll put your tack in the storage room."

Middleton was a big man, easily six feet four and a good three hundred pounds. He led the men into the store and bid them warm themselves. Sitting in the middle of the room was an odd contrivance, free-standing, and a cause of wonder and amusement, with a flue fitted through a hole in the roof. It had an open front, and within its chamber, a small fire burned brightly, heating not only the store's patrons, but a large coffeepot sitting on top. Henry gave his guests tin cups and told them to help themselves, then he disappeared. While the night air wasn't particularly cold, Jamie and Robbie were so exhausted, they were chilled to the bone, and the strong, black coffee felt good running down their throats even with grounds in the bottom of the cup and egg shells floating in it.

Jamie looked around and observed the store was a mix of what Henry Middleton did—customs house, postal route stop, store, home, and, as evidenced by many chairs set askew around the stove, the proprietor of the local social hub.

"Mother, how about some stew for our guests," they heard him say from another room. Middleton stuck his head through the door and told them to come into the kitchen. "We're done for the night. I'll go lock up."

"What is that thing, sir?" Jamie gestured toward the source of the heat.

"A newfangled Franklin cast-iron stove, and you would do well to order one."

Jamie and Robbie were salivating. Each ate two helpings of the beef, potatoes, and carrots swimming in a luscious gravy. Amelia Middleton cut thick slices of homemade bread then slathered a generous portion of butter on each. The golden-brown crust was crisp, and the soft part sopped up the stew's gravy. As they were taking that last tasty bite, the travelers were beginning to nod off. Amelia smiled at her husband and then directed Jamie and Robbie to their beds.

* * *

In the morning, a clatter of dishes and pots wrestled Jamie out of the luxurious cocoon he had made for himself. For one night, at least, he had been able to forgo the trail's hard ground.

Mr. Middleton's sweet talk to the horses could be heard through the window as he fed them with an extra treat of oats. Jamie stuck his head out into the day reveling in the scene before him—a lush pasture surrounded by a crossed-log fence, dense forest beyond, and a long blue mountain range off in the distance. It was a glorious warm summer morning, and the look of the land evoked his dream. He was not far from home now.

"Robbie, wake up. We need to get going."

A mumble arose out of a mountain of quilts and pillows, but Robbie was nowhere to be seen buried under luxury he had never experienced.

A gentle knock came at the door and Mrs. Middleton's soft voice invited them to table.

After the Middletons and their guests dined on a breakfast repast that would sustain them all the way to Bedford, Jamie presented Mr. Middleton with the papers Donald MacDonald gave him before he left Baltimore. Henry unfolded them and read first one letter then another, all the while drinking his coffee. He wiped his mouth on a large kerchief and let out a hardy outcry catching everyone off guard.

"Ah, Donald. I haven't heard from him in years. We came over on the same ship together." He reached for the coffeepot sitting in the middle of the table and poured his cup full again, egg shells floating on the surface. Putting the pot back in its place, he said, "We didn't get properly introduced last night. I am Henry Middleton, and this is my beautiful wife, Amelia. And you are?"

"Sorry, sir. I'm Jamie Kimsey, and this is my friend Robbie French."

"I suspect that rig out there was a gift from Donald. Am I right?"

Jamie gulped the last of his coffee. "Yes, sir."

"A most generous man, and I see by his signature he also gave you his acreage as well. I was there when he bought it many years ago…Yur gonna need the surveyor." He went to the kitchen door and yelled, "Joshua, go and get Jonathan Macrae!" Henry sat down again. "Joshua's a freed slave. He's a good man, and I pay him well because he has a big family, and me and my wife were never blessed with children."

Amelia arose from her chair, added more water, grounds, and egg shells to the coffeepot, and returned it to its rightful place, atop the stove in the store. She kindled the fire.

Middleton and his new friends followed on her heels and sat in pleasant congeniality.

"Why only four horses for that big load?" Henry sort of guessed the reason.

"We had a little trouble along the way, sir. Five men followed us from City Point thinking to rob us. We were three and we beat 'em, but Kenneth, Robbie's friend, got killed. We buried Kenneth in his clan colors overlooking the Appomattox. The ones that got away stole two of my horses."

A chill of sadness settled over the two young men, and only the crackle of the flames disturbed the quiet. A door opened and closed and brought them around to the task at hand.

"Jonathan, you're here. Good man." Everyone was introduced.

The tall, thin surveyor wore a coat and breeches of black broadcloth, woolen hose, a brown brocade waistcoat, a linen shirt with the stock a flurry of lace, a cocked hat of brown felt and a neat brown hair ribbon tied on the queue of his wig—all befitting his station. He also wore gold-rimmed spectacles with which he read the deed.

"I know this land. Remember, Henry? The three of us went together…Oh, I see where Donald has given it to you, Jamie. Fine idea. None of us is getting any younger, right, Henry? How is the old buzzard? I suppose you'll be wanting to get started right away. The iron pins should be totally lost in the overgrowth after all this time."

"Yes, sir, but first I need to do some business with Mr. Middleton."

"Not a concern, young man. I'll come back in an hour. I need to get my instruments and maps."

Robbie went outside to check on nothing in particular.

Jamie knew he must lighten the load of the Conestoga. He wanted his horses fit when he got to Bedford, but, in his Scottish frugality, he did not want to spend extra money to buy two hardy mules to fill out the complement. And so, the well-stocked wagon— six and one-half tons of it—was divided and made lighter by one-third. It was hard to leave behind any part of it, especially for fear of breakdowns—a broken wheel, brake lever, doubletree, tongue—but he promised Middleton he would be back after he settled himself on the land. Everything was set. Macrae rode a big black mule, and Robbie declined to do anything but walk.

West to Bedford, along an old Indian trail, the mood was cheerful. Even Jamie's exceptional animals, with lighter steps, made the twenty-five miles seem as nothing. The talk was cordial—each man having his say or not, as humor or turn of words struck him. Jonathan told about his life when he had been a classmate of a young man named George Washington at the College of William and Mary in Williamsburg in 1749.

"George received his surveyor's license at seventeen, and I was twenty-seven. I was impressed by the young man. Tall boy at six feet. Leading the Virginians, he fought alongside the English against the French and Indians. Later he had a thousand men fighting on the frontier. Heard he was headed to Fort Duquesne in the Ohio territory, but our news in Lynchburg is sometimes slow."

"My wife was killed at Fort Necessity," Robbie told him, sorrow casting a shadow across his face. Suddenly, he brightened. "I heard that Mr. Washington had two horses shot from under him and there were four bullet holes in his coat. He must have been a brave man."

Chapter 7

A New Home—Bedford County, Virginia

JAMIE WAS SEIZED by the grandeur spread out before him. Never had he seen such land since his young years walking the lanes with his father in Scotland. There was unruffled peace in the dark green forests. Sparkling streams watered the deep fertile earth ready for Jamie's sharp plough blade.

Jonathan indicated a turn in the road onto an overgrown track. *How did he have such a sense?* Jamie wondered. No one could actually see it except Jonathan, but all of a sudden, there was a meadow surrounded by stupendous trees—stalwart hickory, massive oak, ninety-foot chestnuts. Jamie coughed, choking on a fly caught in his gaping mouth, and Jonathan and Robbie laughed until their sides hurt.

Their mirth quickly departed as Jonathan unexpectedly left them, yelling, "There it is! There it is!" He said it over and over like a little boy finding a favorite lost toy. The linchpin of his calculations was a lovely dogwood in full bloom but nearly undetectable in the tall grass and heavy brush. "If it hadn't been in bloom, I would have missed it altogether."

At full tilt, he went to where he thought the next pin would present itself, but he disappeared under heavy cover with blades and branches rippling like waves over him, giving away his position. He let out a shout and then a splash was heard. Robbie darted toward the commotion, and Jamie was off his horse in an instant. When

Jonathan surfaced, he was soaking wet and covered with debris, his cocked hat melting over his forehead, and the wig dripping white powder over his coat.

"I miscalculated," he said, a silly grin spreading over his face. "Of course, that fallen tree didn't help. Wonder when…that…happened." His voice trailed off.

Jamie produced a scythe and an ax from the wagon, and Jonathan took out his surveying equipment. Everything was recorded on his map, so finding the positions in the overgrowth was easy to discover with Robbie wielding the scythe and cutting back obstructive growth. Jamie cut branches and mounted them with a shred of canvas banner to mark the perimeter of his land along with the pins. When completed with the coordinates connected, Jamie had 325 acres precisely.

Robbie left the two men to scout for the perfect campsite and went hunting for meat for the evening meal. He found sign alongside the stream and tracked a hare. A flash of moving white caught his eye, but Robbie's musket ball was quicker than the frightened creature. Skinned and skewered, the juicy rabbit meat dripped fat onto the fire.

Meanwhile, Jamie chopped some onions into lard Amelia Middleton had given him, browned them with a goodly portion of oats, and stirred them all together. Round brown loaves of her delicious bread were sliced, and Jonathan held them over the flames.

The hasty puddin', crispy hare, and crunchy toast delighted the three woodsmen as they enjoyed the warm night under a sky filled with stars. Jamie washed dishes at the stream with sand then rejoined his compatriots, who had laid out bedrolls under a canvas lean-to. The three friends talked until their eyelids grew heavy. The red glow of the fire reflected on the white canvas then melded into ink-black sky, and Jamie dreamed of his Mary, wondering.

Jonathan left early the next morning, hoping to beat the heat of the day and make a side trip to see a friend before heading back to Lynchburg. Unwillingly, the three men parted company. They had enjoyed their brief time together as if in some long time past they had been friends or brothers. No words were needed; each just knew it.

Over breakfast, Jamie asked, "Where will you go from here, Robbie?"

The young man seemed older than he was, staring off into the wilderness. There was an understanding of life too deep for words—profound sorrow having reinforced profound happiness.

"You have been kind to me, Jamie. I would stay awhile to help?"

Jamie agreed with a simple nod, and in the next days, they walked the ground to choose suitable places to build, and to plant where the warm sun could cause growth. The earthy scent of his land evoked early memories of his father's farm in Scotland, and it thrilled him to have his own.

They traced a water course along his northeast boundary. The meadow appeared to be a good place to start, and Jamie went to reconnoiter from a high vantage point of a tall hickory tree loaded with underripe nuts. He could see the sinuous track of the river extending toward those far blue mountains in the west and patches of cleared land that held a hope of human neighbors, especially when he started the cabin raising.

Jamie and Robbie began the daunting task of felling trees and clearing land. They took down deadwood first, chopping it into manageable pieces for the campfire. A flock of birds flew away at the sound disturbing their peace. Then the men chose serious contenders from a stand of oak trees for the cabin Jamie would occupy. Their bits sliced into the hardwood; a strong heady odor permeated the air they breathed. But before long, each had stripped to the waist with sweat dripping off their chests and watering the earth.

The ax haft began to torture Jamie's palms and fingers with the beginnings of blisters. On larger circumferences, they turned to a crosscut saw, and the actions tortured his back. The woodsman just laughed at the farmer and tied some cloth strips to his hands.

"That'll take care of you until you can leather up. At this rate, you won't have a roof over your head before the first frost." Together, the pair had only managed a large stack of firewood and eight good-sized logs.

"Well, that was good practice." Jamie's lighthearted remark about their slow progress caused the boy in each of them to race to the river shedding their clothes. Like two buck naked children, they splashed each other, laughing and floating in the slow-moving stream. Jamie took a deep breath and dove down. Many silver fish skirted around them, but he wasn't successful in catching any. Robbie wasn't paying attention to the fish, however, as he perceived his new young friend—white skin rippling in the clear-running water—he was aroused.

Jamie broke ground the next day around a good sturdy tree, the sharp plough turning the clods. He bent down and took a large handful of the rich earth and looked at his friend. Broad smiles swept across their faces. Two fat worms wiggled out of the clump.

Suddenly inspired, they grinned in unison. "Let's go fishing." Robbie made hooks from some pins, attached them to hemp strings and tied each to a sturdy stick which, when dropped into the water, immediately attracted two brook trout. Liberally salted and dipped in egg—another of Mrs. Middleton's treats—then oatmeal, the fish were fried crisp, tender flesh falling off the bones.

A voice as disagreeable as a saw blade yelled, "Guten morgen, der Herr!"

Jamie started for his musket. On alert, Robbie came up from the stream with the cleaned fry pan in his hands.

"Excuse, please. I heard da noise of your axes and tought I would see who dis new neighbor vas. An, you haf a Conestoga. My kinsmen make tose in Kutztown."

Tension dissipated as the man seemed friendly, leaning on a walking stick and conversing enthusiastically. He wore loose-fitting pants of a light color tucked into woolen hose. A short blue coat had a double row of buttons, and a large red kerchief was tied in front over it.

"Mein name ist Hermann Ensch." He approached with an open hand. "Ich bin von Trier…auch…Pennsilfaanisch Deitsch" (Pennsylvania Deutch).

"Willkommen. I'm from Pennsylvania too," Robbie said excitedly.

Jamie scratched his head upon hearing a side of his friend he had never seen before. Herr Ensch was invited for coffee.

The trio sat under the shade of the canvas, Robbie relating that he had known many families in Germantown and west into the French-Ohio territory and had picked up some of the language along the way.

"Dis is a vell-placed property," declared Hermann. "I haf two hundred acres upriver. My Gertrude and I haf six boys to help on da farm. Ve vill help you ven it comes time. Yust follow da river vest unt you vill find us." He got up to leave and said, touching the brim of his hat, "Auf Widersehen."

In the course of ploughing, Jamie ran into rocky outcrops of river-exposed sandstone. This was good news as he would need a base for the stacked rocks of the cabin's four corners. While Robbie was off hunting, Jamie, using chisel and mallet, began the task of cutting the base stones to provide a flat footing for the weight of the cabin. Working the sandstone, though, was slow business.

Robbie came back with a good-sized buck, field dressed and ready for drying. "Get your salt," he said, leading the horse hauling the pallet into camp. Before long, thin strips of red raw meat were salted and rubbed with garlic—found along the river—and hung to dry. A well-salted rump roast was tossed into a large smoking pot hanging over the fire. It was browned on all sides and, with a quantity of water and the last of Mrs. Middleton's root vegetables, made for a slow-cooked stew. Finally, a juicy tenderloin was skewered and cooked for their dinner. However, cornmeal, oats, sugar, and coffee were running low, and Jamie could see that a trek to Middleton's store was at hand. But he looked at the sky and noted a weather change with thick dark clouds moving in. It was not a good time to travel to Lynchburg, and instead his thoughts turned toward Mary. How he longed for her, but he must quickly get at the remaining logs to finish the walls of his cabin. What if she came back early? His reverie was soon disrupted by thoughts of the trusses and flat boards still needing to be hewed out and the shingles to be cut, then overlaid to finish the roof. It was time to call for help from their German neighbors to set the logs. Robbie volunteered and left Jamie working on the last log. Neat stacks lay at each of the four sides.

The long chalk-covered string was snapped in place again and gave Jamie a straight line on the fourth rain log. He straddled it and began taking off the required inches with his foot adze to match the other three. He felt the first raindrop, and just as he took the last swipe, Robbie appeared and so did a squall.

"The family will be here day after tomorrow. It's Sunday—a day of prayer and rest for them…Thought you'd have had more done by now," he said with a grin. Jamie shrugged, and Robbie sliced into the last of the meaty loin, along with the last of the oats and the last of the onions and took shelter under the canvas lean-to while they ate.

"Sorry it's a little meager tonight, Robbie. Got to get to Lynchburg."

Chapter 8

Good Neighbors

ON THE MORNING of the first day of the week with the sun just beginning to flicker through the tall trees, all eight of the Ensch family showed up in camp.

"Guten morgen," Hermann bellowed, waking Jamie and Robbie out of deep slumber.

Jamie crawled from his bedroll, rubbing his eyes and yawning, "Good morning, sir."

Introductions were the first order of business. Starting with the oldest, there was Adam, then Peter, Joseph, Anton, Georg, Jens, "unt my vife, Gertrude," Hermann said proudly.

Mrs. Ensch, ignoring everybody, busied herself poking at nearly dead coals and raising flame with kindling. Once the fire burned brightly, she hung a pot over the heat. An appetizing sour aroma wafted through the camp when she lifted the pot lid and put in onion, peppercorns, and pine twigs, and it was left to bubble all morning long.

On a plank set over a stack of logs, she served breakfast with large quantities of kuchen, the little yeast dough buns twisted in figure eights and thumbprint hollows filled with rum-soaked dried apples. Left to rise in a large covered fry pan, the fat rolls were baked, then slathered all over with butter and sprinkled with sugar. A cup of rich black coffee was the best accompaniment. A hot pot of mashed yellow peas had a stack of bowls sitting next to it. Thick strips of crisp pork bacon were broken over the puree. The bowls quickly disappeared, leaving only two for their slow hosts.

Jamie and Robbie smacked their lips as they tasted the liberal fare, and in between bites, Jamie managed to ask why Mrs. Ensch threw "twigs" into her "stew."

"For flavor," she said curtly, as if he should have known.

Hermann put down his bowl and patted his wife's ample backside. "Sehr gut, meine Frau." He laughed, cleaning away crumbs from his lips with his red kerchief.

She blushed and wagged her finger at him. "Naughty."

Work began in earnest for the men and oldest boys. They ranged in age from twenty-one to nine years old. The younger ones went fishing on what they told Jamie was called the Little Otter River

Hermann nodded his approval of the level, well-placed, and tightly fitted rock piers at each corner. A good foundation, he told Jamie. He was also impressed by the sixteen-inch square hand-hewn oak timbers the two men had made for Jamie's single-storey cabin.

"Okay, boys," Hermann commanded, and the line of Enschs, plus Jamie and Robbie, lifted the first twenty-four-foot log of the first course. It had notches for the floor joists—halved trunks of thin pine trees. Flat boards placed over them made the floor of the cabin. Wooden pins coated with animal fat were pounded in auger-drilled holes to secure it to the sill. One door and two window openings were each faced by short logs and covered with the tie log course. Each crown notch found its home as the logs were set in place. If they refused, the logs were nudged into place by a large wooden hammer called a beetle.

Robbie had a practiced talent for carving crown notches and left his special mark upon Jamie's cabin. But more than once, Jamie found him bent over his maul and mortise ax, tears dripping over flying chips. He wasn't forthcoming with an explanation, but Jamie guessed each salty drop was probably a memory of a time when Robbie built a home for himself and his wife.

When the cabin grew above the tallest of them, Joseph and Anton climbed Hermann's sturdy ladders to the top course and nimbly stepped out on it. Ropes, tied to the next log, were thrown to them, and the log was drawn up over the ladders with the others pushing from below. The boys were agile at the dizzying and increasing height and placed the final rain logs as the topmost course. Two were cantilevered to support the porch roof. Sliding down the ladders, the boys were ready for their mother's good cooking. The sun was settling down for the night, and she had some hungry men to feed.

"Sauerbraten mit spätzle," Mrs. Ensch said. It gave off a delicious, lip-smacking aroma as she plucked out the twigs, tossing them away, and thickened the broth with a slurry of flour and water. Spätzle, little dumplings, were ladled onto tin plates, and the tangy sauerbraten cascaded over them, that beef rump roast sumptuously fork tender.

Work on the trusses began the next day. Eight-inch-diameter logs were stripped of their bark with a draw knife and chiseled out with bird's mouth notches. They were attached to the ridge pole, then flat boards were pinned over the trusses, and shingles were nailed on overlapping each other, making for a weather-tight roof. The gable ends were finished, and it was time for the Enschs to go and tend to their own farmwork at home. Jamie and Robbie would chink the logs themselves using the dried corncobs and stiff horse hair provided by the Enschs. Those items would be mixed with clay to daub between the logs. It was a well-made cabin, and Jamie felt blessed to have such good neighbors.

* * *

The trip to Lynchburg was without incident, but the weather quickly turned cold with frost. Jamie and Robbie had a light load, and the horses seemed almost frisky, happy to be away from hauling the heavy logs and blocks of sandstone. Jamie had a hard time keeping the animals from running all the way to a memory of fresh oats given to them by Henry Middleton who talked sweetly and brushed briskly.

"It'll be good to see Henry Middleton again, don't you think?"

Robbie, depressed for some time, emitted a sullen grunt. They hardly talked at all. When the subject was broached at home, he ignored Jamie's question, preferring the cold outside the cabin to the heat he wanted inside.

* * *

After several months' absence, Henry Middleton was exceedingly happy to see Jamie and Robbie alive and well. Henry heard the bell to cross some passengers over the James and left Jamie to place his order for supplies with Amelia.

"You and your friend will stay for supper, won't you, Jamie? It's almost nightfall, and the trail is not safe in the dark." Amelia's furrows of her wrinkled face showed her fear, and her eyes darted beyond him into the yard.

After a delicious meal, Henry sat with his guests around that same black iron stove with its coffeepot gurgling away, grounds and egg shells swirling about in the dark depths.

Henry echoed his wife's concern. "There are more and more people coming into this beautiful country. It's great for my business and those around town, but not so for the Indians in the area. It has become dangerous."

"What happened, Henry?" Jamie and Robbie were on alert.

"Some folks upriver were harassed by a small party last week, and up in Salem—not too far from you—animals were stolen, and a man was killed trying to fight them off. You need to keep a watchful eye."

A long pause followed, and a chill came over Jamie. He hadn't seen any Indians in Bedford and was worried about leaving his cabin and property unprotected. He shivered at the thought, and Amelia's guests went to their beds.

Middleton asked about the buckskins he was wearing. Robbie left the room to the swirling white flakes outside, leaving Jamie wondering why. "Robbie does the hunting and skinning," Jamie said, watching the door close behind his friend. "He makes them…"

"Something wrong?" Henry asked, sensing a problem. He pinched snuff from his tin and inhaled the rich brown tobacco. Amelia kissed her husband good night and excused herself from the two men.

Jamie stuttered, "I…uh…don't know…I think…he missed his opportunity to leave before the weather set in. He's been in a black mood…Started when we finished the cabin and then the first frost blanketed the land. The leaves seemed to shrivel and die overnight, and he did too."

Robbie never came back into the building, and Henry latched the door leaving Jamie to his thoughts. Was Robbie harboring some dark secret? He seemed agitated and uncomfortable. Maybe his friend's kindness was all that kept him from leaving to his western destiny. Giving it no more thought, Jamie slipped into the deep sleep of exhaustion, right where he was, as the rooms of Amelia's inn were full up. Next morning, he awoke to heat. It was barely light and the fire was dead. All was quiet. He went to the door and found everything outside dripping. The first frost came then left overnight. It was fall and the weather given to change, and the day was already hot.

Others stirred, and Amelia opened the kitchen door. "Jamie, come, have some coffee with Henry and me."

Robbie was already at the table, and a slight smile crossed his face. "Mr. Middleton will load the wagon with the gear you left behind. Have you ordered the supplies you wanted?"

Jamie pulled up the chair opposite him. He looked over the rim of the big tin cup and slurped his coffee. "Ouch! That's hot." He laughed. Robbie laughed. The cold chill was broken—at least for the moment.

"Henry, I need scythe and sickle blades, iron nails, and ax heads to build my house for Mary. Since the Iron Act[13] was passed, they're hard to come by, but do you know anyone in the area?"

---

[13] The Iron Act of 1750 was intended to stem the development of colonial manufacturing in competition with home industry by restricting the growth of the American iron industry to the supply of raw metals. Pig iron and iron bar made in the colonies were permitted to enter England duty free. In the colonies the

There were rumors of clandestine forgers who could make them, but Henry flatly refused to share the information and said he would order them from England. Jamie was angered, not at his friend, but that he would not get the necessary items in time—things that the colonies could produce for themselves. Any further goading of his friend was useless and ill-mannered.

It was hard to leave the friendly couple in Lynchburg, but Jamie didn't want to get stuck by temperamental weather. They hurried home even with horses a bit annoyed by the heavier load. The big brutes did not know that, at least temporarily, they would be treated to a few more days of delicious oats thanks to the Middletons.

They weren't down the road a half a mile when Joshua, Henry's black freeman, rode up, his horses' hooves kicking up dust that had been frosted over the night before.

"Mr. Kimsey," he hollered. Jamie reined in the big team. Perfect white teeth gleamed in a huge smile radiating around his black face. "Mr. Middleton forgot to give you this letter. It came in the post yesterday—all the way from Baltimore." His smile grew broader as he handed the precious correspondence to Jamie. "It smells pretty too," he confided and rode away.

September Letter

The script was from a delicate hand, and the fragrance was from a delicate beauty—his violet-eyed beauty. Guilt suddenly marred the thrilling moment—he had not written a word to Mary. She had never been far from his thoughts, but his mind had been entangled with logs and tools and other pressing things. He breathed in the scent of a brown curl tied with blue ribbon that was tucked inside.

---

following were prohibited: the new establishment of furnaces that produced steel for tools, and the erection of rolling and slitting mills and of plating forges; the manufacture of hardware; and the export of colonial iron beyond the empire. The British policy was successful in its goal of suppressing the manufacture of finished iron goods in the colonies, but colonial production of basic iron and pig iron (which were then shipped to England) flourished under the Iron Act (https://www.britannica.com/event/Iron-Act).

"Well, aren't you going to read it?" Robbie said, rude with annoyance.

Jamie silently perused a few lines. "Ah, she's in Paris," he said. "After Mary and Rebecca left Wales, they went to London, then on to Paris…She's buying her wedding dress." He wiped some tears from his eyes. "Rebecca's going back to Wales to marry the parson…" His voice trailed off.

"What parson? Why did they go to Wales? Who are these women? Jamie, you haven't been forthcoming with me." With no answers to his questions, Robbie ignored him and left him to his reverie, but inwardly, jealousy seized him.

Chapter 9

Trouble

THE CABIN WAS small but comfortable. The beautiful sandstone chimney was a jewel among the logs, and the hearth was perfect to warm the small cabin, bake some corn bread, or cook a pot of porridge.

Jamie placed his sacks of precious corn seed in the cool recesses of the sandstone cliffs and only retrieved what was needed so as not to entice black bears or other marauding creatures. Jamie would consider tobacco next season, but in the meantime, the seed would provide the food and barter needed.

As he followed the lines of his traps along the Little Otter River, hoarfrost crackled beneath Robbie's moccasins. There were more of these mornings, and soon the snow would be flying. He went far afield and came upon the large farm Hermann Ensch had told them about. The owner was a farmer, a blacksmith, and a cooper as well. They needed hinges and barrels, and Colin Mathieson could provide those necessities for Jamie's home. As they talked, Robbie could hear a thick Scottish brogue reminiscent of Kenneth and asked Colin about his homeland.

"Loch Carron, Wester Ross…that's where I was born. My father was a salmon fisherman by trade…"

Robbie, lost in sad reverie, didn't hear much of Colin's narration. Kenneth's warm brogue invaded his mind with longing memories.

"He brought us to the colonies before the first Jacobite rebellion in 1715. War was brewing, and we got out in the spring before Father was 'collected' for James Francis Stuart's battle which began the fall of that year... What was it you needed?"

Robbie hadn't realized Colin stopped talking. "Sorry. About a dozen hinges and five barrels." The two men shook hands confirming the order as snow began to fall.

Retracing his steps through the deepening snow, Robbie collected some rabbits newly caught from the now obscured traps. After he reset them, he was nearing the cabin and thought of calling out for Jamie that fresh meat was coming, but suddenly a doe appeared in a break between the forest trees. He started to load his flintlock, but something was terribly wrong. The deer darted away as terrifying sounds met Robbie's ears: shrieks, whoops, shouts, moaning as in death. *Oh, God! Jamie!*

Running at full speed, he saw the scene was horrifying. Three half naked Indians were on the ground in a mix of snow, earth, and blood. Two were in a mortal struggle with Jamie who was losing the battle. One, whose buckskins were torn and bloodied, was poised with his tomahawk ready to strike, and Jamie was holding his wrist trying to prevent it. The other was mortally wounded and trying his best to pull Jamie down with him.

Robbie quickly raised his flintlock and smashed it over the head of the warrior whose tomahawk was held a foot above Jamie's skull. Over his shoulder, Robbie noticed flames licking at a corner of the cabin, and at the same moment Jamie collapsed in his arms, an arrow sticking out of his back. He put Jamie on the ground and threw the torch, intended to incinerate the cabin, into the snow. In no time, he stamped out the fire gaining momentum. The next moment he carried Jamie inside the cabin and laid him on his small bed.

Robbie gave no thought to the Indians who were outside either dead or dying, because his friend's welfare was all that mattered. His chest heaving from exertion, Robbie ripped away the rest of Jamie's torn buckskin shirt. He could not see clearly as night was falling. Lighting some candles in lanterns, the view of the wounds on the back became distinct. Robbie was relieved to see that most were shallow cuts from Indian knives, but the arrowhead was buried in Jamie's shoulder. He'd removed arrows from folks before, but as he tried to remove it from Jamie, it would not budge. Jamie groaned.

"You awake?" Robbie asked lightly.

"What do you want?" Jamie tried to laugh, but winced in pain instead.

"Just wanted to see if you were still alive."

"Well, just get the thing out of my back," he pleaded. "It hurts like hell."

"That's one nasty pin you got stuck in you." Robbie mulled it over in his mind how he would attack the situation. Stoking the fire with added kindling and another log, he then filled a pot with water from the water barrel and hung it to boil. He stuck his knife in the flames. Offering a stick of oak, he asked, "Can you bite on this? I'm going to try to cut it out."

Jamie bit down hard when the red-hot blade tip cut into his flesh. Robbie swore profusely, and after a few moments he finally noticed a movement from the shaft of the arrow. He turned it just a little, and the arrowhead gave way. The oak stick broke in two, and Jamie's scream in agonizing pain was stifled by unconsciousness.

Robbie washed Jamie's back tenderly, cleaning the hole and sopping up blood with compresses. A few of the cuts were leaking, and he prepared a mixture of dried herbs they had on hand. Garlic was mashed with comfrey, chamomile, wild daisy, and valerian, all mixed with animal fat. This mixture was spread over his back and pressed into the cuts. All night long, Robbie kept daubing the open wounds. He also prepared a tonic of Jopi[14] weed root overnight and gently lifted Jamie's feverish head to spoon the mix into his mouth.

It was first light when Jamie's restless body finally gave in to deep sleep. Robbie's wife had been a good teacher, and he'd been able to staunch the bleeding and prepare a decent tonic. He placed a few more small logs on the fire and collapsed on his bedroll. An emergent

---

[14] Jopi (joe-pye): the roots and leaves could be steeped in hot water and the liquid taken for fever and inflammation.

ache for his Indian squaw, or was it Kenneth, launched itself in his groin. He was tormented with longing.

Kenneth had replaced her. Both men had a desire that couldn't be quenched with a woman. Both had a desire to see what was west of the Appalachian Mountains. They, therefore, teamed up, happy to be on their way to adventure in the far west and away from possible accusative looks and words should anyone discover their secret. But Kenneth was taken away as well—murdered on the trail toward their freedom.

Jamie stirred, and Robbie was at his side. He checked the herb bandages and compress. Everything was all right, and Jamie fell back to sleep.

In the bright frosty morning, a "Hallo the cabin," came with that familiar brogue Robbie had discovered when meeting with Colin Mathieson. "I brought some barrels for your use."

Robbie was aroused from his sleep and went to the door.

"What happened? Are you well?" Colin asked, shocked by the carnage in the yard.

Robbie explained, "After I left your place, I got back to see a damnable attack on my friend. Jamie had already dispatched some, but those last two nearly killed him," he said, pointing at the pile of bodies.

Colin set the barrels down and asked if he could help.

Robbie was short with him. "Come in. All I have to offer you is cold broth and cold coffee."

"No, thank you." He saw Jamie lying on the bed. "I have some medical training. Would you mind if I looked at the patient?" he offered.

Robbie shrugged and pulled back the blanket that covered Jamie, revealing his wounded back.

"Umm. Aha. Right then. Good job. The hole will mend. It's red around the edges. Watch it carefully. Add licorice and thyme to the next poultices. Do you have any dandelion wine? That would help him sleep. I can bring some with me the next time I stop by."

The next time you stop by? No longer could Robbie stand anyone getting in the way of his passion for the young man lying there in the midst of his pain. Angrily, he screamed, "Get out! I can take care of him myself!" Robbie took Colin by the arm forcing him out the door, then slammed it behind him.

Colin was amazed by the contemptuously rude treatment and vowed he would talk to Hermann about the situation.

Robbie saw Jamie's letter from Mary on the table, and anger, fueled by jealousy toward this woman, caused him to want to destroy it in the fire, but his desire was checked by "Who was that?" Jamie asked in a weak voice. "He sounded like a countryman."

Putting the letter back on the table, Robbie said gruffly, "Don't trouble yourself. Here, take some broth?"

Jamie managed a little, but during the day, he fell into a raging fever accompanied by chills. Robbie kept the fire stoked, changed the poultices, and fed him tonic. The red of the hole made by the arrow-head grew larger, and the fire and extra blankets were not enough. Robbie removed his clothes and lay down beside Jamie covering him with his body. The longing grew in him until it became uncontrollable. No matter what, he would rape this man he had called friend. No matter what, he would penetrate this man who had treated him kindly. He was lonely, he reasoned. He deserved this pleasure that was about to be his, but just as he was about to ejaculate before even getting close to the desired coupling, Jamie cried out in his stupor "Mary?" Horrified at what he was about to do, and grabbing his clothes, Robbie ran stark naked from the cabin into the cold wintry night.

Colin kept his word to visit Hermann. The German's face flushed with rage when he discovered a possible misconduct against their friend. "Gertrude, Adam. Vee are going to Yamie's house. Get ready."

Ice lay on the ground and hung from roof edges in long icicles. The Enschs rode their mules so as not to get bogged down in the deep drifts. When they arrived, Adam took care of their animals and Jamie's as well. Hermann barged through the door with Gertrude on his heels. There was no sign of Robbie. There was no fire in the tiny cabin. Stone cold tonic and broth hung over dead ash. Gertrude went immediately to their friend who was moaning and writhing in pain. His back was ablaze and his condition was grave.

Softly, like his dear mother, she spoke to Jamie, "Vee are here to take care of you now." Turning to her husband, she begged. "Vee haf got to get him to our home. He's barely alive."

"No, Trudy. Dragging him tru de ice and snow vould not help him. Vee vill stay da night and decide tomorrow vat to do."

Adam came in, and his father asked about the horses. "They'll be all right. I brought them into the lean-to behind the cabin and gave them some oats. We can hear if anything disturbs them in the night."

The men gathered wood and water for the night vigil. They knew their friend would be struggling between life and death.

Once the cabin was warm, Trudy did as she had done with all her boys—washed Jamie from head to foot—using special care on his back and removing all the old herbs and compress.

"Lift him, Hermann, from da bed," Trudy asked. She changed the bedding under him and then placed a clean cloth over the wounds and covered him well with blankets while she made fresh poultices and hot tonic and boiled more water for her vigil. Jamie was only eighteen, one year younger than her Peter. She treated him like one of her own.

"He hardly veighs more than a feather, Trudy," Hermann gasped sorrowfully.

It was a long night. He and his son slept on the floor. Neither would sleep in Robbie's bed preferring to throw it on the pyre for burning in the morning. Trudy prayed her German prayer book until her eyelids got heavy. She slept fitfully, waking when Jamie groaned or stirred.

The next morning, the weather had cleared, and Hermann and Adam prepared to dispose of the bodies. However, when they appeared in the bright sunshine, an amazing thing met their eyes— the bodies of the Indians were gone! Adam caught his breath and ran to the back of the cabin—the horses were still there. "Thank God," he exclaimed, wringing his hands and making the sign of the cross several times over himself.

"They're all there, Papa," he announced, returning to his father's side.

"Vee half much to be grateful for, Adam."

"Yah, we half much to be grateful for. Come and greet our dear friend," Trudy proclaimed from the porch, smiling broadly.

Jamie was gaunt and still in pain, but he was alive. With her tender care and good food, his wounds began to heal. Hermann went home, leaving his wife and Adam with Jamie until other arrangements needed to be made.

Trudy would not budge when Hermann came back the next day with Peter. Jamie was doing a little better, even sitting up with a number of Trudy's feather pillows placed behind him and taking more of her delicious broth. He didn't ask nor did the Enschs tell what happened to Robbie, but they had perceived what went on.

Colin stopped by that afternoon with his dandelion wine. "I was very worried about him," he told them. Jamie managed a weak smile when he heard the Highland brogue again. But he wasn't much company after a few sips of the tasty wine and again slipped into a deep sleep.

The weather varied over the coming days, and with each day, Jamie grew stronger. One comfortable evening as flames jumped playfully in the hearth, he sat up without help and smiled at Trudy. He told her shyly, "You remind me of my mother. It's been a long time since she died on that ship coming from our home, and I miss her loving care…My sister-in-law Aggie loved me in her stead." He was overwhelmed with sorrow, gratitude, love, and loss.

"It is all right, Yamie. Oh, I forgot." She reached in her apron pocket. "I found dis letter on da table when we found you…ah… Vould you like to read it now?"

"Would you read it to me, Mrs. Ensch?" he asked timidly.

"I vould consider it a great honor." Lifting the seal, she unfolded the letter. "Oh…dis letter is from last year."

Through Mrs. Ensch's thick German accent, Jamie heard Mary's words in her own endearing Welsh timbre.

September 24th, 1757

My beloved Jamie,

This is my second letter that I write to you from Paris, France. Rebecca and I are visiting a couturier who will design that perfect dress which I will wear when we are wed. She is seeking the perfect gown that is all the rage in the upper circles of society here for when we will return to Wales and she will wed Reverend Beecham whom we met searching for our deceased uncle. The reverend is rector of St. Alban's Parish. They will live in the parsonage just a short distance whence we grew up. He has aspirations, however, of becoming a bishop, so the time will not be long before his elevated status will take them from the city that spawned the terrible times we suffered at the hands of our uncle. Remember, I told you about our travails in my first letter?

I trust you are well, my darling. I remember the sensation of touching your strong handsome face. Nothing can erase my memory of it. I see it when I look into a mirror and your gaze looks back at me and into my soul. Our love and innocence were so fresh then. I gave you my heart and thought it a dream that you gave me yours and asked that I share a future with you indelibly linked together forever. I could barely believe that we had within ourselves, at such a young age, that knowledge of our capacity for happiness. My absence from you only makes my heart fall in love with you over and over as I think about that time in front of the ship that was destined to take me away from you. I so look forward to the day when we shall be reunited again, my darling

Jamie. Don't forget me, my love, in the interim of time we are apart.

Life is barely sustainable without you. Close your eyes and remember me as I write this letter from my heart.

Yours forever, Mary.

Mrs. Ensch dabbed at her face with a handkerchief. "Vat a beautiful love letter. I vonder vat happened to the first one?" she said with tears streaming down her cheeks. "She must be a lovely girl, Yamie."

A quiet peace drifted over shared feelings of an old woman and a young man—a wonderful life with her husband and children, and for him, a memory of a young girl with whom a life was yet to begin.

A German Christmas 1758

Jamie was getting his strength back and finally able to care for himself. His dear friends had left him with a promise that he would join them for their Christmas celebration. Jamie was drawn to the idea as any festivities on the birth of Christ were forbidden by a religion in the homeland that saw them a sin.

In Scotland, Hogmanay was the time of joyful jubilation on the eve of the new year. Sweet cakes and small gifts were treats. Jamie's mother knitted warm caps for her boys, and their father, Robert, whittled small dogs or sheep daubed with a bit of real wool for the little ones. On that night, bonfires were lit, and musket fire and the skirl of the pipes rent the air in the vales of Scotland.

Jamie sorely missed his mother, father, and all his family scattered to the winds. And Mary? His heart yearned for her. Harnessing his emotions, he resolved to make a whiskey cake to take to the Enschs' home—a lovely dark cake soaked in Irish whiskey and crowned with a sprig of pine. Henry Middleton had made sure Jamie had his wee dram for cold nights, but the young man wanted to be among friends, not drinking alone at home.

Christmas morning dawned as a bright day with a blue-black sky, no hint of a cloud, and a weak winter sun trying to warm the earth. But the deep snowdrifts, even with his wheelhorse under him, were ice-cold, and his breath stood out in the frosty air. Only the sounds of crunching snow and the friction of rubbing leather kept them company.

The Enschs' cabin was a great log structure with a second storey. Jamie approached the building in awe.

Peter opened the door with a big smile, a handshake, and the greeting now familiar to Jamie. "Wie geht es dir, mein Freund?"

"I'm very well, Peter. Thank you."

"Let me take the Conestoga to the barn. I'll give him some oats and lots of nice hay."

Hermann and Trudy ushered Jamie through the massive door where the warmth of the room and tantalizing aromas of Christmas greeted him. Mr. and Mrs. Ensch glowed in the pride they felt sharing their bounty with their young neighbor. Their sons appeared from all over the cabin, greeting Jamie and making him feel welcome. Trudy kissed his cheek and handed him a cup of hot wassail heady with wine and spices.

A large pine tree stood off to one corner glowing with glittering candles, and gingerbread cookies pierced with red ribbons hanging from every branch.

A mammoth stone fireplace and hearth took up one entire wall of the living area, and it drew Jamie's attention, not so much for the size, but the scene making a splendid appearance upon the mantelpiece.

"What is this, sir?" Jamie asked, sipping his delicious libation. It was a wonder Jamie had never seen before.

Mr. Ensch struggled with the English words, and his youngest boy, Jens—who spoke both German and English as did all the Ensch children—was able to convey his father's words perfectly well. "Do you know the story of the Christ child born in a manger in Bethlehem?"

"I do. Is that what all this is about? Our religion forbade the celebration in Scotland."

"Presbyterian?" Jens winked, smiling, then gave him a tour of the scene. "It all started with an Italian named Francesco from the town of Assisi five hundred years ago. The first scene was a 'living' one intended to educate the people in the worship of Christ. We used to have plays in Germany. I saw one once. But when we came here, Father started to carve small pieces, then we all did it, and some of us add a figure each year."

Festooned with greenery, exquisitely carved people, animals, houses, and trees dotted the landscape of white cloth doubling as snow. Hermann's sons were highly trained carvers and workers of wood. However, the abundance of carvings did not overshadow the centerpiece: a crèche with a tiny baby asleep in a straw-covered manger flanked by the Virgin Mary and Joseph. Angels with ribbons tied to pine boughs floated above.

The boys had been taking their turns at the fireplace hand crank when Gertrude announced the goose was done and moved to the spit with Hermann on her heels. She stabbed the big bird with two large forks and removed it from the rod, placing it on her best German china platter which Hermann proudly carried in procession to the already crowded table. His powerful voice sang out a very old Latin and German Christmas carol

> In dulci jubilo,[15] nun singet und seid froh!
> Unsers Herzens Wonne leit in præsepio und
> leuchtet als die Sonne matris in gremio.
> Alpha es et O.

The feast was begun with a prayer of thanksgiving. It reminded Jamie of the days when his mother, Mary, and stepmother, Aggie, never started a meal or any other activity without thanking God for giving the Kimsey family life. Jamie vowed to continue the tradition instilled in him.

---

[15] It means "In sweet jubilation." Song title: "Good Christian Men, Rejoice" (1320).

Chapter 10

Planting, Building, and Other Things

1759

CHRISTMAS HAD BECOME a pleasant memory as Jamie took care of small chores—drawing water, cooking, tending the horses—and at night, in the glow of the fire and candlelight, he allayed his loneliness with constructive thoughts. He designed outbuildings and the large house he would build for Mary and himself. He planned the planting of his crops. He also made himself write to his beloved. It wasn't that he didn't want to; he just wasn't that good with words. He called her to mind—a young beauty, of course—but how to use words to tell her how much he longed for her, loved her, cherished her. He opened his Bible to the Songs of King Solomon. Now there was a man who could write. Jamie picked up his quill and dipped it in the inkwell. "Dear Mary," he began then sat back in his chair. A small drop of ink fell on the paper. Annoyed, he started in earnest. "I have tarried long enough, my darling." He continued and did not quit until the end of the parchment. He would mail it as soon as the first thaw.

On sunny days, he ventured outside and walked short distances, then longer ones, trudging through the snow building up his strength. As he came across Robbie's traps—sprung by small animals, falling twigs or heavy snow—he reset them. On those walks, he wondered what had happened to Robbie and if he were still alive. Jamie preferred to think he was off traipsing west of those blue mountains, following his dream. There were unpleasant thoughts of Robbie, though. He should have seen the signs, but dwelling on them would only make him mull over terrible things he did not want to remember. His thoughts turned to his brother Benjamin who had told him about those men, and he was surprised it had happened to him.

* * *

When spring was on the beautiful land of Bedford County, Virginia, Jamie's faithful horses easily pulled the plough through the toughest clods and rocky ground and into the fertile earth beneath. He loved those four Conestoga horses, and they in turn loved working with him. Seeds were planted, Hermann's gift of apple seedlings were tended, logs were linked for fencing, and a rise in the land was chosen for a home with a beautiful view. He built a corn crib for the hogs he would buy from Colin. The water was rushing in the Little Otter River, and he would put up a spring house for the milk from the cows he would buy from Hermann. A smokehouse would be constructed to cure the bacon and hams from the hogs and also small game. All this he promised when he wrote to his beautiful Mary.

In the midst of his works, he took the time to go to Lynchburg to post his letter with Henry Middleton. He rested awhile with the amiable man and again shared a meal and coffee with his friends. Word had slipped to Henry about the trouble in Bedford—Indian trouble, that is. "Did Robbie get off on his way west?" was all he asked. "Yes" was all Jamie replied.

Henry gave him his letter, and the bell rang, calling him to his duty at the ferry. "I'll be right back," he told Jamie. But the lonely young man didn't hear, excitedly opening the fragrant sweetness of the parchment. His mind went to his letter to Mary waiting to be picked up at Henry's post. The second page of her letter was on top, and the last line caught his attention. "It is with longing in my heart that I receive some small note from you as you haven't answered my first two letters—"

Henry interrupted, "False alarm. Now, where were we?"

Jamie was forlorn. He wished Benjamin or Paddy were here to sail him to her side.

"Don't worry, my friend. She'll be home soon. Here's the *Virginia Gazette*. There's an advertisement on page two you might be interested in."

They shared the news of the day both from the *Virginia Gazette*, published in Williamsburg, and the *Maryland Gazette*, from Annapolis. Both newspapers circulated all over the colonies. From the advertisement he saw, Jamie was reminded of Henry's suggestion last year that he should buy the stove "invented by Benjamin Franklin in 1741." Jamie thought that the cast-iron box stove, which would "cause less smoke like a regular fireplace and does the double duty of heating and cooking," might please his bride. "It will take awhile," Henry told him, but Jamie would have one and promised to pay from the proceeds of his first harvest of tobacco and corn.

Jamie was on the road for home. Middleton, leaning on the corner of his own house, those notched timbers he himself had hewed, watched the red-haired young man with blond stubble on his chin ride off with the wagon's canvas waving in a good stiff breeze. What had Jamie endured over well-nigh ten months to make him grow so quiet?

With sorrow, Henry walked back to his store, and the coffeepot boiled again and again until thick layers of eggshells and old grounds settled and had to be thrown into the garden. Fresh coffee never quite tasted the same. The bell rang, and he was out the door to bring over passengers wishing to cross the river.

* * *

Jamie felt satisfied with his trip to see his good friends and post the letter to his love. He hoped it wouldn't get lost or cross paths with Mary on her way home especially as it was so difficult for him to write. Her fragrance from the paper tantalized him, and seeing her script, he felt its thrill soothing his longing.

March 3 1758

My darling Jamie,

We remained in Paris over the holidays at the insistence of Rebecca. I have pleaded with her to return with me to Wales as Rev. Beecham awaits her, but she loves the gaiety that life affords here. How I despise the nettlesome and gilded companionship of her friends and long for my dear heart's peace in the home I know you are building for us. I can almost visualize its beauty which keeps me strong from the distracting frills of this life. Rebecca has become a complete bore. She tells me we will be leaving in a month, and when that occurs, we will be living at Gwenyth's Boarding House.

Despite the theft of our uncle's money, it was a paltry pittance of what he actually had. He apparently did not hold a grudge and left a small fortune to both of us even though he had other family. Somehow, he had made a connection with us despite all appearances. It wasn't long after we left that he died in his sleep and the money was held for us with an attorney.

I fear there will be many more months before I can return to your side. My wedding gown is wrapped and packed and awaiting the day when we will be wed. I also have a surprise for Aggie, your little step-mother, a beautiful gown for her use when you and I exchange our vows. I have posted a letter to her asking if she would be my matron of honor. I hope this pleases you, Jamie, as she was the only mother I ever knew.

It is with longing in my heart that I receive some small note from you as you haven't answered my first two letters. Have I done something wrong, my darling, to displease you? Until then, I bid you adieu for now, dearest Jamie.

Your loving Mary

Chapter 11

A New Wife

1760

JAMIE AWOKE SUDDENLY from his reverie in the field, jerked back to the present by the pull of the reins of his impatient team.

How many years had it been? He was twenty, and three years ago his beloved left him. The house stood ready but empty, for he stayed in the small cabin nearby which fit his needs. Besides, he told himself, the big house was too lonely. He worked hard filling up the empty spaces of his mind with ploughs, tobacco, and earth. Jamie was a strong man, bronzed by the sun; however, any neighbor who might pass by his plantation at dawn or dusk would shake their heads at the sight of the sad solitary farmer. They knew the story, and many tried unsuccessfully to help him change his plight by inviting him to parties and church services. He scorned their intrusions. Even Colin's daughter, Patience, was presented to Jamie as a possible mate. She was of marriageable age after all, pretty, and well versed in the Bible, table manners, and sewing. You couldn't ask for more.

Jamie wanted more.

When the tobacco was chest high, Jamie left his land to journey back to Lynchburg for supplies. He always stayed overnight, preferring the company of the occupants of the customs house to the loneliness of the road. Again, he passed the time and dined with his good friends, Amelia and Henry Middleton, and any visitors awaiting transport across the James River.

After Joshua helped Jamie load the wagon with supplies, the Franklin stove, and the iron items he had ordered three years earlier, Jamie headed out of the small settlement that was growing up around Henry's place. He stopped and watched the barge bobbing in the current of the wide river. Then his eyes caught movement on the far side, and the flat-bottomed conveyance jerked to life as it was towed by ropes to the waiting passengers. It was difficult to make out individual people, but Jamie was in no hurry, so he took in the whole scene.

A warm summer wind came across the fields bringing the sweet smell of woods and earth, blooming wildflowers, growing crops—and the morning was fresh with the songs of birds and hum of myriad insects. Jamie shifted in the saddle of his wheelhorse, the leather always uncomfortable on his spare behind. He felt alive and full of unexpected and unexplained anticipation. *What a strange feeling*, he thought, as he gazed off toward the approaching ferry. The passengers on board were at the landing, and he could pick out some women's skirts, a few horses, and a couple of men. *Why would women be coming to this place?* he was wondering when an interruption came from a familiar voice. It was Joshua.

"Mr. Kimsey! Mr. Kimsey, you forgot your molasses."

After securing the reins, Jamie jumped off the wagon, untied the canvas covering, and rearranged a few sacks of flour to make room for the jug. Climbing onto his horse, he said, "Thank you. I'm glad I stopped to watch the ferry. Canna make do without molasses for sweetening." He reached down to shake Joshua's hand.

Everything secured, he slapped the horses' rumps with the leather in his hands, and they turned their muzzles toward home, but just as he rounded the corner of Middleton's store, Jamie caught sight of something. He turned to see a woman stepping from the ferry and shielding her eyes from the morning sun.

The woman was saying, "Well, Jamie, are you just going to ride off and leave me here after coming so far?"

He sat puzzled, looking into a face that seemed familiar.

"Don't you recognize me?" she said in a worried voice, clasping her hands in front of her. Now Mary was scared. *What if he doesn't remember me? What if he's married?* She almost cried in the frozen moment as she held her breath.

Jamie's heart recognized her first and told him to look into the violet eyes. He slid off the horse and saw the teasing brown ringlets caressing the creamy white skin. He peered at her and cried out, "Mary! Oh, my Mary…Is it really you?"

She smiled broadly and threw wide her arms. He entered those arms and felt her womanliness. This was no girl anymore. And she was home. And he was with his beloved again.

* * *

Jamie felt a sense of accomplishment and pride as he presented Mary with the gifts he accumulated during those years of waiting. Their home was clad with whitewashed wood siding and painted green trim and fitted with the new Franklin stove. And in the drying barn was an abundant crop of tobacco.

Jamie sent for his brother, the Reverend Benjamin Kimsey, just four years into his ministry and living as pastor of a Baptist church in Albemarle County. Word was sent back that they could be in Bedford in one month and, as a surprise for Mary, would bring Mr. and Mrs. MacDonald with them.

It was the end of September, and an early frost tricked the green leaves of summer into the rich colors of fall—golden yellow, plain brown, and apple russet. All the neighbors for miles around were invited and a profusion of wonderful food was prepared for the two-day celebration.

Ian, Aggie and Benjamin's oldest boy, plucking at his linen stock, was standing in the parlor where the wedding ceremony would take place. "Mother," he complained, "can I take this thing off? It's too hot."

Aggie stood between rooms, tying the last ribbon around the stems of the nosegays the two women would carry: simple greens, late summer asters, and the lavender Mary brought back with her from France. Its heady fragrance wafted through the warm September afternoon. She debated with herself whether to go and help Mary dress or help the other ladies in the kitchen. A sudden breeze caught a lace curtain, and she had a view of a swirl of falling leaves. *Why not?* she thought and had the benches and chairs set outside amid a grove of sycamore, redbud, and shortleaf pine trees. Then she went and helped Mary with the last-minute bits of finery she would wear.

Jamie was dressing in the small cabin that had been his home when he heard a commotion in the yard and brushed aside the curtains Mary had hung at the window. His heart took a leap at the sight of Paddy, Mr. and Mrs. MacDonald, and two other men. A fleeting thought crossed his mind. *Are those men some of Paddy's crew? This will be a wonderful day.*

Pulling on his stockings, he buttoned his breeches over them then stepped into his buckled shoes. A knock came at the door, and Jamie was so nervous, he jumped. "Come in," he said.

"Are you about ready?" Ian asked, opening the door. An awkward fourteen-year-old, he seemed to be growing out of his shoes.

"Yes," Jamie said, fumbling with the stock. "Can you fix this thing? I've never worn one before."

"Sure thing, Uncle." In a few seconds, he had the fine white pleated linen wrapped around and tied at his neck, the lace-tipped ends spread in a ruffle down his chest. "There. It's done. Everyone's ready. Did you see Paddy arrive?" he asked.

"Yes. Who are the men with him?"

"Oh, just some friends." Ian was barely able to conceal his delight.

"What are you grinning at, Ian?"

"Nothing." He turned to get out of the room before he slipped and told the surprise. "Hurry up!" he called back, tripping over the threshold. Jamie followed, putting on his coat and closing the door behind.

Herman Ensch, his German neighbor, had his dulcimer, and Colin Mathieson, the Scot from Wester Ross, a fine fiddle player, struck up some delightful melodies, old and new. The guests seated themselves, and Jamie noticed Paddy sitting with those two men chatting, but he was unable to see their faces.

Benjamin, Jamie's oldest brother and stepfather, looking somber in his clerical robes, stood on the grass at the head of the rows of benches. With racing heart, Jamie took his place next to Ian. As the music played, his sister-in-law Aggie walked on a bright-colored aisle of fallen leaves wearing a blue and pink silk brocade dress with a sheer snow-white handkerchief pleated around her bodice. Mary had brought it for her from Paris. A wide MacKenzie tartan green and blue plaid ribbon twined around the full skirt and was pinned upon her left shoulder with an ancient silver Celtic brooch. Finally, with Donald MacDonald escorting her, came Jamie's beloved bride. He did not notice the fine white lace that bordered her French ivory damask gown nor the ribbons that formed a cloud twining around her brown ringlets. He saw only those violet eyes brimming with love.

The couple said their vows, promising to be faithful to each other, and Benjamin wrapped the couple's hands in a MacKenzie tartan handfasting ribbon to seal their contract. Then he congratulated them and pronounced, "Mr. and Mrs. Jamie Kimsey, married before God." The guests happily applauded the new couple while joyful cheers came from the younger ones. Ian awkwardly shook Jamie's hand, and Mary and Aggie hugged each other.

Benjamin announced that the celebration would continue with food and drink for all, but first someone special would like to come forward to congratulate them. Everyone beamed because they all knew the secret, including Mary, but Jamie, looking over their seated guests, remained puzzled. The two men with Paddy arose and began their way to the front of the gathering.

Jamie thought to himself that it was strange that Paddy's crewmen would come forward like that, but then, why do they look familiar?

The men removed their cocked hats, and Jamie's heart stopped beating. The apparitions before him were his long-lost brothers, Alexander and Charles. With tears of happiness flowing down their faces, the cherished brothers were welcomed into his arms. Their leathered faces were worn with sun and sweat. Charles's scarred cheek was just a mere memory of the fierce battle of '46. They were toughened pioneers of the new land to which they had been banished as punishment for their crimes against the Crown at Culloden, but what was once feared was turned to opportunity. What should have been misery turned into joy. All three were farmers, but one had answered the call to ministry, and another became a longhunter who had traveled afar.

The celebration lasted for two days.

For Jamie, the world was complete. Everyone clustered about hugging, laughing, and crying with the Kimseys. A cascade of autumn leaves blessed them with their touch. After fourteen years, they were together again.

The brothers stayed a week and got caught up. Alex and Charles had been treated well by MacCorkindale, serving him for seven years. Then as MacDonald had done for Benjamin and Jamie, MacCorkindale was most generous by giving both Alex and Charles three hundred acres on the Cape Fear River in North Carolina where there was a Scots settlement. The brothers worked the land together, but Charles longed for adventure, wanting to go west into the wilderness of North Carolina. Alex, loving his plantation, bought out his brother.

Husband and wife slipped into everyday living with the most beautiful memories of their union and celebration with friends and family. The home that Jamie built was extravagant in love and lavish in tenderness for Mary. Every corner was waiting for her special touch, and she applied it with her own sweet grace.

Chapter 12

Mary and Summertime Babies

THE DOOR BANGED against the house. *No one to hear,* she thought irritably. *Jamie is not in sight or earshot, I'll wager.* "I'll wager," she said angrily. Her moods aggravated both of them, and talking to herself had become a continual habit since Jamie stayed away from her volatile disposition. *Poor Jamie,* she thought. *Poor me,* and she cried.

Mary's first-pregnancy maelstrom sent her storming into their stoned-up root cellar—part of the gift of home Jamie had built for them. Completely exasperated, she wondered what she was looking for. Nothing jogged her memory, but there was the French lavender she'd placed there after their wedding. The sprigs of the plant she purchased in Paris still carried their fragrance and boosted her spirits.

Forgetting her discomfort, Mary recalled the look on Jamie's face when he discovered the whole story of why she left him. Sweetly, at his insistence, the couple kept their letters tied with ribbon inside a fragrant red cedar box, but that first letter didn't show up until after they were married and Mary was with child. *No telling where it had been,*[16] she mused.

---

[16] Note from Gary Kimsey: A little historical context that may or may not be useful in explaining why the letter took so long. Back then, there wasn't a postal system (not until about 1775), and letters were often carried by travelers who dropped them off at local taverns, which typically were the places of social centers for a community. Sometimes an address might be "John Smith,

Eight Months Earlier

After dinner one evening, she read the letter to him as they sat before the fire, drinking tea.

> Jamie Kimsey Esq.
> Baltimore Maryland
> June 1, 1757
>
> My dearest Jamie,
> I write my first pages of love to you from the deck of the Welsh Trader, the ship that took me away from you, to retrace the wake Rebecca and I traveled from Wales. It pulled at its tethers straining incessantly at the quay, like my child's heart bound to yours with cords of love. I recall your words as you looked into my eyes and asked me to be your wife. Your eyes, brimming with tears, are seared into my memory, and I was in torment over leaving you, but my woman's heart knew that my sister and I had a duty to pay back our uncle. Dizzy with love then and now, I can't wait to be your wife...Alas we must do our growing apart for the time being.

Remembering their first kiss, Jamie watched his beautiful wife form the words with those luscious lips he so adored. The life of the soon-to-be mother shone in a refulgence of light, and Jamie was torn between longing and awe.

Massachusetts" and no more. And with such vagueness, sometimes letters lingered forever in a tavern. Some places may not have had a tavern (social place for the community), and the traveler would hang on to the letter until he ran into someone who might know the intended recipient. This could take months, if not years, sometimes.

Mary sipped her tea, and it broke her heart to see Jamie crying. "Do you want me to stop, dear one?"

He wiped his tears and waved away her question, and she continued.

> For the last week it has been impossible to apply any more words to paper as the ship pitched so dangerously we were afraid for our lives. I watch the endless changes in the heavens and the sea and am constantly amazed at its beauty. Rebecca makes friends with every passenger and has a particular flair for flirtation.
>
> The passing is going swiftly for us, and we will be happy to get back on solid ground and cease walking like drunken sailors.
>
> When we landed, a coach took us to our destination—a shuttered and dilapidated dwelling—and we stood there hopelessly defeated in the purpose for which we came.

Mary looked up from the page. "I only had a vague remembrance of the two of us sent to live with Uncle Heddwyn after our parents died of influenza. He was such a crotchety old bachelor, not used to children, and I was frequently sick. He viewed us as meddlesome burdens and treated us as servants, beating us when he could catch us."

She picked up her cup. The tea had grown cold. "Do you want more tea, Jamie?" He nodded his head, and she stoked the fire. Mary continued reading.

> A rotund woman stepped from a tavern across the street, and said "Dead 'e is, ma dearies, 'bout a year." Rebecca asked, "Are you speaking of Heddwyn Crowley?" The woman turned abruptly and walked away, saying as she went, "Down there, at the bottom of the hill, at the

kirk. Talk to the minister." She vanished through a door, a sign above it read "Gwenyth's Boarding House."

Rebecca seemed to think we were in serious trouble, but I suggested we see the minister before we decided whether we were in trouble. The kirk itself was very pretty with flowers and green lawn between it and the parsonage. A stone path led beyond to the graveyard.

And then we met Rev. Beecham—a tall, saintly looking man. And I could see it in her eyes. Rebecca was already smitten and had him reeled in in no time.

"I have to stop and tell you how we got in trouble," Mary said as she poured fresh tea into their cups. "One day Rebecca was dusting the mantle, and she dislodged a brick from the fireplace. Removing it, she found uncle's purse holding a treasure of many coins. She hatched a plan, and put everything back in its place then swore me to secrecy. I was very excited, but what she didn't tell me was we were running away—with his money! We took ourselves to the harbor and found a ship bound for America that very night."

Jamie interrupted, "I'm very much surprised the two of you being so small could attempt such a dangerous journey all by yourselves." He shifted uncomfortably in his chair then sipped his tea.

Concerned for her husband, she asked, "Are you getting tired?" He grinned. "No, go on, sweetheart."

"We had the good grace to meet a family with four children when we went to buy our passage. The ticket master would not sell them to us because we were so young and without accompaniment. Rebecca blurted out, 'Our mother and father have died, and we want to go to America to seek our fortune.' That family became our benefactors. It worked out very well indeed, and we whiled away the time with those children." Mary sat staring at the flames of the fire, lost in the reverie of a happy time within their childhood of misery.

"Oh my, this is such a long-winded letter from a young girl who was so much in love with you." Jamie smiled, and she continued.

> We are staying at the boarding house while we sort out our financial issues, my darling Jamie. As it turns out, our uncle left us a rather large sum of money with a solicitor in Pembrokeshire. I am rather at a loss as to why he did that unless it was we had not a penny to our name and felt sorry for us. We are both very grateful to him and unfortunately spent a large amount of time hating the poor man and living with an enormous amount of guilt over the theft which I do not think he even noticed.
>
> Regardless, dear heart, Rebecca and Rev. Beecham are courting under the watchful eye of Gwenyth, who, it turns out, is his parsonage housekeeper as well, and as soon as we settle our affairs, I hope we will be able to come home. I say we, but I think it will be I myself returning to you, sweetheart, as Rebecca will most probably remain in Wales. She sends you her love.
>
> I miss you so very much and look forward to our marriage. Yours forever my darling Jamie. Mary

Jamie was fast asleep in his chair. She leaned back in her rocker and basked in her memories.

* * *

Mary placed the dried lavender in her apron pocket and wiped her tears on the hem.

Walking back over the stone path to the house, the baby moved in her womb. She was thrilled until she remembered why she went to the root cellar in the first place—potatoes. It was nearly dinnertime, and Jamie would be coming back from the fields at any moment. A leg of mutton roasted on the hanging spit in the fireplace, its drippings splattering into the shallow Dutch oven below. She dusted it with flour and brushed it with melted butter. The leg portion had been a gift from Colin Mathieson to tempt Jamie to consider raising sheep for their wool.

Mary quickly scrubbed the dirt from the brown tubers, then made a small dice and scraped them from the chopping board into the hot fat. Water droplets danced in the pot and quickly she cast on the lid, putting a shovelful of glowing coals on top. The potatoes would brown faster that way.

Taking hold of the hearth's lug pole crane with tongs, she swung it forward. The meat was nicely browned, and she stabbed the juicy roast with a fireside fork, removed it from the spit, and placed it on a platter on the table.

Timidly, Jamie came into the house, not knowing the reception he would get. "Something delights my nose, wife."

Flushed from the hearth, she looked up at him. Her smile told him she was her old self again.

He took her hand and pulled her to him. Again, the child's movement surprised Mary. Alarmed, he asked, "Are you disquieted?"

"Yes," she said with a radiant smile and placed his hand on her belly. Even with apron and full skirts, he could feel movement and held his hand still until the kicking subsided.

"My potatoes!" She quickly pulled away and removed the pot with tongs. Flinging the lid aside, the potatoes were nearly burned. Her face had gone from delight to consternation in seconds, and they were both struck with uncontrollable laughter.

During their meal, Jamie would not stop raving about the burned potatoes—the best he'd ever had, he said. They discussed the fields and crops. Jamie wanted to try flax, but he needed to carve some acres out of the three hundred planted in tobacco.

"What is your thought about raising sheep? I'm sure we could purchase—"

Mary interrupted. "We'll call him James. Would that please you, my love?"

The young couple lingered at the table, and Jamie reached across for her hands. He caressed them in his and gazed at his beautiful wife. His dream came true, no matter the troubles of life getting in the way. "I will be happy to show our boy the ways of a farmer, to teach him to build with his hands, and—"

"And if it's a girl?"

* * *

A pall hung over the land—a thick haze—and a solid curtain of water bled out of the heavens and could not be wiped away for their dead child.

A white pall draped the small wooden coffin placed in the deep hole. It didn't seem right that the white cloth was splashed with mud and dripped black with the rain. Ashes to ashes. The sweet baby was born pink and new with a healthy bawl, little fists clenched, and tiny toes curling, but she turned blue, and nothing could be done to save her. She died in her mother's arms.

Jamie had just come in from the byre after checking on a newborn calf. Strange, he thought later, that the calf lived and the baby died. How much more important was a human. Grim faces of their friends greeted him when he opened the door of the big house he had built. Mournful crying filled their home, and no amount of comfort could dispel their bitter loss. Too numb to feel her sorrow, it was a long while before Mary could let go of the baby and give the lifeless body to Jamie. When she did, he looked at his child and smelled her newness in the soft blanket. He sat by the fire and crooned a lullaby his mother had sung to him when he was small. Now his wife would pack the wee newborn's clothes, diapers, cloths, blankets into a trunk to be placed in the attic—*Sarah's things*, she told herself. Most people buried their dead babies with no names. *Mine will have one*, she cried in defiance and slumped to the floor, tears of loss and sorrow finally falling from her eyes and onto the hardwood.

Gertrude had come. It was her duty, she'd said, having had so many big boys.

"The birth wasn't difficult…What went wrong!" Jamie screamed at the top of his lungs when he was alone in the byre. His baby girl was dead, and there was nothing that could be done.

Many had come for the funeral, and the baby was buried in something Jamie thought he would never have to make on his land—a coffin. The tombstone placed over it read: SARAH KIMSEY BORN JULY 1761 DIED JULY 1761.

Would it be the first of many? He was used to death, he thought. His father, his mother, his brother, and now his own child—how much more could he suffer from an unjust God? He slammed his fist into the byre door, splitting a wide board in two, badly bruising and cutting his hand in the bargain.

Jamie came into the house, blood oozing through his clenched fingers. Mary looked up from her gaze through the streaked window glass. It was driving rain, and the fire had gone cold. She gasped when she saw her husband bleeding.

With a look of anguish, she asked quietly, "What did you do?"

He fell into her arms and cried tears of years of sorrow onto her shoulder. She held him for a long while, then caressed his face in her hands and said, "We will pull through. Now, let's fix that hand of yours."

* * *

After the despair of losing his child, Jamie set his jaw in firm determination and then set his plough to the land. In the heat of the day, his shirt, beset with sweat, was cast aside. The cleansing waters of hard work gave him relief. He would not be beaten by loss.

Flicking the rein at the rump of his Conestoga, the horse could not move. *Slap!* went the leather again, and the animal plodded ahead, its muscles taut with the effort, but the black earth hid a solid mass the plough could not budge. Heat hung on the land, and not a breath of air troubled any leaf. Jamie felt like he was suffocating. He unhitched the rigging and picketed the horse in a grassy area under some trees, then came back to assess the situation. Most of the rock was under the surface and ran for ten feet or more, and Jamie tested the perimeter with his hand. Then he sat in the dirt in a quandary—should he dig it out or blast it to bits?

Shimmers of heat radiated over the land—no sound, but movement everywhere he looked. There was a form—a woman, his woman—coming across the field. She shimmered as well, wearing her grace about her. His heart stuck in his throat. *How beautiful she is*, he thought.

"You come bearing gifts, my girl." Looking up at her, he shaded his eyes from the bright light.

Offering him a jug, she replied, "You look hot and thirsty, my husband. Why are you sitting in the sun?"

He swallowed the refreshment, a glorious tart, sweet apple juice. "I'm contemplating what to do with this damnable rock," he said, annoyed.

"Can't you go around it, dear heart?" She egged him on.

Suddenly he smiled. "It would take two, I believe, using a spade."

Mary gasped as he pulled her down to him. He was wet, and his muscles were hard under her touch. She felt the scars on his back from the Indian attack so many years before, but that concern was whisked away by an urgent breeze coming up over the land fueling their flames. His red curls clung to his face then wended their way through her fingertips. Lips eagerly sought the rising passion, and the ribbon, holding her abundant hair, loosened, and her long brown tresses cascaded over him. Billows of skirts formed a cover over the two lovers in their fertile fields—fertile and true to the plough, Jamie always said. They lingered briefly between accelerations then peeled away like corn silk off a cob and lay breathless, sweating in the humus of the humid afternoon.

Holding hands and watching stalled clouds abandoned by the wind, the lovers suddenly saw a muzzle with trailing reins and two large black eyes peering down at them. The Conestoga had broken its tether and come to investigate the smell of water from a bucket

Mary had brought. They were tickled by the horse's antics and broke into peals of laughter.

* * *

In the fall of that year, husband and wife stood together on the porch of their home enjoying a glass of Hermann Ensch's hard cider. Now, on that rise where Jamie had chosen to build in the dark days of waiting for Mary to return, they watched the setting sun slip behind the mountains and took in the view of their harvested fields. Good crops of tobacco, corn, melons, and squash would give them a substantial income, and the apples from Hermann's seedlings would provide the main ingredient for the Apfelwein from their friend. They breathed in the deep scent of rich land, and Jamie basked in the beauty of his wife held in his embrace. He could not ask for another thing.

A whisper of night graced the sky in purples and darkest of blues, and the sweet enjoyment of another whisper brushed his ear. "We are with child." Even in the fading light, Jamie could see Mary smile, that broad grin infecting both of them with hope and happiness.

Succeeding days of backbreaking work turned into weeks that led to autumn's smoky haze with the aroma of burning leaves. An abundance of newly harvested crops were set to dry—cobs in their cribs, seed for next year's sowing. The root cellar received its hard-shelled squash, potatoes, onions, apples, and herbs. Nuts were set in baskets by the fire for treats and baking, and the earth readied itself for the dormancy of winter.

Samuel Kimsey was born just before the last thaw when bulbs were sprouting from the earth watered by melting snow. The little boy was a joy to his parents.

Chapter 13

Brother Benjamin

BACK IN 1756, the extra year when Jamie decided to stay with the MacDonalds, Benjamin went to a new seminary in New Jersey called Hopewell Academy. He was assigned to live with another Baptist minister and his wife, Richard and Anne Woods, in the town for which the academy was named. However, because of his mentor's large family, the Kimseys were given a small cabin behind the main house which suited Aggie and their growing family—Ian was ten; Benjie, eight; and baby David had just turned two. And, she was very, very heavy with child.

A small stipend was provided by the academy, and Benjamin was given a position with a mercantile to pay for the rest of his tuition. At thirty-one, the well-established Benjamin had considerable knowledge of the Bible thanks to his mother and his wife.

Aggie helped by taking in laundry and sewing to defray costs. She never complained when exhaustion set in or her back hurt, nor did Benjamin complain when his studies kept him up half the night. So as not to disturb his wife, on pleasant moonlit evenings, he would walk the picket-fenced yard practicing his sermons. They were supposed to be spontaneous, but memorizing the written words of other illustrious ministers helped him understand the Baptist's religious views. His dream was to become a circuit-riding preacher who affected his illiterate brethren with the spirit of God. Under the delusion of this dream, however, he realized it was not practical with a family and the constant pain of his war-injured ankle.

Oldest house in Hopewell. Here the first Baptist School in America for higher education was opened in 1757. Now Brown University of Providence, R. I.

Credit: Booklet copy for copying courtesy of the Hopewell Public Library. Photography and editing by Roberta A. Mayer for her book, 1909 Hopewell, New Jersey, One-Hundred Years Later, Blurb, 2009.

Aggie was in constant pain. Her new babe was about to be born, and because her belly was too large for her small frame, Mrs. Woods worriedly sent her eldest boy for the doctor.

Instead of practicing his sermons, Benjamin now paced the yard wringing his hands and praying for his wife. Piercing screams came from within their home, and when they ceased, he ran to enter. But again, his wife's shrill cries penetrated the heavens. Benjamin was stunned and worried. *What was wrong?* "Lord…spare my wife, my love!" he pleaded. *And our baby.*

A low bawling greeted his ears, and then another! He dared to hope.

Mrs. Woods came to the door. "You have twins, Mr. Kimsey. Come in and meet your sons."

* * *

As he stood on the bank of a brook a short distance from the academy, Benjamin was a man on a mission. Wearing his baptismal garb of white shirt and white breeches, he was surrounded by his wife and children, the other ministerial candidates and their families, and Reverend Stearns. He held his Bible in his hands and waited his turn for baptism. Trees lined the banks, and the warm sun shone on the gurgling water as it hurried along. Beautiful singing birds in fine feather flitted throughout branches overhanging the brook. *It was surely a God-filled day*, Benjamin thought.

Handing his Bible to Aggie, he stepped barefoot into the baptismal font. The promise he made during his languishing days in the putrid water of the prisoner ship played through his mind as he was immersed beneath clear, life-giving water.

If, Lord, you choose to let me live, I will give you my life—a life of peace, love, and dedication. But not my will—yours, oh Lord.

The purifying waters of baptism flowed over him, and Benjamin rose full of grace. Hands reached out and lifted him up, saving him as Aggie had done at the end of the voyage from Scotland. Another candidate shook his hand and gave him a towel. Aggie hugged him and gave him back his Bible, and Benjamin raised it to the sky praising God. After two years of formal study, he was ready to begin his ministry.

There was to be no ordination. He and his family were placed in an established congregation not far from Hopewell with a minister who would supervise Benjamin's activities, listen to all his words, criticize, teach, and call him on his sins.

Benjamin's duties were to take up the pulpit on Sundays, attend prayer meetings, and preach to his listeners so much so that his oral communication would "rouse up feelings with tears, feverish exclamations, and even fainting or thrashing about from the divinely inspired words." All these emotional revival meetings would thus bring about many converts.

After another two years in New Jersey, the Kimseys were sent to sparsely populated Albemarle County in Virginia. Brother Jeremiah Pike led his congregation with an iron hand that clutched an iron rod. During the first Sunday's sermon, Benjamin's family was obliged to sit in the front row. As the minister's grandiose words aroused the congregants to a soul-stirring pitch, Brother Pike slammed the rod down on the pulpit. Startled, Aggie stood straight up from her seat, and Benjamin looked at her with consternation. The children were scared into whimpering. Aggie didn't know whether to be embarrassed or ashamed, and Brother Pike frowned at the interruption of his sermon.

"Glory, hallelujah!" she hollered at the top of her lungs.

All the congregation stood, quaking, shouting, "Amen. Amen." Some chanted, "Glory be to Yahweh on high." Benjamin, with his exquisite tenor voice, broke out into a good old-fashioned rendition of the "Old One Hundredth," saving face for his wife and impressing Pike. The congregation joined him, men warbling an octave below, and the women's vibratos, wobbling widely, all chanting the praise of God.

Pike found Benjamin a man true to his word, with a true love of God, but still young in the ministry. While overseeing the young preacher's words and deeds, the men sometimes walked along a glorious trail through a wooded valley a mile from the meeting house. Pike was a bachelor and often asked after Aggie and the children.

"It's a rough go on a minister's salary," the younger man said. "There are a lot of mouths to feed at home." When Pike told him that "Our great Jehovah will provide," and "Benjamin, your faith is small. It should move mountains," Benjamin concluded the man had little understanding for the complications of family life.

Quite frequently, Benjamin found himself annoyed with his host minister, and the annoyance nearly became rage when Brother Pike's sermons focused on his perspective on disciplining children. What did he know about raising children? In Christian charity, Benjamin swallowed his disdain for the man and reasoned that he was the Father's creation after all, and as such needed to be respected. However, when the congregation began shrinking from Pike's harangues about how to care for their own children, and turned toward Benjamin's thoughtful sermons instead, he wondered if the old man had the best interests of his flock in mind when he spoke from the pulpit.

Word had reached the ears of the committee of Hopewell's ministers that trouble was growing in Virginia. Because more people attended his assistant's sermons, Pike gave Benjamin a harsh reprimand for the sin of pride and blamed him for the gossip. But the committee did not see it that way and appointed Brother Kimsey the new minister of Albemarle Baptist Church. Brother Pike's long-term presbyterial service had come to an end, and he was requested to remove himself to New Jersey so they could keep an eye on him, and eventually he was defrocked.

* * *

Aggie was again with child, and it was early in her pregnancy. Smiling at her across the table, and with the large family Bible open before him, Benjamin said in mock blame, "You are so beautiful, my wife, I find it difficult to concentrate on the word of God." She could not respond to his mischievous behavior and left the room needing to eliminate whatever there was left in her stomach even if there was nothing.

A year later, another minister was sent to Albemarle with instructions for Benjamin to begin a new congregation in Bedford County. Good news indeed, as it was the culmination of his experience, and he would be pastor of the growing village in that county, responsible for building a new church. For the time being, he would find a house to rent, but how was his family to survive? That prospect was daunting, but Benjamin could not have been happier as the small town of New London was in good walking distance to the home of his brother. Maybe Jamie would know someone.

To prepare for the move, and before the birth of their seventh child, Benjamin donned his only black suit of clothes and packed a small satchel with his minister's robe and Bible. He and Ian carried what coins they could muster, and Aggie packed food for a few days. After that they would rely on their hunting skills and begging along the way, perhaps in return for a sermon. It was a week's trip south to the Little Otter River and Benjamin Jr., at fourteen, was left in charge of their large family.

* * *

Benjamin and Ian rode along through trees that parted to reveal a charming tableau of a house and acres of lush green corn. "Jamie is a wonder," said Benjamin.

He had wanted to talk to his brother for a long time. Since living with the MacDonalds in Baltimore, the brothers had been separated by distance and the busyness of their lives, and now the elder was most anxious to share his thoughts with his little brother.

They sat on the porch after dinner, watching the glow of the sun's last rays and enjoying each other's company. Then, as the blue dusk settled gently over the land, Mary brought a wee dram for her husband, and tea for Benjamin who did not imbibe since becoming a Baptist minister. The flame of a lone candle united them in the darkness that cast shadow and light over their faces. She lingered awhile making small talk about Aggie and the children, but it was clear the two men needed to talk. *Handsome men, those Kimseys*, she thought, walking back into the house to keep Ian company.

"You've put on weight, brother, and it looks good on you. You were a bit lean last I saw you," Jamie teased.

"Aggie's good cooking adds to my girth." Benjamin smiled, patting his waist. "Those two seminary years took their toll though—school at the academy by day, studying at night, and working at the Hopewell Mercantile any time I could. Ian brought in some money as an apprentice wigmaker—becoming quite good, you know—and Aggie took in sewing. We made it through. Some ministers were harder than others, but I finished, and here I am, a soon-to-be-pastor of my own flock." Staring off into the soft star-filled night, Benjamin became reflective, trying to absorb the reality of what he just said. "I've been assigned New London township to start a church." He waited a minute to let the news sink in.

Jamie did what he always did, even as a child—he put his hands together, almost like praying, and cast his eyes to the floor, listening intently. A moth flew too close to the candle's flame, got its wings singed for its trouble, then tumbled away, wounded.

"So, Ben. You've come for my advice. I thought you always had the right answers," the young man said, smiling with color rising in his cheeks that matched that shock of hair.

Benjamin continued, "I need your assistance finding agreeable help in locating a spot to build it. Would you know of anyone who would be willing?" The accent was on the word "willing."

Jamie shifted in his seat uncomfortably, the chair ill fitted to his spare behind, and started slowly. "It is my opinion that you will suffer greatly if you do this thing. Most of the people settled here are Church of England who ousted preachers sent before you. They don't take kindly to the Baptist way of teaching. Methodists tried, too, as did the Catholics. They were threatened with tar and feathers if they didn't move on. You know we are all required by law to attend the English Church services at least once a month and taxed regularly to support them, so why do you want to anger the residents and risk your life as well as your family's?" Jamie's cheeks burned with ire as he stated the obvious, his emotions getting the best of him. "And you know the town is called New London for a reason!"

Benjamin ignored the warnings. "But I must bring the word of God to them. Please, Jamie, do you know of a house to rent?" Benjamin shifted the discussion to the need at hand.

"Aye, you could do that, Ben, moving slowly at first. Why not have a meeting here in our home. We'll set up a tent and serve food—sort of breaking bread together and getting the people used to the idea of a Baptist in their midst."

Sunday was two days hence, and Jamie and Ian decided to rouse his friends for as large a fellowship as possible. They rode many miles inviting all they came across.

On Sunday, the weather turned gloomy for the new-in-the-cloth minister. But Benjamin was decked out in his robes and stock, the tails of which lay neatly on his chest, and, with Bible in hand, readied himself for a crowd—small or large. He vowed that even if there was only one person to hear the word of God, he would give it his all. Everyone wondered if anyone would come.

At ten minutes past noon, Hermann Ensch, with his family in tow, came into the meeting tent to support their friend and placed dishes of food on the table. Warmly greeted, they were seated in the front row of benches. Colin Mathieson arrived with his only daughter, Patience, and apologized for the absence of the rest of his family due to stomach disorders. They sat on the opposite side of the aisle. Patience was pretty in a pale yellow bonnet and matching dress cinched tightly with a lacy handkerchief at the bodice. Her looks were not lost on Hermann's sons.

A stiff-necked delegation of townspeople approached the gathering flock. Their stern faces were met with broad smiles, and they were immediately seated in the midst of their neighbors. Jamie knew the politics of these men—Loyalists now surrounded by Patriots.

Benjamin's countenance was angelic. He was a devout presence in their midst, literally, as his last-minute decision to forgo the pulpit put him directly in the middle aisle of all onlookers. Despite the dour looks aimed at him, he began.

"My brothers and sisters, you have gathered this day to hear God's word. I intend to part the heavens and bring the Holy Spirit to you, filling you with tender affection from God on high."

All at once, rays of sunshine parted the clouds, and a collective gasp escaped from the attendees.

Benjamin took that as an omen. "Remember, Jesus spoke to the waters, 'Be still and know that I am God. I will be exalted among the heathens.'" Benjamin watched the faces of his uncertain congregation. Some were bored, others belligerent and waiting for a fight with a here-it-comes attitude.

"'I will be exalted through the earth,' Jesus said. We are Christian in agitated days. Summon yourselves afresh to speak, work, live, and enhearten the world. We must keep our eyes on God."

Timid "Amens" were heard from a few of the congregants.

Benjamin continued, "From the Gospel of Matthew, we read that great multitudes wanted Jesus's words. Through his apostles' compassion, he sensed their needs, and though there was no food in the desolate place where they had followed him, he told his apostles to feed them with loaves and fishes. He senses our needs too," he said, pointing to the overflowing table, "and…the danger of temptations. 'What shall it profit a man if he gains the whole world and suffers the loss of his own soul.' The horrors of hell will not prevail. He tells us that 'as I was with Moses so I will be with you. I will not forsake you.'

"Children, you must stand in your father's shoes, take responsibility. Don't be tremulous in spirit. I will be at your elbows, never failing you. Stand with me, stand with the Lord. He will strengthen you and you will go bravely on. These words are for us. Go on with me, and I will be with you. That is his great word for us. Give him the uppermost place in your lives. There is no sacred or secular! You are to be Christian not only here at Sunday noon but also at your shop and store and bank tomorrow. If you are a farmer, wigmaker, lawyer, physician, ironworker, banker, merchant, politician, soldier—give the Lord's cause the first place in your life. Live it to the glory of God. Whether eat or drink, do it all for the glory of God. Do all that he commands you to do.

"These three words: obedience to Christ. Listen, my friends. We will keep his commandments without reservation—obedience to Christ. We miss it if we fail to recognize him. Fail to recognize him as lord and master, and he will fail to recognize you!" Benjamin pointed directly at the leaders of the town. At the same time, the heavens were rent with a glorious resplendent sun that dissolved the overcast—and most of the wanton belligerence.

It is going well, he thought. Now was the proper time. He held out his Bible in his hands.

"Help me, my wife, and children to find a place to live and work among you, and I will be your servant putting the word of God into your very hearts." Then Benjamin suddenly stopped, choked with tears.

People stared at him. Even the delegation seemed to melt before the devout preacher in the long robes with a large family who needed shelter. His stock was soaked with the tears of passionate love for the people.

* * *

Not long after the Sunday go-to-meetin' and the delicious vittles, the town council called Benjamin, his son Ian, and, surprisingly, Jamie, to the courthouse. Jamie had never bothered with the town, and when he needed to replenish his supplies, he always made the long trek to Lynchburg and his friends the Middletons.

A scant mile before town, the three men came upon scattered log cabins and a few clapboard structures. Reaching the center, there was a town square of sorts with an English flag floating above it and flowers planted beneath it—with a short crossed-log fence around all. Cabins seemed planted among neat rows of various vegetables, and pens held hogs while chickens roamed freely. Small children played in yards and the thresholds of doors. New structures were being built, and it appeared that the community was growing.

The town had a sheriff and a judge. Court was the front room of the judge's house. Jamie, Benjamin, and Ian entered on a clean-swept wide-plank wood floor with a desk and two benches. A gnarled old woman, bent with age, skirts dragging, came through a door behind the desk. She looked him up and down with a sneer on her face.

Her voice was harsh. "Sit on the bench, and his lordship will be with thee."

After he settled in behind his desk, the judge, whose face was haggard and grizzled from years of listening to pleas for mercy and of passing judgments and who was well beyond retirement, opened a ledger and wrote something with his quill. "So," he said, "we will provide you with a house and a stipend that comes with it as is custom."

Benjamin's inquiring glance told the judge he didn't understand.

The judge went on, "It is a teacher's stipend that would usually go to a minister from the Church of England who is required to also act as teacher in our town. While we await his arrival from London, the town has decided you should fill that position. However, I must warn you, you probably won't get many, if any, to attend your services. Others have tried before. I warn you again! We didn't cotton to them. What makes you so sure we will to you?" He handed Benjamin the paper. It was a voucher for the rent of a small house and an even smaller stipend than he'd received from Hopewell Academy. Benjamin thanked the judge and left with joy in his heart.

When they were outside, Benjamin showed the paper to Jamie, saying, "It's not much, brother, but it's a start."

Jamie grimaced. "That's not enough to keep a scarecrow alive."

Chapter 14

A Treacherous Town

1768

"Jamie tells me I am to be brought up on charges," Benjamin stated flatly. "He heard it from Henry Middleton in Lynchburg! It was in the *Virginia Gazette*!"

"Charges? For what?" Aggie cried, color draining from her face.

He turned away to stare at the brightly burning fire, wringing his hands. "They call me a liar and disturber of the peace. Sheriff Peter Martin has issued a warrant for my arrest, and I must stand before the magistrate."

"What are we to do?" Tears began to form in Aggie's eyes.

The room was still except for the crackling fire. Suddenly they were interrupted by a wee little fellow with straight blond hair sticking out at odd angles—obviously from a battle with his pillow.

"I'm having a bad dream," Pee Wee said, clutching his mother's skirts.

Aggie picked him up. "Are you still asleep?"

"Yes...I...am!"

She glanced toward Benjamin. "This is becoming a habit."

He turned away, hiding a smile.

Little Pee Wee, with that odor of sweetness that erupted from his innocence and flared about all her children at his age, was placed back in his crib, his rag doll firmly planted under his arm and his favorite blankie tucked up under his chin. Within minutes, he was again sharing his dream with his pillow.

For a moment, Aggie watched her sleeping children. Feelings of thanksgiving and love washed over her. She closed the door and rejoined her husband, slipping her hand in his as they both stood in front of the fire.

Peter Martin appeared at the door of their home with the arrest warrant and seized Benjamin, hauling him before two magistrates who bound him in the penalty of three hundred pounds to appear at court two days hence. Benjamin suffered the tortures of the damned in those forty-eight hours, worrying the floor of their home with his pacing. However, his prayers for peace were realized when there was nothing he could do but trust in God.

Flanked by his brother Jamie, Benjamin and his family appeared at the required time. While the family's presence was not required—nor was it probably wanted—five of their children sat between mother and father, and little Pee Wee fidgeted in Agnes's lap. He told his mother before they went into the large frame building that she was not to call him Pee Wee anymore. He was Humphrey, and that was that!

The courthouse, built the year before, had been moved from Colonel William Callaway's home. He was the first burgess governing the County of Bedford. The long room had two stoked fireplaces warming those of rank and distinction alike, as well as the many spectators who came out on the blustery cold day in the hopes of seeing punishment of the accused. A quarter-circle raised bench with a banister enclosing the business of the court, two sheriff's desks, and a clerk's table completed the simple furnishings along with many benches for observers. Witnesses brought before the court were some of the same men who had given Benjamin a home when first they arrived. They included the complainants David Hase, Archibald

Reah, James Bockhannon (Buchannon), and his brother William; the recognizees[17] had been Robert Risk and John Bell.

Each complainant accounted times when Mr. Kimsey roused his listeners to swoon in the dirt of the road—to madness as they would have it. And then, Benjamin's words bordered on treason; men began brandishing weapons in the air. What actually happened was that the men with the muskets were on a hunting expedition and came upon a meeting of the brethren at Colin Mathieson's house. They joined in and were so moved by Benjamin's words, they threw down their muskets and were baptized on the spot.

Thomas Pullin glared accusingly and railed bitterly, "Mr. Kimsey has lied about adult baptism being the only way to the most high God. His Baptist beliefs are against the doctrine of the Church of England!" This last statement rankled the citizens so much that a decrepit old man in the spectator section raised his walking cane ready to strike Benjamin down and had to be restrained by those seated beside him. The judge banged his gavel while former neighbors now called out for a hanging. Again, the judge called for order with every bang of the gavel. Seemingly endless witnesses were then called into court and swore with their open hands upon the Bible that this man was surely a liar and a disturber of the peace.

The lawyer for the court said, "He cannot meet a fellow on the street without ramming a verse of scripture down his throat."

After the long line of perjurers had been heard from—and no witnesses for the defendant were summoned—the jurors were sent out to deliberate.

While they awaited sentencing, Benjamin shaved off the minutes by whittling.

The more he carved, the angrier he became while awaiting the verdict. Suddenly the toy horse that might have been snapped in his hand and brought back a remembrance of the toy crushed under Alex's foot stepping through the broken door of their ransacked cot-

---

[17] The person in whose favour a recognizance is made; a form of bail; a promise made by the accused to the court that he/she will attend all required judicial proceedings and will not engage in further illegal activity or other prohibited conduct as set by the court (https://en.wiktionary.org/wiki/recognizee).

tage at Inverness. The horror of Culloden, their raped home with its crushed door and crushed dreams stepped on by King George's Redcoats' rampage, and of the murder of his father, mother, and brother Duncan had become a dim memory over the last fifteen years. Now that memory stood before his eyes like a blackhearted nightmare. Baptist ministers were being cited for disruption as the Jacobites had been in Scotland, and the punishment was and would be bestowed accordingly.

The judge entered, the gavel banged, all rose, and the procession of jurors filed from a side door to retake their seats. Some of these men were friends Benjamin had made here in Virginia. Would they become turncoats to punish misdeeds only they perceived?

Today of all days, Benjamin realized that he had become a rebel—a Patriot and a Baptist minister, not a Loyalist and Episcopalian like these men. He loved Virginia with its rolling green hills, blue mountains, dense forests, and agreeable weather, and he hated the thought of losing his home to prejudice and malicious treatment.

The judge asked the jury if it had come to a decision, and in his heart Benjamin knew the outcome would be the same—Scot against Redcoat, damnable traitors to his homeland and now to his country of choice.

Benjamin looked down to see his youngest, Pee Wee, standing before him with a cherub face ready to burst into tears. His cherry cheeks were bright with fright, and he only understood that somehow his father was in trouble.

Benjamin stooped to pick up his child and heard the loud whisper, "Did you tell a lie, Father?" The little face seemed to shrink into itself as if going into hiding. Spectators gabbled and laughed. Others said the boy was being used to sway the jury.

Kissing the apple of his son's cheek, Benjamin smiled and said, "No, Humphrey."

Breathing calmly, he stood to face his persecutor, and with the sweet bairn in his arms, he fixed his gaze on Thomas Pullin who had instigated the fraud and convinced Peter Martin to issue the warrant. In the past, Benjamin had almost come to blows with Pullin over doctrine and the burdensome taxes placed on the colonists for support of the Church of England and forced attendance.

The rest of the jury never made eye contact. Only Pullin met Benjamin's eyes with fixed gaze and clenched jaw. He spoke triumphantly, "We the jury find Benjamin Kimsey…" He paused, delighting in the tragedy he was about to inflict. "Guilty on both charges!" The onlookers broke into cheers.

The wood shavings sat in a pile on the wooden floor—*Dust to dust*, Benjamin thought—and dropped the broken toy carved for his son onto the mound to be trampled upon and spark the conflagration that would kill him. *Orphans*, he thought, *and my wife a widow.* Was it worth it—preaching the love and peace of a just God to men who were closed to it? He was doing what he promised God—no matter if his words fell on deaf ears.

Benjamin was an imposing figure both in the community and as a minister. His lawyer warned him against wearing his robes, but as he dressed that morning and fastened the last button on his waistcoat, Aggie walked in, tying the ribbons on her dark blue cape. The morning chill was on the land draping it with heavy dew, she said. He sat on the edge of their bed knowing she would tie his stock for him as she always did.

"That won't do," she said, glancing at his coat resting neatly folded next to him. He began to protest as she reached for his robes. "Never you mind. If you are to be martyred for a worthy cause today, then you should be wearing the sign of your ministry." Through worry lines, he smiled at his loving wife. She was always a joy to him.

The white stock rested on Benjamin's chest and rose with his sigh of relief when the gavel fell again announcing his punishment—six months in prison. Pullin was satisfied—for the moment. The jurors were sorrowful but relieved; it could have been much worse. Some ministers had been tarred and feathered and run out of town with only their wounds showing forth, or tarred and feathered then set on fire with the torture ending in death. Others had been hanged.

Benjamin stood his ground, and the weeping child had to be removed from his arms, and a chagrined Peter Martin had to do it. He looked at Aggie with pleading eyes to salve his feelings, but she stared him down as he transferred Humphrey to her waiting embrace. Withered to his core, he was only relieved by turning his back to her to lead her husband away to his incarceration.

Peter, however, could not remove the sight of her from his mind. How many times had Aggie come to the Martins' home when influenza struck his wife or children, or an injury brought harvesting to a standstill and her men were there to help? She was always kind and had a good word to say about everyone. A chill went through him, and her look could not drive his devil away.

Aggie was engaged in a fierce battle with her feelings as she watched her husband taken from her. She dared not add terror to the little ones already hanging to her skirts for support. Pee Wee's arms were tightly clenched around her neck. The older boys' combined fear and sorrow showed as defiance, anger, and rebellion. They ran from the court.

Jamie took her home and admired her strength, but then he remembered her faith and courage during the circumstances of the Scottish battle and her survival on the prisoner ship.

* * *

The gaol was built of heavy square timbers in 1754 when the county and its court system were founded. A twenty-by-twelve-foot structure, it was divided in half with a partition of iron bars, the front being quarters for the gaoler when the prison was occupied. Peter handed Benjamin over to Joseph Ray, and was walked through the heavy door. Squealing hinges betrayed its lack of use. The cell was confining with its small straw cot, and a barrel with rainwater siphoned through a hole in the roof, and it was dark. The only window was at the front of the gaol next to the door.

The next morning before the cocks crowed, Aggie was knocking on the gaol door. She banged again. When no one was aroused, she hammered on the window and saw Mr. Ray sleeping in his bed. Yawning, the man opened the door to her while robing himself with a blanket. It was cold in the dim darkness, and he lit a candle.

Benjamin was standing at the bars in his shirt and breeches waiting for Aggie.

"Are you all right, my husband?" she asked, the small bags under her eyes betraying a sleepless night.

Quietly he told her, "I have been praying."

"This might help," she said, handing him his Bible. Noting her husband's mussed robe on the cot, "You have no blanket!" she sighed in her sorrow.

"No...This place lacks for any amenities...Your lips make me hungry, though."

Smiling through her tears, she whispered, "Well, I can satisfy both," and she stood on tiptoes lifting her face toward him to receive his gently given kiss then slipped the quilt through the bars.

Mr. Ray brought her a chair, and the pair talked until sunrise when a tavern wench walked in with a covered tray disturbing their quiet tête-à-tête.

Her bosoms bulged from their constraints, nearly falling out of the tight bodice. *Was she contriving to tempt Benjamin?* Aggie wondered, but then dismissed the thought as un-Christian. The tray held only lukewarm tea and a thin gruel of oatmeal and water with the cold air depriving the meal of any sustenance. Aggie would sustain him to bear his burden and so produced apple pudding dumpling and still-warm milk from their cow. When the aroma met Peter's nose, the gaoler's mouth watered for want of it. His sorry meal was void of comfort as well, and he wished for a tankard of ale and three eggs swimming in thick-sliced bacon fat properly wetting fresh crusty bread.

A few nights later, Peter was spelled by a man Benjamin did not recognize. The man wore a heavy coat and a knitted cap pulled down over his ears and forehead and sat most of the evening slumped at the table with a single taper in a pewter candlestick. A premonition of danger raised Benjamin's hackles. He prayed and dozed on his cot with his back resting against the wall, occasionally waking to see the hulk still there.

When it was nearly midnight, there was a sound, muffled at first as if someone was talking outside the building. A dog barked, a voice raised, a scuffling sound in the darkness, and the door flung open, banging against the wall and causing Benjamin to start. A candle in a lantern flickered violently. It seemed men were tussling with each other, then two of them joined the strange man. The lantern remained outside, and Benjamin could not recognize anyone. The key in the lock and the telltale squeal of the hinges of the barred door alerted him that they had entered the cell. He had not had fisticuffs with any man since the death-dealing confrontation between him and Michael Kelly in Ireland.

In the next moment, violent hands were all over him. A great ball of a fist slammed into his jaw, another hand came from out of the blackness and struck him with a smack straight across his ear, then the top of his head. He flailed about, hitting at nothing and everything and occasionally sliding off someone's shoulder, or side of the head. All his weight crashed into his assailants colliding like balls on a bowling green. Bodies tumbled around, arms and legs flailed up against the timbers and bars of the tight quarters. Someone screamed at the crunch of a broken bone.

On his feet again, Benjamin took a punch to the stomach that knocked him against an edge of one of the wall timbers and into unconsciousness. The last thing he remembered was the acrid smoke of the blown-out candle.

Peter banged on the door awaiting the man with the knitted cap. No answer. The window was ajar. Odd, for it was ice-cold. A heavy fog had settled during the night, and blades of grass were covered with icy dew. He forced the window open further and climbed in. A man lay on the floor moaning—the man with the knitted cap—and he glanced toward the cell only to see Benjamin prostrate in a pool of blood against the back wall. He flung open the door and rang the alarm bell that hung outside. No one came.

Peter cursed this day! Here was Benjamin crumpled on the floor, his lifeblood staining the wood planks. He'd have to get the body back to Aggie but shivered at the thought of facing her again. Peter dragged him out the door and heaved him over the saddle of his horse. At that moment, Pullin rode up.

"I heard the bell. What's happening."

"Well, you should have finished the job! He's still alive but barely. The least I can do is to get him to his family so they can bury him decently."

"Good riddance, I say." Pullin spat on the ground.

Chapter 15

Mercy

Blessed are ye which are persecuted for righteousness' sake, for thine is the kingdom of heaven. Blessed are ye, when men shall revile thee, and persecute thee, and shall say all manner of evil against thee falsely, for my sake. Rejoice, and be exceeding glad: for great is thy reward in heaven: for so persecuted they the prophets... for great is thy reward in...heaven...for great is thy...reward.

JESUS'S WORDS OF beatitude trailed around Benjamin's troubled mind. He was forged in fire, and a hammer was banging on the anvil of his head. Sparks flew behind his eyes, and he woke with a start in his own bed and vomited. The damp cloth fell from his forehead. A whiff of cooking odor passed his nose, and he vomited again. Falling back into the soft feather pillows, he was caught in a vortex of nausea.

Aggie hurried to their bedroom. Benjamin only saw a form twisted and turned at odd angles. He stared, then closed his eyes, only to find that squinting at her did not change his sight. Looking around the room, other objects suffered the same effect.

His wife removed the soiled coverlets, replacing them with a bed rug over his shivering body.

"I can't see you clearly." He strained in pain, grasping at his throat. It felt as if it had been abraded with a rasp.

"Ian, come help me, please. Your father needs to pass urine." The twenty-one-year-old had just come home from Lynchburg when he heard of his father's beating. He gently lifted his father, and Aggie slipped the chamber pot under him. She talked, hoping to distract him from his nausea. "The doctor said your eyes will take time to focus normally. A nasty punch alongside your head has caused the difficulty."

She looked at him with sorrow. Bruises and cuts covered his handsome face. His throat had red, black, and purple finger marks committed by the would-be murderers. The hands—with which he so lovingly baptized the faithful, held gnarled fingers of the dying, ploughed the fields, steered his ship, cuddled his newborns, or shook the hands of newcomers—were mangled and torn. His wounds were swathed in dressings. The chamber pot was removed, and there was blood in the urine.

"Mother, let me spell you for a while."

"I could use a cup of tea." She sighed.

Ian watched her leave the room, his heart following—she had had no sleep for three days straight.

* * *

Aggie, covered by her favorite lap rug, dozed in her rocker. She had made the well-worn quilt while Benjamin recovered from his wounds brought on by conditions on that prisoner ship so long ago. The fading triangles, squares, and trapezoids of wool, silk, and imported printed cottons worked in a crazy quilt design tumbled across the covering once gaily embroidered in fine wool yarns. Later, Benjamin had brought her velvet and satin cloth. Those times were gone now—the days of wealth and trading ships. She awoke startled, in the midst of a dream of days gone by with Paddy; his brother, James Francis; and Benjamin in their shipping business. Her works were made of homespun now.

Ian joined her for tea and replaced logs that had toppled off the grate. She smiled looking at her firstborn son. More studious than the rest, he was tall and thin, and his blond hair dallied along his temples. It seemed to be particularly attractive to his new girlfriend Patience, Colin Mathieson's daughter. He was still an apprentice of a famous wigmaker in Lynchburg, but that man was aged and intended to pass on his business to the younger lad. Ian already had a good following from among the citizens there and, before his father was gaoled, the men of New London. Once firmly established, he would ask for Patience's hand in marriage. He tossed a few more sticks onto the reluctant warmth to renew a brightly burning fire.

"I'm sorry I woke you, Mother. Father's asleep. I'll get Benjie to come and sit with him."

Benjie, coming in from the fields, took up nearly the entire doorframe when he came into the house. Just recently turning twenty, he was like his grandfather Robert—hair black as tar and blue eyes the color of sky—a strapping fellow, good-hearted, and ready to help at a moment's notice.

In his booming voice, he said, "While I'd rather have a good mug of ale, I'll take some of that tea." A big grin swept his face. Striding across the room, he kissed his mother's cheek.

"Shush. Your father is sleeping."

Benjie's face turned to ash. "How's he doing?" Anger washed over him like it had when he ran with his brothers from the courthouse.

Tears trickled down Aggie's face.

"God damn the Loyalists," he let slip.

"Benjie!" Her rebuke stung.

Holding the hot cup in his hands, Ben's head bowed, acknowledging his shame.

A knock interrupted the quiet room. Jamie and Mary had come to call with six-year-old Samuel. She was heavy with child, and their pots were heavy with delicious chicken fricassee and stewed beef collops. Aggie asked her daughter, Polly, to bring in potatoes from the root cellar with a clear admonition to "make sure you cleanse the dirt from the tubers."

After a warm greeting, Benjie excused himself and went to sit with his father. Jamie joined him, and behind the closed door, they discussed the situation. It was the first time Jamie had seen his brother since the trial. "My God!" He recoiled in horror, not recognizing the man on the bed.

"I would wish to beat the men senseless for doing that to my brother, but then I would be no better than they. What does the doctor say?"

"He doesn't think Father will survive except by the grace of God. As angry as I am, we must pray for him."

The family did pray that very night, kneeling around Benjamin's bed. Aggie led the prayers, then late into the evening, sleepy children were put to bed, and the older ones took their turn in vigil.

The next morning, Benjamin was worse. Plump pillows were piled behind him to prop him up to assist in his struggle for breath. Even though the doctor was summoned, he said there was nothing more to do and that all was in God's hands. He gave Aggie a tincture of laudanum to help her sleep. It did not, and after a night of restless, wild, dream-filled sleep, she was angry with the outcome and took her rightful place beside her husband. Polly joined her mother and proved herself a true help by washing bedding, nightshirts, and bandages. Aggie wrung her hands over and over, praying all the while for her husband's recovery.

The vigil went on. After four days, Benjamin was breathing better and began to sit up. He asked for broth, although swallowing was still difficult. The bruises faded a little, and cuts began to heal. Polly changed dressings and fed her Papa broth, then thin oatmeal.

In gratefulness, he feebly tried to hug his only daughter. She threw her arms around his neck, crying, "Papa! Oh, Papa! I was so scared for you."

Benjamin battled serious wounds and demons, aching in body and heart from the violence of a turncoat community set against him. Feeling so accepted after his first sermon at Jamie's house and his plea for shelter for his family, he and Aggie believed they had found a home. But small minds refused to accept the growing tide of religious freedom.

New London continued to be a bastion of the Church of England.

His eyes began to steady themselves, and his head stopped swirling. Focusing on God's words was sweet indeed for a man who had been beaten nearly to death for his beliefs. Death had been the purpose of the attack, or at the very least to scare and force the family out of town.

The Kimseys, however, would not be intimidated.

Chapter 16

Taking a Different Tack

DURING HIS RECOVERY, there was too much time for Benjamin to think. His family was struggling without his stipend, and they were nearly destitute. Oh, they would not starve, thanks to Jamie, but if anything happened to the farm, *God help us*, he prayed in anguish.

He called his family about him. They stood around his bed, and when he announced, "We're poor, my dear ones," grim faces stared back at him, alarmed.

No one spoke until Ian said, "I know I'm just an apprentice, Father, but when you're better, I'll send you what money I make in Lynchburg. I have an arrangement with William Bockhannon..." His voice failed him, remembering the trial and the canceled order with the man.

Solomon had been angry with his father at the trial for not standing up to his tormentors and stomped out of the house. His twin, Hiram, started to cry, not knowing where to turn, and Benjie told his parents that some farmers said they wouldn't be needing their services anymore.

David said, "No one's buying any candles, Papa."

"Nor my wood carvings," William chimed in.

Polly and Humphrey were both on the verge of tears.

"What are we to do, my husband? I could take in sewing…" She looked away from her distraught family, trying not to cry herself. "We could move, but that would split the family apart."

Humphrey crawled onto the bed and put his head on his father's chest.

Cuddling his youngest son, Benjamin remembered something he had not thought of in years. He smiled as the fog of poverty cleared his mind. "What would you think about opening a mercantile. Preaching might go down better if we were to supply the necessities of life. With brother Jamie's help, it just might work."

Each member looked incredulous at the prospect, for the question was how and especially why after their father's poor treatment by the town.

Aggie helped her husband, who was on the mend, sit on the porch after lunch one sunny noon. She thought him rather pallid, and he agreed the bright afternoon would help him grow stronger and lighten his mood. The tap of his cane on the floor cheered her although his old war injury had been made stiffer by the bedridden recuperation, and his limp was worse.

Jamie visited from time to time, and that day, seeing his brother sitting on the porch was a gift. There were other men with him. One seemed like a seaman from his uniform, and Benjamin shielded his eyes from the strong light but could not make out their clothing. Maybe brethren from church? He doubted that. Then who?

"We'd like a sermon, Brother Kimsey," someone declared.

Throwing back his head toward heaven and smiling, Benjamin said, "I would relish the privilege. This is the day the Lord has made. Let us rejoice and be glad in it." It felt so very good to praise God in his high heaven. The men made themselves comfortable on the grass. The preacher went on and on.

"Gawd a'mighty! You always were a wordy bastard, you ole sea dog!"

Benjamin stopped in his tracks. His brows lowered, and he seared the culprit with his gaze.

"Who dares to ridicule the word of God?" he demanded, but his throat seized him into submission.

"I do, you old rapscallion."

Aggie had just stepped foot out the door to listen when she hollered, "Paddy O'Sullivan! Saints preserve us," and she ran to his waiting arms.

Benjamin was totally confused by the flustering turn of events which sent him to his chair.

That night, sitting around the fire, Paddy passed a flask. The non-Baptists, including James Francis and two seamen from Benjamin's shipboard days, had a propensity for strong drink, and talk was free among the friends. Word of Benjamin's maltreatment and others of his bent had reached all the way to Baltimore and throughout the colonies. Such violence was a crime to them and those for whom religious freedom had been a beacon. But Paddy and James Francis had something else in mind than commiserating with their old friend.

James Francis began. "It's been twelve years, my friend, since we've seen each other."

Benjamin noted his graying unkempt beard. A battered cocked hat covered dirty hair hanging over his chest and slumped shoulders, and lines like a worn-out old map covered the shipmaster's face. He looked older than his sixty years, the sea had its way with him, and years of salt and wind had burnished him bronze. His heavy coat in the warm room told Benjamin that his bloated body probably carried the effects of pipe tobacco, rum, and damp sea air. Coughing and excreting sticky green masses of phlegm in the spittoon at intervals interrupted his speech.

"Jamie has told me you're in need of a little cash to help with this fine family of yours. You've produced many hearty boys to carry on your legacy…At sea for years, I never had the time to remarry and have lost touch with my children." He spat again, this time in disdain. "They married English and moved to London!" James Francis stared into the fire and seemed to regurgitate, then swallowing the bitter bile of his vitriol, he washed it down with more rum.

Cheer suddenly took hold of him as the rum danced in his head. "I never was a man of many words as you seem to be." Laughter stirred the excited room, and James Francis triumphantly handed

Benjamin a pouch. "This is your share of the money made from the sale of that ship you captained for our business. I think it will get you where you want to be in your life. I never expected you to be a threadbare preacher." A mighty roar of laughter led him to a terrible fit of coughing.

James Francis could sell you the shirt off your own back, and he had used his expertise and gift of gab to sell the Glasgow ship to one of his contacts in England. King George III paid fifty dollars per ton of the 250-ton well-made Scottish ship, and glad of the expense. Benjamin was glad as well. Divided three ways among the brothers and Benjamin, each share was four thousand pounds sterling.

A few months later, the Kimseys heard talk of the death of James Francis O'Sullivan. The body was reverently slipped into the sea by his crew. His brother, Paddy, took over the business, and he and his good friend Benjamin would continue in a different sort of business—a business that would last through the coming trouble.

Chapter 17

Paddy, His Old Partner

1769

PADDY TRAVELED BACK to New London, Virginia, several times over the year and noted changes in his friend and the town. To the delight of the residents, Benjamin purchased the home his family had been renting and requested permission from the burgesses to build a mercantile. A permit was granted, seeing that their former preacher was putting money into the town's coffers. His tormentors, however, averted their eyes or bowed their heads, slinking quickly away from him as he passed. Never mind. Benjamin was on a mission, and he had long forgiven them.

On one trip, sitting again at his friend's fire, Paddy was a little too comfortable with his rum. This time the fire came from a Franklin stove Jamie had suggested Benjamin install, similar to the one Middleton had at his Lynchburg store. With a scolding click of her tongue, Aggie easily whisked the flask from his hand and stowed it in her apron pocket and said it needed to be "refilled." He would not see it again, however, until he left their home. She furnished both men with cups of steaming coffee and generous portions of pudding made with imported dried figs from the Mediterranean Sea Paddy brought from one of his trips to Boston.

"Your wife is a delicate beauty—and a sly devil," Paddy said thickly.

"My friend, you've had too much anyway." To change the subject, Benjamin asked Paddy how their plans were working for the first delivery of goods.

Between bites of soft figs and crunchy sweet toasted topping, Paddy continued. "The barge will be at the ferry in a day or two, and Jamie will pick it up as planned. He's the only one for miles around with a big-enough wagon. Some of my crew will, with their muskets, attend to his security."

"Good…That's fine." Benjamin stared into the fragments of the waning fire. "You know, I never asked you where nor how you get your supplies…but…maybe I don't want to know."

The room got very quiet with only a small crackle from the stove and a slight hiss of the oil lamps. Benjamin never asked again.

"Back in '57," Paddy began, the work of the coffee seeping into his sinews, "I met me a beautiful young woman, Sally Waitt by name." His brogue was as thick and sweet as Irish butter, bringing back wonderful memories of the two sailors' first years together plying their trade—memories of wild coastlines and dangerous shoals, forbidding forests and savage scoundrels. Paddy let the memories bloom.

Having enough of slouching in his chair, he straightened his back, holding his cup, and stretched forward. The steam from the coffee bathed his face in warm vapor.

Paddy continued, "She was the daughter of a wealthy owner of many a ship in Massachusetts. It was during the time of the French and Indian War, and I had a little money put by. After a while, I asked her father for her hand in marriage."

Benjamin clapped him on the shoulder. "You're married? How wonderful for you, Paddy."

"Well, he was agreeable, and Sally insisted I purchase new clothes. She didn't want me looking like a pauper, although she seemed to enjoy the look of me in my captain's uniform, which is what I planned on wearing." He continued, delighting out loud, "A coat of finest wool, dyed brown, tan lapels with bright brass buttons, matching waistcoat, and, of course, the finest linen small clothes."

"Of course," Benjamin agreed, knowing Paddy's elevated thoughts of himself.

"Women!" They shared a good laugh.

"To continue, I was getting fitted for my suit and seeing what I looked like in the mirror—an abominable peacock with all the frills—but by no means was I overdressed. Then the tailor, working at me from the back, noticed my wig…Ben, stop laughing. And, yes, I was wearing one. As I said, the tailor was touching the hair and bid me remove it. He examined it inside and out and said he'd only seen one such fine example of wig making before…by an eleven-year-old! The name was Ian Kimsey from Virginia. And the most expensive— human hair."

Benjamin was startled. "That's my son. My boy." His face radiated the pride he felt.

"I was grateful I didn't have to dress in that manner all the time. Sally and I were married in early May of '58 by Reverend Checkley at Old North Church, and our reception was a lavish affair. Many of Boston's finest were invited, and I was introduced to Captains Alexander McDougall and Isaac Sears, both from New York. They were among other wealthy men—ship captains and merchants, lawyers, and such. I heard about a soldier-surgeon from Pennsylvania, a captain with the English, wounded during the raid on Kitanning in that same war…Ach, Benjamin…you know me. I don't go in for all that blather, but…Sally's father introduced me to a world I could only guess—privateering. I was always armed as you well remember, but to realize I could be licensed for the work of stealing from English merchant ships astonished me." He let the words rise into the warmed room and sift down over his friend.

"A wounded soldier-surgeon from Pennsylvania? Go on," Benjamin said thoughtfully.

"The sea had taken its toll on the *Eileen O'Rourke*, well-nigh on thirty years old. She was falling apart, so I scuttled her. But I had enough money. And with a small loan from my father-in-law, I purchased another. So now I will be working closely with Alexander

McDougall. He's a merchant and importer, and a fellow Scot of the Isle of Islay." Again, he let his words sink in before delighting Benjamin with more. Quietly, he said, "She's a three-masted schooner—eight guns and twenty-five seamen including my former crew. She's fast as the wind and…I named her the *Mercer*…"

A lull intervened and then a moment of recognition. "Hugh Mercer?" Benjamin's voice quivered in the question.

Paddy nodded.

"He's alive?" Tears formed in Benjamin's eyes and dropped unabashed onto his chest. "I thought he died…"

Benjamin's memories ran back to his childhood when, as a small lad, he had heard the great visiting Presbyterian minister William Mercer from Aberdeenshire who, according to Benjamin's mother, had saved his father, Robert, from sin. Hugh was his son and an assistant surgeon in the army of Bonnie Prince Charlie at Falkirk. Benjamin met Hugh on the battlefield of Culloden. The Jacobite farmer and the Jacobite surgeon liked each other instantly. They shared their passionate love for Scotland, their way of life, and their fidelity to fight to the death for the prince who should have ruled them. Hugh was elbow to elbow with his countrymen, and when they fell, he tried mightily to pull them to safety. When Benjamin saw his brother Charles fighting for his life, Mercer was in the thick of things proving his worth as a superior swordsman, but he was viciously attacked trying to pull another wounded man away from the field. Benjamin was mad as hell thinking the mild country doctor killed. The battle went on, and he himself went down, wounded and unknowing that his friend had escaped. The tie was broken between them as Paddy sailed the Kimseys to sanctuary in Ireland. For months, Hugh had eluded capture, and in the fall of that same year, he himself embarked on a ship headed for the colonies.

Paddy continued. "He had been a captain with the Pennsylvania Regiment in the war. And he lives in Fredericksburg County."

"Here in my own Virginia?" Benjamin's smile drew back into those deep dimples, his eyes radiant with joy. "What a wonder God has performed."

* * *

Paddy told how his ship, the *Mercer*, was a fearless little terrier of a schooner—royal blue and edged in gilt; the copper bottom teasingly slapped the ocean's waves skimming over them with barely an effort. Her sails were full and happy to sneak up on King George's Royal Navy in the night. She was like a favorite horse familiar with the whims of her master, and the reins were not held tightly. Outmaneuvering the quarry, cannons gave them a broadside as a welcome which tore holes in the pine planks and canvas tops, splitting masts into pieces, and lighting the cloud cover with sparks and flame. Paddy pulled her head alongside the big ships without so much as a how do you do. She shinnied alongside, and tentacles tipped with boarding hooks grabbed at the ships, pulling them close to her bosom. His crew boarded the larger manned wreckage and jabbed at the English with Irish broadswords, capturing the mighty ships and killing or wounding her crews. Then she slipped back under cover of the ocean's darkness with the booty—tea, iron implements, molasses, coffee, spirits and spices—belonging to Paddy and shared with his crew and benefactors. For exploits like this, he was a successful and rich man and well-liked both by Alexander McDougall and his father-in-law, John Waitt.

"You didn't take slaves?" Benjamin inquired.

"I cannot trade in human flesh," Paddy cried, disgusted by what he saw and smelled, black bodies burdened with chains and crammed into the cargo holds of some privateers—slave ships. The man named for Ireland's Saint Patrick followed his Roman church's teaching of the dignity of human beings. The *Mercer* was a fine, sleek ship known for agility and speed that Paddy swung between Bermuda and New Jersey, and he would not have her contaminated by slavery.

Benjamin countered, "But you have slaves working your ship."

Paddy's ire got the best of him. He shouted, "Not slaves! Crew! I pay them well enough—the same as my Irishers. They were liberated along with Bahamas sugar and molasses from an English brigantine. They are free to go whenever they like."

Enough said, thought Benjamin, not wanting to enter into a battle with his hot-tempered friend.

* * *

Boston Harbor was becoming dangerous. Paddy couldn't show his face in the city taverns and mostly traveled by night if he had business in town while his ship was being discharged. His privateering was done at night, but there had been occasions when a bright moon or exploding cannon seared his identity in the memory of some unfortunate English sea captain's or crewman's gaze.

One evening, Paddy and two of his men were drinking in a darkened corner of the Green Dragon Tavern, notorious for underground Patriot meetings. Their tankards were empty, and desirous of refills, Paddy motioned for a serving wench. Just at that moment the tavern door opened and closed, and a gust of wind pulled at a lantern, causing light to pass across his face.

"I know you," an angry drunk jeered at Paddy and spat in his face. "You stole my ship." Paddy had had too much to drink and was slow in reacting. Suddenly there was a fist raking his face and breaking his nose. He was out cold on the floor and saved from that captain's English sword by his men and two fellow Patriots.

Awakening in the wee hours of the morning with a tremendous headache, there appeared in the candlelight an apparition bobbing above his head.

"Glad you're awake," the man's voice was saying. "Your men went back to the ship. You can join them later when you're feeling better. For the moment, I'll do the talking. My name is Joseph Warren, physician and soldier, and I know who you are. McDougall told me your background. Happy to make your acquaintance, Mr. O'Sullivan."

A gentle knocking at the door interrupted the one-sided intro-duction. The operating table was uncomfortably hard on Paddy's back, but his aching brain wrestled with memories of what had happened. Nothing was forthcoming, but voices from the hall were moving toward him.

"You have visitors," Dr. Warren announced.

"Oh, my poor love. What have they done to you?" Sally floated across the room in a sky blue silk gown covered by a burgundy bro-caded cloak. She pushed back the hood covering her blonde hair, then held his hand and kissed his forehead. If he had been able, he would have smelled her heavenly fragrance.

Her father was right on her heels. "Who did this thing, Patrick?"

Even though the face at the Green Dragon had been seared into his brain, no name came through the meandering fogginess. Paddy's raspy throat tried to form words. Nothing came out.

"We'll find him, son. Never fear."

"May I give him some water?" Sally asked Dr. Warren. Slipping her delicate hand under Paddy's head, she gently lifted it for him to drink from the glass handed to her. He gave her what passed for a smile if only through two black eyes, and strangely found himself thinking, *I'd rather suckle at your abundant*—Paddy fell into uncon-sciousness. Dr. Warren's laudanum finally did its work, and he could sleep with his dreams of pleasure unencumbered by pain.

If he'd been awake, Paddy would have heard the words spoken quietly by the trio as his wife and father-in-law started to leave.

Dr. Warren encouraged Sally and her father to come on the morrow and, with a slight pause, inquired, "Should we ask him to join us?"

"McDougall told me we should. After all, he has proved his worth many times over, and given money for the cause. Yes, I think we should ask him. I'll talk with him when he's better. Good night, Joseph." Mr. Waitt and his daughter stepped off Dr. Warren's thresh-old and into their waiting carriage.

"No taxation without representation" was the cry from Boston election sermons of the Reverend Mayhew back in 1750 and 1754, the phrase that came to embrace American rights—"the cause of liberty and the right and duty to resist tyranny." The words simmered under the colonists' breaths and drew like-minded men together. Formed in 1765 when the Stamp Act was passed, men joined with Samuel Adams in a secret organization called the Sons of Liberty.

Paddy knew a few of the men—McDougall was one, as was Dr. Warren—and joined them in their endeavors. His father-in-law, John Waitt, was not a member but supported them just the same. The reputable Benedict Arnold was a merchant with ships plying the Atlantic, and he and others of the Sons ignored the tax requirement.

For three-quarters of a century, whalers and merchants running along the New Jersey coast had been using Barnegat Inlet to travel into the bay of the same name behind the barrier island of Long Beach, but McDougall had told Paddy of a place that was easier and safer to access. The base for the privateers was at Wrangleboro (Port Republic), New Jersey, along the Nacote Creek which emptied into the Little Egg Harbor River.

Paddy and Sally stayed at the Waitts' plantation while he recuperated. His men anchored the *Mercer* at Chestnut Neck's wharf, but he longed to be on one of those ships going and coming, sailing the open ocean, trading in the West Indies, and privateering along the way. But he needed to be content with getting his health back, and of course, his beautiful wife's comely body kept him close to home. However, his crew was getting restless with laziness, and finally one day, Paddy said goodbye to his darling Sally at the wharf. To the delight of her husband and family, Sally was with child, and Paddy promised to return by the time she gave birth.

* * *

The *Mercer* entered the mouth of the James River heavily loaded with her crew well armed. Many river rats slithering along the shores and shallows of the river simply waited for a pretty ship like Paddy's schooner to falter. Their avarice flamed at the thought of capturing it, but her armament was a prickly dilemma. She was small, but thorny. Those who had tried quickly got their ass kicked and stayed away from the fiendish Irish captain and her black and white crew.

Barges traveled the broad river delivering supplies to small towns and plantations, most of which had large wharves. Iron goods, cloth, seed, pitch, pine tar, and turpentine were taken off, and tons of tobacco were loaded by plantation slaves. Long lines of men, women, and children bore the burdens of sacks, boxes, crates, and barrels.

Paddy marveled at the wealth of the colonial pioneer plantations along the James—three-storey manor houses, rows of slave cabins out front for all to see their masters' wealth, formal gardens, and thousands of acres of tobacco—not unlike his father-in-law's plantation. Some owners were high up in political power as well.

Paddy was warmed by the thought of his Kimsey friends— good hardworking farmers, religious, and businessmen. But he was in business, too, and while he would fight to the death for his friends, he still made a living by privateering—on the open ocean. River running was a nerve-racking business.

Jamie was waiting at City Point customs house when he received word of Paddy's arrival. The feeling of the place had changed considerably since last he was there. No longer a den of disreputable reputation, it had become a place of commerce and transportation where business could be transacted, where people could make their way up and down the river road with ease, and where the necessities of life could be exchanged.

Benjamin's necessities were quickly dispatched to Jamie's waiting Conestoga wagon. His horses had been retired to their pastures long ago, and six large mules took their places. Jamie joined Paddy on his ship. Money was paid and rum was poured, and two of the crew were assigned as the promised security. Two of Hermann Ensch's well-muscled and well-armed sons had accompanied Jamie, and with this formidable escort, no incident occurred going home.

The friends had worked out a plan for providing Benjamin with supplies for his mercantile and would have to see if it worked out. The rewards of having well-stocked shelves depended on how much could actually be sold in New London town, with former enemies still lurking around him.

Chapter 18

Late Summer

1769

THE GRAND OPENING came, and it seemed as if the whole population hovered around the new mercantile. Little children were given candy, boys and girls drooled over games and toys, and men and women gazed appreciatively at all the provisions for daily life. Quality items such as silks and brocades, fine woolens and leather goods appealed to the wealthy. And prices were fair. At the end of the day, a brisk business had been enjoyed.

Winter Loss
1769–1770

Snow came, and with it the new year. Hogmanay was celebrated on the last day of the old year in the old Scottish tradition, but this time it was different. The gifts exchanged were of a finer quality. In the past, bits of wood carved like animals, toys made of twisted newspaper, birds' nests with unhatched eggs, and maybe a shiny rock or polished stone were given.

Aggie worked her magic with shortbread and bannocks served with a wee dram of Irish whiskey—a yearly gift from Paddy—the only time Benjamin would allow the family to imbibe. This special day, however, Benjamin received a new stock to tie at his neck, the boys got stockings, and there was a store-bought dress for Polly. Aggie always received her children's homemade gifts with joy, and this year she declined any purchased gift, reasoning it was not right for a Baptist minister's wife to seek such attentions.

After the children were in bed and the couple was becoming drowsy in front of the brightly burning hearth, Benjamin rose and left the room. Aggie was surprised. "Are you going to bed, dear heart?" she called after him. No answer. A few minutes passed before he returned with a package tied with a red satin ribbon.

"This is for you," he said with playful eyes and a smile filled with love.

Her cheeks flushed. Was it the hearth? Or was it the fire in her husband's heart?

Delicately pulling at the ribbon, Aggie slipped it off. The paper gave way to a sheer snow-white neck handkerchief to be pleated around her bodice—just like the one she wore at Jamie and Mary's wedding. It was an extravagance she would not consider had it not been given by her husband, and Aggie was overcome by gratitude at his thoughtfulness. She knelt before him with her head lowered and gently folded her hands in his lap. His hands lifted her face to him, and he brushed her tears away. Aggie looked into his handsome features—dark brow and sparkling gaze, a smattering of gray creeping over his temples, teasing curls around the receding hairline he tried so hard to control with pomade. He pulled her forward, kissed her— and a child's cry interrupted their passion.

* * *

In the small hours of the morning, the fire burned low, and each member of the Kimsey family pulled up extra quilts under their chins. A bitter cold covered the land, and a layer of ice collected in the animals' troughs. Benjamin stirred first—he caught a whiff of smoke. His sleepy mind thought the hearth's flames had burned out, and he turned over, curling into his wife's warm body. Suddenly the smell was worse. He threw back the covers and started for the fire-place, but his ankle gave way and he fell to the floor.

Aggie sat up startled. "What's wrong?" In the blackness, she struggled to grasp the oil lamp and was strangely able to see it.

"Benjamin," she screamed and flew out of bed to help her husband get up. "The window!"

They both stared at the flames. Benjamin slipped into his trousers and boots and was on Aggie's heels toward the children's bedrooms. The older boys were in their nightshirts and helping the little ones. Benjamin, Ian, and Benjie ran to the front of the mercantile engulfed in fire and beyond saving.

"Hurry, children!" Aggie commanded, forcing herself to be calm. They all rushed into the yard and stood there in the snow watching their mercantile burn. They counted heads: Benjamin Jr.; William; the twins, Solomon and Hiram; David; Polly; and the baby, Humphrey. Benjamin held his wife and bairn in his arms and watched as the house caught fire quickly—and both buildings burned to the ground. Somewhere in the distance, the fire alarm bell could be heard clanging. No one came.

When an indifferent sun rose that morning, the full extent of the devastation could be seen. Their neighbors had come if only to make sure their houses weren't at risk and force themselves to give token ministry to the Kimseys. Someone gave Benjamin a coat, and Aggie's only friend in the town gave her an old dress and a blanket and made sure the children were warmly covered.

Benjamin and his sons probed the ruins for anything salvageable. He found his metal box containing the money earned from the sale of the ship minus what he paid buying his house, building the mercantile, and stocking it with merchandise. It was fortunate that it was still there, but their home and livelihood were gone.

Three miles away, Jamie had seen the night sky light up and, knowing the history of trouble between Benjamin and the townspeople, decided he better have a look. He arrived just as his brother and nephews were scavenging the remains of the smoldering buildings.

"What's left, brother?" Jamie asked from atop his horse watching Benjamin pick at a burned piece of cloth—the handkerchief he had given his wife that very night. "God almighty. I just knew something like this would happen. Get what you can glean. You're coming with me."

Alight with midmorning sun, a procession of homeless Kimseys rolled along in their salvaged buggy pulled by their horse Gracie over the ice-covered ground to Jamie's house. Fresh snow in drifts sparkled and gave the family slow going over the dangerous path. They were a sorry-looking bunch—sleepy youngsters cradled in the arms of parents and siblings; the boys hunkered into collars of coats or folds of blankets discarded by left-behind enemies; all their faces covered with soot.

Late-afternoon icicles hung from the roof's edge as they stumbled up the steps, and the door was thrown open by Mary. She disguised her sorrow behind a welcoming smile and greeted the bedraggled family.

The next morning found the large two-storey home crowded with thirteen individuals from floor to attic. Wee cousins were doubled up in beds, and older children and adults slept on floors. Both hearths were kept busy warming the two families. Almost everyone slept until afternoon when they awakened with the horror of what had happened invading their souls.

Despite the misery, Benjamin lifted their spirits. "No thought of sadness here, my dearest family. It's better to think on full stomachs and give thanks that we're all together." And Mary, Aggie, and her daughter Polly supplied a splendid supper.

The older boys were sent out to hunt, taking advantage of the sunlight playing on the cold snow. The others collected firewood from the shed, washed dishes, and watched the wee ones.

"Where's Ian?" Mary asked Aggie as they hunted through a large trunk in the attic.

"He's working in Lynchburg. His wigs are highly regarded in the colonies and in England. We're very proud of him…I'm glad he wasn't here to see what happened." And she started to cry.

"Don't worry, Mother…oh…I haven't called you that for so long." They both wept now, but for joy recalling the years that Aggie taught a very young Mary and her sister, Rebecca, in Baltimore. "So many good memories." The two women were more like sisters.

They sorted through the cedar trunk. There were baby clothes from both Samuel and Littleberry, Mary's youngest son. Buried underneath were newborn things from little Sarah who died on her birthday. Again, Mary's eyes brimmed over with tears. "I'm afraid these are too small for Humphrey." Both women began laughing as little Pee Wee was now a plump five-year-old forever racing around in circles.

In her sorrow, Aggie blushed. "I'm with child again."

Mary, with an easy smile and no regret, simply handed her the infant clothes. "Here. Your first gift for the wee bairn."

Mary's attic treasure box also contained her wedding gown, a few maternity dresses, some shifts, and a bolt of cloth obtained when Benjamin had opened his new mercantile.

"Well, let's begin," she said. "I hear Polly is accomplished in the use of needle and thread."

Jamie walked to his old cabin with his brother in tow. "I think with a little imagination we could expand the place and add a second storey." They stepped inside. "How is Ian?" Jamie asked absentmind-edly, touching the logs and stroking his chin whiskers, contemplating the work that needed to be done.

Benjamin was talking in a steady stream, going on and on about his eldest son. "He's twenty-two now and exporting to England."

"Exporting? Exporting what?"

"Wigs. You aren't listening."

"No. I've got my mind on this cabin and how we can make it livable for your family…By God!" Jamie spat on the floor. "Would you just look at this patch? It didn't hold. Oh well, we will open it up again."

Chapter 19

The Kimseys Rise Again

IN THE EARLY spring of 1770 as Paddy was procuring supplies for Benjamin's mercantile, Jamie's 150 acres of three-week-old corn lay lifeless on watery ground. Vegetable sprouts that had pushed through the earth's crust floated above the flooded earth, and yet, it still rained.

In the cabin Jamie built those ten years ago, he found rot in one of the twenty-four-foot logs on the third course—right in the middle. A corncob in the chinking that hadn't been well sealed came loose, and over the years rain caused the clay mud to dissolve around it with the resultant rot. Jamie poked at the spot with an awl and discovered the damage was far worse than he thought. It covered at least three feet of the log, and the rotted piece would have to be removed, fitted with a patch, and re-chinked. And still it rained.

Day after day, Jamie itched to get to the work, but the deluge was relentless. The Little Otter River, which ran from the Blue Ridge Mountains and into the Roanoke River, overflowed its banks, and mudslides and debris washed out the small bridge above his farm. His house sat on a rise, but the cabin was at water level with the creek and straightaway licking at the floor joists above the rock footings.

Finally, the storm gave in to a white hot sun that demanded equal time. Steam rose over the farms of Virginia. Jamie and Mary walked a short distance barefoot into the fields and sank up to their calves in mud.

Completely despondent, he said, "Our corn is lost." A chill of dismay ran down his back despite the heat. He picked up a water-logged, mud-covered plant, then looked out over his ruined fields. What started out as lush green stalks were now floating derelicts. His face flushed with anger.

Slipping her hand in his and with tears in her eyes, Mary voiced their worst fears, "That's our cash crop. What will we do?"

Their tobacco survived, but there was not enough of a growing season left to plant again. The humidity and *musketas* and flies were unbearable. Despite Jamie's protestations, Benjamin gave him needed cash to tide him over.

* * *

With the disastrous year behind them, rebuilding the small cabin and a new season of planting were the order of the day. Jamie felt it would be a rich harvest with the new sediment from last year's flooding settled over the lands of his farm. The Kimseys tilled the land and dropped the seed corn into the new furrows, but rebuilding the small cabin was a priority for the family.

Following the sounds of axes and falling logs, Herman Ensch and his sons came by to help make the work lighter for their old friends. Partway into the business, however, it was decided the cabin should be left alone. They fixed the breech but discovered much more rain damage. Hermann suggested it would make a fine smokehouse, so another site was chosen for Benjamin's family home. Before long the footings were placed, and the framework started. Day after day the work proceeded, and soon a large home was raised for Benjamin, the man Jamie loved not only as a brother but also as the man who had replaced their father, Robert.

The fragrance of new wood, summer blossoms, earth, and crops caused a rush of excitement inside Jamie's body. He just knew it would be a good year because the entire family was working together for life-giving nourishment of body and soul.

Working alone in a far distant corner of his land, Jamie would sometimes hear settlers' axes clearing forest. Spirals of smoke would herald the advent of a homesteader settled into the daily work of feeding his family, and Jamie would feel the tug of his old desire to move on. But home was where his family was—even if it was still in Bedford County.

Benjamin started talking of another mercantile. Where would he put it, asked Jamie. The population of the middle colonies was moving south and west beyond the Appalachian Mountains, and news of itinerant preachers following potential flocks was everywhere. Benjamin had heard there was a growing Baptist community in Pittsylvania County, founded three years earlier along the border with North Carolina. He longed to be one of them.

"I have no flock to look after and teach the tenets of our religion," he explained, walking with Jamie through the rows of growing corn.

"Are you bored, my brother? You have your family to preach to."

"It's not the same," Benjamin retorted.

"Well, we just got you settled. We have a large farm and the family is together. What more do you want?"

"Why don't we go down there and see what it's like?" he begged.

Jamie's color was rising and so was his voice. "And leave the farm? We have women and children. And what about the crops? Why?"

"I...I always wanted to be an itinerant preacher..." Benjamin walked away, leaving his brother wondering what was wrong with him.

They were arguing with each other. Jamie felt bad, and after wrestling with the thorny issue, he gave in. Yes, he would ride with him, albeit nervous about his crops.

For forty miles, the brothers rode along a centuries-old Indian trail that stretched south to the Spanish territory of Florida. Rich farmland was everywhere the eye could see, and the area had a large community of Scots-Irish who were more welcoming than the New London Loyalists.

A Pittsylvania rise showed a splendid vista of buff-colored hills rolling out in endless succession. An abandoned wagon sat decaying, its spokes broken, and the few remaining barely able to hold their own. Rusting chains and hardware had retired long ago, and bunched cornstalks of harvests past sagged with age, clinging to one another, refusing to decompose back to the black earth. Green finger-length sprouts splayed out from rotting pumpkins in fields and looked for support from decaying cross-log fencing.

Taking a good long look from that rise, Jamie swung his leg over the withers of his horse and agreed with his brother that the hills and bottomland of the Smith River looked promising both for their farm and Ben's "itinerant" flock. The brothers discussed the matter of moving.

"What do you think, Ben? Spread out the corn over the hillocks and the faster-growing crops on the flats?" Jamie asked, then mused half under his breath, "I'd like to try wheat instead of tobacco." A big smile swept his face, his eyebrows raised. "Yes?"

"Yes! And I will have a whole new congregation on whom I shall spread the cloak of the word of God." The middle-aged preacher and his brother shook hands on it. However, their dream would be a long time in coming. Ben urged his horse, "Come on, Gracie. Let's go home."

Revolutionary Troubles

Benjamin was excited by the prospect of the move after failing to bring the word of God to New London or open a successful mercantile. He thought he would bring favor on the community; instead, *Pride goeth before the fall*, he told himself. However, his and Jamie's fates were bigger than their personal issues—the Boston Massacre.

Paul Revere's engraving, printed in all the colonial newspapers, depicted the horror and had the effect that the Sons of Liberty desired. Along with many cursed tax acts that swept the colonies and caused grinding and gnashing of teeth, the bloody massacre had solidified the need for fortifying militias with arms and ammunition.

It started at the custom house on King Street, according to the *Boston Gazette*. A Redcoat sentry was provoked verbally, and protesters formed into a mob carrying clubs and sticks. Unarmed men compacted snow in frozen hands. Blood was in the eyes of all, and along with angry shouting and musket butts to Patriots' jaws, the English soldiers came to the gathering riot with the business ends of their guns already primed. Virgin snow fell over the horrible state of affairs. Ice was in hearts as well as accelerating onto the ground. Some Patriots let go their only ammunition, and what followed was a burst of lead balls against innocent snowballs, all of this leading to the threshold of war. In the end, the muck and mire were tragically marked by curled wigs and cocked hats mixed with the blood of three American casualties of war—the first martyr, a mixed-descent African slave named Crispus Attucks and two other Patriots. Days later, another victim, a seventeen-year-old boy named Sam Maverick, died. Theirs was the first of the bloodshed on Boston city's streets. Threats of violent retribution raged among the population as well as the continual irritating presence of English troops.

* * *

1771

Jamie stood in the middle of a row of corn, the smell of summer in the air. It was nearly time for the harvest, and he had spent the morning pulling back husks and checking on kernels in the fat ears. *A few more days would do*, he thought.

But, like all the farmers in his family before him, his senses detected a change in the air before it arrived. When he looked south-east, he caught his breath; the sky was black. Clouds converged on the land, and the wind uprooted trees and crops in its wake, stirring them in a whirlwind, then flung far and wide. Waters of creeks and rivers were uplifted from their beds and whisked rapidly into a froth, only to fall back on the land, flooding everything in its path. Thick in the air was a rank smell of devastation of the land.

Fear gripped Jamie, and he rushed to the house and byre to get the family and animals to safety.

Mary was standing on the porch shielding her eyes from the western sun, her hair and skirts struggling with the unruly wind.

"What's wrong?" she screamed, but her words were ripped out of her mouth.

"Get the children into the root cellar!" Jamie yelled, running past her toward the byre. The animals nervously pushed at the pen's fence. In Jamie's hurry, he tore the gate from its hinges, and with the wind's help, it went flying. His four mules and two cows stampeded past him. He prayed for their survival.

Mary struggled with the root cellar door and was nearly swept away in a blast of wind. After he rushed in, Jamie secured the door from inside, and fright washed the close quarters of the underground fortification. The children, in the arms of their parents, whimpered in wild-eyed terror as the gale whirled above and the ground shook beneath. They were all safe, and yet Jamie worried. He looked at Mary, and in the din, he mouthed, "Benjamin!"

They sat for hours in the dim candlelit earthen den, waiting for the wind to stop. It did, then another sound replaced it, hail pounding with vile rage on their shelter's sod roof. Would the door hold? Jamie noted the sudden drop in temperature and wondered aloud to his wife what manner of storm this was. Toward morning, the candle finally expired and was replaced by a stream of light filtering through a crack in the entrance. Motioning for Samuel, his eldest, to help him, they pushed open the frost-laden door to a bitter sight indeed. A heavy coating of rime covered everything.

"Stay here," Jamie commanded his family. "Samuel, come with me."

Hoarfrost crackled under their shoes. He and his son surveyed the surrounds. Half the roof of the two-story house had been blown away, and broken window glass was everywhere. Curtains had been torn off, or the cloth lacerated by sharp glass daggers was still clinging to their frames. The whole inside of their home looked like a cauldron stirred by an enormous spoon—everything was broken to bits. To Jamie's amazement, the frame was still standing.

The sun rose over the Atlantic seaboard to a clear sky and exhausted landscape exposing the damage done by wind, hail, and frost. Trees were blown down or weighed down with wood siding, shingles, and broken limbs of other trees caught in their boughs.

Jamie and Samuel walked into the fields. The severe wind had flattened their corn, and a strange frost had blackened the green growth. For the second time, the Kimseys lost their crops. Fodder for pigs, Jamie lamented with a sigh.

"What will we do, Father?" His eyes were wide with fear.

Jamie looked at his nine-year-old son, his red hair like his own only tempered by his mother's brown locks. Freckles covered his face which he hated, but only endeared him to his father.

"We will rise again, right Father? We don't let adversity defeat us, do we?"

"That's right, Samuel." Jamie reassured him with a gentle hug.

He had been successful in growing the most enviable of produce, but now Jamie questioned the feasibility of continuing in Bedford County with all the suffering they had endured. Jamie's family met Benjamin's dear ones coming up from their cellar. Their house had not fared much better.

Joining together in the middle of the frost-laden fields, the Kimseys knelt in a poignant moment of thanksgiving, praising God that they were all safe.

Chapter 20

Solomon

1772

FROM THE EARLY years, a strong militia had been formed in each of the thirteen colonies for protection on the western border. After the French and Indian War, Colonel George Washington became the commander of Virginia's militia, and sixteen-year-old Solomon Kimsey was the first of the family to announce he wanted to join the fighting force. His father, Benjamin, with iron determination, was against it.

"No!" was his unequivocal answer, and for three days he turned his back on his son, avoiding the certain struggle. Finally, he knew he needed to speak. "We are Baptists preaching peace, and as such it is our duty to stay away from the disturbances that surround us," he said passionately. Benjamin could see that same passion staring back at him. On the forge, with the hammer of his son's insistence, he began to understand, remembering his own strong desire for the fight in his Scottish homeland—a desire to serve the cause and protect their very way of life. It was taken away, and no amount of unrest between men here in this new land would take away the new life they had set for themselves.

Knowing full well it would not help, he said, "I know how you feel."

"What do you know of battle, Father?" Solomon's accusation stung him. "You profess religious peace, but you allowed yourself to be beaten and thrown in gaol? Why did you not defend yourself?" Tears welled up in his eyes. "I was ashamed of you." He ran from the house.

Benjamin was dismayed that his son had kept his emotions hidden for so long but did not want a confrontation. All his old wounds opened. All the old fighting words and songs and the pipes spurring the clans to defeat the German George II and his soldiers came back to haunt him. Now there was a third on the throne, and he could see what was happening to their Virginia and to the other colonies. He read the stories and saw the fight coming, and it scared him. With neighbors torn apart by quarreling around the heat of his stove, the possibility of war had been a daily occurrence discussed in his mercantile. The daily necessity to pray for peace became more intense, and he spoke openly about it in his weekly sermons.

In the yard, Solomon stopped at the bottom of an old walnut tree that he and his twin brother, Hiram, liked to climb. *Where had the time gone?* Benjamin thought. Solomon was trying to be the man his father wanted but could not understand if he did not know the facts. *How can I tell him?* His stomach churned. He had never told any of his sons his history.

Benjamin limped to his son's side. Solomon continued arguing, determined to win over his father. "That is what the militia means— to defend ourselves against the savages who have ravaged our citizens in the western lands. To kill them and—"

"Yes, that is part of it," Benjamin interrupted, grappling with his proposed words and tightly gripping the cane's head to support his weakened ankle. He continued, "Our colony's bill of rights states that we need a well-regulated militia, and it is our right to keep and bear arms, and defend ourselves by repelling invasions, and to enforce the laws of our Virginia."

Solomon was astounded at his father's knowledge and sudden inflamed passion.

"Yes, I keep up with the news, and it appears that a war will soon be at our doorstep. My son, do you know how I got my injury?"

"Mother told us you broke your ankle on the ship."

"That is what we wanted you to know."

Innocent as he was, Solomon looked at his father with the same saucerlike eyes Benjamin remembered when the wee bairn, sitting on his knee, hung on his every word.

"Grapeshot hit my ankle in the Battle of Culloden Moor in 1746…in Scotland."

Solomon was stunned. "You fought in a war?" he asked, not quite believing what he heard.

"It was a battle that ended the Scots way of life forever and our Clan MacKenzie name." Benjamin hung his head as scenes of the smoke-filled day and starry night a quarter of a century earlier arose in his mind; each was shared with the young man before him.

"You cannot know the anger I felt after the horrible devastation heaped on our homeland. Scotland was just another of England's conquests, and brutal tyranny continued punishing us for many years afterward. Your grandfather Robert and Uncle Duncan, just a wee child, were murdered while they were innocently ploughing the fields. Your grandmother Mary died on that prisoner ship. Your mother and I, your brother Ian, and your uncles Jamie, Alex, and Charles—we were all sold as slaves in Baltimore." Benjamin's chest heaved with emotion.

Brutal devastating tyranny, innocents murdered, prisoners sold as slaves—the hateful words thundered in Solomon's ears.

A few crickets chirruped, filling the awkward silence between father and son. Yellow light from the opening front door of their home spread across the grass and revealed tears on Benjamin's face. Aggie's dark silhouette appeared in the frame.

Solomon saw his father cry for the first time in his short life and felt the color of aroused anger drain from his own face. "I'm sorry, Father. I did not know." *And we were MacKenzies!* he pondered.

With weighty mettle, Benjamin said, "We arose from the ashes of our homeland, and we will arise from whatever will come. You may go if it's your heart's desire." And he limped back to the warmth of the house to his dearly beloved wife.

A humble pie awaited on the table, and Benjamin's battle-field dirk sat beside Solomon's plate, the hide-covered grip emblazoned with the MacKenzie clan crest—Luceo non uro (I shine not burn)—a symbol of allegiance to the clan chiefs from the eleventh century. Loyal, honorable, and tough as nails, battle-hardened warriors clashed in many of Scotland's battles.

Chapter 21

The Soldier

Two MONTHS LATER, all the fine lads of the county were assembled and instructions were read:

> Every soldier shall be furnished with a fire-lock well fixed, a bayonet fitted to the same, a double cartouch-box, and three charges of powder, and constantly appear with the same at the time and place appointed for muster and exercise, and shall also keep at his place of abode one pound of powder and four pounds of ball, and bring the same with him into the field when he shall be required.

Each fellow from Bedford County stood in the long line and waited his turn to read the oath out loud before putting ink to paper—words that said, "Promise until death, guard those western borders, and defend their Virginia from foreign invaders."

Solomon's eyes glanced over it. He knew what it meant and dipped the tip of the quill in the well, sealing his fate with his name scrawled across the paper. It was below his friends' names, Adam and Peter Ensch. Then Colin Mathieson's son affixed his X underneath theirs. Abe and Billy, Zach and Gus, young and old—Solomon's neighbors with whom he had played, fished, or hunted—all ready to give their loyalties to their brothers and their new country.

* * *

Aggie hated the lead balls and black powder in her home, so they were removed to the byre loft, only to be used if her son's supplies ran low.

Solomon was a crack shot. Benjamin taught him and his brothers well, but Solomon could bag more than his fair share of game birds faster than any of his family or friends. Aggie was happy when he came home with quail or duck or rabbit for their dinner. Captain James Callaway looked on his new recruit with astonishment and marked him as an elite sharpshooter.

Aggie took pride in the homespun linen hunting shirts she made for her boys—sturdy but comfortable. Colonel Washington considered it ideal for the militia's working uniforms. Raveled fringe at seams and edges was it's only embellishment. Underneath, Solomon's small clothes consisted of a white linen shirt, a lightweight waistcoat, tan breeches buckled just under the knee over wool stockings. Canvas spatterdashes[18] covered to the calf were buttoned over shins and shoes. He had a knitted wool cap, but preferred a cocked hat similar to his father's, the front angle of which was placed over the corner of his left eye. The cartouche box holding thirty cartridges hung with a strap across his chest. Powder horn, hunting bag, and bullet pouch were strapped so the equipment was on the opposite side, Solomon adjusting it to fit comfortably to his right hand.

The militia was marched to drum and fife, quickly learning the rhythm sounds of the sticks on stretched calfskin and their captain's vocal commands. The company was conspicuously drilled in the town square to the delight of little children and of old men bereft of their youth and yearning with all their hearts to be a part of the

---

[18] Spatterdashes: usually knee-high legging worn as a protection from water and mud (https://www.merriam-webster.com/dictionary/spatterdashes).

fighting force. Solomon was proud of his place in the militia, but Benjamin wasn't so sure when he saw who the commander was.

James Callaway was the son of Colonel William Callaway, the man who, just four years before, had been a willing accomplice with Thomas Pullin, the instigator of Benjamin's arrest. The prejudice had died down over the last few years as throngs of Scots and Scots-Irish colonists turned to the more popular Baptist religion. Benjamin had no church building, but his flock had grown, and he did continue preaching out of his own home and that of his brother Jamie. He stayed away from town as far as possible, though, for fear Callaway would recognize the Kimsey name and thus prejudice his son's chances.

But Solomon had not reckoned on the power of prayer—his father's prayer. Benjamin stormed heaven begging the God of peace for there to be no cause for any war on the frontier and to preserve his son's life if there were.

The men were drilled over and over to make them one body. Spring and fall they marched and fought mock battles. In between, Solomon went back to the fields, planting and harvesting row upon row of corn, wheat, and tobacco for Uncle Jamie. Bored and frustrated in his desires for a real battle, he did not know how soon the conflict would come to satisfy that yearning.

After the terrible storm of '71 and the enlistments in the militia by Solomon and some of his neighbor chums, there was unrest in the western part of North Carolina. The name Tanasi,[19] an Overhill Cherokee village, drifted from place to place and was discussed in the mercantiles. It was an area formed by white settlers in Indian territory. Governor Lord Dunmore called the settlement dangerous. Others called it dangerous enough venturing into land occupied by the Cherokee.

---

[19] The name source of Tennessee.

August 1774

Soon, the militia was called up to meet their commander, fifty-four-year-old Colonel Andrew Lewis. Lewis was Irish born, a pioneer, and surveyor by trade. Most relevant to Solomon, however, he was a veteran of the French and Indian War twenty years earlier. Battle hardened and wounded twice in that conflict, his exploits were whispered among the troops.

Standing at attention, over one hundred men were in formation before Lewis as his practiced stentorian voice carried over their heads. In a matter-of-fact style as if he were talking about the price of tobacco, he said, "Our presence is requested by the Earl of Dunmore, John Murray, our royal governor of the great colony of Virginia. We are ordered to the confluence of the Ohio and Kanawha Rivers to engage the Indians there. Prepare yourselves accordingly."

Solomon's heart jumped to his throat, a slight smile dissipating under the stern gaze of his new commander. Just when he thought he would be reprimanded, was there a smile reflected on the face of his battle-worn leader? Swiftly and efficiently Colonel Lewis turned on his heel and left his troops to Captain Buford to choose the elite.

Lewis requested that his district commanders were to meet at his home in Salem, west of Bedford. Thomas Buford, physician and neighbor of the Kimsey families, and a crack shot himself, was raised to the rank of captain and asked to choose fifty-two of Bedford County's finest riflemen and then join the colonel's officers for the meeting.

"Stand down, men," Buford said, taking the fuse out of the excited tension.

Solomon waited, his heart thumping. Would he be called? He could not catch his breath.

"Thomas Hall, step out...Nathaniel Cooper...John and William Campbell." They began to form a knot around Buford. "Absalom McClanahan."

The list went on and on. Solomon could stand it no longer. He had been counting all the while—fifty so far. Two more to go.

"Mr. Waugh." He was the oldest at sixty-four, and much respected. "John Welch." There it was. All fifty-two.

Solomon endured his defeat and did not let his disappointment show. The air seemed to have stalled, and it was suddenly deadly quiet in the town's square. The men stood fast.

The captain coughed and swallowed water from his canteen. "And Solomon Kimsey."

What? Oh my God, there it was. His own name. He forced his face not to smile. He forced his body not to dance for joy. The grunts of disapproval that dampened the last announcement were ignored by the young man who wanted with all his heart to taste the battle that was upon them.

"Go home to your families, gentlemen. I will send word to you when I return."

A week later, all the commanders arrived back at their counties to relate the orders that were given.

Riding to all the farms of the men in the militia, Johnny Welch halted ever so briefly at the Kimsey homestead. "Buford is back. Meet at the town square tomorrow at noon."

Before his farm chores, Solomon and his mother were on the porch shaking out bed linens and beating mattresses to be aired in the stiff breeze when Johnny Welch brought the news. Solomon stopped his work and was about to begin packing his belongings when Aggie looked at him. Was it ill temper? Was it impatience? Was it worry? He could never offend his mother and just swallowed his pride, continuing on with the bothersome chores. At least he could give her the love of a cooperative son before he was off to the battle. He kissed her cheek.

At noon, they were given their name—Buford's Riflemen—and instructions: bring what ball, powder, and cartridges you have, and food for a few days on a packhorse; fill your canteens; return by 6:00 p.m. Solomon was ready. He'd been practicing the whole week, never missing his target.

That night the men camped just outside of town. There was a chill in the air, and fires cooked food and kept hands and feet warm.

The men ate well; the long march would begin soon enough. Sleep did not come easily, but 6:00 a.m. did.

* * *

Hiram, the Twin

Before the sun was up, Benjamin affirmed he would not go.

Hiram, in his simple ways and never the one to cross his father, looked in disbelief at Benjamin across the breakfast table. He began, "Why in God's great name would you not be there to see your son off? Your father did not support you when you went to fight for your country? Shall you be like him? How did you feel?"

Aggie and the rest of the children, sensing trouble, moved off to do their chores.

Benjamin was startled at the sting of the rebuke. "I was twenty-one and old enough to make that decision. His way was to stay and plough. I respected him, but the clan system was our way of life which was coming to an end, only we did not realize it until the Redcoats were at our threshold. War is an evil thing that men do..." He banged his fist on the table, rattling the remaining dishes, and continued. "You and your brother are eighteen, and I would spare you from the horrors that accompany battle. Your brother is going west. I don't like it, but with all the reports of skirmishes and raids, he will be fighting Indians...in a war! I've read that hordes of surveyors and land jobbers are pushing the Ohio River boundary into Indian hunting grounds and interrupting their ways." He sighed and said quietly, the thought weighing heavily on him, "Perhaps their way of life is being inevitably expunged as was ours." How it hurt him.

Two hours later, both Benjamin's and Jamie's families were in the town square awaiting the departure of their dearly beloved son and nephew, brother and cousin. All were crying as Solomon passed; the weight of his decision seemed to be pressing him down until he saw his loved ones standing beside the road. Hiram stepped out to shake his twin brother's hand, then the other family members joined him. Suddenly Solomon seemed to march taller, his stooped shoulders matching his fellows on either side, with renewed purpose, to accompany the cadence of fife and drum.

On the way home, Hiram sat with his brothers and sister in the back of their wagon, his legs dangling. He watched the trees' leaves, ablaze with golden sunlight in the clear blue August sky and squabbling with one another in a stiff breeze. *Which one would be the first to fall?* he thought. *None rested on the ground—yet.* He shivered and broke into tears.

* * *

The Riflemen would cross the Blue Ridge, down into the Shenandoah River Valley, then over the wild, trackless Allegheny Mountains to the Big Levels.[20] The assembly area was named Camp Union.[21] As the march wore on that day in the bright sunshine and deep blue sky, Solomon had a sweet remembrance of his brother.

"Stop that infernal scratching! It sounds like fingernails on a slate board." He had lost all patience with Hiram. "Pig squeal! Pig squeal!" he murmured over and over, leaving the house in disgust with his musket in hand. *Why did Father give him that damned fiddle.* "I'm gonna kill me somethin'!" he hollered, slamming the door behind him.

Truth be told, Solomon's vexation was only a minor irritation and would soon turn to delight, as it always did, in his brother's accomplishments. Hiram was always a little slow at things, but he seemed to enjoy the way his bow slid across the strings and made its own tunes. Remembering back over the years, the twins always did things together, as if they were one being. They did their chores, they fished and hunted, and they sang songs, even though Hiram could not carry a tune in a bucket but enjoyed them anyway.

Years before, when their father first opened the mercantile, Hiram was enchanted by all the items he saw: candy and sweet cakes,

---

[20] Big Levels: the area of Lewisburg, West Virginia, above the Greenbrier. An area surrounded by the Allegheny Mountains.
[21] Camp Union at present-day Lewisburg, West Virginia.

nuts and candied fruits, and most especially, toys. There were shiny things too: silver, pewter, and chinaware. The sights brought him joy, but as soon as he laid eyes on that fiddle, he was smitten.

"Papa, buy me one?" he asked in all innocence.

Benjamin didn't hear him, being too busy measuring cloth for a customer. The mercantile was crowded that day, and his son was lost among the women's skirts.

Hiram touched the wood, smooth under his fingers. The top was curled, carved in a pleasing scroll pattern. Taut strings wound around some kind of screws. Softly, Hiram set his thumb on one and immediately a lovely sound came forth. He jumped in surprise and almost knocked the instrument off the shelf. He stood there for almost an hour staring at the delightful object with a burning longing in his heart.

Customers slowly left with bundles tucked up under their arms or the promise made of items placed on order or a next-day delivery. Benjamin put shrunken bolts of cloth back on their shelves then crossed the floor to lock the door.

"Hiram, why are you standing there?"

It took a minute for his son to leave his trance before he placed his request again.

"Papa, buy me one?" his eyes brimming with pleading tears.

Under Benjamin's somewhat gruff Baptist demeanor was a heart as soft as downy feathers. He picked up the boy.

"You're getting to be a big boy. Now what is it that you want, son?"

"That, Papa," he said, pointing to the wooden instrument.

"It's not a toy, Hiram. Do you know what it is?"

"No." His child was near whimpering.

Benjamin's ankle was giving him fits, standing on it all day and now holding his heavy son. He put Hiram down and pulled a chair over so he could sit.

"It's a fiddle." He took a long stick from behind and placed the smooth wood rest under his chin and set the stick upon the strings. The sound was scratchy at first, but when it was followed by confidence, a sweet melody filled the mercantile.

"How do you make it sound, Papa?"

"Well, let's see. The bow sweeps across the strings. I press my finger up here"—Benjamin demonstrated—"and the note changes—like this." The difference in tone was clear. "My father taught me when I was a wee bairn, only I was too busy down at the dock watching the ships come in to continue. Would you like to try it?"

The instrument was a little too big, but Hiram stretched himself to fit.

Benjamin corrected the placement of the bow and fiddle and helped his son draw the bow across the strings. It squeaked and squawked at first, but gliding it like a feather, Hiram managed a few successful notes. Somehow in his little-boy mind he had an inkling it would be his lifelong companion—next to his brother, of course.

"Yes, you may have it, my dearest boy, but you must promise to practice every day and take care of it so your fiddle will delight everyone who hears."

Day after day, Hiram practiced—to his family's irritation. Silently gritting their teeth until they could stand it no longer, his brothers taunted him unmercifully. Undaunted, he thought he'd serenade the animals in the byre. Perhaps they might appreciate his persistence more than his family.

Chapter 22

War on the Frontier

SOLOMON CAME OUT of his daydream of Hiram to the task at hand. The march was moving at a good brisk clip out of the low hills of his home and up toward the mountains. The terrain was familiar to him, having hunted with his father and brothers along the Blue Ridge. He took in a sea of green trees, but it would be some time before the old Indian trail they were on would show the glory of God Almighty in riotous color when the season turned.

The men reached a rise where the trees parted and a fork in the trail appeared. An old sign read "Salem" with an arrow pointing south. It was the way to Colonel Lewis's home. However, they crossed the trail and headed west toward the Allegheny Mountains.

A large stretch of land appeared before them, open and well ploughed. Bright orange pumpkins dotted many acres, and tall corn and tobacco awaited harvest. A white farmer supervised Africans tending rows of produce, and he waved as Buford's men passed— then motioned for them to stop. He ordered the slaves to bring water and baskets full of apples. His name was Dan'l Jackson, and he asked the captain where he was headed. Mr. Jackson said he'd seen other groups of men marching by and wondered how far they were all going.

"On to the Ohio," the captain shared.

The farmer spat contemptuously. "The Indians been raiding all around, I've heard. Not much trouble here. Keep an eye out for your pack animals," he warned. Buford asked if the men could camp close by.

The column settled in for the first night, collecting firewood and using the water given them to make coffee. Bread, cheese, and dried meat satisfied their bellies until morning when they would do it all over again. So it would be for many days.

Solomon chatted with Sam Crowley and Gerrott Kelly, acquaintances he'd met through the militia. The pair, not much older than he, lived in the valleys along the Peaks of Otter with their wives and children. They were hunters and fishermen, and asked Sol—as he was now being called by the Riflemen—what he did. He just told them he worked his uncle's farm, deciding not to mention his father's Baptist history.

The march began early the next day after a good night's sleep and a brief morning repast. The men filled canteens from the slaves' buckets, and while softening his hardtack in the steaming coffee, Sol noted the land rising to the west of them. He thought the countryside around them quite becoming. Heavily forested areas opened to well-tended farms, and occasionally, black beeves grazed upon the hillsides. Always, these hardworking pioneers on the edges of the frontier would wave to the men as they passed, and cheer them on.

The heat of late Virginia summer was upon them, and midday found the men resting in what shade they could find. Sol removed his cocked hat and wiped the sweat from his eyes on his sleeve. Colonel Buford wound his way through the makeshift camp, warning his soldiers to conserve their water. He told them, "There are many creeks crossing our path up ahead, and if they're running you'll have your fill."

Afternoon clouds, raked along by strong winds, carried a good downpour into the faces of the Riflemen, cooling them and slaking their thirst. The rains passed swiftly, but the rising steam made the march difficult. Even with the humidity, the men kept a steady pace of eleven or twelve miles per day.

Colonel Buford pushed his men the last seven miles along the trail at the southwest flank of the Blue Ridge that wended its way north into the Shenandoah Valley. He wished to meet up with Colonel William Christian, the commanding officer of the Fincastle County Battalion. By lucky happenstance, Colonel William Fleming of the Botetourt Regiment was just pulling in with his 450 men. Buford's Riflemen were to join forces with him. All three battalions would proceed to the Big Levels following after the Augusta Regiment already gone ahead with the supplies.

Those supplies came through Quartermaster Sampson Matthews's contract which called for him to supply six hundred beeves from the Blue Ridge hills, fifty-four thousand pounds of flour, and all provisions, arms, and ammunition on five hundred pack-horses. The flour was milled from wheat grown by farmers in the Shenandoah Valley, but it was late in coming. Lead balls used for shot came from mines at Fort Chiswell at Upper New River, and the powder was manufactured at Natural Bridge north of Bedford at the James River.

There was much merriment in the camp that night. Butchers slaughtered the necessary number of beeves for the daily ration, and the men, encamped around the flat farmland of Fincastle, licked their lips at the delicious aroma of the roasting meat. Firecakes cooked on hot rocks close to the flames of campfires were made palatable by a good measure of salt thrown in and by soaking in the meat juices on their plates.

Sol was beside himself with excitement, but apprehensive too. He had never been around so many professional army men, soon to be shoulder to shoulder in the fray against the Indians. Most of these veterans had fought the French and Indians during the Seven Years' War and were telling stories in the light of waning campfires. Just as the militia's drummers beat retreat and the camp grew quiet, Sol noticed Colonels Buford and Fleming and Captain Robert McClennahan casting shadows on their tent's wall. The men were obviously enjoying their companionship along with rum-flavored laughter. The three well-educated physicians comprised the Medical Board of the Army. Looking up at the stars, Sol wondered if he would be brave enough and hoped he would not need his commanding officer's doctoring.

Before daybreak, the drummers beat reveille as the signal for the men to rise and the sentinels to cease challenging. The camp was instantly alive with activity and breakfast chores. Impatience for the battle was palpable but checked by the realization they still had 67 miles to Big Levels and then another 150 to the two rivers.

With those thoughts in mind, Sol grumbled to himself as he buckled the belt containing his cartridge box over his hunting shirt, slid the bayonet into its socket on the scabbard, and slung the filled canteen over his head. He rolled the blanket around his food and extra clothes and into the knapsack, slipping each arm into its strap. Musket in hand, he was ready for roll call and inspection of arms by Captain Buford.

Burdened packhorses grumbled, too, as their loads were tightened under their bellies. Flies and dust hung over the backs of the beeves milling around in their corrals. The Riflemen had their own animals picketed close at hand, and Sol began loading his supplies. His father had given his son their good solid horse Gracie to carry the two barrels of powder and two of shot, and all the necessary equipment and food his family could spare for him. Sol placed his hat on his head and picked up his musket. The massive column moved out to face the Shawnee and Mingo tribes of the Ohio Valley.

Colonel Lewis's fifteen companies—1,000 men—would assemble at what Lord Dunmore called Camp Union over the Allegheny Mountains. The governor's half of the army—1,500—coming from Fort Pitt, Pennsylvania, would meet up with Lewis's militia and proceed to the battle together. Sol's commanding officer had no reason to be skeptical. Considering the difficult trail before them, a column of three companies moved slowly as animals and the men trudged over the forested and rock-strewn terrain. At night, extra men were placed guarding the beeves from panthers and wolves. It took nine days to reach the midpoint of their destination.

Captain Matthew Arbuckle of the Botetourt Regiment was a pioneering hunter and trapper who had been to their destination ten years earlier and was appointed as guide to Colonel Lewis. Arbuckle and his men had scouted the river before the column arrived, and while the broad Greenbrier River could be a formidable obstacle, the water level was actually down, making it easier to ford. There was a small three-cabin settlement of ferrymen on the opposite shore who could be counted on to help the army cross, but they had been attacked by a raiding party of Indians with two men killed and all their supplies stolen.

The captain had dealt with these folks in the past, and he and Colonel Lewis conferred on the issue. As the regiments began to assemble, Lewis sent word to Colonel Christian to have his men bring flour and one of the beeves to the front. The river was forded easily, and the ferrymen were happy with the provisions provided. It took all of a day and a half to get the entire army and their copious articles of survival the three miles to where Camp Union would be set up.

Unbeknownst to Sol, a man from his own company had been eyeing him suspiciously all the way from Bedford. George Baley's simmering thoughts ran in streams. *He's not seasoned like the rest of us. What is he doing here anyway? What does he know of fighting Indians? He should be in the fields with his pappy pickin' corn, not out on a dangerous mission.* Baley spat on the ground. The evil thoughts continually raced around his head, and a few of them spewed out to the ears of his mates. "Give him a chance," one advised. "Let the boy prove himself," another defended. Regardless, Sol's presence didn't sit at all well with the veteran.

George Baley knew Benjamin Kimsey, Sol's father, and hated him for his religion and Scottish heritage. John was from the Borders and considered himself English. Plus, he was here for the Royal Governor Dunmore and had fought alongside Colonel Lewis and George Washington with the English back in 1754. He had bragged to his friends that even after a musket ball shattered his arm, he could still prime and fire then reload his musket faster than any man in the militia. The militia had been his home in many border wars, and here was this upstart. Well, he'd wait for a chance to see how much the boy knew.

Finally, most of the regiments arrived, and the camp was busy with activity. There on the Big Levels around the camp, one could thrill at the sounds of men, horses, cattle, fife, and drum. Officers conferred on the next leg of the journey. They would need a number of animals and the amount of supplies to go forward. Those men not on guard lounged on bedrolls, talking and eating. Others found friends or family members from counties not seen since they left home.

August 30

Dunmore, now on the south branch of the Potomac River on his westerly march to the Ohio, had sent a letter to Lewis: "You are directed to move from Camp Union the first of September to join me at the mouth of the Little Kanawha." However, the letter was not received until the fifth of September just as Lewis was preparing to leave on the sixth to proceed as far as the mouth of the Elk River where it flows into the Kanawha. From there they would transport supplies by boats to the Ohio. Lewis's return letter told Dunmore "meeting you would not be possible."

September 11

The men left Camp Union.

Eleven days and eleven camps later, with the tedious job of setting up and tearing down, unloading and reloading packhorses, they arrived after 103 miles at the north side of the Elk's mouth. The men settled into building a magazine and constructing canoes.

Scouts were sent out, details of men were put to work on the conveyances, and tools put in good working order. Knives and tomahawks were sharpened. One thousand men answered roll call.

September 25

Scouts returned with news of tracks of shod and unshod horses and moccasin prints.

September 28

Captain Arbuckle and his men discovered an encampment of 15 Indians but lost track of them in their pursuit. And some settlers sold liquor to the soldiers, a considerable source of disruptive confusion.

The very drunk Baley began a scurrilous tirade, quietly at first so as to stir up only the men resting in close proximity to him. Sol had been sharing a joke with Sam Crowley, and didn't hear the taunting language at first. It became much louder and meant to cause trouble among all those who could hear. Then Baley jumped up and stood over the eighteen-year-old. Sam stepped in to stop Baley but got his ears boxed in the attempt.

Baley pointed an accusing finger at Sol. "You know, I was with your pappy when he was in that gaol back in '68. We meant to kill him that night. He broke my arm. I'll never forgive him for that, so I think I'll take care of you in his stead."

"Wait a minute, Baley," one of his friends interrupted the trouble, "I thought you said you were injured in the fight with them Injuns back in the war?"

Baley was embarrassed caught in a lie, and hit Sol hard on the jaw just as he arose to meet the challenge.

"Why don't you go back home where you belong, you runny-nosed, peevish bairn born in a byre. You still being suckled on your mammy's tit?" Baley came at him again this time with backup from his Loyalist friends.

In a normal fight, Sol could hold his own, but even with Sam by his side, there were too many against them. Coming out of Colonel Lewis's tent, Buford heard the ruckus among his Riflemen and saw that the young man's beating was bad. Men, standing around watching, doffed their cocked hats in salute as he approached. Combatants in various stages of recovery were ordered to remove themselves from the fight. Buford had Baley and his ruffians arrested and taken to the guard tent, and Sol was taken to hospital.

Sol sat on the edge of the cot holding his head and keeping pressure on the draining wound, wondering what the hell happened.

Not even on the field of battle and he was already injured in a camp skirmish. Shamed, he stood before his commanding officer, apologizing for the trouble.

"Never mind, son. Sit down. I know Baley. He's a troublemaker."

"But, sir, maybe Baley's right. Maybe I'm not fit for battle with the Indians."

Buford, a father of sons, smiled at his new recruit. "Watch that wiseacre."

Sol rejoined his regiment, and Colonel Lewis prohibited the sale of liquor otherwise than on the orders of the captains.

September 29

Within fifteen miles of the Kanawha, the scouts discovered campfires along its banks.

October 1

Incessant rain made it impossible to move all day and into the night.

October 2

Captain John Lewis, Andrew's son, led the left column of Botetourt men, Sol among them. Augusta was on the right. Both lines had one hundred men each and flanked the cattle and pack-horses in the center to protect them. They made twelve miles sloshing through the difficult terrain.

October 3

Eight miles were covered.

October 4

The soldiers marched through wilderness and rock massifs.

October 5

Twelve miles over three swollen creeks.

October 6

Thursday. After crossing five creeks, it was late afternoon when they reached the forks of the two rivers. Sol had heard how great the mighty Ohio was, but at low water, it looked more like a lake and the Kanawha an estuary. The triangular-shaped land at the confluence they now viewed was their camp for Dunmore's war on the Indians.

Sweat seeped through their hunting shirts, and exhaustion showed in the faces of those who arrived first, but there was no rest. The men were ordered to do what their bodies balked at—cutting timber. Sol was assigned to a crew of firewood cutters. He winced, hunger gripping his stomach, and following orders, he proceeded like a dumb animal to the chore. Steering clear of men felling trees for the magazine, his ax cut into deadwood, stripping sticks for kindling. Sol bundled them onto worn-out packhorses—terrible work indeed for them and for him.

Soldiers in camp were ordered to roast meat and grind corn for journeycakes—a welcome relief—to greet the work parties when they returned. The Fincastle battalion arrived shortly thereafter, and over the next few days, the last of the soldiers arrived with the rest of the supplies. More firewood was needed.

October 9

Unable to fall asleep, Sol rolled about, fighting his blankets. Pebbles stuck him in the ribs and hips no matter which way he turned. About midnight, he got up to relieve himself. Fires burned here and there, and the sentries made their rounds keeping vigil. Beeves and packhorses snorted restlessly, and many of the soldiers seemed in turmoil in their dreams.

Settling down, Sol pulled up the blanket, finally warming enough to fall asleep.

October 10

Slumber was short-lived. It was still dark when the men were assaulted by the sound of drummers furiously beating to arms, calling for flints, and priming. *What happened? Had it started?* He had been waiting for this moment but was taken by surprise at the suddenness of it.

Bolting upright, Sol had his eyes firmly planted on Captain Buford. He heard whispers flying around the encampment that two men—under orders to do so—had gone out before dawn hunting for deer and had been surprised by a party of Indians. One man was killed, and the other managed to make it back to warn his comrades. Sol's taut sinews became as one with his rifle, and he could smell and taste fear, and his dry tongue stuck to his palate.

Colonel Andrew Lewis barked orders to divide in two divisions. His brother, Colonel Charles Lewis, would lead the first division on the right flank some distance from the river. He ordered Colonel Fleming with his companies of men including Captains Shelby, Russell, Love, and Buford's Riflemen to march on the left flank along the bank of the Ohio.

At sunrise, one-half hour out, Charles Lewis's front line, being exposed in the sparsely covered terrain, was attacked by approximately one thousand Indians made up of Shawnees, Delawares, Mingoes, and Ottowa under Chief Cornstalk. As Colonel Lewis turned to arouse his men to follow him, he was shot dead—a conspicuous mark for a musket ball. Several of his men were wounded, and the Augusta Division was forced to give way to the heavy barrage of the enemy's fire.

The mass of Indians then began their attack on Colonel Fleming's division. As they ran toward the enemy, Sol's heart raced, and he was panting. Shouts of "The reinforcements are coming" gave hope to those in the front lines and emboldened the men. The fighting continued for hours, men on both sides falling all around. Trees and rocks gave some protection from the Indians' armament, but with the difficult terrain, it was hard to maneuver. At around one o'clock, Virginia's finest militia gained higher ground. They were steadfast in defying a most furious onslaught.

Sol was nimble as a young buck—firing, reloading, firing again—as if the actions were one continuous movement. Fleming was down, as were some of his officers, so he kept a sharp eye out for his captain and mates. Musket balls and arrows flew in furious succession. Sol threw himself behind boulders and took cover behind trees. An Indian attacked him. They wrestled like he had done with his brothers many times, but this man's red brown hand was ready to dispatch him with a nasty-looking long knife. One good foot to the man's stomach threw him over Sol's head and onto a large boulder, breaking the man's back.

Getting up, retrieving his musket, arming it, and running was one smooth action for Sol. However, he tripped over a tree stump hiding beneath a mountain of leaves and came up in a somersault, only to see his captain go down, struck in the breast. Had he not tripped, the lead ball would have been his. He was at Buford's side in an instant. Sol tried to staunch the heavy blood flow with the heel of his hand, but no manner of pressure would stop it. Thomas Buford was stunned into shock, but pain did not impede his smile at his recruit, and he died in Sol's arms.

In a hairbreadth of silence, a tomahawk split the air with a fierce spin. Sol looked up to see George Baley in hand-to-hand fighting with a half-naked Indian. He never gave it a thought as he threw himself at the two struggling men to save Baley and to part that flurry of feathers atop the Indian's head. The tomahawk hit Sol's shoulder with a thud. It dug in deep, splitting the bone. Baley dispatched the Indian, then looked down at his former enemy—his own kind—and Sol would never forget the look on his face.

By late afternoon, the dispirited Indians gave up the fight, and the Kimsey son lay on a soft mound of God's most glorious colors when he was recovered by his militia brothers. Sol was still alive but in grievous pain. Gently the men picked him up, Baley among them, and brought him back to the fortification of Point Pleasant, into their makeshift hospital among the other wounded. Those who didn't succumb on the battlefield but died in the magazine were laid to rest there with the newly dead, including Sol's defender against George Baley, Sam Crowley.

The war was over, and the wounded went home either walking or carried. The militia remained behind in case of any uprising. With permission, George Baley accompanied his maimed brothers back to Virginia. Before he left, he gave special care to the man who saved his life.

Chapter 23

Aftermath

SOL DIDN'T KNOW the battle was over and a treaty with the Indians had been signed. He only knew he was back home in Bedford recuperating in the bosom of his family and with a pretty miss at his side. Snow had been on the ground in a light dust, and as Sol began to heal, George Baley visited the Kimsey home, often bringing his daughter, Martha, with him.

The bone was not broken as first thought, so Sol's shoulder was nicely mending.

A gentle knock came in the early afternoon. Martha and George were at the door, bundled against the cold and could they please come in the Kimsey home to talk. Aggie was thrilled with the company, and Benjamin, just back from his daily walk with the Lord preparing his next sermon, shed his heavy coat and sat by the fire to warm himself.

The fragrance of hot cider filled the room. "Would you join us in a cup on this chilly day?" Aggie asked sweetly. "The apples are from our orchard...I'm so happy you have come."

"Father and I are well pleased to be here. How is Sol?" Martha inquired as Hiram took her dove gray cloak to hang on a peg. She had a comely heart-shaped face, accentuated by the center part of her ginger-colored curly hair, the coils of which bounced teasingly as she spoke.

Benjamin excused himself to see to his son, the wounded veteran of Dunmore's War. He helped Sol into his chair close to the fire. Watching the faces of the visitors in the room, he saw there was no doubt the young woman was smitten with Sol, and Sol's eyes showed the feeling was mutual.

Aggie served the refreshment, and Hiram got the giggles watching the young couple staring intently at each other and both of them blushing at revealing their feelings.

Pleasant talk contributed to the congenial air, but George, all of a sudden, seemed nervous. Aggie asked after his health.

"Concern yourself not for me, my good woman, for I am in need of a confession which has plagued me for many a year."

"George, you do not have to do this," Sol implored him.

"You know it needs to be done, my brother."

Benjamin and Agnes were puzzled by what appeared to be a difficult relationship between their son and this man.

"Sir," he looked at Benjamin, "your son saved my life at the battle, but…I should have been butchered…for my sins against you." Tears of release began to flow, and the crackling fire was suddenly deafening in the room.

Baffled, Benjamin finally said, "I don't understand, George."

"Remember that night at the gaol, Mr. Kimsey?" He could not be so familiar with Sol's father as to call him by his first name. "I was the man with the knitted cap, the one who replaced the gaoler, Joseph Ray."

Benjamin's thoughts ran back over the terrible events when he was nearly beaten to death in Bedford town's gaol. The horrid remembrance hit him hard. Forgiving the men was not automatic. Even as a minister of God's word, it took a few years to get over the assault.

"You were the one I never knew."

"Yes, my arm was broken in the fight…We did not succeed in killing you…Thank God."

So, it was a plot, then. After all the made-up accusations, the trial was a sham. Benjamin was scorned and shamed by a town prejudiced against a man for his religion and his freedom of speech.

"Forgive me, Mr. Kimsey, for my crime against you. And...I carried my crime to your son as well. For that he has forgiven me. Would you do the same? Say that you will forgive me?" he pleaded.

Benjamin, in good conscience, knew he must free this man from his guilt, not hold him accountable, and erase their aching pain of long-ago hurt.

The two families were bound together, when in the spring Solomon Kimsey married his love Martha Baley—his Mattie, he called her, a dear little tender name for his redheaded beauty.

June 14, 1775

The Continental Army was formed. The *Gazette* carried the story, and ten rifle companies were called from the middle colonies. Virginia agreed to send two, with Daniel Morgan named commander. He recruited ninety-six men in ten days, assembling them at his home in Winchester on July 14. They marched out in fine fashion, covering six hundred miles in twenty-one days to Boston.

Sol longed to be one of them.

With gentleness, Benjamin again recognized his son's determination and said, "I still see you wince when you place the rifle against your shoulder. Do you think it advisable?"

"Father, I knew Morgan at Point Pleasant, and his exploits were exemplary. If Colonel Lewis agrees, I could handle the rigors, and maybe he could get word to Winchester of my desire."

Sol, fighting against everything that was telling him he wasn't ready, rode to Salem seeking his former commander in chief.

Colonel Lewis greeted him warmly. Andrew, while pleased to see his former recruit, was skeptical and proved himself right when he tested the young man's injured shoulder. "It's still pretty raw, Sol. Maybe you should wait. You need to heal."

He missed his opportunity. When the response came to Sol in late July, the men had already marched north.

But then came a surprise.

> Solomon Kimsey Esq.
> Bedford County Virginia
> July 12, 1775
>
> Sir
>
> I remember your deeds plainly on the field of Point Pleasant and would welcome your expert marksmanship and exemplary spirit in our present situation, but I regret to inform you that time does not allow for me to recruit you. Please know that the Continental Army would welcome you in the near future as I believe there will be regiments forming soon if this conflict does not subside.
>
> Your servant
> Brig. General Daniel Morgan

It was a good thing he had to wait. Sol's Martha was with child.

Chapter 24

A Different Direction

Summer 1775

THE SUN, WHEN it got hold of things, burned with the fury of hell and temperatures the hottest ever seen. No rain for over two months caused Jamie's crops to fail for the third time. Again, with no means of livelihood and unable to pay his taxes, he would have to sell. He walked the rows of dried brown stalks listening to the depressing crackle. His boys tried to salvage what they could for the pigs. Sol, his dear nephew, was still recuperating and unable to help.

Mary could not stand to be in the house another minute. Trying to cook at the fire was not to be, with sweat pouring down her face and her gown soaked. She followed her husband out to the fields and took what water there was available, the Little Otter River being nearly dried up. Jamie had dug a well some years back for such emergencies, but the bucket seemed to go deeper each day. How could they and their neighbors hold out if the rains did not come?

She found Jamie slumped in the middle of his crops, holding dead stalks and drowning in depression. So as not to startle him, Mary began humming as she moved along the sad dry corn. He turned to look and alarmed her with his bloodred face. They sat in the dirt saying nothing—just drinking the lukewarm water and not finding any satisfaction in the process.

"We should move to the shade?" she asked, teasing him.

He smiled at her. "What shade? There's none to be had for a hundred acres."

Dead silent heat hung on them.

"Let's move."

"Where, may I ask, dear wife, should we move?"

"You and your brother have been talking about that land south of here for five years. So, why not sell and move. We can pay the tithe and get a smaller place and…We can do this, Jamie."

A gentle breath of air rustled the dead stalks.

"Remember that hard year before Samuel was born…," Mary reminded him.

Jamie's mood quickly turned to desire when he recalled their tryst in the fields after the terrible loss of their dear Sarah. Mary again dispelled the present to prepare for the future. The Lord was nudging them on.

Jamie's hunger for his wife dried up like the cornstalks in his fields when he saw his eleven-year-old son Littleberry running toward them, yelling at the top of his lungs, waving the *Virginia Gazette*, "Pa! Pa! We're at war with the British. They've taken over Boston, and Paul Revere sounded the alarm to roust the Massachusetts militia. We beat 'um, Pa! We beat 'um at Lexington and Concord."

Pittsylvania County[22]
1776

They were all in agreement, 200 acres 25 miles from the North Carolina colony would suit the Kimseys just fine. In three wagons, including the Conestoga, they left Bedford together when the tax was satisfied from the sale of Jamie's farm. Benjamin slapped the rumps of his horses with the reins and never looked back, focusing on the trail before them. However, despite the difficulties the families had suffered, Jamie did scan the disappearing view behind him. He

---

[22] Pittsylvania County, Virginia. In 1777, the western part of Pittsylvania County became Patrick Henry County.

couldn't forget his first farm and cabin, where he waited for Mary's return, and of course, their wedding. Brothers were reunited, and babies were born. Mary placed her hand on Jamie's arm, knowing his strengths and weaknesses and now loss, but as they traveled toward their new land, along the Smith River, at a place called Rock Castle Creek, she knew that nature would open wide its arms to welcome them. It was already preparing for their arrival from six years ago, when Benjamin and Jamie first saw it and struck a bargain with it. The old wagon and rusted chains would be completely gone by now, but still the land from that same rise would show those buff-colored hills rolling out in endless succession and many acres of woven vines dotted with orange pumpkins. The land was ready for their seeds and would supply them with plenty of timber and water—it was ideal.

Jamie smiled at his wife.

They built homes of clapboard, not log, and high enough off the ground so the Smith River would not swamp their land.

While the Kimseys sweated on their buildings, so did the Continental Congress on its decisions. It took a long time for John Adams, Thomas Jefferson, and the other representatives to hammer out their words during that Philadelphia summer. Like the hot, humid air, those words rose to a heated pitch, then finally rested in black ink on parchment.

George Washington had sent letters to Congress for more men and more money and finally captured their attention by reporting that forty-five British ships were off Staten Island with twenty-five thousand lobsterbacks massing against his five thousand troops.

After many revisions, the Declaration of Independence was signed by the fifty-six men of the thirteen colonies, stating that the United States was to be free of English rule.

No more would the British lines of Redcoats push them into subservience. In King George's eyes, those who held the quill were traitors, but George Washington read the Declaration to his troops, spurring them to action. Published in colonial newspapers, it was read by ministers in their churches and on backwoods pulpits. Men read it in doorframes and at breakfast tables. Benjamin read it to his family.

When Jamie and the Kimsey men sunk their ploughs in the earth in southern Virginia, they became neighbors to plantation owners Governor Patrick Henry, a founding father, and General Joseph Martin, a farmer and brigadier general in the Virginia militia.

On July 12, British ships opened fire on New York. Troubled by the growing despair of the land sinking into war, the Kimseys did not hesitate in their work of tending crops that would produce a bountiful harvest for their survival and that of their countrymen.

Hungry for action, Sol devoured news in the *Gazette* when it came, anticipating the call for more men. He received a beautiful new American longrifle from his father, with a graceful stock and long smooth barrel. Its sight was more accurate than the old muskets, and he practiced on it daily through the summer, even though his shoulder sometimes balked.

Washington called for more enlistments as soldiers were leaving at the end of their one-year term. In mid-September, Congress arranged for raising the Continental Army and authorized 15 regiments. From Williamsburg, Virginia's capital, Governor Henry notified his officers to begin recruiting. The *Gazette* announced that companies of the 15th Virginia Regiment of Foot would be raised in various counties on Virginia's eastern shore. Recruitment was not going well, and Washington had to write to the officers to forward their men to him as fast as they could arm and clothe them. The enemy would not wait, and neither could he.

* * *

Captain John Gregory was put in charge of recruitment at Nansemond County, Virginia. He came from a large and famous family well-known in the colonies. By the time Sol heard the news, it was late in the year and two hundred miles to the eastern shore. To be eligible for the 6 2/3 dollars per month offered them, he would have to sign up by December 31. He could now see his desire to have his own land for his family fulfilled, but he must hurry.

"Take Girlie," Benjamin said.

It was a long, difficult, and cold trip crossing creeks, rivers, and other land features Sol was unfamiliar with, but he was determined as he rode his favorite horse. She surely wouldn't win any races, but Girlie was dependable, strong, and patient when all Sol's siblings bothered her with their love. Sol cared for her by finding friendly farmers along the way who allowed them to rest in their byres overnight, and for a coin, Girlie could share feed with the other animals, especially when those men found out where Sol was going: to sign up for Washington's army.

* * *

Captain Gregory was helping his recruitment officer set up for what they hoped would be an onslaught of men. Sol proudly strode across the creaking courthouse floor, his booted feet in strict cadence as the soldier he was and attracting the attention of the two men. Gregory turned around just as Sol made his way to the table. He noted the youthfulness of the stranger, but the eyes told a different story. He was battle hardened. Sol removed his cocked hat.

"Good morning." Gregory proffered an outstretched hand in welcome. He was smartly dressed in a dark-blue coat with buff lapels and cuffs, pewter buttons, and buff waistcoat and breeches. He wore no hat, and his natural dark hair was pulled back and tied in a queue. He was a handsome man with a square jaw and prominent English nose.

"Good morning, sir." Sol took his hand and looked directly into the captain's steel gray eyes. Was it hardness or strength he saw there?

"Have you come far?"

"Yes, sir. From the new county named for Governor Patrick Henry."

"I'm John Gregory, captain of the 15th Regiment, 1st Company. My assistant Jonathan Edmunds will be with you shortly. We have a few more items to assemble before the others arrive. May I ask your name?"

"Solomon Kimsey, at your service." He gave a slight bow as was custom.

As the two talked, Captain Gregory surveyed this new recruit dressed in his ash-colored hunting shirt, leather trousers, and knee-length black boots. *Ready for action, this one*, he thought.

"That's a fine rifle you carry. Are you any good with it?"

"Yes, sir. I was with Captain Buford's Riflemen from Bedford County in '74."

John Gregory was astounded. He knew the deadly aim of the shirtmen from the backwoods and had heard of Solomon's exploits in Dunmore's War from Colonel Daniel Morgan.

"Welcome, Solomon," his soon-to-be commanding officer said. "I'm happy you have chosen to fight for the cause of freedom."

Men traipsed in behind Sol, but he took no notice, concentrating on the paper before him. The men were enlisting for three years, not for the duration of the war as Congress preferred. He signed. It was December 31, 1776, and he realized he would miss Hogmanay with his family. The men were requested to assemble in the foyer of the large room and wait to be called. Sol had time to reflect on the tearful goodbyes when he left his family in Patrick County.

Martha was worried sick. "We have a young child and a baby on the way, Sol. What will I do without you, my love?"

He caressed her beautiful face and enfolded her in his arms. Her tears dropped on his shoulder. "I know it will be difficult, Mattie, but you will have our families to care for you. We are in troubling times, and the call for Patriots is strong within me. I must go and represent our family." He kissed her tenderly.

It would be difficult for Uncle Jamie, too, who relied on Sol's hard work for the Kimseys' farm, but his parents were a different story. While Benjamin was resigned to his son's decision, his mother was not, and told him so in no uncertain terms!

Sol smiled, but his reflections were interrupted by some of the local women of Nansemond County offering coffee and cakes to the men about to pledge their oaths. Some of the newly enlisted stood around and talked to the women. Many of the young girls flirted with the new recruits, making them wish they hadn't signed up at all.

Sol got up off the hard bench and walked outside with his coffee. There was a light drift of snow on the ground, and his thoughts were mixed about home and where his new regiment would take them. The men were recalled inside the courthouse, and Captain Gregory asked them to raise their right hands as he read the oath. His voice resounded in pride as a Patriot and a captain in General Washington's Continental Army. He imparted that pride to these men, ready to give their lives in the defense of the new United States of America.

"I do swear that I will be faithful and true to the colony and dominion of Virginia; and that I will serve the same to the utmost of my power, in defense of the just rights of America, against all enemies whatsoever."

"I do!" came the reverberating reply from all the new smiling soldiers.

"Congratulations, gentlemen."

They were instructed to camp just outside of town and, with the canvas supplied them, to set up tents and wait for orders.

Chapter 25

The Revolution

1777

THE NEW YEAR began, and the soldiers were provided an extra set of clothes—hunting shirts, breeches, and stockings. A ration of ball and powder was also included. Sol volunteered Girlie to the wagoner as she was used to pulling the family's wagons. The soldiers settled and, in a short time, got acquainted with their brothers-in-arms.

In the morning, the drummers beat reveille, and once the men assembled, Captain Gregory announced that after their breakfast they would march to New Jersey to join General Washington. "Enjoy your food, men, provided generously by the townsfolk. It will probably be your last home-cooked meal—we have a long walk before us."

Sol noted an amused smile on his captain's face; Morris Town, their destination, was four hundred miles north.

* * *

It seemed they marched for days without end and prayed they would not be caught in blizzards to slow their progress, which would make for a very uncomfortable trek. When it didn't snow and the sun brightened the countryside, it was magnificent. Sol particularly enjoyed the coastal views and vowed he might come back some day.

While keeping his mind on the tasks at hand, like digging latrines, cutting firewood, game hunting, guard posting, and setting up camp for the officers, he recalled another of the family he'd left behind.

Sol took very good care of his boots, paying special attention to the soles, hoping they would have a long life for the difficult march ahead. He remembered with fondness his brother, David, the cobbler in the family, who had presented them to him as a going-away gift. And it suddenly struck him that his father and uncles came from Scotland, and after hearing from Benjamin of the last battle lost to the British there, Sol thought proudly, *Maybe that's where I get my desire to fight for our cause.*

Captain Gregory's troops were conveyed across the James River at Burrell's Ferry. Next, they then marched to Yorktown to a place where the *Virginia Gazette* called the "Ferry...inferior to none in the Colony." It was run by women with men wending the oars. They crossed the York River landing at Gloucester Point and headed for Richmond to connect with other regiments. Growing up in south-western Virginia, Sol had had only a hint of the country for which he would soon fight.

Morris Town, New Jersey—Winter Quarters of George Washington

After George Washington's defeats of 1776, his misfortune turned to glory when, spurred on by one of his spies, he crossed the Delaware River on Christmas Eve and surprised and overtook the Germans at Trenton. January 3, 1777, also saw victory for him at Princeton, twelve miles away, where a hard-fought battle was won. But his friend Brigadier General Hugh Mercer was brutally killed by British bayonet blows. Nonetheless, the tide was turned, and the victory stories were told around the campfires encouraging the new recruits moving fast toward the action.

Sol learned about Mercer's death and hoped against hope that his father would not hear as he and Hugh had been friends during the Jacobite rebellion of '46 in Scotland. Sol felt sorrow for his father, knowing he would be pained to hear of the tragic death.

Washington marched his dwindled army thirty-eight miles to Morris Town where he placed his men strategically between the capital at Philadelphia and the city of New York, ever watching the movements of the lobsterbacks. American militia companies, sometimes with Continental Army support, went on a foraging war, engaging the British whenever they were confronted and arresting any British attempts to acquire animals and fodder.

The Virginia recruits arrived at the end of February, and other regiments appeared by spring, swelling the army to nearly ten thousand soldiers. Sol's regiment was hoping for battle action right away, but besides expanding the encampment, they spent their wintering, with mud up to their knees, building a fort—a guardhouse for army provisions overlooking Morris Town. Irked by not engaging the enemy, he and his comrades dug the earthworks for the redoubt's bristling abitis, which meant more cutting of wood. Whispered away from their officers' ears, the New Jersey regiments laughingly called it Fort Nonsense, "totally indefensible and built to keep us busy."

March saw Pennsylvania and Connecticut troop enlistments ending, and one thousand men dwindled to five hundred under Major General Benjamin Lincoln, who was left to command the new post—Fort Nonsense at Bound Brook. In mid-April, the British marched from their headquarters at New Brunswick with four thousand troops and routed the Americans with no difficulty, causing the abandonment of the post and theft of important papers, artillery, and provisions confirming the attitude of the soldiers. Washington responded by sending a large force under Major General Nathanael Green—not including the 15th Virginia Regiment of Foot—and to retake the stolen goods. Lives were lost and wounds sustained. Washington decided the place was not worth it, so on May 26 he withdrew the garrison, then moved part of his army to Middle Brook. The men grumbled their disdain but obeyed, and Sol's teeth ground down a little further with the lack of fighting.

In May, regiments from their home states were formed into brigades in the Main Continental Army. Sol was in the 3rd Virginia

Brigade under Brigadier General William Woodford. Within that brigade were the 3rd, 7th, 11th, and 15th Regiments. Within the 15th Regiment were ten companies. The men from Nansemond County were in the 1st Company. Their standard infantry weapon was the French Army musket, which fired a one-ounce ball and had a fourteen-inch socket bayonet. Sol was allowed his American rifle until it got shot out of his hands on a skirmish while harassing the British threat along the Hudson River Highlands. That fine rifle his father had given him was replaced by the much inferior musket, annoying him with its less-than-accurate action.

On this foraging war, others were sent out to torment the Redcoats on the roads leading to the capital of Philadelphia. Sol and the rest built latrines, cut wood, marched endlessly, practiced saluting and battlefield maneuvers, and learned regulations for the baggage train and guard duty.

It all began soon after Sol's march from Virginia. His intense pride made a hasty retreat when annoyance crept into his thoughts. Hunger was the first grievance, whirling around his belly back to front. After being fed by the good citizens of Suffolk town, the soldiers marched on rations given them as part of their kit—flour, salt, and a pound of fresh beef for each. After a few days and with a long march ahead of them, it was scant pickings—firecakes and foraging.

At the Battle of Point Pleasant, the militia officers had made sure their men had quite enough victuals to last—six hundred beeves, thousands of pounds of flour, and cornmeal and other provisions given them along the way by wilderness farmers. The march took two months, but the battle itself lasted only one day, and they never went hungry. This revolution had already stretched two years and looked like it wouldn't end anytime soon. Others were fighting, but the Virginians were doing nothing but digging holes and piling up the earth. The battle idleness was not good for morale. Sol wanted to be in the fray.

In between camp chores, he was ordered to guard duty. He now patrolled with the French musket given him after his rifle had been splintered to pieces. Always watching for any untoward movements, Sol's eyes took in the terrain, memorizing it and noting any suspicious changes, especially at night. He tried to keep his mind from wandering, but things tended to fester with him. His father had told him that, and it was still so.

Late one afternoon, Sol was patrolling the perimeter of the camp. Skeleton shadows of leafless tree limbs stretched across late-season drifts of snow. The blue-black sky had not a cloud, and the ever-increasing chill in the air of the exhausting day seeped under his hunting shirt. His back hunched automatically against it, but a slight skid beneath his boot sole checked his posture as did the presence of another soldier coming toward him. The man's face was half hidden by a heavy scarf wrapped around his neck and shoulders. Sol was on alert and was about to lift his weapon until the other man spoke first, his musket raised in a defensive posture.

"Who are you?" the man demanded.

"Private Solomon Kimsey from the 15th."

Lowering his scarf, a broad smile flushed across his face. "Hello. I'm William Shell also from the 15th, but 9th Company. Call me Will."

"Captain Foster?"

Will nodded.

"John Gregory is my commanding officer," Sol said with pride.

From the camp, there was an aroma of cooking.

"Smells like boiled beef. Wish there was some onion. Where are you from, Sol?"

"Henry County. You?"

"Bedford. We just moved there from Frederick County. Do you have any relatives in Bedford? Your name sounds familiar."

Just as Sol was contemplating how to respond, a man on horseback rode up behind them. The setting sun over the Wachtung Mountains had turned the sky gold, and stars began to show themselves in the east.

"You two are supposed to be on patrol. Get on with it. I'm going down to headquarters and will be back late. Don't shoot me in the dark."

"Yes, sir, Captain Gregory." Both men stood at attention and saluted.

Relaxing after the captain disappeared over a rise, Sol asked Will, "Did you notice his smile? His Excellency is residing at Arnold's Tavern. I'll bet that's where the captain's going."

Both men chuckled and went about their business on guard in the cantonment and would join the others for whatever meager dinner was supplied when they were relieved.

* * *

At the end of May, after the debacle at Broad Brook on April 13, General Washington broke camp and took his troops, tents, and headquarters closer to the post, staying at Middle Brook. One-third of his men limped or were carried on wagons from illnesses or wounds sustained during the battle. They were there for only one month. Washington was playing cat and mouse with the British, and Lieutenant General William Howe moved his Redcoats to Staten Island on June 30, trying to draw the Continental Army out of the protection of the mountains. Two days later, Washington moved them again, this time to Pompton Plains thirty-six miles away.

There had been another brief conflict called the Battle of Short Hills on June 26, the Continentals under Brigadier General William Alexander while the New Jersey and Pennsylvania Brigades took part along with Daniel Morgan's Riflemen. With his 500 and the other two brigades, 2,500 men harassed the English. A running skirmish ensued, and the Americans retreated. But even with heavy artillery fire from the British, the heat on the battlefield got to the enemy who fell back from pursuit, allowing Alexander to retreat back to Middle Brook.

It seemed as if Sol and his regiment were doing nothing but packing and unpacking, then repacking their supply train, putting up tents, and moving earth around when they set up each encampment. Aside from going out on skirmishes, they were not called up for a real battle. Sol's thoughts went to Daniel Morgan's Corps. Envy took control of Sol. How he wished he was with Morgan.

July 4, 1777

The sweet freshness of spring was long gone, and the soldiers endured blistering heat. The first anniversary of the Declaration of Independence was celebrated in camp that day with a generous portion of rum all around. General Washington had it read to his troops the year before, and Sol remembered his father, Benjamin, reading it from the pulpit. The day ended with most of the men drunk on empty stomachs.

Finally, Captain Gregory's and Captain Foster's men, along with others, about one hundred chosen in all, were sent out by the commander in chief to find provisions in the form of meat and whatever else could be scrounged from the countryside. Sol was relieved to be out of the camp with its white tents reflecting the ever-increasing temperature and the stench of ten thousand men.

They marched through the mountains that he viewed not much more than hills, really. There were three ranges, each with views of New York, Newark, and New Jersey—perfect for Washington to eye the British movements. With the rising elevation, the air became a little cooler. Rivers and streams with fresh clean water ran alongside and intersected trails the patrol covered. Many had working grain, grist, and sawmills. The Continentals took what they could get, and some Patriot supporters even gave the men baked goods from their own larders, offering cider or ale to wash it down. Sol, along with his friends, were exceedingly happy to fill their bellies.

The companies were out about a week with the wagons full of provisions and a number of beeves tethered to iron harness rings at the rear, when the forward scouts returned to the commanders with the news about a detachment of Redcoat spies heading toward General Washington's camp. The captains quickly ordered the men and equipment off the trail to hide and keep the animals quiet. Those who weren't muffling horses and cattle prepared to meet the enemy.

Sol's heart raced at the oncoming sound of rhythmic marching. The British cohort was coming closer by the second, but just as the Patriots were holding their collective breath, a cow snorted, and suddenly chaos erupted. Musket balls slammed into tree trunks and men's bodies. Angry shouts and cries within the fighting forces filled the forest. Dusk and smoke settled over the intense battle which was short-lived because the numbers were small and the English were unable to see the Americans clearly in the thick stand of trees and growing darkness. When the smoke dissipated, wounded and dead British strewn over the trail and into the trees were kicked over the embankment to the water below. The entire skirmish had lasted about fifteen minutes. When a full moon rose over the ghastly scene, each captain reviewed their companies.

"Is anyone hurt?" Captain Gregory called out.

The soldiers emerged from the trees onto the trail.

"Tully, sir," Will Shell from the 9th reported.

Others listed only a few names.

Captain Foster ordered the men to "put the wounded in the wagons. There's enough light for us to get off the mountain."

In the morning, the companies limped in to camp. Washington was informed at Arnold's Tavern of the skirmish, and the men were congratulated upon their defeat of the British and the successful scavenging.

It wasn't until the next morning that Sol Kimsey did not answer roll call. An investigation was required and inquiries made of the men involved. No one had seen him, and Gregory ordered out a search party to find him.

* * *

Sol awoke on his side with a throbbing headache and the stench of blood all around. His hand went immediately to the source of his pain and followed a concavity along his scalp, but trying to move only made him nauseated. Rays of sunlight filtered through the dense stand of trees and warmed his body resting on the damp ground, but he could not recall how he came to such a state of affairs. The music of gurgling water at the bottom of the ravine was enticing as his thirst was strong, but he lost consciousness and dreamed of his wife. She came to him and lay beside him with her arm outstretched over his body. He could feel her large belly alive with the life of their unborn child.

"My love," he heard himself say to Mattie.

"Where are you my dearest, Sol?" she asked tenderly. "Come to me, sweetheart."

He stood and looked down at the body on the ground and cringed in horror.

"Oh, God! No!"

Voices on the trail, heavy with a brogue he didn't know, woke him with a start from his dream. He moaned and tried to call for help, but nothing came from his dry throat. He made an effort to raise his arm but wasn't sure if it was accomplished. Someone was moving him, carrying him, placing his lifeless body in a cart. Was he alive? He looked back with one eye to where his body had been and saw nothing. Was he dead?

When the hunters had come upon the scene, they saw the remnants of the small battle that had taken place and searched for anyone alive. There were none except this young man, a Patriot they knew from his hunting shirt and musket beside him. They gleaned what they could from the bodies of the Redcoats, picking them clean and taking the Patriot soldier home with them.

The pleasing aroma of food filled Sol's nostrils. He was only able to open one cloudy eye to see a woman holding a bowl of something steaming.

"Water?" his voice scraped like nails on a bit of slate.

With tender understanding and placing the bowl on a side table, the woman lifted his head gently and placed the lip of the cup to his mouth. Nothing tasted sweeter to him than that refreshing dew from heaven above, unless, of course, it was the succulent contents of that bowl. He tried to sit, but the action caused his head to swim. He had not noticed there was another in the room who lifted him to receive the sustenance he so desperately needed.

Soup of a fine quality was spooned into his mouth. He coughed at first choking from his raw throat, but with each succeeding mouthful, he began to feel better. After a while, he became exhausted and closed his eyes.

Until that moment, the woman had not said a word, but then, she spoke softly, "Are you all right, Sol?"

He opened his eye again, this time the view was crystal clear, but he could not believe what he saw. "Am I dreaming? Mattie? Is it you?"

"Yes, my dear one. I am here."

Was it simply a coincidence or a very strange miracle that these hunters came upon the very man their kin was looking for?

"Where am I?" His voice was hoarse.

Chapter 26

The Deserter

July and August

"HUNTERDON COUNTY, NEW Jersey. Father has family here. Do you want more soup?" she asked, picking up the bowl.

He waved the offer away. "How did you get here? I was…where was I?"

"I followed you, and I thought you were in Middle Brook with the troops. Father and the cousins were watching the British marching over the mountain to sneak up on Mr. Washington. Father said there was a skirmish, and they found you barely alive."

The fog was clearing from his brain. "I remember…Why did you come?"

"I wanted to be with you in the encampment, but the family was firmly against it since I was close to my time," Mattie related, "but I simply had to be with you, Sol. We were set to leave tomorrow for Mr. Washington's camp."

Women did that in those days of war—followed their husbands from camp to camp washing and mending clothes, fixing meals, and giving comfort to them.

Mattie looked like an angel in her cream-colored cotton gown printed in rose-colored flowers. The bodice was laced to a stomacher to hold the gown together and underneath was a petticoat of cream-colored linen. Those laces were broader at the bottom to make way for her burgeoning belly.

Mattie's tenderness toward her husband would not be checked even when her aunt gave a rebuke. "You need to rest, my child. I can care for him."

Irritated, she told the woman, "I need to change his bandages," and began removing the cloths binding half of his head and one eye.

Sol's hand went up to hers. "I don't want you in camp, Mattie. Washington keeps moving the soldiers, and your time is nearly here."

"But at least we should contact your regiment and let them know of your wounds."

"No!" He squeezed her delicate fingers.

She shrunk back from his angry rebuff. "You are ill-humored with me, Sol." Strain was beginning to show, and tears flooded her eyes. Uncomfortable silence bruised the space between them.

Once the bandages were clear of his head, she gently washed the area where his hair had been sheared and noticed there was still seeping. Mattie bound it again with fresh cloths.

Being at once uneasy and suddenly disquieted by movement from her child within, she changed the subject. "It's starting to heal and looks much better today. I'll get your lunch." Stepping through the doorframe of the room, she didn't react when he turned on his side away from her. Quietly, Mattie set the latch of the door, leaving him to his angry thoughts.

On the second day, Sol knew he might be in trouble. He'd seen other soldiers desert for many reasons, but if he went back now, he could probably convince Captain Gregory that the party had left him for dead, and he would be exonerated. The trouble was—he did not want to go back. Mattie had hardly recognized his thin body when her family brought him in. He was always lean, but starvation combined with hard labor did not make a soldier worth his weight. Farming was looking better to him. "Nothing like farming," his Uncle Jamie always said. Yes, he would go back to that good life when he got out of the army—if he got out.

Sol sat on the edge of the bed, drowning himself in guilt and envy. Fueling his resentment was the thought of Colonel Morgan and those five hundred riflemen in the thick of battle harassing the retreating English all over northern New Jersey. The Virginia regiments were constantly moving around with the bulk of the army, waiting for General Washington's orders—always waiting and no action. Maybe he would desert and take his wife back home. The envy quickly dissipated, however, when a sweet baby cry called him to his wife's side. He stood up too fast and the room spun around.

Unsteady legs followed the sound, and Mrs. Baley roughly rebuked him. "Get out," she yelled at him. "Your wife's not ready to receive you yet."

Sol staggered outside, shading his one good eye from the bright sun. Laughing, Uncle Baley helped him off the porch and under a large tree where the shade was refreshing, and Sol's head stopped twirling.

"Here, have some cider. She's always like that. Thinks us men can't take the sight of our wives giving birth. Seems odd since it's not much different with the animals. Brought up that way, I guess." After a moment, he continued, "Guess you're gonna be in a speck of trouble with your outfit."

"Yes, sir, I probably am."

"You gonna go back? I hear the punishment is harsh."

"Yes, sir, it probably is, but I can't leave my wife and child just now."

"Sol, you don't need to call me sir. My name is Tam. There's rumors of a big battle. Up till now it's been skirmishes. You'd better think on it." Uncle Baley was giving him sound advice, but Sol couldn't "think on it" when Mattie called to him. Trembling, he rushed to her side, ignoring the dizziness that accompanied his every move.

Aunt Baley clucked like the old hen she was and left the room.

"Come sit by me," Mattie invited, raising his hope for forgiveness for his ill temper.

His dearest wife, beautiful in her bloom of motherhood, cradled the infant.

"Welcome your newborn daughter, Sol." Mattie urged her husband to take the child in his arms. In trepidation, he took the wee bairn and fell for her instantly.

"What will we call her, wife?"

"Would you consider Joanna Ruth Kimsey, husband?"

"I think that's a fine name."

She was so tiny in the instant of life. The baby opened her eyes and looked at Sol, unsure of what he was about. He wondered, *Was she memorizing the quality of her father?*

Solomon did what he said he would—stay with them for two months—but he was now a deserter, someone who abandoned his responsibility. Like most in the Continental Army, he felt that being away from family and farm was vile. But there was something larger involved—he must not abandon his duty to the ideal to which he swore an oath.

Sol was gone for July and August, and yes, Uncle Baley was right, he was in more than a little trouble when he returned to his unit. Tam and his nephew, Joshua, who had aspired to be in the militia, accompanied Sol back to the encampment at Middle Brook. The discordant sounds of ten thousand men talking, laughing, going about chores, marching to orders and drumbeats, were gone, and the three sat astride horses on a rise looking down, mouths open at the site of the completely empty camp.

As they moved onto the grounds, they saw a small detachment of men billeted in one of the officers' old cabins. A corporal stared, his weapon pointed directly at them.

"What has happened?" Sol asked, not believing his eyes at the deserted cantonment.

"Why do you want to know?" The corporal was suspicious, and the barrel of the musket followed his sudden recognition of a possible deserter.

Sol had lost his hat in the skirmish along the mountain trail and so lifted his hand to salute the man who was obviously superior, in more ways than one. The fresh scar sparked the corporal to recall the men who went out for provisions just prior to the army's departure and who had returned minus one of their comrades.

A captain in his unbuttoned waistcoat and rolled-up shirt-sleeves, who Sol recognized, stepped out from the cabin with a rather tousled woman staring from behind. Surprised, the officer said, "His Excellency has taken his men south to Pennsylvania..." It appeared that he was deliberating.

"What is your name and these two?"

"Private Solomon Kimsey, sir"—he saluted, calling attention to his bare head and accompanying scar—"and Tam Baley. His son, Joshua, wants to join the New Jersey militia."

"Well, then, Private, you are under arrest for desertion. I could shoot you right where you stand, but since His Excellency is in need of every man he can get, I'm going to send you south to face whatever Captain Gregory should mete out to you. Corporal, see to his transportation."

So then, this captain knew who he was and knew his commanding officer, but Sol could not remember his name.

Uncle Baley and his son stayed astride their horses, but the captain relieved the prisoner of his. Sol was restrained and placed in a wagon on top of a pile of iron implements to be sent south for the army.

"Well, at least you don't have to walk all the way to Pennsylvania," Tam said. "Odd for a deserter, don't you think?"

Tam rode about ten miles with the pair when Joshua told his father to take his horse and go on back home. He'd stay with Sol and do his duty in the militia.

Before leaving, Uncle Baley tossed his hat up to his niece's husband. "We'll take care of Mattie and the wee bairn and see that they get back home safe and sound."

Sol raised his manacled hands in acknowledgment and placed the hat on his head, grateful for the protection it afforded his scar from the sun.

Many miles were covered in the waning light of the long day before they finally stopped. The wagon master and his two companions were kind and shared their repast with the travelers, but they were quiet on the road and kept to themselves in camp. Sol and

Joshua weren't bothered by the men, and the pair talked together quietly so as not to disturb them while they slept.

"I noted that your family still has a strong brogue from the old country. I thought your kin had been in the colonies for a long while."

"Yes, we have been," Joshua considered, "though I suspect it may have lessened over time. The only one who won't change is George, Mattie's father. He maintains his royal ties and will until he goes to his grave…but I guess you knew that."

He agreed and told the younger man about Dunmore's War and their disagreeable encounter that miraculously turned to Sol's benefit in marrying Mattie. Joshua wanted to know more about the war, but Sol was getting tired and his head pounded in pain.

In the days that followed, the wagoners became friendlier, and the five men got to know one another and their histories. They figured that Sol had been a deserter, but what was that to them? All three had worked in one of the many iron forges in Hunterdon County and made a good living turning smelted iron into useful items for the Continental Army.

The talk inevitably turned to the war, and Joshua drank it all in. Sol thought about the last eight months since he'd enlisted in the army and about having only one skirmish with the Redcoats to show for it. But that skirmish led him to Mattie and his new daughter, and the realization of his important duty to his country and his small son waiting for him at home. He was still anxious to get in the fray, but he felt sure there would be trouble enough. Whatever punishment was to come, he would take it with sustainable faith and trust that he would eventually return to his family.

The Continentals were not where they should have been along the Neshaminy Creek. The travelers had to ask local inhabitants for directions and were pointed across the border into Delaware to a place called Wilmington. Crossing Brandywine Creek, the quartermaster welcomed the wagon with its heavy load of iron implements and its strange manacled passenger. Washington had requested these supplies which were late in coming because of the continual movements of his camps. Finally, here was the necessary equipment. The wagoner reported that he had a deserter in tow, and a flurry of curiosity rippled through the encampment.

Joshua helped the unsteady Sol off the wagon. "So many men... Where did they all come from?" Sol asked of no one in particular, gazing out across a sea of men and tents. It was the beginning of September and very hot, and Sol's tongue lolled out of his mouth for want of water.

General Washington was staying at the George Forsythe House at Quaker Hill, not far from where the encampment waited for their next deployment. Captain Gregory and a small detachment of men escorted Sol and Joshua to the general's headquarters.

"Oh, I'm in trouble now...I'm in trouble now!" Sol uttered in dread.

The house was a large redbrick structure, three storeys high, encircled by a tall iron fence. An arbor of protecting trees lined the street. Sol, in a haze of dehydration, saw three front doors and was pushed roughly through a tall scroll gate toward the one on the right wing. Four stairs led to a black glazed entrance with a menacing-looking brass door knocker, but no matter how he tried, he could not put one foot on the first tread. His guards pressed him harshly through the entrance when it was opened to them. On the left, a row of stairs led to an upper floor, and on the right, the knot of guards, prisoner, and draftee traversed a long hall leading to an open area and a cluster of officers.

The men parted, letting someone pass through. A general, who stood at least a head taller than any and, at the least, weighed in at seventy-five pounds heavier than Sol, asked politely, "What has transpired, Captain Gregory?"

"Explain your two-month desertion, Private Kimsey," Gregory demanded with disdain.

Sol was speechless before the man he now recognized as his highest commanding officer, General George Washington. What could he possibly say to this man who began his military career in the French and Indian War where he had two horses shot from under him, and it was reported there were four musket ball holes in his coat.

"Sir!" The lowly private stood his tallest and doffed his hat in salute, still wearing the unwieldy manacles and revealing his scar showing through a new growth of hair.

Feeling very small and close to fainting, Sol wanted to tell his story thinking it would probably not make any difference to Washington. He did not relish having his neck stretched or his back scarred with lashings and decided he would plead for mercy. He prayed to the good God that his punishment would not include hanging and leave his poor wife a widow and their two children orphans. Sol's wrists and arms were getting sore from being bound. If that was his only discomfort on this day, he would be grateful. And then, something occurred that made all the difference.

"What is your defense, Private Kimsey?" Washington pursued him, aggrieved.

"General, sir." Sol coughed violently. Washington motioned to an aide, but Sol was oblivious until the man handed him a glass of water, which he guzzled straightaway. "Thank you, sir. We were sent out on a scouting party, and to find beeves and provisions for the troops. We were ready to come back to camp when our scouts detected a cohort of Redcoats hurrying to discover what you were up to in the encampment. I got shot..."

"I can see that," Washington stated, staring at the white scar. "How are you feeling?"

"Better sir, the dizziness is gone...and so is my wife..."

There was sniggering in the company.

"She came to join me in the encampment, but our daughter decided to be born at her Uncle Baley's home in Hunterdon."

Only one was not successful in hiding his smile—Washington himself. Considering that this private had been left behind alive by his comrades, reminding all the abandonment of Colonel Hugh Mercer during the French and Indian War, and the fact that they had possibly prevented detection by English spies, the general said, "You need say no more, Private."

Sol wasn't finished. "Sir, excuse me."

Captain Gregory was ready to hang Solomon right at that very minute.

"May I introduce Joshua Baley. He wants to join the New Jersey Militia."

"See to it," Washington said, smiling broadly to his aide-de-camp. "As for you, Private Kimsey, flogging with at least one hundred lashes is the usual punishment, but I fear our upcoming clash with General Howe is about to become reality. We have no time for such trifles when your punishment may soon be at the hands of the English for returning to your Patriot fervor. You are exonerated."

After the deserter and new recruit left with Captain Gregory and the guards, Washington told his officers, "Gentlemen, prepare to march. I believe General Howe is at the front gate."

Chapter 27

Brandywine Creek

September 6

"THE GENERAL OFFICERS are to meet at five o'clock this afternoon at the brick house by White-Clay Creek, and fix upon proper picquets for the security of the camp."

It was at the Hale-Byrnes house where General Washington met with those officers, twelve in all, who led his divisions: Majors General William Alexander (Lord Stirling), New Jersey and certain Pennsylvania regiments; John Sullivan, Maryland; Nathanael Greene, certain Virginia regiments; Anthony Wayne, other Pennsylvania regiments; and Adam Stephen with the 3rd and 4th Virginia Brigades. The 3rd was Sol's 15th along with the 3rd, 7th, and 11th under Brigadier General William Woodford. The 4th Virginia Brigade was under Brigadier General Charles Scott and included the 4th, 8th, and 12th, and two additional Continental Regiments: Grayson's and Patton's.

In a letter to his family after the battle was concluded and the Continental Army was licking its wounds, Sol wrote.

> Dearest Father,
>
> First, give my love to Mattie, little Sol, baby Joanna, and the rest of our families. Sorrow at our parting at the end of August was consider-

ably debilitating to me especially in the discomforted state of my head. I am sure my beloved wife related the incident where I was considered a deserter. What shame I felt, but that has been finished, and I find myself back in the good graces of Major General Washington, Captain Gregory, and my fellow 15th Virginians.

I was swiftly swept up in a force of over fourteen-thousand Continentals almost as soon as I returned. Under Major General Adam Stephen, a Scott from our colonial militia who had fought with His Excellency in the French and Indian War, we marched immediately for one of the many crossings of the Brandywine River to a place called Chadd's Ford, the most direct route between Baltimore and Philadelphia and where Washington thought we would meet the main force of Gen. Howe's army and prevent them from taking the capitol. When we arrived, we were given our orders and spread out over five miles defending each ford.

Stirling's Division of Pennsylvanians and New Jersey was on our right, and Sullivan's Maryland boys were on our left. Our two brigades were on high ground along the east bank— all Virginians. We waited for two days while our officers had a council of war with their General.

On the morning of the 11th, reports came that Howe's Army was marching straight toward us. My stomach churned, and I was dizzy with fright, my musket allowing me to keep upright. Wary shock rippled through the soldiers standing ready for the beat-to-arms from our drummers, but the air was let out of the pipes as Sullivan reported that the information was wrong. But at once my pipes were filled with patriotic fervor!

Howe had taken a hill on our right flank, we opened fire on the advancing British troops. Green was ordered to assist Sullivan taking over Stirling & Stephen's divisions, but Sullivan wasn't in place and the Redcoats advanced on our left. We were in full battle mode and I no longer felt any fear. Reloading and firing, reloading and firing, red coats littered the field of battle combining with our men in hunting shirts covered with red blood. It suddenly became hand-to-hand as we were close enough to spit in the enemy's faces.

We were now attacked by a German Maj. Gen. leading 8,000 of Howe's troops directly across Chadd's Ford, Stephen fell back taking our Virginians quickly north to meet the British. We were on high ground at the Quaker Birmingham Meetinghouse one mile north of Chadd's Ford. We held firm aided by our battery of artillery. It didn't work, we fell back. Stirling had to retreat facing a bayonet charge, and we were scared thoroughly spit less by those prickly implements of death.

It was getting dark, but with reinforcements helping us, we stopped the pursuing British for an hour, letting the rest of the army retreat. Most of them escaped. Our three divisions fought for time and saved Mr. Washington's Continental Army. Our spirits were not defeated, though, because we exhausted the British who did not follow as we marched toward German Town the next day.

Father, we proudly had a new flag over our heads made with red and white stripes and a circle of white stars on a background of blue.
Give my love to mother, and Mattie and the wee bairns.

Your son Sol.

When General Howe enveloped the capital of Philadelphia, he was disappointed to find a deserted city.

Depleted by high emotions in the long fatiguing flight and thinking the enemy was at their heels, all Sol wanted to do was sleep. Only by sheer guts did he pull himself along with his comrades. They looked like beaten dogs—bloody and bandaged, dirty and sweat soaked. Food and a warm bed were what he wanted, but the march lasted well into the next day, and when the army finally stopped, there was no thought of his surroundings. On any other day, he would have noticed a glassy blue sky streaked with clouds, beautiful open farmland, and sage green forests of oak. Sol simply wiped his face on his sleeve as word went through the troops that, similarly exhausted, the English had not pursued them.

Sol fell asleep with his head on a rock and his musket cradled in his arms. Two hours later, he awoke to Captain Gregory's voice, "Fifteenth, you're on guard."

Sol dragged himself to the perimeter along with his exhausted regiment. The warm September night was not wholly unpleasant, but the lack of sustenance was. He hastened to arm his musket in case those lobsterbacks should sneak up on them in the night, and he made note of who was present and who was absent sick. Several of their boys had been injured in the fray—musket ball holes, broken or missing limbs from cannon balls, or those killed in the action. The picquets would form a chain of sentinels patrolling the plantation of Pennypacker's Mill where those wounded were cared for in the temporary hospital. It was just east of a large creek from whence the march to Brandywine had taken place and to where the Continental Army had returned. All night long an empty stomachache was Sol's only companion. He wondered whether, since the army had no provisions for them, they would all just fall down and die.

With first light came relief for his hunger when he and his messmates were surprised with a day's ration of beef and flour. Sol stuck his bone-studded portion on a sturdy stick to broil over the fire and, while salivating briskly, mixed his flour with water to make firecakes. He relished the taste of those biscuits that had soaked up the splattering meat drippings on the rocks below. Picking the last sinews off the bone with his teeth, Sol kept that bone in his mouth, sucking on it and not wanting to forget the taste until the next day's ration—whenever that would come.

The drummers, beating to roll, interrupted his rapture.

Germantown
October 4, 1777

For Sol's 15th, there were four enemies that morning—the distance, the fog, the British, and General Adam Stephen, Sol's commanding officer. Eleven thousand of Washington's troops advanced in three columns on a surprised General Howe who was inhabiting Philadelphia. Most of Howe's army was encamped at Germantown on the outskirts of the capital.

Washington's fourth column and his left wing were under the command of General Nathanael Greene, leading his Connecticut and Virginia regiments. They had been camped the farthest away and arrived late, stumbling into what they thought was the enemy. Not knowing who they were firing on through a cloudy veil of smoke and fog no eye could penetrate, they only aggravated the beginning of the end by inflicting casualties on their own Continentals, Major General John Sullivan's right-wing Maryland regiments. Meanwhile, a number of British took shelter in a large well-built stone mansion house, and even when matrosses touched the burning tips of their linstocks to ignite cannon to bombard the Redcoat refuge, it would not fall. Time and ammunition were wasted and ineffectual.

Before momentum was lost in disorientation and retreat, Sol, with guns ringing in his ears, engaged a lobsterback. Both had lost their muskets somewhere on the battlefield, and the soldierly melee threw them together in a personal wrestling match. Sol took the advantage and pulled the soldier off balance by his white shoulder belt. The smell of sweat-soaked wool assailed Sol's nose as they fought hand to hand. Dirt smudged handsome faces, and dark hair was littered with cartridge paper. They lost footing, each holding a moment over the other, rolling this way and that. The enemy hand grasped a wayward bayonet and thrust to slice the immediate target of Sol's soft belly. Without knowing how he did it, Sol's Culloden battle dirk entered the chest of the Englisher. At that killing moment, with dripping blade in hand, Sol and his father, Benjamin, were one. Piercing British blue eyes and the wet wool smell scorched themselves into Sol's mind. He hated wool.

Again writing to his father, the soldier son related that

> the whole campaign was a complicated attempt which fell flat and caused many casualties. We lost two battles in less than a month. Afterward, Washington moved us a half a dozen times ending at a place called White Plains where we, his exhausted and bloodied soldiers, began building redoubts and defensive abatis in case Howe attacked us. He didn't and Mr. Washington marched us where I and my mates would spend our winter encampment, a place called Iron Forge. Father, I was never so tired and hungry in all my life. If given the opportunity, I would have put my head down and died right where I was. My worst feeling, however, came with the knowledge that my commanding officer, who we all looked up to, Colonel Adam Stephen, was drunk upon the battlefield of Germantown and there is talk of his court-martial.

Eight months later, another letter arrived, and Benjamin read it aloud to the family gathered together on a warm summer's evening. The letter was crushed and torn in places, and he gently unfolded the parchment.

> Dec 1777
>
> Father, I write from a place they now call Valley Forge. A wide expanse that, I am sure, would be delightful in summer, but it is like hell

frozen over at present. God, I am so cold. My stolen coat from our last battle feels as thin as a summer shirt, the holes letting in the breath of the men around me. Maybe that's why we haven't died yet, that collective breath is actually keeping us alive. If I could think of another thing, though, it would be my belly, the scraping emptiness gnawing at me. I remember eating something a few days ago that caused me to give it back to the countryside. Nothing since then to give my gut relief. I can't feel my feet, but they mindlessly follow the bloody footprints of the soldier in front of me.

The snow is relentless. On a night like this, if I be at home, I would be warmed by the fire, hard cider in hand, and my beautiful Mattie by my side under a thick quilt. We would be preparing for Christmas and Hogmanay, and on that day the musket fire would be heard for celebration not killing.

Abruptly we are stopped. The officers pass down commands from General Washington. We love him and care not what we suffer, as long as he leads us. There is not a twinge of envy for the man in the warm cloak sitting atop his fine steed to be headquartered in a farmer's house. We have marched into hell for him and our cause. Grateful for stopping, we would go to sleep in the snow, but we are ordered to build shelters. We begin clearing the forest round about. It's a good thing, for if we had lain down, we would surely be dead by morning.

Our shelters are up as crude as can be, not the fine houses made by you and uncle. Master builders you surely are, and I have learned much from you. There is no time for fine now. My hands are nearly frozen from the clay I tamp in the cracks between the logs. It will hold as there is no time to remove the bark. Some soldiers bring rocks inside the poor cabins to make hearths and chimneys—the thought of warmth makes me dizzy with the thrill. Finally, the 16x14 foot structures are complete and there is room enough for 12 inside each—with hope the hearths will keep us from freezing to death.

The mood in camp is changing, and the boys begin looking covetously at my boots, the ones David made for me. I never wore spatter-dashes because my brother always kept me in boots. Even now, nearly without soles, I wouldn't take them off for fear they would be stolen. After a year's worth of constant marching, the soles finally gave up the ghost with large holes allowing rain, snow and mud to seep in. Some twine I found to hold them in place rotted away, which causes me to search for more. The covetousness was too much, however, and even I longed to chew on a tasty stew. We in our 12 man cabin cut those dirty boots in small pieces and boiled them with some small flour from our infernal firecakes and a piece of onion one of the boys had in his pocket. I could almost kill for a little salt to savor our soup. The talk is of mutiny.

Again we are chopping, this time for fire-wood. I go out nearly barefooted again and again, and then I have to go to hospital because I can't feel my toes. I remove the makeshift coverings of leaves and bark and discover some of those appendages have turned a horrible black tinge. They remove the offending toes, bandage my foot and decently give me a pair of stockings but won't let me go back to my barracks. It's a good thing, for if the others saw my feet bathed in those socks, they would surely fight me for them.

The holidays and 2 months have passed me by. Laudanum and a little soup with beef and corn have kept me alive. I feel sorrow for my brothers, but I am hobbling and hear that we have a visitor in camp, Baron Von Steuben. A German, they tell me, who will whip us into shape. I can hear the drummers, fife players, and him counting in German eins, swei, drei. His orders are given to one who speaks French. He speaks French, and the two foreign languages combine to make a finely tuned ensemble that we march to. The squelched mutiny has turned to hope. And some women, when they saw our plight, busied them-selves with needle and thread and presented us with shirts. Somehow the quartermaster finally procured breeches, coats, and shoes.

June Pennsylvania

I see by my original date that I had not mailed this letter to you. So many lives were lost to desertion, sickness and death...but the rest of us have survived and they took me off the sick-present roster. I will soon hobble-march with my brothers northward again into New Jersey. As we leave this place, I am sure the green grass will grow back to cover the fields our boys have watered with their blood and tears. Your loving son, Sol

With renewed confidence in well-rehearsed tactics, the Continental Army was stronger and bayonet ready, and they marched in proud formation away from the mournful fields of ice, snow, and suffering. After reconnaissance told him the British abandoned Philadelphia and were on their way to secure New York, General Washington led his men in repeated exhausting skirmishes on the heels of the Redcoats. In the summertime heat, the two armies finally clashed at Monmouth. Sol hoped all the suffering on those horrid Pennsylvania fields would be turned to glory in New Jersey.

The shoes which had been given him fit well enough, but the condition of Sol's foot with its missing toes made a long-distance march nearly impossible. Riding in an invalid wagon, he had time to review his first year and a half with the Continental Army and how far he'd come, and also remember with love and affection his wife and children and the rest of the Kimseys. Sol had sacrificed much during that time but was bolstered by two letters he'd received—one from Mattie and one from his father, Benjamin, held close inside his pocket next to the 6 2/3 dollars for the month of May.

Monmouth
June 28, 1778

Sol wore his new shoes and set Uncle Baley's hat firmly upon his head, which managed to stay with him during the suffering time, and he would fight the battle, no matter the pain in his foot.

Sol wrote again to his family.

> Colonel Lee, sent in advance with his men and artillery, became confused with orders and strategy, and he called a retreat. General Washington was right behind him with the rest of the Army and caught the men leaving the action. He promptly turned them around while cursing Lee mightily, but we beat those British when the day was done, We lay down exhausted from the fiery furnace of the day's scorching temperature, and even though our guards kept a watchful eye, they did not catch, nor did we see the enemy sneak away like dogs under cover of the night. Both sides claimed victory, but I think our Continentals scared the devil out of the British. We let 'em know the Americans weren't

the incompetent oafs they thought we were before the hell of Valley Forge shaped us. With the heat of the battle and the heat of the day, I had forgotten my pains, Father.

Please give my love to mother and the others, and deliver the enclosed to Mattie. Oh, how I long to see you again.

Until that moment, Mattie had not received a letter from Sol directed to her personally. Aggie calmed her daughter-in-law's fears knowing the circumstances were not favorable to much more than relieving himself of the horrors he was experiencing. She suggested Mattie go into the garden to read her correspondence.

"Do you want me to go with you?"

"No, Mother. I'd rather be alone."

Mattie sat on a low tree branch of an ancient oak. It was nearly touching the ground and perfect for climbing into the upper branches. Her babies were too young, but the Kimsey cousins enjoyed the sport. Ben and Aggie's boy, twelve-year-old Humphrey, usually led the pack which included Jamie and Mary's young ones: ten-year-old Littleberry, seven-year-old Ellie, and five-year-old Lizzie. Their sixteen-year-old Samuel was too busy with farmwork and his new love, Penelope.

Mattie was languishing for love, but she held off reading Sol's letter, calming herself in the beauty of her surroundings. Her in-laws had a beautiful farm, and the wildwood in which she sat gave off a delicious fragrance and the heady breath of Mary's lavender box hedge. It was a warm, drowsy afternoon, and a few dogwood flowers still clung to their parent. She opened her letter slowly. It had her man's uncomplicated script—no fancy flourishes for him—written in the field with lead pencil. She took a deep breath.

Dearest Mattie,

I hope you forgive me for not writing sooner. It gives me such pause to confess how much I love you and how much the very thought of you brings tears to my eyes. My regiment boys laugh at me (even though they shed tears when they write to their sweethearts), but I need to tell you of my heart's longing. You have heard from my letters of this damnable war, so the thought of your tender compassion, as it was at your Uncle Tam's and the birth of our baby girl, Joanna, sustains me on the battlefield when I know you and our children are waiting for me to return. Kiss little Sol and our baby girl for me. I will try to write more, but I know not where we go next or have a moment to write and tell you how much I miss you. Just recall that I do and do not forget me, Mattie.

When this thing is over, I will come and get you and the babies and we will move to a place of magnificent beauty along the Atlantic Coast and have our own farm.

Your dearest and most ardent husband.

Aggie pressed Sol's letter to her heart and she wept.

Benjamin received one more letter from his son—nearly illegible with holes and dark stains. Were they blood?

Jan. 1779...another winter hell hole...if I survive...11 more months to go before I am done...damnable war. Our regiments are being shuffled...Va. 11Th & 5th now. I got my wish, Father...under Col. Dan'l Morgan...3 mos...My good Capt. John Gregory since the war began... on furlough...sick...home...son, Sol

By the time Benjamin received the January letter, it was early summer. He tried to absorb what his son was telling him. Was Sol injured? Coming home on furlough? For good? There was an article in the *Virginia Gazette*: "After an illustrious career in the Continental Army, Captain John Gregory resigned due to ill health."

Chapter 28

The Revolting Southern Campaign

1778

IN HENRY COUNTY, the Kimsey farm was growing, and Jamie was happy with the progress—eighty acres of tobacco, fifty of corn, the rest in other vegetables including cabbage planted later in the year to escape the pests.

"They are pests," Benjamin said in the middle of the discussion of worms, his mind obviously pointing someplace else. "I refuse to sign that damnable oath."

"But, brother, it is required of us all." Jamie tried to reason with him.

"They are forcing us to choose sides—Patriots or Loyalists—and thoroughly antagonizing the Baptist population even more. We are Scots staying out of such things."

"Do you hold allegiance to George III? Is he your king? Or do you renounce him by owing your fidelity to Virginia and our United States of America which have given you so much these long thirty years." The familiar bloom of Jamie's face spread with anger.

Benjamin shot back, "I won't sign!"

"You stubborn Scot!" Jamie spat and put his name on the paper along with Benjie Jr., but Benjamin Sr. flatly refused.

Later that year with those who had missed the oath or had refused to sign, Benjamin found himself waiting his turn in line at the courthouse. Looking rather sheepish in front of Sheriff Robert Hairston, he limped to the table and signed the document promising his faithfulness to his country. After all, his family retorted, despite some religious intolerance he'd suffered, and the issue of slavery, which he detested, he should be grateful. He was surprised when he had to wipe away his tears seeing his ink-infused signature on the oath's surface.

1779

Abram Penn's magnetic and commanding presence brought the men of Henry County together to form a militia, and he was named its captain. He was a prominent and wealthy citizen who had fought with General Andrew Lewis in the Battle of Point Pleasant. Promoted to colonel in March 1781, Penn would lead his Virginia men to join General Nathanael Green in North Carolina preparing to meet the enemy.

1780–1781

It was the duty of all Virginians to be ready to defend their colony. However, the farmers could not leave their crops to rot in the field and would abandon the battlefields for the harvest, so they were generally exempt and left alone. The Kimseys' Virginia had been rarely touched by the war, but now the enemy was suddenly at their back door, and the Virginians were sorely unprepared for the conflict. At forty, Jamie volunteered for the militia.

On the day he left, Mary stood on the porch crying. Jamie held her in his arms, and it broke his heart to leave her. Samuel, his firstborn son, was by his side, along with Hermann Ensch's sons, Adam and Peter, who had come down from Bedford County to join them on the march. Mary looked in disbelief at her husband, son, and their friends in green hunting shirts and overalls ready to march south with their militia. *Another separation*, she thought. A short one, she hoped. So many good boys hurt or dead in the southern conflict already.

Lord, bring them back safely, she prayed.

After British misfortunes at Quebec and Saratoga, they had turned their strategy to the Southern Colonies, gathering Loyalists along the way and leaving New York City in the hands of Sir William Howe and his German mercenaries. On December 26, 1779, thousands of soldiers left Rhode Island and sailed for the Savannah River in Georgia, then they laid siege to Charleston in May and sent the captured Patriots' regiments to hell in English prison ships. In 1780, skirmishes and battles continued throughout South Carolina and into its northern sister.

January 4, 1781

The turncoat Benedict Arnold, in the red coat of a brigadier general, sailed up the James River to City Point. Nine hundred troops disembarked and marched, unchallenged by a few hundred local militia, and entered Richmond, the very heart of Virginia. They burned it to the ground.

Jamie wasn't a soldier but a simple farmer hardened by work in the fields. The only enemies he knew were severe weather and pests. He had listened to the letters from his nephew Solomon from that terrible valley called Iron Forge, but knowledge of what he was about to do didn't sink in until he faced this new enemy and had to follow orders to cock his musket and shoot that deadly ball into the midsection of a man—possibly another farmer. Besides Redcoats, there were Loyalists—people who held allegiance to the king—who bled out on that earth that they had broken with their own ploughs and tilled with all the muscles and sweat of their bodies. Killing was not to his liking one bit.

Jamie found himself marching uncountable miles until he thought his feet and legs would give out. He starved and went without water. He fought in North Carolina cow pens, fields of furrowed rows, by rivers and ponds, a hacking massacre on a race path, at a courthouse and fort on the way to meet General Nathanael Greene in Hillsborough, South Carolina. Greene was Washington's most gifted officer and ordered to lead the Continental Army in the southern war while Washington himself was in the north ready to take on the British in New York. Jamie found himself stretched nearly to the end of human endurance, but he vowed to keep up.

In the thick of things, with fire and smoke all around, Jamie would catch a glimpse of Colonel Lee's famous Legion. They were cavalry soldiers and experts with swords. He admired their dexterity, and one man especially caught his eye. He sported a helmet covered with bearskin and a cluster of red feathers on the left side which trembled in the course of battle. The man was curly headed, blond, young, and fighting with tremendous bravery.

Through the spring and summer, Colonel Penn led his Virginia Militia under General Greene deep into the south where Cornwallis was devastating South Carolina. They were then ordered to Virginia.

All efforts of America's struggle for power with Britain happened in the late summer of 1781 when Commander in Chief Washington, at his officer's advice and that of the French, turned his attention away from New York and toward the south. Washington's troops marched four hundred miles from New York, and they were joined by militia forces from every colony all to gather at Williamsburg. Lord Cornwallis had been ordered to dig a deep water port between Gloucester Point and Yorktown for the promised ships carrying their reinforcements. But when they looked up from their work, they were caught off guard by the advancing Patriot troops now pushing their English redcoat backs to the mouth of the York River.

Yorktown
October 6, 1781

The Patriots marched fourteen miles from Williamsburg to the outskirts of Yorktown. When they arrived on the evening of the sixth in stormy weather, before darkness descended on the field, Washington took a pickax and ceremoniously struck the first blow to the ground to begin the first parallel trench, and the troops followed suit and dug all night long.

Despite the cool weather, Jamie sweated through his clothing. His comrades were in front of him, and a stranger worked beside him. A waning full moon in a turbulent sky cast a moment of pale light over them. Jamie noted his uniform—short buff coat lapelled with green and rows of gilt buttons. He wore buff small clothes, leather breeches, and black knee-high boots splashed with mud. His chest was crossed with black leather belts They spoke briefly when the line of men stopped.

"I'm Jamie Kimsey from Virginia," he said over the din, shaking hands with the man.

"James McCracken from South Caro—"

"Move it," an officer reprimanded in a harsh whisper, and the line moved.

The pickaxes and shovels continued, and McCracken concluded, "A matross with Light Horse Harry Lee." It was that same soldier mounted on horseback Jamie had seen in the previous campaign—the one wearing the bearskin helmet.

At dawn, the enemy saw the trenches and over the next few days were struck by Washington's heavy artillery placements. There were fourteen big guns aimed at the British and nearly nineteen thousand men, including over eight thousand French regulars, facing nine thousand Redcoats, many of whom were sick and most exhausted. The turnabout worried Lord Cornwallis as he looked toward the sea at twenty-nine French warships. *Where was his promised backup?*

October 19, 1781

Yorktown. The last battle was done and the war over. The end was awkward but to the point—the ceremony of surrender. Brigadier General Charles O'Hara, second in command to Major General Cornwallis, who, it was said, feigned illness, tried to give the sword of surrender to the French commander General Rochambeau. He, in turn, indicated the commander of the Continental Army where it was to be proffered. However, Washington signaled that Major General Benjamin Lincoln should receive it for the atrocities committed against the United States at Charleston. Thus, the sword went around the field of surrender, and thousands of muskets and swords were placed at the feet of the victors.

Now what? The officers were spent, and there was no longer need for giving orders and men no longer receiving them. Jamie leaned on his musket in a daze.

"For home," someone said.

"Yes, my fine lad," another replied, placing his one good arm over the shoulders of his brother.

All over the fields, others shouted like sentiments to their comrades. Broken men walked off in twos and threes. No longer bound, soldiers headed north, south, or west. On the east, the York River, in front of them, was full of America's allies, the French fleet. Jamie reached for his hat and found that his head was bare. Apparently, he'd lost it somewhere without notice on that wide-open rubbish heap that once had been rich tobacco farms. Routed and abandoned redoubts stood ugly and stark, their abatis askew and damaged. Bodies and parts lay in the same blood-soaked ground as smashed cannon, heaps of shots and shells, fractured muskets and pistols. The disordered earth was scoured by burial details, taking up their grisly tasks. Others wandered the death field for friends and family. Some just wandered off. Somehow, among all the devastation, Jamie found his son.

"You're wounded." An icy reflex sent Jamie's hand to the side of Samuel's head where a neatly wrapped bandage sported a spreading red leak.

"A damned musket ball nearly tore off my ear. Hurts like fire. Got it bandaged, though, by a pretty Molly Pitcher from the town who was carrying a bucket of water and some clean rags. Can't hear so well, Father, but I still got my head on my shoulders." Samuel smiled.

"Let's go home, son."

Weak from hunger and pain and revolted by utter destruction, they walked off the bloody field without looking back. Crossing by the blasted-out earthworks of redoubt number nine, Jamie fell over an unseen body. It twisted eerily and came to rest on its back.

Samuel recognized him first and cried out, "Oh my God! Peter!" It was Hermann's son.

On his knees in front of the half man, Jamie stared in horror. He could not stand and vomited from the sight and stench of burned flesh, sulfur from gunpowder, and bloody gore—Peter's entire lower torso had been torn away by a damnable cannonball. Samuel helped his father to his feet. Leather straps still crossed the soldier's chest holding his canteen and powder horn intact. His chest and face were splattered with blood, and his arms were outstretched. "As if crucified," Jamie mumbled.

Samuel started to look away from the wretched scene, but a glint off a gold chain hanging from Peter's waistcoat pocket caught his eyes—his pocket watch was intact! Samuel carefully removed it, unbelieving that it could have survived. Father and son walked off, the memento held close to Samuel's heart.

Two hundred fifty miles toward the setting sun would be a long walk home. Jamie and Samuel had no money nor transportation but came across a makeshift hospital staffed by some of the Army's surgeons. Injured men staggered toward any relief they could get. From the town, some women donned in bloodstained aprons proceeded efficiently about their duties of assisting the surgeons. Samuel's bandaged ear was checked by one of the surgeons who pronounced it well wrapped then dismissed the young soldier. Mixed with the acrid smell of metal and blood was the breathtaking aroma of warm food. Jamie and Samuel were offered bread and soup. They sat down on a grassy slope to eat. The soup was redolent of chicken broth and vegetables of the best kind. Chunks of chicken parts made for toothsome eating.

Two men, walking along in a daze, presented themselves and asked if they could sit with them. Despite the dirt, powder smudge, and faces covered with matted beards, one began a conversation with a moment of recognition.

"Hello. I remember you from the trenches. You're Jamie Kimsey. Glad to see you made it out safely."

"Ah…you're the matross…James McCracken, that right? From South Carolina? And I saw you fight with tremendous bravery after Hillsborough in Lee's Legion."

"Yes, sir. Thank you, sir. Call me Mack."

Jamie introduced his son Samuel, and then, looking at the other, he said, "I don't know your name." His features weren't immediately recognizable.

"You should, I'm Adam Ensch. Tough times, huh?" he said soaking his bread in the broth of the soup and consumed it greedily, crumbs and drops of stock clinging to his beard.

A woman with hands full of tankards of ale offered them to the men. Jamie was thankful that he could wash the stench of vomit from his mouth. "Surely are, Adam. Surely are."

It was a warm welcome, indeed, for the men, but bittersweet for what they had to tell him. It wasn't necessary. The watch chimed from Samuel's pocket, a lovely Viennese melody, "Auch du lieber Augustin." It had been a gift from Hermann to his son Peter.

Stunned silence, then tears. Adam swayed from the pain of his suffering and choked on his bread. Sorrowfully, their former friends and neighbors buried their Peter in the hallowed ground of the fields of Yorktown.

McCracken left the field to go home to South Carolina with his Legion under Colonel Lee. Adam, Jamie, and Samuel walked fourteen miles to Williamsburg in the hope of finding some work to pay their way back home. Williamsburg, denuded of its status as capital of Virginia the year before, had become just another town, especially when the shadow of Cornwallis was removed. Many wayfarers from the fresh battlefield tramped this way to get to their homes, so it was no surprise there were few jobs to be had. Luckily, Adam had a silver coin that would provide them with a room in the tavern for the night. By sharing a bath, they could at least get clean. Jamie was the last stepping into the now chilly water. The two boys had a good laugh at his expense. The tavern keeper, having a son who fought early in the war and had given his life for the cause, had it in his own heart to give them suitable clothes by way of thanks. Their stained hunting shirts would keep them warm enough, but winter was setting in.

A sumptuous breakfast awaited the three soldiers. They drank their coffee and ate their bacon while discussing the strategy of how to get home. The conversation drifted to the next table.

A man turned in his chair and said, "Where are you from, gentlemen?"

"Henry County, sir," Samuel related.

Adam followed with "Bedford County."

"Well, I'm riding to Green Spring Plantation at the river to see a friend who weathered the battle there in July. Would you care to join me? Perhaps you could catch a boat up the James River to City Point."

Jamie threw his head back with a hearty laugh at the odd coincidence. Everyone thought he was daft, for twenty-five years before, he had traveled that same route to establish his home. It was an agreeable circumstance.

The coach was waiting, but before leaving, the tavern owner gave them one last kindness.

"I make a good wage here in my establishment and was going to leave it and my small farm to my son and only heir. I would like to give you this, knowing you are Patriots who fought for our freedoms and survived. Please use it in the name of my son, George Nelson. My brother, Thomas, survived the battle intact. I hear his house is still standing in the town even though it's pockmarked from cannon fire."

The pouch contained enough money for the men to return to their homes and more.

"Your kindnesses will never be forgotten, Mr. Nelson." Jamie shook his hand in grateful friendship.

From the James River to City Point, then to the Appomattox River, the men parted company at Petersburg. With Peter's watch safely tucked in his pocket, Adam journeyed to his home to bring the sad news to his family. Jamie and Samuel proceeded southwest to Henry County and the bosom of their own dear home.

Reconstruction of homes and businesses decimated by war, reconciliation of families ripped apart by Loyalist attitudes and Patriot sensibilities, and replanting of abandoned farmlands, all this and more needed to be accomplished before they could be one united country.

* * *

The snow lay on the ground in great drifts when Jamie and Samuel finally returned, and Mary knew there was something dreadfully wrong with her husband. Being unable to work his farm, then confined to the house for weeks on end, Jamie was sullen and given to fits of anger. He barely acknowledged his children, and he was cold to her, rebuffing any comfort she wished to give him and leaving her longing and loneliness unattended. Christmas and Hogmanay came, and neither husband nor wife could find any cheer.

Eventually the thaw began with a few bright days. But there was no thaw between them. Jamie seemed strangely repulsed by his wife, who had given him so many children. Perhaps it was the war, she reasoned wisely. Maybe there were things he saw or had to do that made him this way. It all made sense to her, but she was bewildered that he found no comfort with his wife.

Spring was in the air and so was romance. Samuel had finally asked his love to marry him, and there were wedding plans to be made. Of course, the ceremony would take place at the Kimsey home.

But when the day came, Jamie was nowhere to be found. Littleberry and Benjie went to search for him with no luck.

The nuptials were performed by Samuel's Uncle Benjamin, and Penelope and Samuel were married "in the sight of God and all here present". Mary cried, dabbing at her eyes and runny nose. She hoped that "all here present" would know it was from her oldest son marrying the prettiest girl in the county and not from the embarrassment and shame that fell on Mary's shoulders at the disappearance of her husband.

Henry County
September 1782

Even though comforted and encouraged by her children and a new grandchild on the way, Mary could hardly bear up under the burden of her husband's absence to her. He was in the fields from sunup to sundown and came in only for dinner. One evening he was late.

"You must be famished," she stated simply, not expecting anything in return.

He turned on her, grabbing her wrist, glaring wildly as if he could kill her on a whim. His face turned ash gray. He wheeled around and went from the house weeping.

Mary cried herself to sleep that night and most of the next day. Jamie had disappeared altogether.

"I saw him in his hunting shirt carrying his musket about twenty miles from here," their neighbor was saying as he stood on Mary's porch. He handed her a paper scribbled with a note.

She went inside and sat by a warm fire. She was surprisingly cold for such a warm day. She wrapped her shawl around her shaking shoulders and gently unfolded the note.

> You must find yourself another to keep your bed warm at night. I'm off to the far blue mountains and will not see you again. You have enough to keep you at ease.

> Jamie

That was all it said. No reasons, no excuses, just those words scrawled across the paper—and not even looking like his writing. It seemed as if someone had grabbed her by the throat and suddenly she could not breathe. *Why is the door still open?* she wondered. Arising from her chair, she staggered toward it and collapsed on the floor.

With a horrible headache, Mary awoke the next morning in her own bed to see her daughters, Elizabeth and Eleanor, standing above her. Nine-year-old Lizzie was unfolding a damp cloth to place on her mother's forehead.

"Thanks for sending Littleberry for us, Ellie," Samuel said as he and Penelope swiftly entered the room. "We came as soon as we could. How's Mother doing?"

Mary's voice was weak, and she was annoyed at the trouble she was causing, "I can speak for myself, Samuel! I'm at ease."

Ellie handed him the note.

As he read it, Samuel's face darkened into an anger Mary had never seen before.

"I'll find him, Mother, and bring him back. I know he doesn't mean it. It's the war."

"I know, son, but don't bother. He has his own road to travel now."

"No, Mother, you're wrong. He needs you…and us," he added, sorrow replacing anger.

Mary was ill for a time until she realized her marriage was over. Of course, Samuel could help her out as would Benjamin's sons who were still working the farm. But the thought forced itself to the front of her mind that she should look for another to replace Jamie. The idea repulsed her. He was her love, her only love. No one could take his place. But what about her young children?

Finally, she decided. At least another year would have to pass before she would allow herself to make that kind of dreaded decision.

Fall 1784

By autumn, no one had found Jamie. While there was still hope, Mary resigned herself to that fact and kept at her chores every day, every week. Months flew by until the day arrived that she would remember forever—the anniversary of her wedding. Fastening the last pin on one of her girl's wet dresses hanging on the clothesline, she didn't have to remind herself. It was at the forefront of her thoughts from the moment she got up. Early before the children awoke, she had gone to her dresser and removed the bonnet that she wore on the day she left Jamie to go back to Wales so many years before. It was old and faded and the lace a little shabby, but she held it close, breathing in the lingering fragrance of lavender, reviving her memories of when she returned for their wedding.

It was the end of September, and again an early frost tricked the green leaves of summer into the rich colors of fall—golden yellow, brown, and apple russet. A day not unlike the one she experienced at this very moment—the day of her marriage. All the neighbors for miles around had been invited for the two-day celebration. Others came from great distances and would stay over. With Donald MacDonald escorting her, she walked toward her beloved Jamie.

They said their vows before family and friends, promising to be faithful to each other. Benjamin wrapped the couple's hands in a MacKenzie tartan handfasting ribbon to seal their contract, then he congratulated them and pronounced, "Mr. and Mrs. Jamie Kimsey, married before God."

* * *

At the clothesline, Samuel startled her with "A Penny for your thoughts, Mother."

Flustered at being caught in the act of a sweet remembrance of things past, Mary quickly concealed the bonnet in her pocket and turned her attention to her new grandson. "Let me hold him?" Mary asked. She hardly had a chance to cuddle and tickle the boy when he started to fret. Penny, with the "new mother" look about her," sighed. "I awoke him from his nap. I guess he's still sleepy." The fertile soil of Jamie's family had produced his first grandchild, Samuel Crowley Kimsey Jr., to honor his mother. But would Jamie ever know?

"Samuel, you've done well by marrying Penny. She has a kindliness of manner, and those blue eyes of hers cannot hide her joy in her love for you and the baby."

Samuel was all smiles. "We've brought some folks by to have a picnic." Suddenly the entire Kimsey clan was swirling about her, and it became a day that helped her forget her sorrows.

A cornucopia of food graced tables, and quilts were laid on the grass. Jugs of ale and rum were passed among the men who drank, and there was apple juice for the children. Off to the side of the porch, bright green watermelons were piled high into a large tub. Benjamin's boy, eighteen-year-old Humphrey, picked a likely candidate. Placing it on a table for the execution, he wielded a large sharp knife and began cutting slices from the heavy fruit. The warm sweet juice oozed from the green rind and then down the chins when a recipient bit into a delicious red wedge. The challenge of who could spit the black seeds farthest became a fun game.

Mary enjoyed the scenes of lively conversation with everyone enjoying one another's company—all eating fried chicken, corn bread, and cakes; children playing; and the sight of her clean clothes flapping in a good breeze. The sound of dissonant notes floated across the air until they became one, the finely tuned instruments to be played in the shade on the porch. Her nephew Hiram began first with his fiddle setting the tempo and was then joined by her daughter Lizzie as accompaniment on the dulcimer. It was a slow-moving waltz. Adding a shrill fife and brisk drum left from the war, David and William turned the dancing to a quick Scottish hornpipe with boots and shoes keeping the frisky rhythm, and twice as fast was a reel in four danced by the younger members of the family. As the families rested, Hiram bowed a slower piece, and to everyone's astonishment, Benjamin took Aggie's hand and began to dance to the music, throwing Baptist caution to the wind. It didn't last long, however. The pain of Ben's old war injury was too much, and he and Aggie left for their home.

Samuel took Mary's hand. "Would you like to dance, Mother." She feigned shyness but thought it would be fun. He could not resist pulling at the blue ribbons hanging from her pocket. "Oh, no, Samuel. Not that."

"Go on, Mother. Tie it on your head."

She reluctantly complied.

As they danced, Benjie suddenly interrupted and whispered something in his cousin's ear. Both men smiled.

"What intrigue are you two about?" Mary wanted to know.

Samuel danced in circles. She was getting dizzy and wanted to stop, but he whirled her around then let her go when another's hand took hold of hers.

It was Jamie.

She nearly fainted. It was fortunate that his arm was around her waist. He danced with her, and Mary's familiar scent reminded him of their parting when she left for Wales. She wore that same blue bonnet with its bits of lace; brown ringlets were now tinged with gray; her face, a creamy white and rose-red blush, wore a few wrinkles of graced time. But those violet eyes were not dimmed by time even if there was sorrow behind them, and the vermilion lips Jamie wished so to kiss. His heart raced between love and despair; his mind reeled between passion and loss. *Have I lost her forever? How could I have let this happen?*

Hiram continued playing lively songs old and new—poems that had been set to music from over the sea in the early years from England, Scotland, Ireland; colonial songs like "Whiskey in the Jar" and "Yankee Doodle"; and sad songs, like "Johnny Has Gone for a Soldier." When everyone had settled into just listening, Hiram changed the mood with a very old Scottish tune from the Hebrides his mother, Agnes, sang to him, his twin, Solomon; and all their brothers and sister as bairns.

Family members departed the cool evening to the warmth of the house, but Jamie and Mary remained, listening to their nephew. He was playing just to them. Stars began to appear as darkness was drawn across the sky by the setting sun. Jamie beckoned Mary to come close and then pulled up a colorful corner of the quilt with which to cover her. She did not protest to his placing a doubtful arm around her. Hiram started to sing to his violin's accompaniment.

Bye, bye, sleep in peace. Mother's right beside you.
Bye, bye, little one, sleep the sleep of peace.

The words seemed to pull something from Jamie that he did not want to release. A chill ran through him, and he twisted uneasily.

He held tightly to the fear of the familiar face of sorrow that he was used to and that he did not want to let go.

There was awkward silence between them. Jamie did not know how to begin.

She did, "What happened?" Mary unwaveringly adhered to her resolve to find out why he had left her.

Hiram sang.

Turn, turn around from your play.

"The war changed me. I was so angry and…I was afraid I would hurt you."

Come and sleep the dreams you may.

"Benjie shamed me into coming back, reminding me how much I missed you."

Sing the tune, sing the tune, pass it to your own bairns.

"I was in the barn all the while. I waited until Ben left…I couldn't let him see me, terrified by what he might do…and say. I don't know if I can ever face him again."

Sing, oh sing the hymn of peace. Bye, bye, baby, sleep in peace.

"Thank God Samuel and Benjie found me. I was destitute on those mountains, barely surviving, lonely and with no hope. I prayed for death so you would no longer bear the burden of my anger."

The longer the song went on, the more it seemed to pull at him. No longer able to bear the pain, he fled from Mary's side to the byre away from his torment, but he should have known better.

Inside, it felt like home. The smell of the animals, corn in the crib, seed in the bins, hay in the loft for the winter cold, even the dust from the floor. He closed his eyes and, for an anchor, seized the worn splintered planks he had fashioned with his own hands. *Why did I leave? I don't understand.* Quietly, Mary went to him. He felt her presence.

"I am…so ashamed," he whispered into the night air, afraid to look at her.

She touched his arm with her hand. He turned to face his wife.

"You are my love, and I am unworthy of you." Tears streamed down his face and onto his long beard tinged with gray, his words unlocking the horrid chill of the offending torment. "So many times, I sat in front of a fire and stared off into the long dark night, my own shadow playing out behind me trembling, mocking me for what I had done to you and the family. Over and over I resolved to come home, but the minute I turned to leave the mountain, my resolve gave way, and I just couldn't do it for fear you and the family would shun me—would cast me aside as the coward that I am."

Mary took him in her arms, those arms she had opened wide to receive him many times before. "Let it go, my love," she whispered gently.

He cried in her embrace as he had done when their daughter Sarah had died, tears of years of sorrow onto her shoulder. She held him for a long while, then caressed his face in her hands and said, "We will pull through, and we will rise from this."

Their bed was a marriage bed once more, and gently the seed of longing slipped inside his beloved.

The wee bairn was born May 30, 1785, their eighth child, a little boy called James Jr. after his own pioneer father in Henry County, Virginia.

Chapter 29

Buncombe County, North Carolina—A Breach of Love

1790

"WHAT ARE YOU going to do over there that you cannot do here?" Benjamin reasoned.

"It's getting crowded. I am suffocated by the encroaching population."

Jamie's anger was getting the best of him. He slammed the cabinet door, breaking it off its hinges. *I should have fixed that damned thing long ago.* Irritation churned in him.

"Why did you come here if you're going to argue with me?"

"Sit down, brother. Let us discuss this amicably."

Jamie softened a little.

"I was just on my way home from the church. There's a hole in the roof. Would you fix it for us? By the way, where are Mary and the children?"

"Most of them are at their chores, and Mary took Junior to visit with Aggie."

They sat across from each other in the kitchen of his finely built cabin, comfortably warm on a blustery spring day. A gust of wind blew down the flue and swirled ashes onto the hearth rug. They both breathed simultaneously, not that either one noticed, as they had done since Jamie was a wee lad and Benjamin was his fifteen-year-older brother.

"You are a master craftsman. I noticed and said so long ago when we were burned out of our home in Bedford and you and Mary took us in. I never felt so lost in all my life trying to do the Lord's work and having the whole community turn against us, but you were there for us as you've always been. The farm was a masterpiece of design, and our own house, which grew out of that kindness, a thing of beauty. I was hard-pressed to leave it and move here. But here we are again, and your family is the recipient of another magnificent homestead."

Jamie was pleased by his brother's regard, and an appreciative smile relieved a tense situation. But the arguments were not quelled and came again. He pushed a folded paper toward Benjamin, left the table, and went to the now doorless cabinet. Taking a bottle from it, he filled a small glass and turned.

"Do you want some?" He took a large swallow and stared out the window.

"You know I don't drink! And why are you? That was never your habit."

"Not since lately. It kills the fire in my gut—at least temporarily." He turned toward his brother. "I want to move on, Ben. Please don't let us be separated by your obstinacy."

Benjamin unfolded the paper. It was a certificate for fifty acres of land in a place called Franklin.

"What's this for, and where is Franklin?"

"It's a 'reward' for my service in the militia—nothing that I sought after, of course. One of Colonel Penn's militiamen rode all the way here from Henry County to deliver it last week. I talked to the family, and they were willing."

"Willing, huh?" Ben's attitude showed the scorn he could not hide from his brother. "I'm sixty-five, Jamie, too old, and anyway, Aggie is happy here. We are respected members of the community, and you are too. You would do well to remember that."

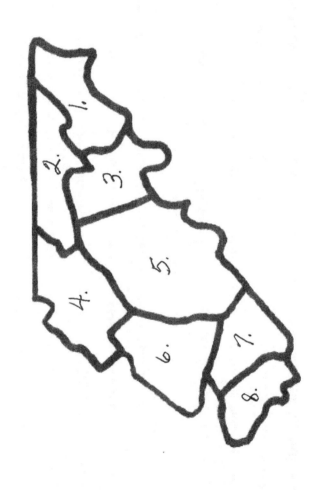

The State of Franklin in 1786: 1. Wayne (Johnson and Carter Counties); 2. Sullivan; 3. Washington (includes Unicoi); 4. Spencer (Hawkins); 5. Greene (includes Cocke County); 6. Caswell (Jefferson and Hamblen Counties); 7. Sevier; 8 Blount.

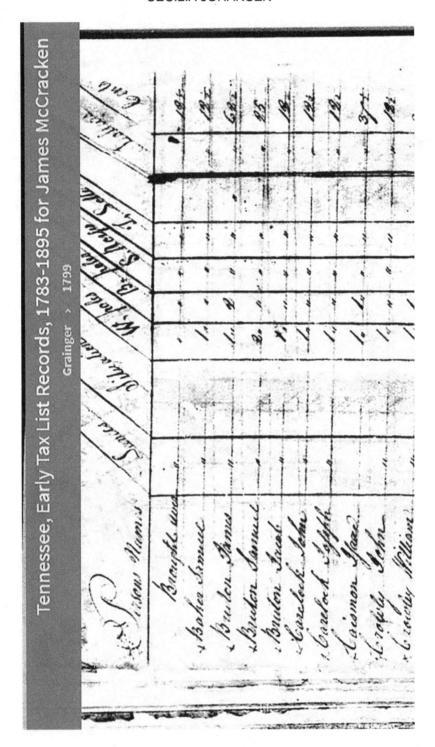

Tennessee, Early Tax List Records, 1783-1895 for James McCracken

Grainger > 1799

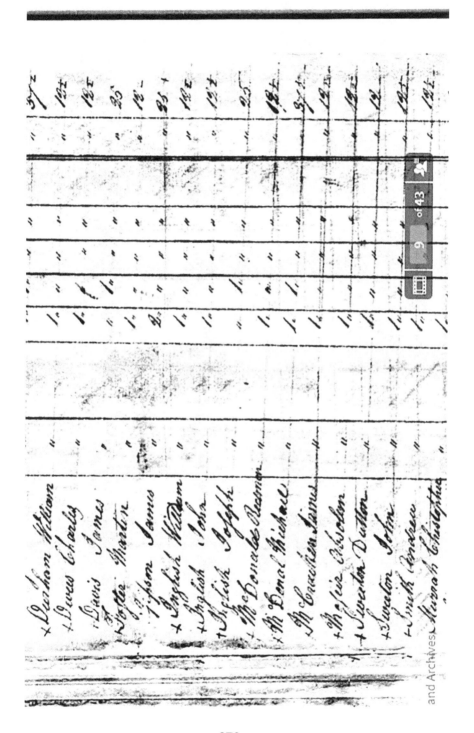

Jamie looked at Ben, not quite comprehending his age after all the years. His receding hairline had deepened, and the black hair like his father's was now gray, pulled back, and hanging in a queue over his ministerial robes. There were wrinkles at the corners of his eyes, and, when did he become so stooped?

"I don't want to be respected. I want to move on into new lands to the western edges of North Carolina. I want to break new ground that has never been dug before. I…I have looked westward for years and wondered what was out there and how glorious it would be to plough fresh land." Through the window, his anguish searched the horizon.

Ben watched his brother. He had a reminiscence of the six-year-old Jamie popping out from the family's hiding place in their cottage at Inverness so long ago. The red hair of that little boy had not dimmed much—just a few gray hairs mingling in. He was fifty. The freckles were gone, but he was still lean, his spare behind not quite fitting the chair in which he sat. Ben smiled looking down at Jamie's knee-high black leather boots. They were a gift from David, the cobbler in the family, and replaced his old, worn-out shoes.

"There are Indians out there—savage ones. You know that." Ben was getting desperate.

"They were here, too, when we came. That makes no difference to me." Jamie swallowed the rest of his rum, fortifying himself. "I can't talk to you anymore." He turned his back to his dearest brother and adopted father, not wanting to hurt him. *But he's hurting me,* Jamie cried out in his soul.

"You're talking nonsense." His words came sharply, rising in volume. "Why are you trying to tear our family apart like this? I do not understand." The ugliness of anger was taking its toll, and that telltale vein popped out on his forehead.

Frustrated, Jamie turned and threw his glass at Benjamin, missing him purposefully and crashing the glass in pieces against the hearth's stones. "You bastard Scot!" And he started out the door.

Benjamin rushed his brother, not knowing where the strength came from, and grabbed Jamie's shoulder. "Don't you call me that and turn on me, brother mine. You turned on your own wife once, don't do it to me. I'll not take it."

They were facing each other, bodies tense, clenched jaws, and ugly, contorted faces ablaze with angry determination. Jamie pushed Benjamin's arm away with such force that the older man lost his balance and nearly fell.

"So…there it is. You and the whole family have harbored my abandonment of Mary all these years. Never forgiving me for my crime. You don't know what it was like—the carnage and fear, starvation…and the murder of farmers like me…those just wanting to till the land, not kill each other."

"You should have stayed!" Benjamin growled.

"I couldn't. You should have known that!" Jamie charged out of the cabin. "I have my chance and I'll take it!"

"Family doesn't treat family like that!" Benjamin yelled after his most beloved brother, his fists beating the air, his chin quivering and tears soaking his stock. He had to let him go, just as he let go Solomon to his own private war.

The families were inconsolable, and the breach between the brothers was severe. Nothing could bring them back together. The clan was broken.

* * *

No one came to wish them well on their journey except Hiram, the fiddler. He was simple and unable to understand the rift. Their families were one, why all this terrible sadness? All the cousins had grown up together as if they were siblings. "Why, Uncle Jamie? Why are you leaving us? It breaks my heart."

He left without an answer as if he knew there was none, and as the family in their wagons pulled out of the yard, Jamie could hear the soft mournful strains of the violin coming from the byre where Hiram always hid himself when he was sad. Jamie shivered, as he did after the war, when he heard that same lullaby that brought him back to his home and loving wife. This time he would not return.

Following the French Broad River on a path called the Wilderness Trail, the three wagons pressed on toward their destination that was spelled out on the papers Jamie held: "Free land for those willing settlers ready to break ground and defy the elements—50 acres—State of Franklin[23]—meet at Bean Station." He wasn't sure exactly where it was, but trusting the ancient path would lead them to their goal.

Only a few days out, there was another group of wagons following them within earshot. Jamie, Samuel, and Littleberry pulled their teams off the trail into a stand of trees, thinking to let them pass or discover if they were up to some mischief. Muskets at the ready, the women and children waited in the trees—but he noted that the party was well equipped with packhorses and two beeves. Not much of a threat, he guessed. Just other pioneers.

---

[23] The State of Franklin was an area located in today's Eastern Tennessee, United States created in 1784 from part of the territory west of the Appalachian Mountains that had been offered by North Carolina as a cession to Congress to help pay off debts related to the American War for Independence. It was founded with the intent of becoming the fourteenth state of the new United States. The concept came from Arthur Campbell of Washington County, Virginia and John Sevier of Augusta County, Virginia. They believed the Overmountain towns should be admitted to the United States as a separate state. Campbell's proposed state would have included southwestern Virginia, eastern Tennessee and parts of Kentucky, Georgia, and Alabama. Sevier favored a more limited state, that being the eastern section of the old Washington District which was then part of North Carolina.

Although many of the frontiersmen supported the idea, Campbell's calls for the creation of an independent state carved out of parts of Virginia territory caused Virginia Governor and Kentucky land speculator Patrick Henry—who opposed a loss of territory for the state—to pass a law which forbade anyone to attempt to create a new state from Virginia. After Virginia Gov. Henry stopped Campbell, Sevier and his followers renamed their proposed state Franklin and sought support for their cause from Benjamin Franklin. The Frankland movement had little success on the Kentucky frontier, as settlers there wanted their own state (which they achieved in 1792). Sevier's State of Franklin included the following counties: Sullivan, Wayne (modern Johnson & Carter Cos.), Washington (includes modern Unicoi Co.), Spencer (modern Hawkins Co.), Caswell (modern Jefferson & Hamblen Cos.), Greene (includes modern Cocke Co.), Sevier, and Blount (https://en.wikipedia.org/wiki/State_of_Franklin).

The wagoner shouted, "Whoa!" to his mules. "Hello to you, sir. Are you going our way?"

Jamie recognized the voice. "It depends where you are going."

"The new State of Franklin, to till the ground and raise my young 'uns."

"Well, Mack, shall we travel together for safety and mutual support?" Jamie's broad smile convinced the sojourners they had met were friendly travelers.

"You know my name?"

"Yes, of course. We dug many a trench together at that terrible battle back in '81."

"What fortunate luck." Mack jumped off the hard seat of his wagon and heartily embraced his old acquaintance.

"You still look like a young buck, my friend. You must be thirty—"

"Thirty-six in truth," said Mack. "This is my family." He turned to them.

Jamie was very impressed as the proud young man pointed out each member of his family—his wife and five young daughters—the youngest a babe in arms, and his eldest child, eleven-year-old John, who drove their second wagon! Mack's hair was darker blond, and he had the browned skin and muscular physique of a farmer.

Junior eyed the scene with wonder. *How in the world did they meet up with someone his father knew?* "Look, Papa." Five-year-old Junior pointed to the little children. "See how they cling like baby possums to their mama." But, the most unusual sight of all was the light color of the six-year-old girl's hair. It curled around her head like a glory. Never did he see hair of that color before—as bright as the sun on a summer day.

The two families took sustenance together, sharing bread, jerked beef, and fruit. From the old-growth forest surrounding them, there was an enchanting coolness. And when the children's laughter ceased, the sound of rushing water led Mack, Jamie, and Littleberry, with Junior trailing them, to a winding stream splashing over rocks along an open meadow. They filled their jugs and returned to the wagons. While Samuel filled the barrels, Mrs. McCracken changed her infant's soiled diaper, and she and Penny tried to corral their little ones. Suddenly Mary turned and cried out in alarm, "Where's Junior?"

Fright swept all in the camp. Blank stares on the faces of the three men convinced her their boy was missing.

Littleberry was the first to run back to the stream with Mack and Jamie following, calling out the boy's name. Even if the lad had been a good swimmer, the swift moving current would have been too much for him. Mack checked the thick growth of the forest around about the stream, and Jamie and Berry ran along the bank.

Jamie was sick at heart and unable to call out with a thick knot of fear caught in his throat. In a boulder-filled pool, he waded in up to his hips and reached under, hoping against hope his hand would not hook his son's body. It didn't.

Berry advanced slowly over a precipice where a waterfall splashed on rocks one hundred feet below. Jamie could hear him calling and calling until the sound was drowned out by the gushing water. Jamie cursed God almighty for letting this horrible thing happen to his little boy, then shrunk back in horror from what he had just done. *God forgive me. It was my fault for not watching him.*

The face of the cliff was not difficult to surmount. Berry climbed easily over moss-covered rocks and straggling trees, root anchored along the descending fall of water. He was only gone a matter of seconds when suddenly he reappeared at the top of the cliff. "Pa, come quickly!"

Oh, God! Oh, God! No! Please don't take my boy!

Mack had caught up to them, and the view from the top was stunning, but movement below revealed someone. Was it Junior? They hurried, scrambling down the cliff's face. Was that an Indian? And what was he doing? Jamie was thinking the very worst—kidnap or kill the white child. The dark man in skins, fringe, and feathers saw them coming, and the motion from the arm of the man was not threatening in the least. It was beckoning them. When they reached him, Junior was hanging over the Indian's arm, spewing forth water that had nearly drowned him. In sign language, the story was easy to understand. While fishing in the large pool, he saw the boy carried over the waterfall, and caught him midstream before he hit the rocks. Junior was placed in his father's arms. The boy, now revived, immediately cried for pure fright and being reunited with his father. The party thanked the Indian with a pouch full of tobacco. A large smile spread across his weathered face.

* * *

The trace[24] stretched out before them. Annoyances of wagon creak, canvas billow, biting flies, leather squeak, and the uncomfortable hardwood under their behinds disappeared when they saw the good land ahead of them, and Jamie loved it all. Mary tucked her arm under her husband's, sensing his pleasure and enjoying it with him. He had been afraid of bitter recrimination from his wife when he left her after the war, but none had come. And then the break with Benjamin.

Now, with the unfortunate accident almost losing Junior, his failings continued to infest his mind, and he wondered why she stayed with him. Mary was a remarkable woman. That was all there was to that. He would, therefore, not permit all the bad he'd committed to mar the moment.

He changed the reins to his left hand and slipped his right arm around his wife's waist, pulling her closer. Jamie glanced behind to see the younger children asleep and the older ones quietly talking, walking alongside the wagon. Mary looked at his weary face and was surprised by his kiss.

"Are you tired, my love?" he asked.

"Not so much. How far do you think we've traveled?" She pushed the bonnet off her head to let a cooling breeze dry her sweat-filled hair. Despite the flush and toll the trip was taking on her, she was a beautiful woman even after thirty years of marriage and nine children.

---

[24] Trace: path, trail, or road made by the passage of animals, people, or vehicles (https://www.merriam-webster.com/dictionary/trace).

He stared ahead. "'Bout sixty-seventy miles or so, I'm guessing. Maybe another few days." Then turning back to her, he said, "You never said a word about the quarrel with Benjamin."

"I've always understood your close bond to your brother. It is sometimes unseen, but there nonetheless. You are both thrifty and resourceful, hardworking, determined, and you've stuck together through thick and thin all these long years. I thought you'd never part from him. But now I see you driven by something else. What is it, Jamie?"

"It's part of our nature as Scots. A drive to push forward, to rise from any ill fortune or travail, but...there is a destination that I haven't met yet. Something out there pulling me on, and I couldn't let Ben chain me to that bond you talk about. I needed my father when I was six, but he was gone and my brother took his place. I am forever grateful to him, but it was time. I'm glad you and the children are with me, my dearest life."

Despite the difficulties, crossing the Nolichucky and Holston Rivers, nightly wolf howls and panther cries, and nearly losing their youngest son, the Kimseys finally came upon the intersection of their Wilderness Trail and the Cumberland Gap Road at Bean Station. Nestled in a long beautiful valley, the fort had a tavern and mercantile. Their land was properly marked, Jamie was told, just follow the trail south. The Kimseys and McCrackens found themselves squarely in the heart of Cherokee lands in the place called the State of Franklin.

Chapter 30

Tanasi

1792

THE VERDANT ASPECT of the land beyond Bean Station was more than Jamie ever envisaged. Abundant hardwood trees, water, and rolling hills would provide for all their needs. He and Mary were well pleased, although the daunting task of building without help from Ben's family would be formidable.

How his heart suffered without his big brother!

He wished he could have turned Ben's heart to move with them, but the wrath he felt at the time would have to be squared with his Lord. He remembered the admonishment of Mary to "let it go, my husband. It has been settled." There was so much work to be done on this new land, and the divide between the brothers would have to be set aside for a spell.

Meeting up with Mack McCracken, a fellow warrior with Jamie at Yorktown, was fortuitous. His family was still young, but with the many Kimsey hands, their first order of business was for a small cabin to house the McCracken bairns before the coming winter. Mack assisted with the felling of trees and preparing the logs. Samuel and Littleberry would hunt and lay traps. The bags of salt and garlic bulbs, purchased at Bean Station, would be used to cure the meat. Hogsheads of molasses and sacks of seeds of tobacco, corn, wheat, and cotton would fill out what they carried with them from their farms.

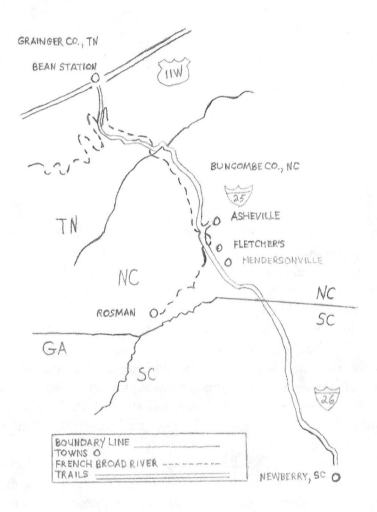

From the *Tennessee, Early Tax List Records, 1783-1895* James McCracken lived at least periodically in Grainger Co. in the 1790s. Amazingly, the route from his home in Newberry, Union Co., SC is on a direct route through Asheville, Buncombe Co., NC via the Howard Gap Road. Fletcher, in Henderson Co., was first settled in 1795 when Samuel Murray decided to move his family to the mountains of western North Carolina. His family made the difficult journey from SC up the old Howard Gap Road which, in areas, was little more than an old Indian trail.

The outpost of Bean Station was situated at the intersection of the Old Wilderness Road, a north–south pathway that roughly followed what is present-day U.S. Route 25E, and the Old Stage Road, an east–west pathway that roughly followed what is now U.S. Route 11W. Total mileage approximately 220 miles.

Another interesting note: There is a Kimsey Creek and Kimzey Creek Rd. in Arden, NC. It is an unincorporated community located in southern Buncombe County.

Fortified Bean Station had reminded Jamie of Middleton's Ferry in Lynchburg back when he first moved into Bedford County. He reminisced about this as he swung the ax to fell one tree after another, after another, clearing the land for homesteads and planting. The fact that both bounty land claims were next to each other was pure luck. Mack had three hundred acres for his service with Light Horse Harry Lee's Legion in the Southern Campaign. Jamie held 150 acres, rejoicing that it was not the expected fifty rewarded for his time in the militia and the last Revolutionary War battle at Yorktown.

This was the frontier, close to Indian territory for sure, but more than likely in it. He really didn't know, but the fort at the station was there for a reason. They would all have to be vigilant and keep a sharp eye.

* * *

Junior looked between the stakes of the simple palisade fence surrounding the garden. It bordered on the farm of Mack's cotton fields where the girl with the golden hair lived. She was sitting on the back step of their cabin reading a book. They had hardly exchanged two words since their families settled south of the station. Clouds floated lazily across the land causing light and shadow, but even in the shadow, the glory of her hair remained. He longed to free the locks of hair held back by pink ribbons. He fell for her instantly, thunderstruck by the emotion he felt.

The girl glanced up from her book, peeved by the intruding eyes but not so much as to make her angry for the interruption when she saw who it was. She quickly brushed the tears from her freckled cheeks.

"Are you all right?" he asked her. Surprised by his own concern, he quickly apologized. "I'm sorry if I startled you." *What did I just say?* His thoughts were all jumbled.

"No mind. I was reading about a lost love."

"Oh...Oh?"

"What's your name, little boy?"

That word stung. *Little! I'm not little*, he railed. His size had just not caught up to his manhood—yet. He had just turned seven at the end of May.

His parents called him Junior, but he didn't want to tell her that, and he wished he didn't have such a common name. There were too many Jameses anyway, including her father.

"James," he said boldly, finally showing himself from the security of the fence.

"May I call you Jimmy?"

What? Oh, joy! The innocent question caught him off guard. *She can call me anything she likes.* "Sure," he stammered. The way she said it pleased him very much. He was lost.

"You're one of the Kimsey boys, aren't you?"

Don't I stand out from the crowd of my family? She sure did—out of Mr. McCracken's children, she was the prettiest.

"You have a fine-looking farm. Your father works very hard. I've seen you working beside him."

So, she's been watching me too.

"Hannah Jane," her mother called loudly from their kitchen.

"Oh, I have to go. I hope I see you again," she said, and she was off in a flurry of white homespun and yellow hair.

In a fog, Junior was not quite sure he'd heard his father calling him. *My feet don't seem to be touching the ground.* Jamie's smile and command, "We've got work to do, son," brought him back to earth.

"Yes, sir."

* * *

Not all days were workdays. In the Kimsey household, Sundays were reserved for worshiping God and reading scripture. But Saturday mornings they usually went hunting for deer or small animals caught in the traps they laid or maybe fishing for whatever they could find in local creeks or the river.

Jamie and Junior set off with their poles. They scrambled down an embankment and over a dead fallen tree. There were a number of them littered along the clay-colored shoreline. Changes in the level of the river's water claimed any tree whose roots had been exposed to swift moving currents, and on that day, tangled dead branches held turtles in their grasp as they comfortably sunned themselves.

The sun scorched the earth and burned the skin of father and son alike, but they paid it no mind when their only thought was on the catch. If Jamie could snag their dinner, Mary would make a tasty soup out of the useful parts, and the hard shells properly worked would make helpful tools and such. Along the striated bank, he broke off flinty rocks to make arrowheads that night after supper.

Sweat ran down Jamie's face and under his shirt. Looking up and shielding his eyes, he studied the cloudless deep blue sky.

He ran his sleeve over his wet brow as Junior copied his papa's actions. In the water directly in front of them, a fish stuck its head above the surface but decided it was too hot and dove down again. Another followed, but Jamie was too quick for the laggard and netted the silver fish before it could decide otherwise. Their poles were useless in the hot morning river, but nevertheless, "Mama will be pleased," Junior said.

The boy looked up at Jamie. "Shall we go home, Papa?"

No answer, but the cloud of a faraway look shaded his father's face. "Um…no, boy. Let's pick some dandelion greens. She'll like that."

Junior was growing fast, and his voice would soon change. Jamie would have to get used to that when the time came, but it wasn't what he wanted. Jealously he wanted to keep the child small and close to him. He still remembered the heartache he'd caused Mary and the family by deserting them like he did. But when Junior was born, the bonny little boy almost made up for the horror he'd experienced in the Southern Campaign and at Yorktown, the sorrow he'd caused Mary, and not long since to Ben's family. Junior's idolizing presence made all the difference, and the pain was set aside for a time.

Occasionally, however, in the hour before dawn, Mary found her husband standing over Junior staring at his sleeping child, unable to sleep himself with night dreams of remorse torturing him.

"That catch won't feed half of us," Mary teased, chiding her hunter-gatherers when they returned home sunburned and sweat soaked. "Good thing I stewed a chicken—at least each will get a morsel." Mary knew it was good for her husband to be with the boy.

That night after dinner, the stifling heat hung over them in the close quarters of the cabin. Mary finished the dishes and put the towel on the table. She followed the path of candlelight out onto the stoop. Standing there in the cool, fresh night air, her slim frame cast a long shadow over the yard. Jamie followed and wrapped his arms around her waist.

"Thank you for the turtle soup. It was delicious," Jamie whispered in her ear.

After thirty-one years of marriage, that's as romantic as it gets, Mary thought, smiling.

* * *

Samuel and his wife, Penelope, had a small farm close by his parents. Combining the brute strength of man and beast and the sheer determination of the pioneers, their cabin was erected, fencing put up, and a garden plot planted.

Mary secretly hoped that Penny and Samuel would have more babies soon and enjoy the happiness that other children would bring. She adored eight-year-old Sammy Junior, but two beloved daughters after him had died and rested in Virginia's dark soil. Mary cried afresh and prayed for her beloved family.

* * *

One snowy night in late December, Jamie, rocking in tandem with Mary, and just on the cusp of falling asleep in front of the fire, heard their cow bellowing in distress.

Berry's head appeared out of the darkness of the loft above. So as not to wake Junior, he whispered, "Did you hear that, Pa?"

But Junior did hear. Yawning and scratching his head, he asked, "What's happening?"

"Nothing, boy. Go back to sleep. Get dressed, Berry, and let's check on her. She's due anytime."

He grabbed his hat, and Mary placed the warm wool scarf around his neck as he put on a heavy coat. Jamie and Berry took their rifles from the pegs on the wall, and Mary set candles in the lanterns for them. When Jamie opened the door, the wind howled through the small cabin, whipping the snow in a froth across the wooden floor and Mary's rag rugs. The candles flickered, and the fire's sparks and warmth drew up the chimney. Mary said a silent prayer both for the cow and her men. Going out in that kind of weather was dangerous. She pulled her shawl closer around her shoulders and worried.

Plodding through drifts of heavy wind-blown snowfall was tedious indeed; their footprints immediately filling in behind them. Visibility was limited, and as they approached, Jamie lifted his lantern. On alert, they cocked their guns and cautiously approached the murky darkness within. Their ears were assailed by a terror-stricken yelp, and a large wolf flew out of the byre, knocking Jamie's rifle out of his hands, causing a misfire. Berry turned to see a heap of gray fur, limbs splayed, and red blood flowing onto the frozen snow. Fearful of another predator inside, Jamie and Berry cautiously entered the byre.

The two-year-old heifer was in extreme distress with sac and fluid on the byre's floor, and the calf's feet dangling behind her. Jamie lit another lantern and hung both in the stall.

Berry stroked her flank and slowly approached her head, all the while talking softly to her as he had done so many times before. She lay down, and the contractions continued until the birth sac was completely out. After a few minutes of rest, she stood and turned toward her baby, broke the sac, and nudged it with her nose. The calf struggled to stand on the wet floor, and with a few wobbly steps, the calf suckled for the first time.

In that time just before dawn, they discovered bite marks in the heifer's back legs and reckoned the wolf had smelled the birthing and squeezed itself through a small breach in the byre door. The heifer, having none of it, kicked the predator away from her unborn calf just at the time Jamie and Berry were entering the byre.

The men cleaned the stall and put down some fresh straw for mother and baby.

With the byre door secure, they labored through the deep pristine snow drifts back to the house but stopped short, pleased at the sight. Jamie's favorite time of the day was the gloaming, but in all his years, he had never seen that scene played out before them as it did on this fine day. The snow had stopped and lay about in softened forms covering the land and their homestead. Their breath hung in the ice-cold air, and with the dawn parting the earth from the sky, ambient blue light enveloped the virgin valley where they chose to settle. Jamie clapped Berry on the shoulder and smiled a wide grin. Smoke spiraled from a new fire, and a whiff of hot coffee invited them home.

* * *

March was a muddy month, warm one day and cold the next. As Hannah milked the cow, the kitten toddled toward her and sat in the straw to watch the curious goings-on. Quite suddenly a stream of warm sweet milk hit the small brown fur ball squarely in the face. Scared, the kitten hurried back to the safety of its mother, but when it stopped and pawed its face, the kitten found the milk was delicious, and it sat patiently watching.

"So, you're back?" And she sent another stream from the cow's teat at the fur ball.

This time the kitten didn't hurry away but opened wide her mouth to receive the warm sweet milk, surprised that it wasn't coming from her mother.

"I think I'll call you…Whishy, because you have a white throat under your chin." The kitten mewed loudly as Hannah finished filling the bucket.

There was a snickering outside the barn door.

"Johnny! Is that you out there?" Silence.

"John, if you're trying to scare me, it's not working." Leaving her chores, Hannah stuck her head outside the door and turned it from side to side, expecting to see her eldest brother.

"It's me."

"Me who?" she asked, teasing the one behind the barn door.

"Me…Junior. Hi, Hannah," he said, leaving his hiding place.

"Why are you hiding from me? I always like to see you."

Hannah delivered the bucket of milk to her mother and asked if she could stay out and walk awhile with the Kimsey boy.

"Yes, you may go, but be back to help me with dinner," her mother requested.

"Yes, ma'am. Come on, Junior. First, let me get the kitten."

They went down toward the creek, but Junior froze, stopping short at some big boulders above the water. "Can we sit in the grass up here on the bank?"

Hannah had advanced a little further, hoping to walk alongside the running stream. It was peaceful there; she liked hearing the sweet sound of gurgling and watching the silver-spotted fish chasing each other in the current. Opening her mouth to protest, she stopped short, remembering his fear. "Sure, we can," she hollered. "There's a better view from up there anyway. I'm glad you came to visit me."

Braced against a rock, Junior's fearfulness subsided as soon as she joined him. The kitten squirmed in her pocket. Hannah gently took it from her apron and placed it in the grass between them. The wee thing wanted back on her lap but was too weak to accomplish the task.

"Do you want to hold her?" she asked, panting from the climb. "I'm calling her Whishy because of the white under her throat. It's a Scottish word Pa taught me. The cow has it too." She placed the ball in his hands.

"Ouch! Whishy bit me. What sharp teeth she has. I don't think she likes me." He gave the kitten back to Hannah. Whishy wobbled a bit, and its head lolled to the side until Hannah placed it in her lap where the little thing promptly fell asleep, purring.

Hannah watched the creek going about its business, but Junior could only stare at the beautiful girl beside him. "Your hair is so pretty, Hannah. I noticed it from the first time I saw you in your Pa's wagon the day I almost…" His voice trailed off.

"I was so scared for you," she said softly, tears flowing onto her apron. She wiped her eyes with the backs of her hands.

"I'm sorry. I didn't mean to make you cry. Please don't cry, Hannah. May I touch your hair?"

He held a soft strand, which was certainly the nicest thing he'd ever felt. She took his hand and touched it to her cheek and held it there for a while.

"I think we should go back. Mother will be needing me to help give the little ones their Saturday night baths and then set the table for dinner."

"Hannah, wait." He leaned over and kissed her cheek, the same one to which she had held his hand. She smiled in the pleasant feeling, then quickly kissed his lips.

* * *

"Did you have a nice time with Junior, dear?"

"Yes, Ma." Hannah set the wood bowls and spoons on the table, but her wise mother noticed her eldest daughter had more than a friend in that Kimsey boy. Her cheeks were flushed. *From the walking, or the kissing?* she wondered.

* * *

Junior ran through the field, slithered under the cross-log fence, and hurried straight to the house where his father was in the yard sharpening the scythe. Junior sat himself down on the porch step, watching.

"Where've you been, boy?" Jamie never missed a turn of the grindstone, sharpening the blade to a good edge, his leg constantly turning the stone in endless circles. The screech of the metal on the stone rang through the hot late-afternoon air.

"At the McCrackens'. Can I try, Pa?"

"Not yet. Your legs need to grow a little more before you can reach the pedal. I'll tell you what you can do. Help me put the grindstone away." They walked it to the shed.

"Their cat had kittens, Pa. Hannah let me hold one, but it bit me right through my finger."

"Well, your Ma can fix that. Let's go in for dinner. I'm famished."

"Me too." He took hold of his father's hand. Jamie lovingly looked at his little son by his side.

1793

"Whoa, Gracie Lou." He stopped to adjust his hat and wipe the sweat from his face, his mule grateful for the respite. As Jamie worked that spring, the strong rich smell of the plough-turned earth and the aroma of fresh sweet grass and flowers bothered by bees made him think of heaven. *It surely must be*, he thought. Then with a mere flick of the plough line, his command was gentle, "Git up, girl." The animal was happy to oblige. All his livestock seemed happy to oblige whether they be hens laying in their nests or fat, corn-fed pigs grunting in their mud wallow. When he first came to Virginia, he had those sturdy Conestoga horses MacDonald had given him, but when they were no more, mules were the chosen work animal. Back and forth, he cut the ground, acre after acre yielding fishing-pole worms Junior kept in a jar with holes poked in the lid.

Through the frayed linen curtain, Mary saw her men coming up the trail from the fields and dumped water into the basin in the dry sink. Her eyes sparkled in mischief when they entered. "Wash up, my hardworking farmers. Come in and join the others of your family waiting patiently for your return. Eat and drink. You must be exhausted with all that backbreaking work you do."

Jamie eyed her suspiciously. "What are you up to, wife?"

She went about her work ladling soup into their bowls and setting bread on the table, never mind the meal took the entire morning to prepare, and the evening meal was cooking in the Dutch oven over the hearth; a pile of needy clothing requiring mending awaited her hand; and even before she sat in her chair, Jamie tore a loaf into pieces, dropping them into the bowl, and began talking with Berry about the planting.

"So, you can't even wait for your wife and mother to seat herself? Am I to eat alone when you go back to the fields?" Mary was getting vexed and in rising ill humor with her family. She knew her place and would complain with a hope of sympathy, but muddy boot prints spread over her freshly swept floor. *They don't even notice*, she thought.

Junior did notice something was wrong. "We forgot to thank the Lord, Pa," he said with the spoon halfway to his mouth.

"Sorry, boy." Jamie was chagrined. He swallowed and bowed his head. "God, we thank you for this bounty spread out before us and which we have grown to your honor and glory. Amen." He stuffed his mouth with a crust.

"And, God, we thank you for our Ma who made this delicious soup." In all his innocence, the wee lad gave his mother thankful appreciation for her labor, and when Jamie left for the fields, Junior held back and swept his mother's floor.

* * *

Jamie announced he and Berry would go to Bean Station and trade his hand-hewn tools for deerskin pelts at the fort, buy supplies they needed, and possibly barter for a bull.

"I'll miss you, dear one," Mary said, trying not to show the fear she felt of being left alone and exceedingly worried about the danger of the trip itself.

"We'll get back as soon as we can." Jamie kissed her cheek. "Samuel and Penny are close by if you need help."

But Mary cried when he left, worn thin by the work of her hands. Her tears would not abate no matter how hard she tried. At forty-nine, the years weighed heavily upon her, and she enumerated her losses. Sarah, their daughter, had died as an infant when she and Jamie were first married. There was no longer a close companionship with Aggie, her dear adopted mother and loving friend—*God, I wished Jamie hadn't torn our family in two like that. We could have talked it through.* She only confessed that to herself, never wanting to hurt her husband further on top of the guilt he already suffered. Because of his own temper, he had lost his brother Benjamin. Continuing her burden of woe, Mary's sister, Rebecca, was only a long-ago memory as she settled in Wales with the Reverend Beecham. Eleanor, her eldest daughter and an accomplished clothier, lived with Benjamin and Aggie until such time she would wed the young tailor she loved. Mary wondered if she would ever hear about the marriage or grandchildren. *How I miss them all.*

Suddenly, her bundle of joy came rushing through the door, and her words rushed out to greet him. "Sit down, Junior. Here's a little cake and some milk for you. You remember Father said they would check the traps on the way back. It'll probably be at least three to four days or possibly a week before they return. We'll need to be watchful, son. Oh, and bring in some more firewood."

"Yes, Ma." He finished his cake and cup of milk and rushed outside to do his chores.

While churning her cream, Mary wished for her daughter Elizabeth's return. At nineteen, she stayed with the McCrackens to help take care of their young children. A plain, quiet woman, not given to argument or cunning, her strength was the love of children, but Mary wondered if Lizzie would ever find a good husband in this wilderness.

There were enough supplies to hold Mary and Junior until the men returned. She busied herself with sewing and thought they'll all need warm gloves before the coming winter. The wolf's hide was waiting to be made into lining for hoods and moccasins as well. She sighed.

A few days after the men left, Junior went to the byre to check on the calf. Mary was sitting on the porch in her favorite rocker—the one that Jamie made especially for her—patching Berry's overalls. Without warning, Junior screamed at the top of his lungs. Mary flung her sewing down and grabbed the gun propped against the railing. Running toward the byre, she didn't get far when a furtive Indian came through the door with the boy wiggling mightily in his arms. From behind, another Indian was struggling with the calf. Neither was ready for what they faced—a white woman taking dead aim at their heads, gun cocked, and waiting. She squinted through the sight and put her finger on the trigger. Despite her terror, Mary held her ground, her long skirt shifting in the breeze, hiding her knocking knees.

Mary did not recognize the voice coming from her throat. In controlled rage, she barked orders, "Put my son down! I know you understand what I'm saying. I heard you both speaking our language at the fort." They hesitated. She took one step closer. Junior's eyes were wide with fear.

"Put my son down!" she commanded in measured cadence.

Mary, fearful she might shoot her son, had one chance with one shot, and took another step closer. "Remember what your Pa told you, boy?" Junior went slack, and the Indian lost his grip. The other dropped the calf, and Mary's ball took the ear off one, and whistled through the hair of the other. Both ran like the very devil was after them.

With her ears ringing from the blast, Mary nearly fainted after they left, but staggering to the porch steps, she sat and wept tears of relief. She took her beloved boy on her lap. Junior hugged her tight. "Ma, don't cry," he said, caressing her face until she stopped shaking. They clung to each other for a long while.

Late the next afternoon, Mary rocked in her chair on the porch enjoying the warmth of the day's final hours. She fingered the extra lead ball in her apron pocket. Junior played close by with his wooden top winding the cord around the axis. He let it go several times setting it to a dizzying speed—the last spin headed straight for the gun sitting at an arms distance from his mother. She caught the top just in the nick of time.

"Junior, be careful, son. Play with it on the ground."

"Yes, ma'am." He hung his head, not liking the uneven ground which wouldn't allow it such a good spin. The porch boards, even with the gaps between, were much better, and if you did it just right, the top spun perfectly without getting stuck. He let it go again and watched it twirl round and round in the dirt for a good distance, but abruptly the sounds of wagons and mules racing into the yard caught his attention. A cloud of dust arose around them with the mules in a lather and their nostrils flaring. Jamie and Berry flew off the seats.

"What in God's name went on here yesterday?" Jamie's face burned bright with concern.

Berry pressed his mother. "Are you all right? Two Indians came into the fort with incoherent stories of some wild woman scaring the skins off them. We pushed the mules as fast as they could to get to you."

Junior's chest swelled with pride. "You should've see her, Pa. I didn't know if Ma could do it, but she held those old Indians off and told me to do what you said, 'stop struggling and go slack.' They didn't know what to do, Pa, and I just run like a scared jackrabbit."

"Junior, help your brother unload the wagon and let the team out to pasture." When they went off to their chores, Jamie took her in his arms. "Oh, my love. You are such a brave and beautiful soul. If I'd lost you…my life would be worth nothing…nothing…I promise you, I'll never leave you and Junior alone again."

The news of the standoff and threat of Indian encroachment put the lone farmers in the valley on alert, but there were no more incidents with Indians that year. Junior later found his top hiding under a mountain laurel tree, and Mary found peace in the warm embrace of her family.

* * *

One beautiful autumnal day, glorious in the valley's first coloring, Mack stopped by the Kimsey homestead, bringing Lizzie with him. He pulled up his team. "Whoa, boys." Mack jumped down from the wagon. "I brought your daughter back home as we have no need of her services anymore," he said as Jamie came from the byre to greet his friend. Mary came from the cabin, wiping her hands on her apron, surprised to see Lizzie home. She invited Mack in to discover why.

Jamie poured the last of their Apfelwein, purchased in the spring at Bean Station and reminiscent of Hermann Ensch's hard cider years ago.

"Delicious," Mack said after taking his first taste. "Truly an amazing flavor."

"It's a great story I'd like to tell you sometime," Jamie said, dreading what was coming.

"Wish I had the time." He took another sip, as if fortifying himself for what he was about to say.

"What has happened?" Mary was apprehensive.

Mack took a deep breath, and Lizzie sniffled in the background. "We're leaving the valley."

"But why? Where are you going?" The dread was realized. Jamie could not deal with the thought of their friends leaving.

Mack explained, "We're going back to South Carolina. With Mollie's mother sick and my brother unwilling to care for the family homestead, it is imperative that we go." He said they would remain there until matters were settled then come back to the valley as soon as they could.

The announcement was a stunning blow, especially to Junior. What would he do without the golden-haired girl he'd come to love? But Lizzie had a small treat for him from Hannah. The young cat named Whishy had come to live with the Kimseys.

* * *

The sparse homesteads in the valley produced an abundant first harvest that September. Jamie, Berry, and Samuel needed Mack as the fourth hand, so with him gone back to Union County, they enlisted the help of Mary, Lizzie, and Penny. Junior drove the wagon pulled by Gracie Lou and her brother Taddy. At eight years old, Junior was becoming quite a hand with those mules. He'd grown two inches since his arrival in the valley and was nearly up to his father's shoulder. The women tied on their bonnets and tucked up their skirts. Shoulder to shoulder, the trio harvested the corn in cadence to the tune of an old Baptist hymn.

> Must Jesus bear the cross alone,
> And other saints be free?
> Each saint of thine shall find his own
> And there is one for me.
> Whene'er it falls unto my lot,
> Let it not drive me from my God,

Let me ne'r be forgot
Till thou hast lov'd me home.

"Why did we leave North Carolina?" Mary complained, pushing her hair back from her forehead and placing the drooping bonnet back where it belonged. A mischievous wind had caused the strings to become undone.

Lizzie laughed. "For a better life, Mother. Where's your spirit of adventure? Keep singing."

The words of "Must Jesus Bear the Cross Alone," sung by the women's sweet voices, made the work go faster—and a little easier. Sister Penny's harmony made the cross of hard work almost bearable.

After each backbreaking day, the work was still not done with animals to be fed and watered and milked, and a supper of cold porridge to set upon the table. More than once, Junior, doing the milking, caught himself falling asleep and nearly dumping the bucket onto the straw-covered floor. Mary reminded Jamie that a hog needed butchering, and Junior should learn by watching. The boy was already capable of providing a plucked chicken or skinned rabbit for the pot and feathers for a mattress or fur for gloves.

* * *

Another winter came, and Penny was with child. Mary was beside herself with happiness and began sewing clothes for the little one. Her heart forgot her vexation and sadness and rejoiced with the thrilling prospect holding a baby again.

Chapter 31

The Talk

"Her water broke," Samuel said, greeting his family at the cabin door. Unruffled as ever, he had his arms full of cloths and a bucket filled with hot water steaming in the cold winter air.

Ever the calm one, Samuel, as a ten-year-old following the bitter storm of 1771, had left the safety of the root cellar with his father to assess the damage to their home and crops. "We can fix it, Father" was his guiding principle then, and with family, they began the process of moving on. He was similarly stouthearted by Jamie's side when they fought in the Southern Campaign. The only time Mary saw Samuel angry was when Jamie went missing for those years after the war, but even then, Samuel "fixed it" for his mother.

The women hurried into the cabin, doffing coats and scarves, and rolling up their sleeves. Penny was gripping a beam to the side of the hearth and holding her belly, moaning in the waves of pain. Lizzie and Mary helped her to the bed, but the baby decided it would see the light of day before Penny reclined. Lizzie hiked up Penny's shift, and Mary was there to catch the wee one as he slipped from his mother's womb. The sound of the child's cry carried over the quiet snow and into the byre where men, and it seemed even the animals, awaited the birth. Lizzie called to Samuel to come see his son, and there was rejoicing in the Kimsey home.

After Samuel went in the house, Jamie and Junior lingered in the byre with the stock. A cow, a horse, and a few chickens were all he had. Junior stepped up on a board of the stall and petted the back of the bay with the beautiful black mane and tail.

"Pa. How'd you meet Ma?"

"Oh, I guess I've never told you." Jamie was feeding the horse hay while patting the animal's strong neck. "Well, she and her sister, Rebecca, came to live with the MacDonalds when we were indentured servants to them in Baltimore. Mary was a very little girl—just four years old—and I was seven. She used to chase me all over the place. Drove me crazy!" He stopped and smiled, remembering their games. "Your Aunt Agnes, my dear little mother, needed help when she was pregnant with Benjie, and the girls were a godsend."

"When did you know you loved Ma?"

Jamie was trying to figure out where this conversation was going. "Well, I guess I always knew, then when she went back to Wales with her sister, I was afraid she'd forget me, but she didn't. Why do you ask?"

"Oh…just wondering."

"I'm wondering what Hannah is thinking about right now?"

Junior's eyes brightened.

"You miss her, don't you?"

The boy valiantly fought back tears.

Jamie went around the stall and hugged his son. "I'm thinkin' you'll see her again. Let's go inside and see the new baby. Maybe we can get a good cup of hot coffee."

Jamie winced when he heard that his own brother's name was chosen for the little baby boy—Benjamin Kimsey. Smiles went around the circle of happy family members, but Mary hurt for her husband when she saw his face and knew his heart.

* * *

"Look what Whishy caught, Ma." The long tail of a rather large rat hung out of the cat's mouth.

"That's nice, dear. You take it outside and let her have her feast. That cat is a good mouser."

Lizzie remained behind to help Penny and her newborn, and was most pleased to be with a baby again.

The heavy snow lasted another two weeks until a warm spell hit, sending puddles to the edges of the drifts. Jamie took advantage of the lull to check for leaks in the roof, shoveling off the remaining mass that trickled like rain on the overhang. There were none. The windows were snug and dry as well. He cut a path to the byre and forked hay from the loft and into the troughs and made sure the animals had water. Soupy melted snow was everywhere, and mud stuck to his every step.

"Rake out the byre, Junior. Then we'll put down fresh straw."

The sky was clear blue, and he did not smell another storm on the heels of the last.

"It's warmed up considerably," he commented, entering the house and shedding his heavy coat. "I'll chop some wood later. What's for supper, Mary?"

Junior was on his Pa's heels. "I'm hungry, too, Ma."

"Wash up," she said. "Chicken and biscuits. Beans for dinner. Maybe tomorrow, Jamie, if the weather holds, you could check your traps for a nice fat rabbit. I could fry it up just the way you like it, Junior." She smiled at the boy and placed the iron skillet on the table. White gravy bubbled up around the browned biscuits. Dried green peas cooked plump, and great orange rounds of carrots colored the delicious-looking dish.

"My favorite, Ma."

She laughed lightly. "Everything's your favorite, son."

Overnight it froze, and when a weak sun rose the next morning, storm clouds shot over the mountains and raced down the valley. Jamie went out to check the closest traps and did find that rabbit for Junior. When he started back, mud and debris were encased in a sheet of ice. Even though he stepped with great care, his feet went out from under him, and he could hear the break of his shoulder as it slammed against an ice-covered tree stump.

Lying prone on the trail and in severe pain, Jamie could not move. Fear seized him. Alone in the wilderness, there was no chance of survival in the sharp and violent cold. He was foolish for letting himself get caught, but he let his love for his son blind him to the elements. While regretting his mistake, he forced himself to think and listen for anything familiar.

He could hear the stream's current where he found the rabbit in the trap. The frost's crackling was audible as it formed in twisted angles of ice in the water. Tree branches scratched together in a rising wind over the rime-covered land, and frozen droplets on clumps of stiff dried grasses were ripped cruelly from those straight sentinels along the trail. He fought unconsciousness by calculating how far off he was from the path to his home. Was it feet, yards, or miles? Confused, he couldn't remember. The weak setting sun filtered through the trees, shifting shadows. Snow began to fall.

Shivering, he thought about his cabin with hearth, candle, and the love of his family warming its interior. They sat around the table, the one he fashioned with his own hands, and ate Mary's good food placed upon it.

Close by, Jamie thought he heard men talk and horses whicker,[25] but neither he nor the phantasms—if that's what they were—could see the other in the snowfall. He begged for charity with icy lips, but received none—*even the dogs under the table receive scraps from their master, Lord*, he prayed. The children would take care of Mary when he was gone, but Junior, he would miss his special boy, the one born out of loss and gain. Jamie cried, and wayward tears froze along his cheeks. His body would be buried soon and found only when spring came. Death was surely on him. He gave in. His breath stopped, and his dead mother's voice was heard. "Not yet, my son. Not yet. You have more love to give."

* * *

---

[25] Whicker: the sound a horse makes in anticipation.

Jamie awoke in his warm bed with powerful hands roughly handling his shoulder. "It's not a break," said the man who stood over him. "Let's sit him up. Right. Now hold on, Mr. Kimsey. This is gonna to hurt like hell," he said, and immediately snapped Jamie's shoulder back into place. Jamie groaned in agony. "Bind him well, missus. He shouldn't use it for a few months."

Jamie winced in pain as Mary wrapped and tied the cloth around her husband. She kissed his forehead. "Lie back, sweetheart, and rest. I'll bring hot soup for you. Junior will keep you company."

The boy crawled onto the bed and sat beside his father. "Does it hurt awful, Pa?"

"Yes, son. It hurts awful bad." Jamie turned his face away, not wanting Junior to see his tears. But Junior did see and drew closer to his father. His small arm gently slipped around Jamie's neck, and for the first time, he saw his father suffering.

When Mary returned with hot soup, Jamie—with the effects of laudanum finally giving him rest—and Junior, curled up next to him, were both fast asleep.

The next morning, Jamie awoke to throbbing pain and Junior's big eyes staring down at him. "Help me up, boy. I gotta move."

"I don't think you should, Pa. Your shoulder…"

Jamie threw back the covers with his left arm. "Come here and give me a hand up."

The cabin was quiet and comfortably warm. Mary was asleep in her rocking chair, and Berry was just coming in carrying a bundle of firewood. The icy blast of the open door caused Jamie to shudder, realizing that yesterday he very nearly lost his life. *Did my mother really come to me?* he wondered and brushed it off as one of those phantasms.

"What are you doing out of bed, Pa?" Berry asked, thinking it was pointless to trouble his stubborn father with a silly question. "Here, sit by the fire. I'll stoke it and get some coffee going."

"How did they find me, Berry?"

Berry poked at the dwindling fire with an iron and set another log on it. "I went out to look for you and came across some men along the trail. That big longhunter who fixed your shoulder last night is Clark Biggerstaff. He and his partner were coming north from Knoxville to look for deer. There's a fort south of us and a settlement. The men are still here."

Mary awoke from a deep sleep and saw her husband out of bed. She wanted to scold him. It would do no good, but she frowned at him anyway.

Lizzie climbed down the loft's ladder to help her mother. "Mornin', Ma," she said.

"Mornin', daughter. I see your obstinate father didn't listen to Mr. Biggerstaff last night."

Jamie hurt too bad to argue.

"Good mornin' the house." It was the voice of the man who set Jamie's shoulder.

"Come inside and welcome, sir," Jamie greeted him.

"Ah, Mr. Kimsey. How are you feeling?"

"I'm alive, thanks to you and my son."

"You were lucky we heard you. Another few minutes and you would have been a-knockin' at those pearly gates it says in the Bible. A seasoned farmer like yourself—"

Jamie interrupted the man, "The weather changed on me... Should have known better. Thank you, Mr. Biggerstaff."

"Call me Clark." His partner was close on his heels. "This is my friend, Jim White, lieutenant colonel commandant of the Knox County Militia."

White pushed back his fur-lined hood and removed his gloves and strode to Jamie, taking his left hand in greeting. "Glad to see you alive, sir."

Clearly there was a houseful of people. Berry brought benches from the porch into the cabin, took their coats, and made coffee. There was hot water for tea and porridge to eat, and Junior protested wildly when he was sent to milk the cow as he would be away from the interesting gentlemen. However, when Junior was busy at his chore, Mr. White came into the byre. The cow lowed, and Junior brushed her side with his hand. With long practice, he easily exchanged one nearly full pail to put an empty one under her with no break in the milking. The rhythmic splash of the warm sweet milk always made him hungry.

"It's a good family you have there, boy. Your brother took proper care of our animals, and I'm most grateful," he said, patting his horse's flank. "How long have you lived here in the valley?"

"A couple of years, sir. Moved here from Buncombe County with the McCrackens. They came all the way from South Carolina but went back shortly after."

Mr. White could see the youngster's face grow serious. "Oh, they went back. I'll bet it's kind of lonely so far away from your neighbors, isn't it?"

"Yes, sir. My brother Samuel and Penny—they have a new baby and another boy my age—live just a mile away, so it's not so bad. I do wish Hannah—I mean the McCrackens, that is—were back."

"Did they have children too?"

"Yes, sir."

"Looks like you have enough milk there for two full buckets. Let me help with that, and we'll have a nice chat over breakfast with your Pa and Ma."

Coming in from the byre, Mr. White left his bucket and excused himself. He went to the horses and untied from the travois a large bag of cornmeal from his own gristmill, and a deer haunch. "These are for you," he said to Jamie, coming back into the cabin. Then he posed a question to his hosts. "Have you had any run-ins with the Cherokee since you've been here?" From the look on their faces, he guessed they had.

Over the meal, he began, "Back in '86, I built a fort, and now there's a new settlement growing around it called Knoxville. It's at the confluence of the French Broad and Holston Rivers which both flow into the Tanasi River. The town was named for Henry Knox, our first secretary of war. You may remember him from the revolution, Mr. Kimsey."

Jamie nodded but only had scant memories of him from the *Virginia Gazette* years ago. His pain was getting worse.

"We're looking for pioneers like yourselves to be a part of that town. It's been platted for sixty-four-acre lots. There's a waterfront, a

First Presbyterian church, and four lots set aside for a school for boys like yours."

Junior was sitting with Berry on a bench, and the brothers looked at each other wide-eyed and very much excited about a formal school.

"And we have a newspaper called the *Knoxville Gazette*. I'll leave you a copy. You can see for yourself information about our governor, William Blount. He was appointed by President Washington three years ago for the Territory South of the River Ohio, they call it. He's from North Carolina—perhaps you may know him?"

Jamie was trying to concentrate through his pain and the muddle of laudanum Mary gave him. The family was excited by the visiting gentlemen talking about the new town, especially Lizzie. There was a connection between Clark Biggerstaff and his daughter. He noticed and then promptly fell asleep.

"Oh my God! Jamie," Mary cried out. "Let's get him to bed. Too much excitement for him…I told him, but he wouldn't listen. Stubborn Scot! Lizzie, see to our guests."

"I'm so sorry, Mrs. Kimsey. I think we've overstayed our welcome. Come on, Jim, I think we should be going," Clark said. "You're mighty isolated up here, folks. Give a thought to moving closer in."

Berry and his mother were able to carry Jamie to the bedroom. He was always thin with a spare behind, he'd say, so it wasn't difficult to lift him.

Junior walked out with the gentlemen, and Lizzie followed after retrieving two small cakes she'd made.

"Mr. Biggerstaff, these are for you and Mr. White on your journey back to Knoxville. We so enjoyed your visit, and I should like to see your town someday." She looked up at him—an attractive and imposing figure sitting astride his horse. He took the package, touching her hand with his. "It was like a lightning bolt between us," she told her mother later.

The gentlemen rode off. Lizzie stood there in the cold snow and watched them go down the trail. Clark turned back to look and raised his hand. She waved back.

"Come on, Lizzie." Junior pulled on her sleeve. "I'm freezing out here, and what about Pa? Thank you for the supplies, sir," he hollered after the visitors, and they were enveloped by the dark forest along the trail and disappeared from sight.

* * *

Jamie's shoulder felt better after a few weeks. The days grew longer, and the snow receded to the shadows of the valley. The last frost melted into the ground, and it was time to plough. But a thought nagged at him, and he brought the family together on a Sunday afternoon. Jamie read from the Bible after their supper. "From Ecclesiastes chapter 3 we read, 'To every thing there is a season, and a time to every purpose under the heaven: A time to be born, and a time to die; a time to plant, and a time to pluck up that which is planted.' While we've been lucky having had only one incident with the Cherokee, after reading Knoxville's newspaper, I believe we may be vulnerable to more attacks. We seem to be in the center of their land, and I fear for our lives. What would you think of moving closer to the fort and new town?"

"You've never asked us before, Father," Samuel offered. "As for me and mine, we would follow you anywhere."

Jamie was truly humbled by his son's trust. "I know, but we've always had Benjamin and his large family for support and protection. In my rage, I have endangered us all."

Berry looked around at the faces of his loved ones sitting at the table. "I'm in. Wouldn't mind trying that fancy school Mr. White talked about. How about you, Junior? Would you like to go?"

"But what about the McCrackens? What if they come back and don't find us here?" Junior's face could not hide his emotions.

From across the table, Mary took Jamie's hands in hers. "We could try it for a while. Lizzie, what do you think?" She knew what her daughter would say.

"I'd like it, too, especially that nice Mr. Biggerstaff." She could not hide her smile.

After all had left, Junior could not sleep and sneaked out of the loft, down the ladder and to the front window. He looked through the streaked window glass, staring at the yard and trees washed by beautiful moonlight. The pane was cold against his fingertips. But what about Hannah?

* * *

It was a fine spring morning when they started out. The bloom on the countryside was spreading its fragrance, and Jamie breathed deeply of it. The last of the canvas was tied down, and everyone but Junior was ready to go. Mary went inside their empty cabin to make sure nothing was left behind and found her son.

"What are you doing, boy? Everyone is waiting for you. We're ready to leave, and…you haven't even packed your belongings yet. What is the matter with you?" Mary was thoroughly exasperated.

"I don't want to go," Junior screamed at his mother. "I don't want to traipse to Knoxville. I don't want to go to school. What if Hannah comes back and we're not here? She's gonna wonder why I left her. Can't we stay, Ma? Please can't we stay?" His pleading watery brown eyes were breaking her heart.

Junior seemed to grow right before her very eyes. This wasn't a childish love; this was a nine-year-old with a man's heart. He actually loved the girl. A feeling of motherly jealousy passed over her, which she thought unseemly. But not so maybe, because she herself had loved Jamie when she was only four. It didn't come to fruition until much later, but here was her dear son in love with Hannah, the young blonde McCracken girl.

"Why don't you write her a note? That way, if they come back, and she comes by the cabin, then Hannah will know where you are. Would that make you happy?"

"Yes, Ma." He was suddenly a shy boy again and hugged his mother tight.

The family was holding the reins and awaiting Mary and Junior. Down the trail they went toward another adventure. Choosing his own path, Junior walked beside his cousin Sammy. Jamie looked back in astonishment that their youngest didn't want to sit with his parents.

"What happened?" Jamie asked, smiling.

"He's growing up, husband. He's growing up."

* * *

About fifty miles, Mr. White had said. Just follow the trail south. Knoxville is where the three rivers meet. The trail—if you could call it that—was just wide enough for their wagons; however, the Conestoga's larger height and breadth caught tree branches as it rattled along and threw them backward, causing those who walked behind to have a care. These trails were mostly used by bison and other animals for routes to salt licks in places only they, and the Indians who hunted them, knew about. They were also paths for warring tribes from the north and for longhunters bringing in pioneers seeking those Indian lands for their settlements. Jamie had seen those longhunters at Bean Station when his family came to Tanasi.

As they traveled along the Great Valley, there were elongated heavily wooded ridges on either side. Once in a while, trees opened to large meadows with streams sparkling in the midday sun. The hum of bugs, birds, and small mammals was audible to one who listened for them. It was no wonder, with sights and sounds such as these, that movement west was so enticing to those hungry for land. Jamie could have put down roots anywhere along this valley, watered abundantly by the long river, but the Cherokee hunted this place and didn't like interlopers on their lands.

It took two and a half days before the family finally spotted settlers' cabins and farms set close together. When they arrived, they saw Jim White's cabin, sitting on a bluff overlooking the vast river. It was in a quadrangle of several fortified log structures surrounded by an eight-foot-high wooden palisade. On the land side was Governor Blount's large mansion. The Kimseys rode right up to the fort.

White and Clark Biggerstaff just happened to be coming from his cabin and welcomed the families.

"How did you get through?" Clark asked in surprise, searching the faces of the family.

"Why do you ask?" Jamie said.

"We've had a dispatch from some longhunters down from Bean Station. They said there was some violence among the settlers and the Cherokee up by your place. Many have been burned out, and there was killing on both sides. It's a miracle you made it out alive. Let's get you folks settled. There's a piece of nice bottomland 'bout a quarter mile south with some others who moved closer in to the fort. Set up there and come here immediately if there is danger. Do you need anything?"

"No, sir. We have everything necessary for a while," Jamie replied.

The men shook hands, and Jamie noticed Clark's hopeful glance toward Lizzie.

"Those cakes you gave Jim and me were fine victuals, Miss Kimsey, and I'm really glad you made it through."

Chapter 32

Knoxville

THE KIMSEY FAMILY, being of the land, had never lived in a town. Jamie remembered visiting Inverness one time when Robert, his father, carried him on his shoulders to buy a horse. The well-trampled road to the castle on the bluff over the River Ness was muddy with carts and animals, locals in worn woolens, men in red uniforms, and women wrapped in moth-eaten shawls and threadbare skirts, all trailing in the muck of the busy village. Odors of fish and cooking, peat fires, urine, and feces cast a pall over hovels and stone buildings that made up the town. Men and women hawked wares. Chickens cackled. Geese honked. Dogs barked. It was an unwelcome cacophony to those who preferred fresh air and the solitude of their lords' lands.

Baltimore, Maryland, had been a large port city, but the family was too busy working as indentured servants for Mr. MacDonald then, and visits to the city were rare. When he did go, Jamie remembered refined citizens wearing nicer clothing—men in fine coats and breeches and women in fancy dresses. Taverns and churches, dances and banquets, and all the crowds of a busy life were more than he could stand for more than half a day. He simply preferred the solitude of crops growing at the master's farm.

In Bedford and Henry Counties, where small towns had sprouted, pioneers built fine wooden or brick homes and birthed aspiring politicians, lawyers, and statesmen. Bedford had been a terror for Benjamin, and when weather destroyed what the Kimsey family created, they moved to Henry.

The family had left Virginia for North Carolina to a new county called Buncombe, a settlement where the quiet of their farms was pleasing to the ears, and the wholesome sounds of nature satisfied their souls. But, Jamie's restlessness crept into his thoughts in the evenings when the work of his fields was done and the work of his hands began—fashioning tools or toys. But, in the gloaming or on starry nights, after the children were put to bed, Mary would find Jamie on the porch always searching the sky toward the land in the west. Now they were here, in Knoxville with the Cherokee. In the past, small towns swelling to cities had pushed the Indians away, and this new proximity of diverse populations was something he hadn't considered.

Knoxville was a new frontier town, surrounded by a stockade of timbers standing as high sentinels protecting a cluster of cabins— with human sentries ever vigilant for trouble. Plain cotton was worn by the women with mop caps on their heads and aprons tied around their waists. Buckskins and hunting shirts were worn by the men who scouted for Indians and sought meat for their tables.

Samuel quickly cleared a wagon to make a snug refuge for Penny and the baby. The rest of the family slept under their wagons as they cleared their small plot of land. Jamie worried about getting a permanent shelter for the family, but was warned not to do so until peace could be established between Governor Blount and the Indians. They erected a canvas tent supported by tree poles with a temporary shingle roof to protect it from rain.

Clark called on them one day and watched the progress of hewing each shingle by hand with hatchet and adze. He marveled at their work. Mary, Lizzie, and Penny—with the baby strapped to her back—went about cooking their midday meal. When Lizzie saw Clark approaching, she excitedly rubbed her hands clean of cornmeal remnants and pushed back locks of hair from her forehead. "There's a well-seasoned pot of shucky beans on the fire. Would you care to join us?" she asked hopefully.

Clark responded with a grin. The flour on her nose tickled him, and that red hair was a wonder. "Yes, if it's not too much bother. Are those leather breeches you're talking about…the kind you dry on strings? I remember my mother, bless her soul, sitting of an evening threading the surplus beans to feed us through the winter. But I wouldn't want to deprive anyone their due."

Jamie approached, noting the sparks between Clark and his daughter, and brushed wood shavings from his hands before taking Clark's hand in friendship. "We most assuredly welcome you to our camp, Mr. Biggerstaff, and to our repast."

"I brought more canvas for you. Looks like you could use it along the sides of that fine-looking shelter you're building."

The men talked away the afternoon discussing the peace talks. They were going well, Clark said, and the next day would tell the tale. He arose to leave, the boys said their goodbyes so they could finish their work before they lost the light, and the women went off to clean up. Clark tarried a bit and touched Jamie's arm. "May we talk, Mr. Kimsey?"

The pair walked off a few yards. "I didn't want to scare the women, but I think you and your sons should be prepared. These talks are a tricky business, and we never know what the sides are thinking. I will let you know by a sign if there is anything afoot that should concern you. But get your womenfolk into the fort if there is any inkling of trouble."

Jamie nodded in understanding but noted Clark hesitating. "Is there anything else you wanted to say, Mr. Biggerstaff? And please call me Jamie."

"I will, if you call me Clark. Uh…one last thing. Maybe untoward, but may I walk out with your daughter sometime, Mr. Kimsey? Sorry…Jamie?"

"She has a mind of her own, and yes, you surely could ask her." The men parted with a handshake. Jamie couldn't help but smile at that prospect, and he would study the character of this man who wished to 'walk out' with his cherished daughter. Clark was a man of resolute action, the trait of a Scot from the Isle of Skye.

Jamie stood on the bluff and followed the big south-flowing river with his practiced eye. How far did it run? It seemed never-ending. Did it discharge into other rivers and eventually to another ocean similar to the one they had crossed coming to this land? How high would it rise in the rainy seasons with the Holston and French Broad emptying into it? Being flooded out once in his life, Jamie did not relish the possibility again, but for now, the Kimsey men would plough the earth and tend the ground along the big river. He thought to himself, *There's still time for planting and harvesting a corn crop.*

* * *

Clark and White discussed the peace renegotiations and concluded they had gone well. They hoped they would not have any more trouble with the Cherokee. "We will keep close watch tonight for any trouble and double the sentries just in case," White ordered.

Clark was preparing to leave when they were interrupted by someone knocking at the cabin door. Jamie's lad, Junior, was standing there looking expectant.

"White, here's a young man who will follow in his pioneer father's footsteps. What can we do for you, son?"

"My name's Junior, sir, and I come with an invitation to share our victuals this evening."

"It would be most pleasant for me to do so." Clark winked at Jim when he left the cabin.

As they walked along back to the encampment, Junior said, "I hear you like my sister, Mr. Biggerstaff. Is that true?" Junior's remark caught Clark by surprise.

"I surely do. Would you think I might be worthy of her, young Kimsey?"

"Yes, sir...if you mind your manners."

What might have been a happy evening ended in panic. Halfway through their dinner, gunshots were heard from the ramparts of the fort responding to bloodcurdling cries coming from the forest and spreading over the settlement. Bursts of gunpowder and burning torches wagging through the fading evening light lit up the trees as outbuildings were set aflame. The terror of women's screams filled Knoxville, and citizens ran for the protection of the fort, some arriving with arrows following close on their heels.

The Kimseys were further out than most, and Clark stopped their flight toward the stockade. "Get under your wagons," he commanded while smothering the cooking fire with dirt. "Stay low, and keep the baby quiet," he said, moving forward toward the fort.

In the dust, Lizzie suppressed her desire to call after him, and Penny held the baby close to her bosom, muffling its cry. Clark was shot and landed hard on the ground, emitting a grunt and cursing his luck. His gun discharged as it fell with the ball smashing the leg of the offending enemy.

Jamie crawled after Clark. "Are you hurt?" he whispered.

"Shot in the arm. Nothing broke, but it hurts like hell."

Jamie and Clark made it back to the wagons, and Clark sat against a wheel. He was bleeding profusely. Lizzie was immediately by his side and helped him to remove his coat. She tied a cloth tightly around the wound.

* * *

The battle was short-lived. The militia was on alert while the wounded were pulled to safety, and all waited to see if the enemy would attack again. Others remained on guard on top of the palisade. Moving ever so slowly, the eyes of the living looked over the dreadful view of no less than forty bodies strewn about the surrounds of the fort. They were mostly Cherokee, but some citizens of Knoxville also lay dead amid smoking torches dying in the sunrise.

When it seemed safe and the wounded limped back to their homes, wives and children began searching for their loved ones. Jim White left the fort to search for Clark and, finding him well tended by the lovely Lizzie, said he would send a rider after Governor Blount who was returning to Virginia after the peace talks.

"We have to go after those who broke the treaty," White said forcefully.

Clark agreed and proceeded to gather men to go after those individual Cherokee who had resented the original treaty and were unable to be persuaded by their tribal members.

* * *

In the fall of 1794, the McCrackens returned to Tanasi from South Carolina only to find their home burned to the ground. Beautiful timber, hand hewn by Mack's and Jamie's boys, lay in a charred rubble. Mack was stunned. The family wandered the grounds looking for anything left behind, but nothing remained of their dwelling. What happened?

They traveled on to Samuel Kimsey's place and found a burned-out hovel. Mack sighed, then took in a quick breath. What about Jamie and his family? On down the road a mile, they found the same awful scene, and again the McCrackens picked through remnants of burned logs cold in their disarray. There was no sign of their neighbor's former home. What would they do? Mack had not the man-power to begin again.

Hannah began to cry. What happened to Junior? There were no signs of foul play, no bodies, no clothing, or pots and pans showing anyone had even lived there. She walked around the still-standing fireplace. The chimney had fallen inward and was just a pile of broken rubblestone. Something odd caught her eye. Bending over, there was writing on the floor of the fireplace. She pushed away debris on the hearth with her foot.

"Pa! Come quick!" Hannah hollered.

Mack was immediately by her side. "What is it, girl?"

"A message." She cleaned the surface, blackening her hand in the process.

> Deer Hannah We moved to Knocksvil.
> Come quick. I love you. Junior.

Their friends had moved south. Were they driven out by Indians? Were they all alive?

Mack's choices were limited to turning around and going back to Newberry or continuing on and finding Jamie.

"I'm at a loss, my family. What should we do?"

"Let us go south, dear. I don't like the look of this, and we know there is a settlement in Knoxville," Mollie pleaded.

The three oldest McCracken children spoke their minds. John, Jane, and Hannah, catching the concern in their mother's voice, said they should continue especially with winter coming on their heels. Mack turned his teams south toward their friends.

Chapter 33

The Reunion

JUNIOR SHARPENED THE ax blade to a good edge for his father, his legs finally long enough to turn the stone in endless circles. The screech of metal on grindstone rang through the crisp autumn air. Around him, maples burned red, and the golden glory of tulip trees caused him to pause and look up from his chore. His ears caught the sounds of horses, then his eyes focused on something emerging from the trail through the forest. It was a wagon, then a second and a third. Junior stood straddling the grindstone, staring toward the emerging scene. Jamie was coming from the byre, and Mary set foot outside their temporary cabin.

"Did you finish, boy?" his father asked.

Junior didn't answer, just staring toward the trees. Jamie turned around to see what was he was looking at.

"Pa...Pa! It's the McCrackens!" Junior nearly tripped as he sprinted toward their old friends.

Hannah ran past her family and straight into Junior's arms.

"You're taller," she said, holding him at arm's length.

"And so are you, Hannah." At eleven, she had blossomed in all the right places. Junior wanted so badly to kiss her the way Pa kissed Ma but thought it too forward.

Mack wondered what had happened and why the Kimseys were living in a temporary shelter. There was a lot to catch up on while sitting around the large campfire that night. The chilly air in mid-October required coats and blankets as they not only shared supper but also swapped stories about the time the families had been apart.

Mrs. Smith, Mack's mother-in-law, had died, and his brothers were straightened out about their farm in Newberry. They had paid Mack his fair share of the land. That was all there was to it, he said. The time for leaving South Carolina, when all was settled, was not opportune for them, and the McCrackens stayed another year. Come hell or high water, that prime land in Union County would either make or break his brothers. Mack didn't care because he had money enough, but now with his farm gone in Grainger County, they would have to start all over again.

"What happened up there?" Mack asked.

"After we left," Jamie said, "the Cherokee attacked the farmers, burning and pillaging nearly every family. Most got out with their lives, but some were murdered and scalped in their fields. A tragic event." He hung his head. "It was only by God's grace that we got out in time, on the advice of our new friend…Ah, here he is now."

Clark rode in to see Lizzie but instead found a large crowd in the Kimsey camp that night.

"Come have some supper with us. This is the McCracken family. Mack, meet Clark Biggerstaff," Jamie said with a big smile on his face.

The folks warmly greeted one another, and Mack especially embraced Lizzie. She was delighted to see them again, especially those young 'uns she'd looked after. How they had grown, and she noticed some new additions to their family.

Clark bent down on a knee by the fire and refilled his cup with good strong coffee, bracing himself. Lizzie, on the other side of the brightly burning fire, was hugging and kissing those children she had not seen for several years. One child clung to her skirts, and another she held in her arms. It was a scene he had so longed for—growing a family with her. There was an aching pain in the pit of his stomach. This was the night he had waited for. But there were so many souls around her; how could he interrupt such a tender moment for her.

He must. It had to be tonight, or else he would never have the courage again.

Unknown to Clark, Lizzie had watched him the whole of the evening. Only temporarily distracted by the sweet remembrances of the little ones, she longed to be by his side. The younger babies began to fuss, and Hannah, noticing something in Lizzie's eyes that she herself felt for Junior, immediately announced it was time to put the babies to bed. Her mother agreed, and the families began to disperse. Jamie said he would help his friends picket the horses and get all settled in for the night. He walked by Biggerstaff, winking at him. "What are you waiting for, man?"

The fire glowed on the trees surrounding the campground. Men, women, and children left to secure the areas where they would bed down. Tomorrow, Jamie would see to helping Mack set up a temporary shelter and talk with both Biggerstaff and Jim White to make permanent arrangements.

Lizzie still stood in the same place, opposite the man she had grown to love. Would he meet her halfway?

Clark set his empty cup on a convenient rock and decided it was now or never. He quavered in his boots. What would she say? If the answer was no, what would he do?

Lizzie moved toward him, regarding the man she wished to be with for the rest of her life. A Scot he was—a tall, proud, handsome man with gray-blue eyes, the color of the sea around his home on the Isle of Skye. His garb was the belted kilt—shades of muted moss green and purple gloaming—with fur sporran and chain protecting his manliness from a sudden gust of wind. A cream shirt was covered by a dark green woolen jacket. His dirk and claymore were affixed to his belt. He carried the drape of that great kilt over one arm and approached her.

Clark studied her expectant face. She was a beauty all right, with fire in her hair and on her cheeks like her father. But even with Jamie's strength of character, Lizzie still had the daintiness of her fair Welsh mother.

She was silent. He swallowed. "Elizabeth Kimsey, I wish for all the world that you would be my wife. I have loved you from the moment we met, and that love has grown stronger as I have seen the quality of your attributes. If you say yes, I will love and cherish you for all our lives together."

"What's been keeping you, Clark?" Lizzie asked, throwing her arms around his neck, and they kissed ever so tenderly. "I would love to go through life with you."

Hannah watched the lovers from her bedroll under the wagon, tears rolling down her cheeks. *How long until Junior and I are together?* she begged God, falling asleep with that prayer on her lips.

1795

It was Saturday, May 30, and a day of jubilation. Junior was ten years old. There was a birthday party at Clark's cabin for the young man with presents and a table filled with food, including a delicious-looking cake covered with a frosting of beaten egg whites and sugar Mary made for her boy. Everyone laughed as she rubbed her arm from the tedious job, but more so because the children kept swiping their fingers through the concoction. She tried slapping their hands but couldn't stop them. "There won't be any icing left if you children keep it up."

Jamie gave him a new rifle. "It's time to replace the old musket," he said. There were other gifts: a small shell and arrowheads dug from the earth when the new cabin footings were placed; a new hatchet from his older brother Littleberry; some candies wrapped in paper and tied with string from Mrs. McCracken. Clark and Lizzie, newly married, gave him a hunting shirt sewn by his sister's own hands. And dearest Hannah gave him a bird's nest with two tiny eggs inside. He treasured that gift almost as much as his new rifle.

In the eventide, babies were asleep in arms and young ones yawned loudly, and after they were put to bed, some entertainment was at hand in the yard of Clark's home. On the ground were placed two swords crossing each other. Then the rhythmic beat of a small skin-covered hand drum began, and a dulcimer played. Mack stepped out of the darkness into the firelight. He wore his kilt and loose-fitting shirt. With his arms lifted overhead, he began dancing a Scottish sword war dance. His bare feet executed the steps with strength and vigor on the dusty ground between the blades and moved to a fever pitch. Sweat had soaked his shirt through and through by the time he finished.

Jamie listened, watched, and remembered. His eyes followed the fire's sparks ascending toward the stars in the heavens, and he heard the drone and whine of the pipes in his mind. Wait! A knot twisted in his throat.

Where was that sound coming from?

He looked around thinking he was back in Scotland, but no, it was coming from the throats of Mack, Mollie, and their oldest boy, John. They mimicked the sound of bagpipes with mouth music.

When the pipes spurred the Scots to patriotic fervor for the last time in '46, the enemy considered the skirl a treasonous weapon and was no longer permitted to be heard in their homeland, but men and women in the back country of the Appalachian Mountains took up the creation of the sounds with their throats. When German folk, like his old friend Hermann Ensch, had brought the dulcimer to the New World, it was close to the sound of the pipes adding to the magic.

After everyone retired, Jamie and Mack rested their backs against a large hollow log. Junior was asleep with his head in his Pa's lap.

"Where did you learn to do that?" Jamie asked, astonished.

"Our father taught us. I've taught John, but he's more interested in hunting than the music, or the dance. There were ten in the family, including three girls… Say, we never got around to talking about the homeland or our families, did we? Never had time, I guess." Mack wiped his sweaty face on his shirttail, which had come loose in the heat of the dance.

"Where were you born, Mack?"

"Galloway—southwest coast of Scotland. With the English right across the border, the persecution of us Presbyterians got to be too much, and our family was struggling to live and breathe. We were made to attend the Church of England and taxed heavily for it, but my father, like so many other of Scotland's lads from the Lowlands, refused—and we were forced out. We made our way to Ulster in Northern Ireland. Scots-Irish, they call us here.

"Father settled us on the Little Pee Dee River in South Carolina. A number of his brothers followed his lead, and we prospered even though the land was swampy and difficult. He moved us to the fertile land in Union County. That was where we buried him and mother." There was a catch in his throat. "Where do you hail from? Somewhere in the north, I'll bet, although you don't have much of a brogue on you."

"No. I could work on it, however."

Mack caught the joke, and both men laughed. Junior stirred, and Jamie said to his son, "Why don't you go back with your Ma and the others."

Junior yawned. "No, Pa. I'll stay with you and Mr. McCracken." He rubbed his eyes and went back to sleep.

Jamie continued, "Beauly Priory, our ancestral home. We were tenant farmers and moved to Inverness when I was just a bairn. My father was caught up with the Jacobite rebellion in January of '46, but our MacKenzie chief refused to send his clan to support Prince Charles at Culloden in April. My brothers fought, however—Benjamin, Alex, and Charles. I was proud of them…But Charlie boy's attempt at the throne failed on the backs of all those dead Scots' clans!" It was a scornful remark which quickly turned to anger when he blurted out, "My father and brother Duncan were butchered there in the fields!" It hurt him so to utter those names. He stared into the darkness beyond the campfire.

Mack sighed, remembering the history told him by his father. "So, you were MacKenzies then. How did you get the Kimsey name?"

Jamie realized he had a choice to make—either refuse to talk about it or trust this man he had befriended. He chose to trust and related the story—even the part about Benjamin.

"I was six years old when we fled from the English. Benjamin thought we could find refuge in Ireland, and that's where he changed our name to Kimsey, thinking we would be spared from arrest by the enemy. We were not, but that was our name from then on, and we were sold as servants in Maryland."

Jamie drew in a deep breath, taking a moment to continue. "Ben and I had a break a few years back. I wanted to move, but as stubborn as we both were, neither of us would budge. Our family had been together since the war...but now..."

Jamie hung his head in exhaustion from the long day and the story told. Mack felt deep sorrow for his friend and wondered what other horrors there had been in his life. He placed his hand on Jamie's shoulder. "I guess we should get some sleep." He got up to leave and started to say something, but thought better of it and left his friend and Junior in peace.

The next morning when Mary awoke, she found that her husband and son had decided to sleep elsewhere. Lizzie stepped from the cabin to shake the flour from her apron.

"We're going to make breakfast, Mother. Where's Pa and the boy?"

"I don't rightly know. I saw them with Mack. They'll show up when they smell the bacon."

* * *

Mary was getting on Jamie's nerves. "How many times must I complain? What are we going to do about this leaky roof? Every time it rains, it's the same old thing. How on earth do you expect me to cook our meal when all the pots are sitting on the floor filled with water, dearest?"

That last word was like a slap in the face. The simmer had just turned to a boil, and as patiently as he could, and with drops of water plopping in at least a half dozen pots around them, he told her he'd fix the shingles as soon as the rain stopped. "I can't go up there until it's dry. It's too dangerous."

"But I complained about this last month and the month before. Jamie, please. We need to build our home if we're going to stay here in Knoxville...Are we going to stay in Knoxville?" She gave him an incredulous stare.

Suddenly the roof gave way and drenched them both. Jamie thought it was funny, but Mary did not see it that way as they were now destitute of home.

"Don't worry, my dear. It will be done."

And it was done. Jamie; Littleberry; Samuel; Junior; Mack and his boy, John; Clark; and some of Clark's friends worked together. And in no time both the Kimseys and McCrackens were snug in rainproof cabins. Jamie thought about expanding to three rooms at some future time, but Mack was content that there was a good solid roof over his growing family. Mollie was pregnant again—their eighth.

* * *

1796

The Southwest Territory was admitted to the Union as Tennessee, the sixteenth state on June 1, 1796. Knoxville, the new capital, had a growing population of about seventy-five thousand—sixty thousand settlers and ten thousand slaves. Governor William Blount and then his successor John Sevier both tried desperately to contain the onslaught of settlers—to keep them within the Indian treaties' boundaries—but they just kept coming and treaty lines were pushed to outposts built to protect a dwindling number of Cherokees from aggressive settlers.

With all these people and stifling encroachment, Jamie felt trapped and was as restless as a squirrel saving up nuts for the winter.

There was more, though. He felt that Knoxville was still not the right place for his family. Another place, maybe, or something else. That old feeling made him scratch his head. Why was he so restless? Despite his fifty-six years, he yearned for a new place. Sometimes he would walk the banks of the Tennessee River staring down its long breadth to only God knows where, he thought. Other times he would take Junior with him, and they would fish. Mostly he was alone. Until—

"What's wrong, Jamie?" Mary recognized the same old problem as they took in the last remaining sips of light coming back from one of their walks. It was a grand evening, and she did not want it to end.

"I feel fenced in, my girl. Always the same old longing. I…want to move away from the crowd."

Or was it something else? For a fleeting moment, and quite inexplicably, he thought of Ben's joy in the ministry: *when he presided at our wedding; when he moved with joy to be close to us, his family; and always that joy-filled desire to preach the Gospel to all—even in New London. Where is my joy? It has always been with the land…but what if I followed that path?* He drew back and dismissed those wild notions when Mary commented regarding another move, "That will hardly endear you to your family and friends. We can't go." Mary could hardly contain her happiness and could not keep the surprise from him any longer. "Lizzie is with child."

When he heard he would be a grandfather again, Jamie laid down his restlessness and picked up the plough. Tilling, planting, and harvesting were his life, but the only thing he loved more was his family, and now the exciting news about his Lizzie and Clark. He buried his desperate discontent among the furrows.

* * *

The onslaught of white settlers continued pushing the Cherokee west. The Indians pushed back in kind with raids, scalpings, murders, and abductions of women, children, and slaves—adding them to their own existing slaves. The militia was sent after the culprits, and the Kimseys and McCrackens remained cautiously vigilant, keeping their rifles and families close by.

Other counties had been formed and were being created to the north and west. The revolution was still going on when Fort Nashborough was built on the Cumberland River and Nashville was populated by settlers led by longhunters. Planting corn, the settlers left their mark in the fields. Further west were Robertson and Montgomery Counties. And in eastern Tennessee, the ploughs meeting the earth pushed south in Blount and Cocke Counties.

February 1797

The weather had been mild, and Jamie wanted very much to check his traps before it soured and a possible bounty of fresh meat was left to spoilage or predation. Littleberry and Junior went with him. When they were about two miles from the fortification of Knoxville along Third Creek of the Tennessee River, their first set of traps was visible and contained a pair of squirrels caught by their legs. Littleberry went on ahead to the second trap while Jamie showed Junior how to reset the snare. Slogging along the course of puddles and mud from the previous storm, they caught up with Littleberry.

A disagreeable wind suddenly picked up, darkening the sky with nasty-looking gray clouds, and the men decided to make their way home. The weather turned really foul in no time at all with howling wind and snow turning to sleet. In haste, the father and sons moved forward, Jamie making quite sure Littleberry and Jamie stayed close. He lamented that they were only wearing hunting shirts. It had been such a lovely morning that no thought had been given to wearing heavy winter coats—a mistake he hoped he would not regret.

Mary was at the window staring into the white space beyond, anxiously awaiting her men's return. She glanced at the coats hanging on the pegs beside the door. *They should have taken them*, but the thought was short-lived when figures appeared on the porch. She drew open the door, and there they stood, the most pitiful souls she'd ever seen. She kissed Jamie's and Berry's nearly-frozen cheeks as they stumbled through the door and settled them in front of the fire.

"Here, warm your hands around these." Mary gave each one a cup of tea.

"There's a stewing chicken for your supper." They both looked well enough, but when she kissed Junior's cheek, she uttered a sharp cry as she felt his face with her hands. "My God, Jamie! Something is wrong with him!" Despite being cold, he was burning up.

"What?" Incredulously, he went to his son.

Berry looked at him worriedly. "We need to get those wet clothes off him, Ma."

Jamie carried Junior into their bedroom and dressed him in his own nightshirt. Mary was close on his heels with a bowl of steaming broth. The boy swallowed a spoonful, but he was in extreme pain, causing tears to well up in his eyes. There was only a rasping whisper coming from his throat. "Thanks, Ma."

Mary drew the covers over him and sat on the bed. Berry brought a cold compress for Junior, and he and his father stood there helplessly.

"You and Berry get into warm clothes and have some of that soup. I'll take the first watch." Mary warned them, "If his fever doesn't break by morning, I'm afraid we'll have to go for the doctor."

Junior cuddled into her loving embrace, and she caressed his feverish brow with the cloth, singing softly to him. He fell asleep in her arms.

She never uttered a word of rebuke.

* * *

By morning, the storm had passed, and the winter sun sparkled upon tree limbs laden with drifts. A featureless landscape with only an occasional rooftop and the fort's palisade showed above the white blanket. During the night, Jamie had fallen asleep with Junior's head on his chest.

Mary moved silently into the room and touched her husband's shoulder, startling him. Junior moaned when he did so, causing the damp cloth to fall from his forehead. She replaced it, and put a hot poultice from ear to ear on her son's neck.

"The boy is still burning up. Berry is eating breakfast now, and I've asked him to fetch the doctor. Go and eat, and I'll sit with Junior."

Berry had to use snowshoes to plough through the frosty landscape. It was slow going and took him half an hour to get to the fort where the doctor's house was. Dr. Hunt wasn't there, he was told by the man's missus. There was an emergency, she said, and Berry would have to wait.

Berry could think of nothing except his little brother. He prayed and walked the floor and sat on the hard bench and then walked the floor again. He was getting agitated just as the doctor walked through the door.

"It's good to see you again, Berry. How's your family?" he asked, pumping the lad's hand and removing his hat and coat.

"Not well, sir. I'm afraid I'll have to ask you to come to our cabin. My brother Junior is sick with a bad fever."

Dr. Hunt was welcomed by the Kimseys. He shed his coat and scarf into Jamie's hands and headed for the bedroom.

"What have you done for the boy so far, Mrs. Kimsey?" He sat down and checked Junior's throat. The boy coughed violently.

Wringing her hands, Mary told him, "I put a warm plaster around his neck and had him flush his throat with sal prunella."[26]

"Hmm…That's fine…fine…It's quinsy,"[27] the doctor pronounced and bent over, listening to Junior's chest. "I hear a wheezing." He placed his hands on Junior's face and gently brushed the boy's hair from his moist forehead. "And ague,[28] of course. This malady has gone around the settlement, I'm afraid. Bad weather."

Junior managed a slight little smile when Dr. Hunt produced a licorice stick from his bag and handed it to Mary.

"Put the sal prunella in posset[29] if it's easier for him. Also, keep the warm plasters on his neck. If you have some dried leek, soak it and add honey to the juice. Burn a little of the dried and add that. Junior can take some on the licorice—just dip it in the mixture. Here's a few sticks for afterward." He winked. Jamie joined them in

---

[26] Sal prunella: a mixture of refined nitre and soda for sore throats. Prunella is a corruption of Brunelle, in French *scl de brunelle,* from the German *breune* (a sore throat), *braune* (the quinsy) (https://www.infoplease.com/dictionary/brewers/sal-prunella).

[27] Quinsy: peritonsillar abscess (https://www.merriam-webster.com/dictionary/quinsy).

[28] Ague: a fever marked by paroxysms of chills and sweating that recur at regular intervals; a fit of shivering (https://www.merriam-webster.com/dictionary/ague).

[29] Posset: a hot drink of sweetened and spiced milk curdled with ale or wine (https://www.merriam-webster.com/dictionary/posset).

the outer room and heard, "If his fever doesn't break in a few days, I'll come back and bleed him."

Jamie helped the doctor with his coat and hat. "Berry, would you walk Dr. Hunt back to the fort?"

"Not necessary, Mr. Kimsey. But send him if Junior takes a turn for the worse."

Jamie pressed some coins in the good man's hand.

Mary searched her cupboard for the necessary ingredients for the medicine, and Berry cooked the squirrels for their supper. Jamie went to sit with Junior, but the boy was drowsy and having trouble breathing.

"Papa…hold me." His voice gave out in a fit of coughing. Jamie eased him up onto his own chest, and Junior's breath came a little easier. Jamie pulled up the covers and held his son in his arms just as Mary came in with the warm plaster. She wrapped it around Junior's neck and gave him a little laudanum.

"Thanks, Ma," Junior whispered.

Mary kissed his feverish forehead and Jamie's for good measure. "When he's asleep, come have your supper."

But after an hour, Jamie didn't come, and Mary went to look in on them. Both were fast asleep, but she was taken aback by what she saw. There were tears on Jamie's face. It was a tender moment she would remember all her life.

* * *

Junior was slow in recovering and tired easily. Berry kept an eye on him up in the loft when the immediacy of his illness was less urgent and he could move out of his parents' bed.

The snow shrank to small mounds in shadowy corners and behind woodpiles, and sticky mud puddles were everywhere. The story of the boy's illness went around the settlement, and Hannah was the first one at the Kimseys' cabin. Her face was flushed from running, and she was so out of breath, it was difficult for her to talk when Berry answered the door.

"Junior, your beloved is here!" he yelled through the house.

Coming down the ladder from the loft, Junior was panting from the exertion and heartily embarrassed by his brother's announcement—but yet secretly pleased she was there.

Mary was at the door before Junior. "Come in, Hannah, and make yourself at home. Have some tea. How's your family?"

"Just fine, Mrs. Kimsey. Mama sends you her best wishes and some small cakes." She placed the basket on the table. "How did you folks survive the storm?"

"Junior, would you bring the cups, dear," Mary requested sweetly. She sat next to Hannah on the straight-backed settee, forcing Junior to sit in the rocker and thoroughly annoying him by sitting between the two.

Wanting to be the center of attention, Whishy, the cat, getting rather gray in the whiskers, had given up the loft for the preferred fireplace rug and leaped into Hannah's lap just as she took a dainty sip of tea. She petted him lavishly, commenting on how handsome he'd become since last they had seen each other. He promptly curled in a ball and, with his tail entwined over his eyes, went to sleep.

Annoyed as he was, Junior could not take his eyes off Hannah. He wanted to say, "I've missed you so," but Mary said, "Junior, where are your manners. Hannah's out of tea."

Junior went about his duty, but even though those cakes looked delicious, he'd lost his appetite in Hannah's presence.

"I heard about your sickness from the gossip in town. Are you feeling better, Junior?"

"Yes, thank you. I hope to help Pa with the ploughing in a few weeks."

Frowning, Mary was incredulous.

Hannah finished her tea. "Junior, maybe with your mother's permission you could come outside and walk a bit?"

"Not just now, dear. The wind is rather blustery, and he might have a relapse."

That was her final word, no matter how Junior longed to be out and about with his "beloved."

Chapter 34

Forsaken

ANOTHER YEAR AND Junior was as tall as his father and working hard with his brothers Littleberry and Samuel, the McCrackens, and Clark Biggerstaff. There wasn't much time to see Hannah with all the work. Junior's sister Lizzie and Clark had another baby. They still lived within the fort's confines, but Clark had purchased some prime farmland close to the Kimseys' compound and wanted to start building soon.

Knoxville continued to grow and prosper. More and more settlers were bringing their hopes and dreams with them to the burgeoning community. Many thought they had unfettered access to Indian lands beyond those borders, and Jamie began to feel the pressure of "all these people" and then they heard the news that the McCrackens were going back to South Carolina.

"What?" Junior screamed. "It can't be! You can't! Again? Hannah…no…"

He was heartbroken. He cried. Unashamed, he cried. Junior didn't care why they were leaving. All he knew was his precious Hannah was going out of his life. *How could they?* He had been planning and saving a small pittance here and there, working in any stolen moments for other farmers in the region who might give him a coin or two for his efforts. They knew what he was doing and applauded him for it, but what they did not know was Junior wanted to ask for

Hannah's hand next year. There was a good piece of land on a bluff above the compound. He would have it—and his Hannah.

Jamie wondered about the cause of the frenetic burst of activity in his son, and this day, as the McCrackens tied the last cup next to the water barrel, the light of understanding dawned on him. *Oh, God! All this time he's been preparing for his life with her!*

Hannah and Junior walked up to the bluff overlooking the long broad river. They wondered together where the river ended. Perhaps in a far western land; maybe in an ocean somewhere; or into a great divide of mountains. The separation they felt was already painful. They knew they were meant to be together. Mack said they were too young. She told Junior that, but not the rest. Hannah did not want her father's words to hurt him. *Junior is not yet a man.*

They held hands, walked awhile, then stopped in the deep wood. The odor of the land was strong in their nostrils. Potent desire arose with the closeness of their bodies—where two would become one—and the moment was right for the kiss he'd always wanted to give her. Junior took a step closer, and Hannah did not back away. He looked in her eyes and saw the same love he had for her.

Suddenly shy, Junior asked, "May I kiss you, Hannah?"

She drew near. He hoped it wouldn't be awkward when he touched her lips. He really didn't know what to expect. Would she cry? Would he? Bringing her to him, he felt the delight of holding her in his arms, her breasts pressing against his chest, and a sudden throbbing in his groin. They kissed again, this time with a passion neither had ever known before. Junior didn't want it to end.

"Hannah Jane!" Mollie's voice cut like the crack of a whip, a cutting of skin, a strike of a fist. From the edge of the wood, she called, "It's time to go!"

Hannah's cheeks were wet with tears of love and longing. "Will I ever see you again, James Kimsey?" She ran away from him, her passion expending itself in the labored exertion of her limbs.

"What were you doing out there, daughter?"

"Nothing, Mother! Absolutely nothing!" She went to the back of the wagon with John and the other McCracken children to walk to God knows where, she thought, sorely distressed. Hannah wanted no more questions.

John was ready to tease his sister with a smart quip until he saw her face. Mercifully, he refrained.

* * *

It was dark and a long time after supper when Junior finally came home. He went straight to his bed in the loft, no longer the inexperienced lad he had been before that day. Jamie and Mary stared after him, wondering. Junior was junior no longer. He was James Kimsey and would not give up his dream.

Jamie and Mary spoke quietly together that night.

"What will we do without our very good friends the McCrackens…never mind their solid help in everything we've done here. I will miss them tremendously," and she thought, *The value I place on Mollie's friendship. How will I fare without her.*

Jamie didn't know how to respond. He felt the same way but more so because of his son—and he told his wife that.

Mary sat for a moment before speaking. "I knew they were close, but I didn't want them 'to stir up love before it's time' like it says in the book of Solomon."

"It's too late for that, Mary. He loves Hannah with a love I've only seen once before."

Mary looked at him with a blank expression on her face.

"Don't you remember? It was you and me. I loved you from the first time I laid eyes on you. You were only four years old and a big pain in my neck the way you used to follow me around. Drove me crazy," he said with a gentle laugh. "Junior's already planning on asking her to marry him. He's got eyes on that piece of vacant land."

Her smile turned to a thoughtful frown. "No…It can't be? The poor boy." She turned her face toward him.

They rocked in tandem as the fire burned brightly.

"Jamie, can I ask you a question?"

"Yes, of course."

"When Junior was sick last year, I came into the room, and even though you were asleep holding him, I noticed the tears on your face. Why were you crying so? I know you were worried."

Jamie sat for a moment and remembered the thing he never told his wife or his son. The fire crackled and spat out a log which tumbled onto the hearth. He stood and grasped it with the tongs, placing it back where it belonged, then held to the mantelpiece for support and spoke slowly.

"You know I love all our children dearly, but Junior was always a special gift to me. I'll never forget the harm I caused you all, but when we had him, I absolutely knew I was forgiven." He took a moment before continuing. "When Junior was sick, I prayed to God that night to spare him and take my life instead. Our good God told me 'No. You will care for this boy as he will grow into a fine man. I have special work for you and him to do.' I heard his voice clearly, and, Mary"—he faced her—"I wish to become a Baptist minister, as Ben did following his promise to God so very long ago."

This revelation was a grand calling. She took his hands across the space between them and was filled with joy.

The quiet in the room was only disturbed by a creak in the loft above them. Junior and Littleberry had been listening from their beds. Berry patted his brother's shoulder, and they both turned over and went back to sleep, silently blessing the parents they had been given.

Chapter 35

The Mississippi Territory Question

1800

WITH THE NEW century came much movement in the land. Trappers, hunters, and surveyors came from the north through the Tennessee Valley along the Holston River and from the east along the French Broad. At the confluence of the rivers, men traipsed into Knoxville and headed straight west into the fertile Indian lands of the Mississippi Territory[30]—barrens they were called—lands the Indians had cleared and cultivated for centuries. Settlers, bringing slaves with them, were close on their heels, eager to drive their sharp plough blades into the malleable earth. Their wagons were filled with children, pots and pans, and cotton seed.

While Jamie cast a wishful eye toward their destinations, he had more important things on his mind. He was apprenticed to a Baptist minister in town who was astonished by what his pupil already knew—until he found out who Jamie's brother was. The minister

---

[30] The Territory of Mississippi was an organized incorporated territory of the United States that existed from April 7, 1798, until December 10, 1817, when the western half of the territory was admitted to the Union as the State of Mississippi and the eastern half became the Alabama Territory until its admittance to the Union as the State of Alabama on December 14, 1819 (https://en.wikipedia.org/wiki/Mississippi_Territory).

knew Benjamin by reputation, and even though Jamie was a little old, his sixty years did give him a background for the recruitment of souls ripe for converting. In Knoxville, there were many Baptists and Methodists ministers in the field, but Jamie never worried about what he would say. Neither his seedbeds of souls—nor his furrows—would go wanting.

Junior bought his land. It was only five acres, but he cleared it himself. Jamie visited him on occasion in between his own works and was astonished and extremely proud of his son.

"Berry comes over from time to time and helps, Pa, so does Sam, but mostly I shape the logs for the cabin. They provide the muscle." He smiled broadly and stuck his hands in his overalls pockets. Looking over the progress he'd made, Junior remarked, "I think I know how you felt so long ago waiting for Mother to return from Wales—bury the longing in hard work. It makes it a little easier, doesn't it, Pa?"

"Yes, son." Jamie walked away with tears in his eyes, the clear vision of waiting for his Mary to return brought to the forefront of his memory, and the intervening growth he experienced becoming a man. "You'll see her again, boy. I just know it."

* * *

Time flew by for the Kimseys and Biggerstaffs—Lizzie and Clark having two young 'uns running around and getting into everything. It was all Lizzie could do to keep up, especially since she was pregnant with their third child. Grandmother Mary cared for the babies more and more as Lizzie grew in girth and Junior cast an occasional jealous eye toward the fun she was having with the little ones. He remembered when his mother played with him like that. Thinking that way was a waste of energy, he reasoned, and got back to the work of making furniture for his Hannah, hoping that they would give his parents grandbabies too.

The cabin was finished, and his fields were planted. It wasn't much, he admitted, but he was proud. Now, if his woman would just come back to him.

* * *

The year 1804 brought more surveyors, this time from the Nashville area and deeper into the Mississippi Territory. They laid out plats of land, and public sales were held through land acts. Jamie began again tasting the thrill of moving into that virgin territory, even though those lands were inhabited by Indians.

Junior had no desire to forge ahead from the known into the unknown. He wanted something more permanent. "Stable and long-lasting!" he yelled, startling a deer that bounded away at his exuberance. "You're lucky, my fine friend, or else I would have had you for my dinner tonight."

Over his nineteen years on earth, the family had lived in many places. He liked the Knoxville area and thought Hannah would feel the same, although they had never really discussed staying in one place. Actually, they had never really discussed anything. Mack was another pioneering spirit wanting to go where the hills were greener, but Junior had neither his father's craving for the next green hill nor Mack's.

The quiet fall forest surrounding Junior's cabin was showing its colors and disturbed only by his footfall as he headed toward the shed. He needed nails and a new plank to replace one of the porch steps badly warped from the last rain. Summoning all the power of his strong arms, he banged away at a nailhead and oddly felt a strange cold prickling of his skin. He looked around and saw nothing. One more nail would take care of the step, but the same prickling bothered him again. He stood and looked around, rubbing his arms. A ray of sun filtered through the tall trees, and someone was standing there—a woman with golden hair. She was walking toward him.

"You're taller," she said.

"Hannah...I've been waiting for you." Junior took her in his arms with no thought that she might have grown away from him. But no, they were together.

"I have missed you so, James."

She was even more beautiful. They kissed as if they'd never parted.

Her family had returned, bringing others that came with them. Mack pulled his wagons, family, and stock into the yard of his former home, pleased that Jamie and Clark had watched over his land to make sure no squatter tried to take over Mack's extensive holdings while they were gone. Even their garden was producing vegetables, which were grown to feed the town's indigent—especially widows and orphans—until Mack returned. The fields went fallow, however, but Mollie was pleased to open her home and find it just as she had left it. She put the children to work sweeping out the dust and making a good fire to cook their first meal in their old home.

In the gloaming, a great bonfire was lit for the homecoming celebration. The darkening sky was a purple cloak surrounding them, and emboldened stars made a great swath across the sky to dance with the rising sparks and spirits of the merrymakers. Old friends and new gathered together to share a common meal and any newsworthy tidings of the homes they'd left behind.

Jamie was not home, Mary told Mack. He was out spreading the word of God to those coming to settle in Knoxville or those just passing through to find open land. "He is a Baptist minister now," she shared. Noting the pride in her voice, he wondered why such a change had come about in his old friend.

As the men settled their wagons, the women gushed about new babies with fat pink cheeks, or deep dimples, little baldies or heads full of dark hair. Toddlers running around their mother's skirts—and some clutching a loved toy or blanket—were picked up and swung in circles. Older boys and girls were given approving nods for "growing like a weed." All were treasured and all ready to take their first steps with their parents into the unknown.

Jamie, coming from the far distant border of the town, saw the hullabaloo and hurried forward to see what was going on. He joined his wife.

"What's happening, Mary?"

"The McCrackens have returned, and they brought others with them."

Clark passed Jamie to join Lizzie. "I can't believe they're back. Isn't it a wonder!"

An evening mist gave off a chill in the autumn air, and babies needed their mother's breasts and warm beds. Little ones were tipsy with sleepiness, and it was time for the elders to talk of important matters.

"Gather around, my friends. I have some things to share with you," Mack began. Just noticing Jamie in the crowd, he reached forward to shake hands with him, a broad grin spreading across his face.

Samuel and Penny were sitting on a tree stump. He took off his coat and put it around her shoulders. Lizzie went back with her little ones, and Clark leaned against an old tree trunk. Jamie sat beside Mary, his legs giving out after a long day of proselytizing for God. He squinted, looking beyond the fire at some men he didn't recognize. Hannah and Junior, holding hands, stood beside his parents and listened intently.

Mack started in earnest. "Dear friends and most cherished neighbors." His eyes glanced over to the Kimseys. "I have some exciting news for you. About two hundred miles due west of this town of Knoxville in a place called Rutherford County, there is virgin land, cheap for the taking. There are two rivers running through it, the Duck and the Stones." He took a deep breath.

Clark sneered, "And how many Cherokee running through it, McCracken?"

A ripple of sniggering ran through the crowd.

"Chickasaw, my friend, and as friendly as they come. The federal government has negotiated with them for that land. I tell you true, the seeds we plant will grow the bonniest of crops. I have brought these honorable gentlemen with me—James English from

Virginia, and my neighbor Clem Hancock, from Laurens County, South Carolina, ready to—"

"What are you suggesting, Mack," Jamie interrupted, "that we pick up stakes here in this our new home and turn around traipsing west into God knows what? I, for one, am settled in Knoxville," he stated bluntly to the astonishment of his wife. She placed her hand on his arm and looked at him in disbelief. All looked at him in disbelief, and Mack just stared at him.

Junior felt confused—happy, on the one hand, with what he thought was going to be his new life with Hannah in Knoxville; strangely embarrassed for his father, on the other; and third, totally surprised by his father wanting to stay where he was.

Junior stepped in. "Mr. McCracken, if you are suggesting that we all pick up and move, then I think we need to consider what you are talking about. We need to study on your ideas and discuss them." He didn't want to say anything until he'd had time to talk with his father about why he had such a change of heart, and especially knowing his penchant for those greener hills beyond.

In the coming days, Mack's suggestions caused a rumble of discontent in the settlement which accompanied the usual hard labor of farmwork and care of small children. Junior and Hannah were kept apart by those obligations and something more important than their love—family always came first, and never the breakdown of that bond as had been between Jamie and Uncle Benjamin. That offense had been a disturbance of the family's survival together.

It was late in the year, a time of turning leaves and hunting game. "Indian summer" was a new term for it. The temperature during the day could be warm or mild and the need for an extra blanket at night. And then the winter hit them. It started simply with a few flurries. Junior, shucking the seed corn from the ears, thought, as a good gesture, he would share his bounty with the McCrackens.

Hannah answered the door, and Junior could see the longing in her eyes. Mollie asked after his family.

"They're all good, ma'am. I brought this seed corn for you folks for next year's plantin'. There was an abundance."

The McCracken children, all busy at chores, were suddenly everywhere, the younger ones happily hanging to Junior's legs. Mack and two of his eldest sons, John and William, who had been out hunting, came in the cabin at that moment with game. They hung their rifles over the door.

"We've been out your way, and you've done a fine job of it, boy, building that cabin. I have seen the pride in the eyes of your parents. Yes, you've done a yeoman's job of it, for sure. Here, sit by the fire. The cold's comin' in off the river, and the snow's comin' down hard."

"Thank you, sir, but I should be getting back" was all Junior could get out of his mouth. Hannah offered him a cup of tea. He declined, not wanting to give away his strong feelings in front of her parents. He was surprised by Mack's compliment but wondered if they actually approved of him. Hannah's pleading eyes said to stay.

Mrs. McCracken salved his discomfort. "James, please tell your family that we are having a Hogmanay celebration and all are invited."

"Yes, ma'am. I will tell them. They will be mighty pleased."

He glanced again at Hannah before he left, flustered by the inexplicable frustration he felt. As he walked back home through the thickening snow, he had to smile—Mrs. McCracken didn't call him Junior. *Maybe they like me after all.*

* * *

Hogmanay
1804

Junior peered in the mirror—the only one in the house—atop his mother's forty-year-old pine dresser handmade by his father. Wayward waves of hair stuck out from his head at odd angles and made him feel anxious. He took her yellowed ivory comb and pulled it through his hair, hoping the brown locks would straighten out, but the teeth promptly hit a snag. With a good yank the knot broke free of his unruly mop. He considered a jar of pomade sitting there but hesitated because the smell was nasty—animal fat and some sort of fragrance. There was a party at the McCracken home tonight, and he wanted to ask his Hannah to marry him. So, plunging his fingers into the jar, he spread a good deal liberally on his palms then ran the oily goo through his hair with the comb. One last glance in the mirror, and he thought himself looking older with the slicked-back hair away from his face. Lastly, he tied a ribbon to the unplaited queue that hung down behind.

"Junior! You ready yet?" His father's voice interrupted the grooming. "Lizzie and Clark are here. Samuel and Penny will meet us at the house. Come on. Let' go."

With the finishing touch of his cocked hat on his head, Junior joined his family members who were laughing at the arrival of the smell before the man himself.

Snow fell gently over the sleigh. A lantern on either side lit the tips of cross-log fencing along the trail. They hadn't far to go, but the women did not want to wet their skirts in the drifts. It was bitterly cold, and they huddled together swathed in woolen capes and scarves.

The McCrackens' cabin was large, made to accommodate their eleven children. Through the windows, candlelight spread over the snow, and when Mack heard the sleigh bells, he opened wide the door, and the glow from within made an inviting path to their threshold. Mary presented Mollie with a basket of cookies, knitted mittens, and small carved toys for the children while the older boys put the horses in the byre. The middle children helped with coats and bonnets, and the little ones played hide-and-seek around legs and full skirts.

Among all of this seeming chaos, Junior was transfixed by the beauty of Hannah Jane. Her hair, done up in curls, ribbon, and a pine sprig, looked like a golden crown. She smiled demurely at him, and his heart caught in his throat. The young men of both families took notice how the eyes of the couple betrayed the depth of their love, so they annoyed them unmercifully with boisterous hooting.

Festive dancing, drinking, and eating—this holiday promised to be the best of all, but Hannah had no appetite with all the butterflies dancing in her stomach. She wondered, *Would this be the night?*

* * *

Before the guests arrived, Hannah, standing barefoot in her shift, had appealed to Mollie with tears in her eyes, "Mother, I think I'm going to be sick."

"I can understand that, my darling girl. I felt the same way when your father asked me to marry him. This is the most important night of your life. Here, let me cast the dress over your head." Hoping to distract her, Mollie continued. "Shall we use a ribbon? Or...how about a small sprig of pine nestled in your hair?"

"But, what if he doesn't ask me? I shall be crushed!" she cried as the finely woven wool dress settled over her. Mollie tied the satin streamers in a large bow, accentuating her daughter's tiny waist.

"Turn around, dear." Now Mollie's eyes filled with tears. "Oh my! You are breathtaking." Mother and daughter hugged. "I am so happy for you as James will make a fine husband. Now, how about both a ribbon and pine?"

* * *

Mack drew everyone's attention by raising his glass to wish all a happy and prosperous new year, and all responded, "Hear! Hear!" with a clink of glasses.

Seeking his time alone with Hannah, James took his chance when everyone was at last occupied with the delicious meal before them. The couple, unseen by their families, slipped away to a cozy corner by the hearth. The aroma of pine and dried berries, apples, and cinnamon permeated the air. James took her hands in his and kissed her.

It was fifteen years since they had first fallen in love, and as small children, they were not cognizant of the sacrifices demanded by love. But much had transpired over those years of waiting, causing a deep knowledge of the other and making their love stronger. James felt surprisingly calm. The time was ripe.

"Would you marry me, Hannah Jane?"

"Oh yes, James."

In the glow of candles and fire, ardent light danced in her eyes as he slipped a slender silver band on her finger. His farmer hands had been fashioning it for weeks from the band of one of his mother's thimbles. Caressing her face, he kissed Hannah again.

Joy-filled laughter and crying interrupted the couple's tender moment. But it was almost midnight, and Samuel took James's arm, wrenching him away from his beloved and, with him, led the men outside with muskets at the ready. Wild cheering and applause accompanied a burst of gunfire that lit up the star-filled sky for Hogmanay. The women then gathered in a knot around Hannah. Like her, they were bursting with joy over her engagement.

The new year had begun.

* * *

In the first days of 1805, heavy snow fell and drifts were halfway up the windows. It caught Junior at his parents' home, and the bad weather even prevented the young couple from exchanging their vows, so their marriage was postponed until all their families and friends could join in the celebration. Memories of the happy time at Hogmanay and Hannah saying yes to his proposal remained in Junior's dreams and consumed every waking hour. The days dragged on. No one could leave their cabins except to gather wood and feed the animals—and those tasks at great risk to themselves.

Despite the weather, the Kimsey families kept busy as best they could: blades sharpened and oiled to keep from rust; guns cleaned; cabin checked for leaks, and any cracks repaired; games were played, and the Bible read with lessons taught every day. But nerves were on edge in the close confines of their cabins, and Mack's suggestion of moving on was vexing them all. Awakening one morning, Junior threw off his covers in a sweat. He went down the ladder to the kitchen. A strong sun shone over Knoxville, and he pushed open the cabin door with much effort to step outside. Limbs of trees were dropping, drenching melting snow. Cracking was heard all over the settlement as those same limbs broke off from the weight, and God forbid that there was any structure beneath. Junior worried for his cabin. That snowstorm would be in people's memories for a long time to come. It was the heaviest anyone could remember.

The shovel was inside the door in preparation for such a difficulty, so Junior didn't bother with the cup of tea his mother was offering. He started right in clearing the path across the farmyard, his heavily muscled arms flinging the wet snow up in great heaps. His father, with Berry on his heels, plodded through the mud and into the byre. Jamie ascended the ladder to the loft to check the roof. It was solid with no leaks. He then pitched hay through the trapdoor into the manger below. Berry cared for the animals while Junior went to the roof to shovel off the snow.

As he worked, Junior ached for his love. He imagined her with him, settled in the house he had built, and when it was easier to pass over the snow, he went to his own land—their home-to-be—and discovered a very large tree had fallen and destroyed his cabin. He was heartbroken.

Meanwhile, the men of the families Kimsey, McCracken, and Biggerstaff, plus James English and Clem Hancock, came together to discuss the move from Knox County to places unknown. Published in the *Gazette*, reports from longhunters, surveyors, and Indian agents confirmed their friends' stories of good land in the west and whetted the settlers' appetites. The idea was enticing, but freezing rain had replaced the snow in the early spring, and everything was mud then ice, thaw, then more mud. Even if the decision was yea all around, they could not leave until the rain stopped, which it did the first of April.

Suddenly, there were newcomers in Knoxville with cash to spend. Mack had said that would happen. The folks pressing in from the Carolinas and Virginia made good on their investments, and their families made a good return for their years of hard work. Despite the collision of tree and cabin, even Junior made a good bargain for his land. Jamie was convinced there would be souls to convert in the new settlements, and he surprised his family with an unexpected change of heart.

Chapter 36

Grievous Affliction

THE WESTWARD TRAVELERS found the land wild yet fair to the eye. New green growth penetrated dried clumps lining an old buffalo trail—just barely wide enough for an old buffalo, but not much more for their wagons as they passed. As with all the places they had lived, trees were plentiful. Elder, ash, pine, and black locust would be useful for tools and building. Cherry and crab apple would give delicious fruit; sassafras and elm would be good for medicine; sourwood gave honey, syrup, and sugar.

The land flattened out, but the cold had not quite yielded to the idea of spring. There were frozen patches along the trail that required caution, lest there be a possible broken ankle. Summertime meadows were just beginning to green up, and occasionally a doe and her fawns were to be seen. The prospect of fine game hunting was discussed around the campfires in the evenings as the women of the caravan wrapped themselves in shawls and men slipped on warm coats to ward off the still low temperatures. Families snuggled together under rope and canvas lean-to tents upside their wagons while sentries patrolled the perimeter of their camp, keeping a close eye on their corralled stock.

They were out about a week and a half—slow going it had been with heavy wagons carrying everything they owned—when Jamie's boy Samuel and Mack's son John, acting as forward scouts, returned with the news that there was a wide river in front of them. The train was led to a large meadow where the men could assess the possibility of crossing. They had made their way across shallow rivers and small streams many miles back with no incident. But this one was different.

Jamie stood looking across this new obstacle with hands on hips. Mack shaded his eyes, hoping to see better in the glare. Clark chewed on his cigar.

"When did you take up smoking?" Mack asked.

"Waiting for my children to be born. Jim White got me started when he slapped me on the back with the first and stuck a celebratory cigar in my mouth. Didn't know what to do with it until White lit the end and said 'breathe.' I did and nearly choked to death. Been smoking ever since."

Mack laughed, and Jamie said, "They stink."

"That's why I just chew 'em around others. How are we gonna cross this thing?"

"Tomorrow is the Sabbath. Why don't we rest in that meadow back there and study on it. Might have to build some rafts—plenty of trees." Jamie had a lot of experience with that back in Virginia. In his brief view, he studied the current, mentally calculated the width, and knew they would need to test the depth with a pole, wading or swimming. He was a fair swimmer. Rope across maybe. But what about the wagons? If it were deeper than the height of the wheels, it would spoil the contents. Many things to think about.

Up early, Jamie began thumbing through his Bible to ask for guidance for the preaching and forgiveness for the brevity of the service. Exodus came to mind when a dove's shadow crossed the holy book. Albeit not a white dove, he still took it as a sign. *God works his own ways*, he thought, smiling to himself.

Before breakfast, everyone gathered in the center of the ring of wagons, and Jamie began a brief service with an even briefer sermon.

"God's words were clear for the Egyptians and for us in this hour of our need." Before he could get another word out of his mouth, he was interrupted by a small child—one of Mack's. She was bawling loudly and clutching her little hands then pointing toward the river. Her little shift was muddy and covered with grass stains. Mollie ran to her daughter. *Where was this one? I thought all were accounted for!* She looked at her husband, searching for an answer.

Mollie lifted the little one in her arms. "What's the matter, darling? What's happened?" She hugged the child comforting her, but the girl would have none of it, crying all the more.

She held up two fingers saying, "Water." She pointed again, whimpering.

"Oh, God." Hannah looked at Junior.

"Go!" he said.

Jamie ran past. "Watch the stock," he yelled at Junior. Mr. English and Clem Hancock stayed with him. All the others went to the river's edge.

The river's current was strong and running high, being a tributary of the Cumberland in Nashville north of their position. Jamie and Mack ran full out to join the close-knit kith and kin already at the shore. Canebrakes lined the river on both sides up and down as far as the eye could see and as the forest would allow. The two men wormed their way to the front of the crowd, and there Jamie saw Lizzie, completely incoherent with fear. She was up to her waist in water holding to a large branch of a fallen tree. Someone said a girl had drowned, another said there were two of them. In a blink, Clark appeared above the surface, grabbed a full breath and submerged again. Jamie was in the water in an instant. Many minutes went by while folks thought Clark drowned, but he reappeared and saw Jamie in the water beside him.

"What can I do, Clark?" Jamie yelled at his son-in-law.

Gasping for air, Clark screamed in fright, "The girls…are in the canebrake…somewhere. I can't find them. My girls! I can't find them! Help me, Jamie!" The two men went underwater together.

Jamie was closest to the cane in the middle of the river and had to keep a strong hold to it so as not to be torn away by the current. Grabbing the next clump of cane, his hand hit upon an arm—a little girl's arm. His stomach turned, and as he surfaced, bearing his granddaughter in his arms, he vomited. The vomit drifted off downriver.

Jamie handed the child to someone, and taking a deep breath, he descended again and stopped short. There before his eyes was

Clark afloat and frozen in time with his daughter clenched tightly in his arms—their hair drifting eerily in the current. His head inclined toward her, and his eyes were wide, staring at the girl. Jamie took Clark's arm and guided his body to the surface.

Arms were everywhere grabbing, pulling, helping. Mary sobbed on Jamie's shoulder. No one could pull Lizzie away from her dead husband and children. She pounded on Clark's chest—in anger or trying to awaken him? Caressing his face, she kissed him. Her kiss would surely wake him. At last, unable to revive him, she gave up and gathered her little girls in her arms rocking them, singing their favorite lullaby to them, fondling their little faces. Delirious with grief, she straightened their dresses. "Momma will wash your dresses and tie your hair up with ribbons." She kept her promise as Jamie and Mack dug the graves and set roughly wrought wooden crosses to mark the spot, each bearing the name of the one who died.

How did this horrible thing happen? was the question they all asked. Mack queried John and William, and neither son knew the answer. They were at the Sunday meeting. Standing nearby, Robert, his seven-year-old, seemed to be hiding something.

"Robert, what do you know about this?" Mack was stern, and the boy trembled in fear.

"Some of us wanted to go fishing…Please, Pa. I'm sorry," Robert was inconsolable.

After all had left the horrific scene along the shore, Berry had found several makeshift poles with strings attached and brought them into camp. He handed them to Jamie. They were children after all, but no one had noticed the two little girls.

* * *

Jamie choked on his words when they buried Clark and the girls, his forty-four-year-old memories of daughter Sarah caught in his throat. Mary knew that he was thinking about the death of their first child and moved to his side, taking his arm. It gave him courage to continue.

"Thank God!…Yes, thank God for his holy will." Jamie swallowed hard.

Everyone, incensed, stared at him. Was it God's holy will to drown a loving father and his small children?

Jamie knew what they all thought and held up his hand. "Yes, thank God for his holy will that gives us good, good family and friends surrounding us on this horribly solemn day." He felt the preacher come out of him and to just speak as a father. "My friend, Clark Biggerstaff—ah, and what a friend he was—saved my life once. He married my darling daughter Elizabeth, built her a solid home, and gave her two beautiful little girls and granddaughters to Mary and me." He looked tenderly at them with tears in his eyes. And the Baptist minister surfaced. "Harden not your hearts today as we know for a surety that these loved ones are with our heavenly Father in his magnificent kingdom—the kingdom where we shall all be together one day." That was all he could say.

Grim melancholy permeated the camp. Fires crackled in the darkness. Little children were fed and put to bed, but no one else had an appetite. Families huddled together in the midst of horrendous grief. Maybe the next day would bring some relief.

The scouts found an easier ford—wider and shallower—and they left that place of death.

* * *

The easy rolling hills seemed to green up as the train passed, and shadow and light played tag as endless tumbling clouds rolled across the land. In an open barren, surrounded by tall grasses and massive trees, they again corralled the stock and settled for the night. Berry, Junior, Samuel, and John, went off with Clem to hunt while the women started their fires. The period of grief and mourning diminished as the pioneers went on with the chores of daily life—all except Lizzie.

Mary kept an eye on her daughter, but the young woman refused to talk and, in the evening, would walk away from camp to be by herself. Day after day Lizzie was alone in her grief. She sat watching. *Watching for what?* Mary questioned. Lizzie lost the love of her life and the children of her body. *Was she waiting for them to return?* Mary was vexed. *She needs to get back to work. Oh, that was harsh!* Mary was ashamed of herself for criticizing her daughter.

The scouts returned to camp following tree silhouettes stretching east across the land in a clay-colored sunset. There was one more river, they said—not much more than a creek, really, but easy, and about ten miles beyond, there was a settlement. That announcement brought cheer to the travelers' hearts, and that night the women's fires cooked delicious haunches of roasted deer. Rabbit was fried, and corn bread batter was poured on top of the fat to cook in the juices. After the days of mournful hunger, the dinner was especially delicious.

Collins River, it was called. The long line of wagons with billowing canvas covers crossed it without much trouble over a rocky bed. After the earlier fatal accident, Clem had now tied his horse and pack mule to the back of Clark's wagon and had driven it for Lizzie. She sat beside him, morose and silent, but when they came to the river, she herself filled the empty barrel with fresh water bubbling over the rocks. Clem tied the barrel on the side of the wagon, but on the spur of the moment, Lizzie decided to take the reins of her mules and her wagon containing all her worldly possessions—including Clark's bags of seeds and apple seedlings ready for planting on a new farm. The water cup and her washtub, clanging together, made a joyful noise.

"You are a strong woman," Clem told Lizzie.

Her eyes, now open with gratitude, saw kindness in that nice-looking fellow who had helped in her hour of grief. She knew pangs of loss would surface and wash over her from time to time, but she could move on. It was done, and she had to think of her family and the baby she was carrying—Clark's baby—about to be born.

Chapter 37

Fortune and Love

1805

THE WAGON TRAIN had left the Cherokee behind and pushed west straight into Chickasaw wilderness, where several ceded land treaties existed. Jamie, Mack, James English, and Clem Hancock left the train in the clearing close to the settlement and rode to the land office at Nashville fifty miles north. Samuel, Littleberry, and Junior stayed behind and took care of the camp, women, and children.

The night the men returned, a meeting was held after dinner. Mack spoke for the others. Smiling broadly, he announced simply, "Each family has received 160 acres. We were registered for six shillings each."

There was an incomprehensible gasp. All eyes stared at Mack, not believing what they heard.

"Where?" asked Junior. "Is it here?"

"No. The land is fifty miles south of here deep in the Alabama Territory.[31] All is ready for clearing and the plough. The surveyor said it is beautiful land and one day will become a state. He also told us that east along the Flint River is a settlement called New Market, and another west of us at a place called Athens."

---

[31] The Alabama Territory existed from 1798 until 1819.

"When do we leave?" Junior seemed to be the only one asking the questions.

Jamie spoke for the first time, "We put it to you, our families and friends. The thought is to wait for a few weeks while we replenish our supplies and purchase what necessities we will need. There is no mercantile where we will be going, so if anything is needed, we best git it now. And anyway, we have a wedding to perform!"

Junior gave Hannah a surprised look.

June 25

Mollie opened her chest in the back of the McCracken wagon and unwrapped the blanket. She took the beautiful dress in her hands, shook out any dust particles, and smoothed the fabric. Hannah was getting dressed in the lean-to at the side of their wagon.

"Are you about ready, girl?"

"Yes, Mother. I'm just primping at your mirror."

"You're what?"

She came out of the lean-to. "Primping. It's a new word. I heard it used at the mercantile in the settlement. I'm making myself pretty for James. How do I look?"

"Beautiful, but I think you'll look even prettier when you cover your shift with this."

"Oh, Mother! It's beautiful. When did you make this?"

"When we were back in Knoxville." Mollie gathered up the linen material and dropped it over Hannah's head. "It has an empire waistline I was reading about—the latest style from France, the article said."

It was somewhat low cut with an embroidered bodice and designed to show the shift beneath with its pretty lace ruffle just above the bosom. The skirt fell straight to her toes. Mollie had purchased a special wide blue satin ribbon and tied it in the back. There was a matching cap to be tied up under her chin. Hannah had put her long hair in a bun, but there were wispy strands of hair curled around her face and at the edge of the cap.

Jamie was suddenly homesick thinking of his nephew Hiram and wishing he was with them. His musical talent on the violin would have been a welcome addition to the ceremony. Jamie was dressed in a plain white shirt and his best Sunday breeches, shunning his traditional black robes and white stock, the ones like Benjamin used to wear. He wasn't that fussy. He was very excited to officiate at his youngest son's wedding, and Hannah would make him a fine, fine wife.

There was a local Methodist minister in the small settlement down from Nashville, and he and the mercantile owner were invited to the wedding. No Baptist minister was in residence, and as yet, there was no church of any denomination. Jamie had been asked by some residents if he would stay, but he turned down the offer. Other things were calling him, he explained.

The camp was ready, and Junior and Hannah walked from their family's wagons. All circled around the young couple as they held hands. Jamie opened his Bible.

"Dear friends and family. We are gathered here in God's sight on this beautiful day." He stopped for a moment, breathing in the incredible fragrance of this most breathtaking day and calming his heart. "We are so honored and blessed to have each of you here to witness the union of this man and this woman and to celebrate with them their love.

"Hannah and James, you have come before us with the intention of committing your lives to each other. You know the sorrowful difficulties of life, but you also know the joy it can bring. It is easier when we have someone to share all of it." He glanced toward Mack and Mollie, and his dear love, Mary. "The vows you will take are binding for life, and so, if you are prepared to make this serious commitment, turn and face one another and join your hands."

They did so.

"James, in taking Hannah to be your wife, do you so promise to honor, to love, and to cherish her in sickness as in health, in poverty as in wealth, in hardship as in blessing, until death alone shall part you?"

There was just a moment of distraction when Junior heard his father call him James for the very first time in his life. "I do," he said, looking into Hannah's beautiful eyes.

"And, Hannah, do you so promise…" Hannah had memorized those vows and promised God she would always be faithful to her man. Oh, how she loved James. She would never forget his face at that moment. He was radiant with joy.

"I do so proudly," she said.

A rustle of delight rippled through the congregation.

"In front of these witnesses, I pronounce James and Hannah Kimsey as husband and wife. You may kiss your bride." Everyone cheered. Jamie's youngest boy was married. He suddenly felt very old indeed.

Taking Hannah in his arms, James's kiss was tender on her lips. Their dreams had come true.

* * *

James bought his own wagon and four sturdy mules, and he and Hannah followed the pioneer train to their new home, and life began in earnest for the young couple. Neither was a stranger to hard work. Some of the men went off to hunt, others felled trees, including James and his father. The women gathered wood for fires and set about roasting pigeons and kneading dough, and so it began all over again.

Jamie thought it a pleasant surprise when his family, Mack's family, James English, and Clem Hancock received land contiguous to one another. Each tract surveyed was marked by pins from a particular tree or feature of land. Jamie's description read thus: on the west waters of the Limestone Creek beginning at a pine with a fork at the top, thence to the northeast at a black walnut with deep bear scratches at a notch ten feet above the ground; then four poles to an elm and crossing again a fork of the Limestone.

It wasn't precise, but the settlers had been promised that in the near future there would be definitive plats from a new land office to be created in Huntsville.

The McCracken cabin went up first as Mack had the most young children. Samuel's was next, and the others were all finished by early fall. A stockade was constructed for the protection of their animals, and each family built pens for their own fowl. Byres and cross-log fences could be erected later. These men worked for all, and any new farmers arriving in their midst became good friends.

In the fall when all the leaves left their colorful ways and returned to the bosom of the earth, another little girl joined the Kimsey family. A sweet baby, Clark's baby, she was the delight of her mother and grandparents. Lizzie could mourn no more. She would smile instead, for as the weeks went by, Grace looked more and more like her father.

When Jamie and Mary built their cabin, he calculated for his brother Berry in the loft and a separate room for Lizzie and the child. It would be private until such time, well, as God's will for her manifested itself. For now, he and Mary would simply enjoy their time together.

* * *

A tall young man arrived at a well-built cabin where he thought he might get direction. He set the brake, tied off the reins, and stepped down off the wagon's seat. It was a vividly brilliant Sunday morning, and he eyed the beautiful land around the settlement. He knocked on the door, and the woman who opened it frowned at the stranger, not recognizing him although she did not know every one of her neighbors.

"May I help you?"

"Yes." He removed his hat. "Could you point me to the home of Mr. McCracken?"

"You've reached it."

Son John came up behind her. "What can we do for you, sir?"

"I've just received a piece of side land on the west, and noted the name of Mr. McCracken on the plat map and was wondering if he was from the same family I knew in the Carolinas."

Mollie rubbed her cold arms. Despite the strong sun, there was a hint of fall in the air, and John invited the man in out of the cold and took his hat. She poured tea and, handing him a cup, explained that her husband was helping Jamie with the Sunday service.

The young man wrapped his cold hands around the cup. "Oh, you have a minister here? That's wonderful 'cause I'm gonna be lookin' for a wife soon."

Daughter Nancy walked in. "Gracie's asleep. I thought I'd take a break and have a cup of—oh, hello." She smiled at the fine-looking stranger with prominent brow, dark eyes, and several days' growth of beard. "Who's this, Mother?" she asked.

"Goodness! I'm sorry for our bad manners. We didn't get your name."

"Oh, sorry, ma'am. My name is Jacob Simpson from Georgetown County, South Carolina." He stood and bowed gracefully, then he shook John's hand. "They recently divided up the county, so now it's called...Horry County...ah...along the Little Pee Dee River." He was getting tongue-tied looking at Nancy and dropped his cup; he deftly caught it although splashes of hot tea burned his hand. His faced turned red in pain and embarrassment, and Nancy turned her face away to hide her smile.

"What's going on here?" Mack asked, coming inside.

John replied, "Here's a man who says he knows your family from the old time."

"Sit down and tell me all about it," Mack directed although he did not recognize him. "Bring him another cup, Nan."

"I knew your family, sir, before they moved to Union County, South Carolina." He swore he wouldn't fumble with the cup this time.

Gracie began to cry, and Nancy excused herself. When she came back, she had the baby in her arms.

Jacob's face fell. "Is that yours?" he asked, crestfallen that she might already be taken and confused as to who was whom in this family.

Mack nearly burst out laughing and quickly cleared his throat. This boy was obviously shopping for a wife. "Now tell me, Jacob. How do you know my family?"

They were interrupted again with a knock at the door. Mollie opened it.

Muffled voices burst into the room.

"Thanks for taking care of the baby, Nan. My throat's much better today." Lizzie took the child in her arms. "Oh, I'm sorry, Mr. McCracken. I didn't realize you had company. Father could really use your help again. He's almost ready to start the service."

Jacob's story would have to wait. He didn't know what to do with himself. Here were two beautiful girls in the same room and family members he couldn't quite sort out.

"Why don't you join us for the service, Jacob, then you can meet the rest of the settlers," Mack offered.

The church services were being held in Jamie's living room until such time that a small church could be built. Later, when Mack and Jamie were talking together, Mack commented that "Jacob probably didn't hear a word you said for staring at all the pretty girls at the service. Lizzie seems to be the target."

* * *

"Two weddings—oh, what a happy day!" Jamie was ecstatic, and the announcement went out. "Nancy, daughter of Mack McCracken, our most esteemed friend, is marrying our fine neighbor James English. Elizabeth Kimsey Biggerstaff, our most precious daughter, is to wed Jacob Simpson, late of South Carolina, at a double ceremony. Welcome one and all on this glorious day, a day of celebration."

Lizzie wore a store-bought dress of cotton with vines of tiny yellow flowers trailing through the skirt's folds purchased for her by Jacob at the mercantile in Nashville. She was well pleased at his gift. Her only other adornment was a narrow yellow ribbon holding her auburn locks so they fell over her shoulder.

As the couples walked toward him, Jamie looked deeply at his daughter, and the memories of her played out in his mind—from a little child to the grown woman she was at this moment. Now she was different—wiser, complete, with a depth of soul only she could understand. He had his own understanding of life, as only a man could, but this woman—Jacob would have a fine match for life.

Nancy, two years younger than Hannah, wanted to wear her sister's wedding dress with a few modifications to make it her own. Mollie made a lace overlay on the bodice and took up the hem—Hannah being taller. There was a matching lace cap for her head, and her long black curls cascaded around her shoulders.

The man she was marrying—James English—was acquiring great wealth after he built his first sawmill. He was selling his services to the settlement's residents, and they in turn could make clapboard homes to be whitewashed for beauty instead of the cruder and tediously built log cabins. Construction went faster, and they could have smooth wood plank floors and cupboards on the walls, headboards, footboards for the bedstead, and also firm foundations for feather mattresses.

Mack and Jamie had discussed the couple when it first appeared they were in love. English was an ambitious young man. He wasn't hard to look at, and she would never be poor, of that they were confident.

Late Fall 1805

Fragile. All of life is fragile, Jim thought. He was half naked lying on his side and up to his shoulder in the animal's birthing canal as he twisted and turned the breach. A last pull on the sac spewed forth water and blood over his bare chest. As dawn had approached, the calf was in distress, struggling to give birth. Jim had gone to her side, but there being nothing he could do. She lay down and died. Now he cried for the orphan in his arms as he wiped away the vestiges of the membrane. He tenderly carried her to another stall.

"You are a mess," Hannah grimaced, coming into the byre at the moment he was sharpening his hunting knife on the strap. She had a bottle of milk for the baby collected from its struggling mother the evening before, clean clothes for Jim, and her six-year-old brother Jeremiah, anxious to get a first glimpse of the little neat.

"Jeremiah, run to Mr. Hancock down the road. Tell him what happened and to bring one of his lactating neats," Jim requested. "The mother has to be dressed immediately."

The boy pouted, rocking back and forth from foot to foot, hovering over the calf and dying to pet the newborn. "Git!" Jim commanded.

"Hannah, help me," he implored.

She nodded and tied a leather apron around herself, then handed Jim the chain. First, he removed the animal's head, then knotted the back feet together, threading the rope's free end with the chain over the pulley and fastening it to the winch. Between the two of them, they managed to get the animal to a height where Jim could comfortably work on it.

While he was busy with the hide, Hannah guided the bottle's nipple to the baby's muzzle. It began sucking happily, slurping noisily until the last tasty drops were consumed. The wee creature in her lap—weighing five stone and healthy for a newborn—was exhausted from its ordeal and fell asleep immediately.

By the time Jim had skinned the cow, they could hear Clem's wagon pull up outside the byre. He brought a good healthy heifer with him, her teats nearly touching the ground.

"What happened, Jim?" his concerned neighbor asked, bringing in one of the barrels that had been tethered to the wagon.

"It was a breach, Clem."

"Ah," he exhaled and went to work without further discussion.

The men split the meat—two barrels each of salted beef. Jim shared his half with Hannah's large family. Clem left his friends, saying, "I'll be back when the calf is weaned off."

Jim, divested of his trousers, shivered in the cold nakedness of the early morning ground fog. His teeth chattered as he doused himself with water and rubbed the bar of lye soap over the goose bumps on his skin.

"Go inside for your breakfast, Jim. I'll finish up here." Hannah suggested.

It was deliciously warm in the house. Jim poured a cup of coffee, drowning it with cream and sugar. In the middle of the kitchen table, an iron skillet held scrambled eggs, potatoes, and strips of bacon laced across the top. He sat for a moment and wolfed down spoonfuls of the glorious yellow concoction right out of the pan but finally gave in to his sore back, resting it against the chair slats. The hot coffee made him too comfortable, and it only took a moment for his eyelids to close. He was startled awake with a jerk, feeling his cup falling sideways at his wife's call.

"Damn, I'm glad you caught me. Almost spilled my coffee. Got to get to the old tree stump. Been thinkin' about it all the time I was working that calf. How's she doin'?"

"Fine. Jeremiah's looking after her. Put on your coat. It's still cold out there."

He pulled an old stained linen fringed hunting shirt over his slim frame. Hannah heaped the leftover contents of the iron pan onto a slice of bread and covered it with another. "Here. Take this with you. I'll bring your dinner later."

"Thanks, sweetheart. I'll need it." He wiped his mouth with his sleeve, not quite managing the remnants of his breakfast stuck to his mustache. He kissed her cheek.

Hannah loved the smell of her husband whether it was his sweat, the odor of the food about him, or his clean smell after the Saturday-night bath. He was a man of the earth. He was her man.

Jim finished the last bite of his breakfast while walking around the difficult task that was ahead of him. He wished he had more coffee to go with it, but as tired as he was, the remainder of the felled tree needed to be removed, and it was too big to pull out with a horse team. When they first came to the area, he guessed it was about three hundred years old with its many rings. The root spread was as wide as the branches had been and took up a large portion of his planting area.

A snag stopped his shovel cold. Again and again he dug deeper in the rich earth only to find a grasping arm outstretched and ready to receive nutrients but grasping the earth for dear life instead. Using the ax, he drove the blade into the wood, chopping and cursing over and over until only the stump remained and he thought his arms would fall off. He was boring several holes in the ragged surface when

Hannah joined him in the field. They sat on the massive obstruction to enjoy their meal of ham and beans. More than once, as they talked, she caught him distractedly staring west.

"I wonder what's out there," he mused, wanderlust grabbing at his resolve to do something he thought he would never do. *Just like Pa.* "Oh, well…Go on back to the house. I'll blast this thing out."

"Jim, when were the hunters due back?"

"Two days ago. Wish I could have gone with them, but that heifer…Couldn't leave her. They should be back soon." In trying to soothe Hannah, a stinging sensation rose on the back of his neck, a premonition. Something was wrong.

"Be careful, sweetheart."

When Hannah was far out of sight, Jim charged each opening in the stump with black powder. He made a hole in the granules with a pricker, tamped it with clay, then pulled out the tool. Filling a few hollow straws with powder, he placed each into a hole and attached touch paper[32] to the ends. He struck a match to one tip and ran like hell, diving headfirst behind the stacked roots just as the powder exploded. The blast sent shock waves over the ground and splintered wood flying through the air. Fragments were everywhere, but with the plough, he would turn them under and let them rot naturally. A big smile enveloped his face at the thought of the extra fertile acres that would provide more food for his family.

* * *

Grinding work and alertness to the movement of the Chickasaw kept the new settlers busy. Not at all happy with the encroachment of the white man on their hunting grounds and the treaties with the federal government, the Indians continued to clash with the white settlers.

---

[32] Touch-paper is a slow-burning paper fuse treated with solution of potassium nitrate or saltpetre used for lighting flammable or explosive devices such as fireworks (https://en.wikipedia.org/wiki/Touchpaper).

363

The Kimsey, McCracken, English, and Simpson families bonded together for mutual comfort and protection—a mighty force to be reckoned with. Each shared the fruits of their labor and the intertwining of their families by marriages, and each family had an arsenal of muskets and pistols from the war, hunting rifles, and a great larder of gunpowder and ammunition in case of assault.

More often now, Jim found himself in the fields or on their porch watching the sunset—just standing there looking. There was an unnatural draw, a pull of something beyond the horizon that he found he shared with his father. But, he would awake from his reveries, remembering the imminent beginning of his new family growing within Hannah.

Chapter 38

Buncombe County, North Carolina

1805

AGNES HEARD HIM singing. She listened carefully, shushing the children—what was it? "Listen to Grampa," she said to their eight grandchildren and two great-grandchildren. "He has a beautiful voice."

It was the "Old One Hundreth," Benjamin's favorite. "You're singing it too high for the congregation, my love. No one can reach the beauty of your voice," she often complained.

But he didn't care. "Let them sing lower. It's all for the honor and glory of God anyway. He's pleased with all who sing his praises."

Benjamin's eighty-year-old voice was still clear and strong drifting over the heads of the women watching their children, across the backyard of his home and business, and onto the street beyond. Many a time Aggie saw passersby linger, listening to the Baptist minister who moved the community of Buncombe County to worship.

The sermon from John chapter 21 that warm summer morning had been about Peter, the first apostle. Benjamin connected with Peter because he recognized himself as a sinner. Three times Peter denied knowing Jesus, even as the savior was being accused of blasphemy, tried for his crime, and hung on the cross. Peter ran away and cried bitter tears and would only believe when he saw the empty tomb. Like Peter, Benjamin would lose his temper when pressed, and there were other things, other things that bothered his soul.

Benjamin bowed his head, then raised it and began softly—something unusual for him.

"The disciples had just made a large catch of fish, and as they were coming to shore, Jesus stood waiting for them. 'Come and dine,' he called to them. By the Sea of Tiberius, he had a charcoal fire cooking fish on it and bread to feed them, but they didn't recognize him. After they dined, Jesus said to Peter, 'Simon, son of Jonas, lovest thou me more than these?' Peter replied, 'Yea, Lord, thou knowest that I love thee.' Jesus replied, 'Feed my lambs.'

"Again, Jesus asked if Peter loved him. Peter was hurt to the core, but the answer was the same. 'Feed my sheep,' Jesus patiently taught him. Grieved, Peter said, 'Lord, thou knowest all things. Thou knowest I love thee.' Again, the same three words, 'Feed my flock.'... Lord, I have done all these things. I've never regretted being a minister...I never forgot my promise..." He clenched his hands, his knuckles turning white.

Startled, Aggie looked up at him that he was suddenly deviating from scripture.

Collecting himself, Reverend Kimsey continued, "Jesus told Peter, 'Verily I say unto thee, when thou wast young, thou walkest whither thou wouldst: but when thou shalt be old, thou shalt stretch forth thy hands'"—he looked at his hands—"'and another shall gird thee'"—and then he looked at Aggie—"'and carry thee whither thou wouldest not.'" Benjamin's voice was barely audible. "He must increase...while I must decrease."

This was not his habit at all. The end of his sermons were usually bombastic, bringing the faithful to a fever pitch. What was wrong? All looked around in astonishment and searched the eyes of their fellow congregants for answers.

Aggie was seized with fear. She peered at her husband for any telltale signs. Many times, she heard this sermon about Peter and how he was to die on a cross, but not like Jesus asking his tormentors to place the cross upside down. Was Benjamin foretelling his own death? She bit her lip, drawing a small drop of blood. Quickly wiping it away, she was drawn back from her fear by Hiram's violin introduction of the final hymn.

After the service, the Kimseys had planned a picnic on the lawn of their home, and Aggie's fears disappeared in the fun and games that ensued. The men and boys of the family were at a good-spirited game of ninepins. Benjamin had carved the pins years before when his children were little and fashioned a ball out of corn husks wrapped with leather and tied with string. Many times over the years, his hands formed other balls for his family who still delighted in the game.

"Father," David complained, "this thing is falling apart."

"Well, make another," he told him.

William pleaded with him, "Come on, David. Roll it. You have only one pin left. If you knock it over, we win."

The ball just missed the pin by inches. "I'm getting too old for this," David whined.

"We won, Papa. We won," Benjamin's six-year-old great-grandson ran to him laughing, and he took the small boy on his lap. A large whoop ran through the family.

Shut out of the fun, the girls were in ill humor. "Go play hoops," the boys snapped back as they launched another ball toward the pins. "First one over the finish line wins," one of the girls hollered and picked up a stick, tapping the rim of an old barrel ring, sending it down an embankment as she ran alongside to keep it rolling. "Don't let it fall over or you're out."

Benjamin sat in his chair watching his large family. Pretty colors of summertime dresses caught his eye. Shirtsleeves were rolled up, and all were barefoot, running and having fun in the long grass just like in the old days. Agnes sat on a colorful quilt with Polly and her daughters-in-law. Tree limbs cast shadows over the bowling green. Yellow lemonade quenched thirsts, and many of the picnickers came back for another piece of fried chicken or a slice of cake.

It was a pleasant afternoon, only overshadowed by the fact that some family members had moved away from the homestead. Jamie had broken with the family and moved on to Tennessee, and after the war, Solomon moved to Currituck County along the coast of North Carolina. The family had not seen him for twenty-five years.

David wheedled the boys into a new game and rolled a ninepin ball, sending it down the slope on the side of their home and missing the pins altogether. "So sorry. I'll fetch it!" he yelled breathless, sweating profusely and thoroughly enjoying the day.

David stopped short as a stranger stooped to pick up the ball. Aggie watched from her position on the quilt. She shielded her eyes. Who was it? Her boys were laughing, shaking hands, hugging. "Benjamin," she called to her husband and pointed to a large group of people coming their way. "Help me up, Polly," she asked of her daughter.

Benjamin struggled out of his chair too. His eyesight wasn't good anymore, and he couldn't imagine what the commotion was. Everyone was running to the newcomer.

Stiff from sitting on the ground, Aggie made it over to her husband and held firmly to him. "Ben…" She nervously patted his arm. "It's…Solomon! My God in heaven, Ben. It's Sol."

The Kimseys encircled Sol's family with hugs and kisses. Sol clasped his brother Hiram tightly in his arms, holding him with special affection, and Aggie, who barely recognized their son and daughter-in-law, Martha, nearly fainted at the sight.

"Mother!" he sobbed on her shoulder. Then, in his happiness, Sol picked her up and swung her around in a circle. Back on level ground, Aggie held to him to study his aged face and grayed hair. "How is he, Mother?" he whispered in her ear. "I was afeard for him. I had a dream…"

"Go to your father, son."

"My boy! Oh, how I've missed you." Father and son shook hands, then Ben embraced his long-gone son.

Ben and Aggie stood apart from the crowd, admiring each child and grandchild presented to them. Mattie came to their side and held on to Aggie, happy tears running down both their faces.

Mattie related that most of the kin remained behind, but Sol and members of her family desired to move west. She commented on each of her children's progress as well as the sadness of the lost ones over the years.

Sol's large extended family had a compound on the eastern shore, each son or son-in-law with many hundred acres. Knowing how his father hated slavery, he did not relate that some of the family owned slaves to prosper their lands.

* * *

The outing over, all had gone home satisfied and happy, leaving Aggie and Benjamin to consider the life they had begun with their love. Now aged, they thought of their large family carrying on the Kimsey name.

Late that evening, Benjamin began making a list of needs for the mercantile.

"How much silk yardage will we need, dear?"

Agnes knew what the ladies in the surrounding towns enjoyed. Times and tastes had changed, but even though her clothing had always been plain cotton or wool, she watched the trends and could help her husband with all the modes of bonnets, stays, ties, and ribbons. She caught Benjamin's head nodding over their shared list.

"Darling one, why don't you go to bed? I'll finish up, and we can go over it in the morning."

He stood to leave, but, with a sudden rush of passion for his wife, drew her to him. "After all our years together, those green eyes of yours still make me dizzy. Don't take too long."

When Aggie crawled in bed exhausted, Benjamin held her close and remarked in an uncommon lack of humility, "I have become so old. How can you bear to look at me after sixty-four years of marriage? My hair and beard have become gray and thin."

"Not so much that I've noticed," she responded with a yawn.

"Your eyes must have failed you, woman."

"It's just a mask you bear, dear heart. You are still the brave, strong warrior I married so long ago—even if your feet are like ice. Good night, Benjamin." She tilted her head toward him, smiling, and they kissed with the long, deep devotion they had held through all their years together.

"It all goes so quickly." Benjamin sighed to his sleeping wife.

* * *

Aggie awoke to the birds singing, and her soul smiled at the thought. Then she turned over…the love of her life was dead. Numb, she summoned the family.

Reverently, she washed Benjamin's body, remembering his last sermon…

> Verily I say unto thee, when thou wast young, thou walkest whither thou wouldst: but when thou shalt be old, thou shalt stretch forth thy hands and another shall gird thee and carry thee whither thou wouldest not.

And remembering the misery of the English prisoner ship…

> Laying him on the English wool, Aggie stripped away what was left of his foul rags. She gently cleansed the filth from his colorless fragile skin, dried him and dressed his wounds.

She laid Benjamin out on the tidied bed in his black suit and ministerial robes and straightened the ends of his stock on his chest.

Then Aggie dressed herself in her dark-blue wool dress, a fine white handkerchief folded neatly over her bodice the only adornment. She brushed her long gray hair and began to pin it in a severe bun at the nape of her neck. She always wore it like that, but somehow it wasn't right. Unseemly, she looked in the mirror this way and that and decided she would curl the locks and tie them with a ribbon just the way Benjamin liked it. She recalled.

Slowly, tenderly, he touched her face then reached back to untie a yellow satin ribbon holding the long locks in a cluster of curls. She was wearing her hair that same way when he first met her. He pulled the curls forward over her bosom, then kissed her lips. A long left-behind passion bloomed in them, and they made love for the first time since their union in Ireland.

The remembrance of that moment in time caused tears of grief and loss to flow. She was bereft of her husband and lover, friend, and companion. As hard as she was with the slings and arrows of life, she was tender of heart, and her loss was deep and bitter.

A long dark line stretched through town toward Ebenezer Baptist Church—some walked, others rode in carriages or wagons, or on horses. With her son David supporting her, Aggie walked behind the wagon that carried the plain wood coffin containing her husband's body, a plain wood cross rested on his bosom. The family, politicians, businessmen, friends, and Benjamin's congregation followed—all in Buncombe County revered the preacher, merchant, husband, father, grandfather, and great-grandfather.

Inside the church, and to Aggie's surprise, Sol delivered the eulogy.

"Years ago, when our country was on the brink of war, I heard my father speak of the necessity to pray for peace. Being a strict Baptist, he was opposed to violence. I told him I was ashamed of him standing for peace against the threat to our way of life. I saw my father cry for the first time in my life." Head bowed, Sol tried to compose himself. "You see, I was an unruly fellow and told him I wanted to answer the call for Virginia's militia. He gave his permission…after I harangued him unmercifully." Sol laughed lightly, and the palpable sadness in the church was relieved. He continued, "I had thought him a coward. My own father! A coward! Far from it—he was a hero…a prisoner and beaten for his beliefs. In the end, he told me, 'We arose from the ashes of our homeland, and we will arise from whatever will come. You may go if it is your heart's desire.' He was the inspiration for my life and for my brothers and sisters as well. Honorable and courageous, we loved him for the truth he proclaimed and the great man he was, but most especially for being our father. Benjamin Kimsey lived and died for his beloved kin and faithful flock. Now he rests in the arms of our heavenly Father."

Hiram touched the bow to the strings of his violin and played his heart out for his father. There were many tears for the loved man. Benjamin was laid in the dark earth with his adopted Kimsey name in the place he chose to give his affection.

Chapter 39

The Parting

1805

THE WHIZ AND thud of an arrow splitting his breast bone sent screams tearing at the black sky and with it a deluge of rain and frightful rolling thunder descending upon the hunting party. Lightning lit Jamie's tormented face in violent waves of dazed pain and showed his white beard spattered with blood. It wasn't just the weapon protruding from his chest at which he stared, it was a brutal vision accompanying his imminent death.

The men around him—his son and friends—had taken defensive positions after the assault but were helpless in the instant the death-dealing blow took place. Musket and rifle shots pierced the air and smoke from exploding powder sunk to the wet earth as did two bodies of the attacking Chickasaw. The rest ran off, dissatisfied that they had only killed one encroaching settler. Jamie looked straight into the eyes of his son Littleberry as he dropped to the ground on his knees.

"Benjamin!" Jamie's breath came in sobs. His arms outstretched.

"Father?…I'm Littleberry."

While the others stood guard in case the enemy would return, Mack was at Jamie's side instantly, not believing what he saw. He bent low over his friend newly related by marriage. "Jamie, hold on…" Wild weather lashed away his words.

Jamie grabbed Mack's hunting shirt, pulling him low, gasping, "Forgive me?"

The two men holding him tenderly stared in disbelief as Jamie's head fell to the side, and he groaned his death rattle in their arms.

At that instant, three men appeared out of the dense forest.

"What happened?" one man yelled. "We ran after them, but the devils already disappeared into the mists." His mates held their defense, preparing for any more aggression.

Littleberry's tormented face looked at them. "My father is dead."

The hunters joined the knot already assembled around the party's fallen comrade. One of the men dressed in buckskins, his fringe shedding the continual deluge, came closest and stared in disbelief at the pierced victim.

"Charles, what is it?" one of the trio asked his friend.

The man moved in closer, and strangely the hunting party made way for the newcomer. Even though the body was drenched with rain-diluted blood and mud, there was recognition. Why Mack moved back, he did not know, and why Charles took his place was a mystery. The stranger with the scarred cheek glanced at Littleberry, seeing the relationship, then he looked down at the man clenched tightly in the son's arms.

"Oh, God! No! No!" Tears of memory ran down his face. "May I hold him?" Charles held out his arms and waited breathlessly. All were astonished when he said, "This is my brother…Jamie."

Littleberry let his father go to the stranger's arms. How did this thing occur? Was it true?

When the party returned home with carcasses of deer ladened on packhorses and the body of Jamie carried by travois, they were greeted in the yard apprehensively by the Kimseys and McCrackens. Joy turned to wailing with Mary the first to see.

"I knew it…I knew it…I told them, but they doubted!" she screamed out in shock and horror, staggering forward through the mud toward her beloved husband with Junior on her heels. Sheets of rain crossed the yard, and the sky gave a long, deep, rolling peal of thunder as if crying for the death of the brothers Kimsey. She held her man, sobbing onto his drenched shirt. Lightning cracked a tree, cutting it in two pieces that fell side by side. Mary had had a vision before they left. She told them not to go—it was too dangerous. Her dream was confused, and even she could not believe it. Both brothers would die, but when? Both families would not believe, but assigned another to go with the hunters, and now Mary beheld her dead husband.

Someone was pulling Mary off her man. She was angry and violently resisted. The man was firm but gentle. "Mary! Mary, don't struggle." He held her by her shoulders. Unbelieving, she looked at his face aged by many decades and damaged by that English sword nearly fifty years before. The rain stopped, and the sun's rays shot through the black clouds.

"Charles?" She collapsed into his arms and poured her sad tears onto his chest.

One month later, word was received from Agnes of the very day and hour Benjamin had died. The occurrences were exact. For generations, the families would tell the tale over campfires not even thought of yet.

Desolated by his father's death, Jim mourned the old farmer and his Uncle Benjamin, the old warrior turned minister. Scots brothers together—and now they were gone. With them, two wars had melded into the past. No more, Jim prayed. But then his sorrow was replaced by envy—envy of the setting western sun. How he wished he could go there. For the present, he would lovingly feed his family, just like his Pa.

And a New Beginning

Charles MacKenzie felt no need to keep the name Kimsey. His brother Benjamin had sought to change it when the English arrested them in Ireland. It hadn't worked for the family, and it wasn't necessary when Mr. MacCorkindale purchased him and his brother Alexander for work in the tobacco fields of Virginia. The last he saw of Jamie was in 1761 when he and Mary were married in Virginia.

The other brother, Alexander, went back east and worked the land MacCorkindale had given him, but Charles had no desire to pick stubborn bugs off tobacco plants.

From North Carolina into Kentucky, he'd followed a man named Daniel Boone and stayed awhile in Boonesborough where he met like-minded mountain men. They formed an alliance: go forth, hunt, fight when necessary, and settle when you're too tired to move further west. At seventy-four, it struck him that he fit that last requirement.

Even with his friends, loneliness along the Indian trails had become something to contend with in his advancing years. He thought he'd die somewhere alone on one of those trails, meeting one of those Indians on whose land he hunted.

Mary, at sixty-two, was a rare beauty, he caught himself thinking. He swore he would leave as soon as his nephew Littleberry and the other hunters of the Kimsey and McCracken families would go out again and bring back the needed provisions for their many members.

Sleeping in the byre, Charles awoke one morning realizing he had been in one spot for two months. What was he thinking?

The delicious aroma of breakfast caught him brushing bits of hay from his clothes. What was he doing? His life had been sleeping in his clothes, slapping on his beaver skin hat, and continuing on his way, musket tucked up under his arm. If he found a good creek running fast and cold, he'd shed his clothes and bathe bare-assed, catching a fish if one passed his way. The only time he might slick down his hair was if he entered a fort or town to trade skins for ball and powder and supplies—although no one really cared what a mountain man looked like. Only the pelts were attractive to the proprietors.

Two months, even with three square meals a day, was way too long for any man to stay put, and Charles's two friends were getting restless. They prodded their friend to come with them to St. Louis and they would head west—that was their plan. Here they were expected to do chores for the widow, Mary, so they gave Charles the evil eye when carrying a load of wood for the fire. It's getting late in the year, they said. We want to be up the Mississippi to St. Louis before the snow flies, they begged. Charles waved them off, delaying. Why was he delaying? You can go anytime, he told his friends.

For that day, Mary would not dress in mourning black. Work was awaiting her hands, and she wanted to get back to normal, even though she missed her Jamie terribly. By candlelight, she laced up her petticoat over the shift then cast the dark-blue cotton gown over all and tied her apron over the skirt. She adjusted the cap over her hair but left the strings free.

It was early, just barely light in the east, when a tap at the kitchen door startled her.

"Can you use some help?" Hannah called out.

Mary was pleased that her new daughter-in-law was there to help prepare the meal. She had wanted to have a talk with the pretty blonde woman.

Hannah stirred the porridge so it wouldn't scorch, and Mary set slices of cured pork in a hot frying pan, sending the smell wafting through the house. She continued slicing into the slab and cut her finger in the process. Just as she cried out in pain holding her hand, Charles appeared at the door.

"Do you need me to milk the cow...Oh, you're hurt! Let me help." He produced a cloth from his pocket and tied it around her finger to staunch the blood.

Mary saw the Scottish blush bloom on his ruddy cheeks from the cold air, and especially when she looked at him. He did not immediately remove his hands from hers.

"Thank you," Mary said quietly, embarrassed for her clumsiness. "Yes, we could use more milk for our baking this afternoon." She neither removed her hands from his nor turned aside from his steady gaze—a mix of pleasure and awe.

Hannah knew it right then and there. Jim had even suggested it to his wife, but she wouldn't believe him.

"But do you think he'll stay around?" she asked. "After all, he is a wandering man."

"I'll talk to him regarding the prospect," Jim offered.

After their meal and everyone went to do their chores, Hannah stayed to clean the dishes for her mother-in-law. Charles came in with another bucket filled with warm sweet milk.

"May I have a cup, Mary? It's delicious. Don't get it very often unless we find an occasional farmhouse along the way. Not too many of those in the wilderness. Too dangerous."

"What's keeping you here, Charles?" Mary delicately inquired when he drank the milk. "Your friends are getting restless. Will you push on with them?"

He pulled out a chair and sat his tired frame on the hard surface. Mary seated herself across from him, placing her towel in her lap. Neither noticed Hannah had left the room.

"I'd be lying if I said I want to go." He stared down at his hands scarred with years of hard work and fights with Indians and wild animals. He thought about the precious woman sitting with him at the table, the woman who had been married for so many years to his brother. Why would she want him?

"You have family here, Charles," she stated bluntly. Her forthright statement startled him.

He started to speak when Jim bungled in.

Hannah, on her husband's tail, winced. "Jim! For heaven's sake."

"Oh…I'm so sorry, Mother. I didn't realize you had company."

"No, it's quite all right. I'm glad you're both here. If Mary is willing, I would like permission to court her."

Mary looked at the man who had traversed the western lands all his life. She suddenly remembered her Jamie when he had left her and went missing for three years in that same wilderness. That unhappiness was a long time ago and would never be related to Charles, but she wondered if he, too, would again long for the freedom of the far west and leave her. She thought herself a plain woman. He had never been married. She had married for love. What did he look like under that beard and all that long hair? He was a lot older. Would he leave her a widow for the second time in her life? She had so many questions.

Hannah suggested Mary could perhaps give him her answer that evening at the McCracken's home.

Charles left the house to attend to any chores he thought needed to be done, but his friends swayed his resolve and they went into the woods to hunt.

"I suspect there is more to this delay than we understand, Charles. Is that right?" one asked as they scouted along for tracks.

"If you intend to stay, maybe you should clean up so's she knows what she's gettin' under all that filth. She may not like the view," the other said and broke into a hearty laugh. Charles was not amused and despaired as to how to go about it. The men took him by his sleeves and marched him to the McCracken's home, where Jim and Hannah were helping her mother with the preparations.

Hannah answered the door. "Jim," she yelled. "Your uncle is here!"

Mary and Littleberry rode the distance to their in-laws' homestead that night. She didn't know what to expect and sought out her son's advice.

"Berry, I haven't asked what you think of the situation with your uncle. He's just shown up on our doorstep, and it's been many decades. By all accounts from your father and Benjamin, he was a good man despite his wandering life."

"I think it's too soon, Mother. Charles would need to prove himself to me before I would allow him to court you. I believe Junior would agree, and I could take care of you myself."

Mary would defer to her sons before allowing her emotions to rule her own desires—if it came to that. She would see what the night would bring.

As usual, the McCracken home was a chaos of happy souls— adults and children alike—and Mollie McCracken was again with child. *Where was Charles?* Mary wondered. All sat around a very long table and waited for the curious stranger who claimed to be uncle and brother-in-law.

Mary was engaged in conversation with Hannah's youngest sister, Lettice. The fifteen-year-old was the spitting image of Hannah, only with amber-colored hair and green eyes, and both were being interrupted by two-year-old Nimrod who demanded he be called Roddy. His white-blond hair curled around his forehead and big ears.

"You need to go to bed, Nimrod. Mother says so." And Lettice whisked the little fellow away to tuck him in.

"Who are you?" everyone heard Lettice ask as she ascended the stairs with her little brother. All heads turned toward the landing. A man stepped off, disturbing their convivial gathering. There was stunned silence in the room.

Jim stared, noting the striking resemblance to his father and uncle, and asked the question everyone wanted to know. "Uncle Charles? Is that you?"

They all sat there with their mouths wide open at the stranger's entrance, then gasps and whistles one after another around the table.

"What do you think?" He turned in a circle. "I haven't seen myself in twenty-five years!"

At the sight of him, Mary dropped the cup of water that was halfway to her mouth. She felt awkward and fidgeted with the mess in her lap as Charles sat down next to her. He took her hand in his, calming her anxiety. She stopped and looked at him.

His beard was gone. He had a rather pleasing-looking face, even with the four-inch scar on his left cheek given from an unkind cut of a Redcoat soldier back in '46. Deep lines reflected a long life. The unkempt gray hair, which had been hidden beneath his hat, was drawn back and tied. Buckskins were replaced with a rather nice linen shirt covered by a brown waistcoat, and brown breeches completed his new outfit and revealed a slim frame that hadn't been apparent before. The donated clothes fit him well enough, but no one's shoes fit his big feet, and he was forced to wear his worn out Indian moccasins—not exactly matching his style of dress. It caused laughter to fill the room. Not one could believe it was the same man.

"I'm so sorry I startled you," he said to Mary as the food was served and the attention was off him.

She found him comfortably attractive, a good likeness of Jamie and Benjamin, especially around the eyes. Staring at him, Mary said, "You're really quite handsome." She suddenly lost her appetite, and she wouldn't be a widow for long.

Chapter 40

Madison County, Alabama

December 13, 1808

WHILE THE KIMSEYS prepared for Christmas and Hogmanay, Madison County's seat was established as Huntsville[33] north of the Tennessee River, but the area was still known as the Mississippi Territory and had its own governor and taxes. The boundaries of their settlement had been drawn in error, however, then redrawn again on a plat map, and Tennessee's state line[34] was then corrected when the surveyor's mistakes were discovered. The Kimseys were definitely in Chickasaw country.

Jim wasn't concerned for the present, but he knew that settlers were pouring across the Appalachian Mountains just as his father, Jamie, and Uncle Benjamin had done. A steady stream descended into the Tennessee River Valley from Virginia and North Carolina. And just a few years before, two men sent by President Thomas Jefferson became the first to find a path of discovery to the Pacific Ocean. Reading about their travels whetted Jim's appetite for the west. "I'd like to go there someday," Jim said to Hannah over a cup of tea.

---

[33] Huntsville, Alabama, founded in 1805, incorporated in 1811.
[34] The state line is along the 35th parallel.

"I'll bet Charles would have loved to go as well, but I bet he'd say, 'I'm too old and prefer your mother to the open road.'" Hannah grinned, and Jim raised his cup to his new stepfather who reminded him so much of Uncle Benjamin. *Wonder what it was like back in their days in Scotland.*

The Kimseys would stay as they had always done: planting, living, having babies, making friends, and leaving many family members behind as they spread out across the United States. This new country over the western borders was pristine with plenty of game, good soil, and comfortable weather. The Indians had cleared, by burning, barrens for themselves to plant their crops then moved on as treaties pushed them away. It was rich land ready for the plough without ever having to be cleared.

It was early spring, and against Jim's better judgment, Hannah went out with him to work the barren on their land with their fifteen-month-old Samuel strapped to her back and one-month-old Mahala in a basket set in some shade. Yes, they named him after Jim's oldest brother, Samuel, and his son, Sam Jr. She would tell those who asked that it was the Scottish way—to share the names of their beloved children with those who came after.

As he ploughed, Hannah cleared rocks from the path in front of him. It was hot work, and the boy was heavy and fussy. Without warning, she vomited in the field and collapsed to her knees.

Jim rushed to her side. "I'm so sorry, Hannah. You shouldn't have come out. I simply wanted to get a good start on the garden in the pleasant weather. You're a stubborn woman, Hannah Jane. Here, have some water and sit down." He passed her a cupful from the bucket and unfastened the boy from her back. Jim put him down on the ground next to his sister.

Husband and wife sat together watching their babies. "Let's go back to the house and get supper," he suggested.

Samuel suddenly pursed his lips and let go his bowels. Hannah laughed. "It's a good thing for both of us you put him down."

As they came in the cabin, Hannah wiped the sweat from her face and neck. "Will some jerked beef and bread be enough for now?"

"Yes, of course. Let me clean this little guy up first. He's caked with mud and excrement." Jim walked past her, holding the boy at arm's length, the smell following in his wake. Hannah retched and ran out the door and into the yard. It was a false alarm, but she wondered if she was pregnant again, or was it just the heat.

When Samuel was sufficiently clean, Jim brought him back to his mother. "I've a surprise for you. I'll be right back."

When he returned, he found Hannah resting in her rocker and Samuel napping in his crib and Mahala cooing in her basket.

"You look sheepish. What are you up to, Jim? What have you in your hands that you are hiding?" She stood and tried her best to get him to show her, first one hand and then the other. "Come on, Jim. What's the surprise?"

She was bursting with excitement. How he loved seeing the delight in her eyes. He could not keep it from her any longer, and produced two nice fat oranges.

"Where did you get these? They're beautiful."

"The other day when I was working in the fields along the trail to New Market, some men stopped me and asked if I wanted some. They were on their way to the new mercantile in that town and suggested we come in for supplies. 'We have all the necessities of life gotten from the coast at Mobile,' the man told me, and…they have new cotton cloth."

Hannah's eyes lit up. He now wished he'd had coins in his pocket to buy her some that very day.

"Can we eat them now, Jim?" she begged.

They sat and ate their jerked beef and buttered bread, and when they removed the orange rind, it gave off a spicy aroma that made her mouth water. She had never tasted anything so delicious in all her life. Letting the peelings dry on her kitchen windowsill, she could pick them up at any time and inhale the treat that Jim had brought her.

Permission given by The University of Alabama Libraries Special Collections.
Map of Madison County, Alabama, Showing Original Boundary

MAP OF
MADISON COUNTY
ALABAMA

ADDED
1836

DETACHED
1837

ADDED
1826

ADDED
1819

CHEROKEE

ADDED
FEB. 6, 1818

REDSTONE
ARSENAL

NEW BOUNDARY BY ACT OF FEB. 6, 1818	
BOUNDARY EXTENSION TO FLINT RIVER 1819	
BOUNDARY EXTENSION 1836	
BOUNDARY REDEFINED ACTS-1826, 1841, 1887	
AREA DETACHED 1837	

Chapter 41

The Days the Earth Shook

1811–1812

Two Hogmanays had come and gone, and another was on the wintry horizon. It was much anticipated as usual, but would be especially welcome as family showed up on their doorstep—Solomon and Hiram, Benjamin's twin sons. They were much older now, midsixties, but Jim only remembered Hiram and greeted him warmly at the door. "And you must be cousin Sol? What a pleasure to meet you. I've heard of your valor in the war. Come in. Come in and warm yourselves. Hannah, look who's here," he called to her. She was carrying two-year-old Hiley, trailed by three-year-old Mahala, and five-year-old Samuel, both hanging to her skirts.

Jim took their coats, and Hannah welcomed them then excused herself to put her babies to bed. "Would you like tea, or something a little stronger?" she offered. "Jim will take care of you."

"Tea would be fine," Hiram said. "It's very good to see you again. Father missed Jamie ever so much when he left. Indeed, we all missed him. Of course, we have missed you all."

As simple as he was, Hiram always went straight to the point, never able to mince words. He had been taught to always tell the truth.

"Did you bring your families with you?"

Sol related, "No. We've left those who are with us in the settlement up in Tennessee—Flat Creek. Many Kimseys and related families are living there now. We want to be with them and build our homes and plant our crops."

Hannah returned with a sigh and a smile, announcing, "The children are finally asleep." She walked over to Jim's relatives, taking their hands in greeting. "I was about to dish up supper, and we would be very honored if you would eat and stay with us."

"May I see to your wagon and team?" Jim offered.

Sol nodded for Hiram to go with him. When they left, he helped Hannah set the table and fetched water from the barrel on the porch. The delicious aroma of stew and corn bread filled the house when Jim and Hiram came in out of the cold.

It was comfortable sitting around the table when Jim started. "I'm sorry I'd never met you, Sol…Oh, is it okay if I call you that?"

"Sure. Solomon seems rather biblically formal to me. I think Mother prayed me into existence and then Hiram was a bonus." Sol, with a broad grin on his face, clapped his twin's shoulder. "When we were kids, no one could tell us apart—even Mother. We had great fun getting into trouble. As we've aged, I got the rougher look of the Kimsey bunch, but Hiram developed the refined features of both our parents. His looks attract many of the womenfolk as do those seductive violin strings. I'm told he has a lady friend back home."

Hiram turned scarlet, uncomfortably self-conscious with Sol's teasing. "I'm gonna bring her out just as soon as I find a place. Lookin' forward to that," he said with pride.

"Hiram's been with Father and Mother all this time caring for them, but after the war, I had moved on to Currituck on the eastern shore of North Carolina with my wife and family. I hadn't seen him or the kin until just before father died. We were all amazed when we found out that Uncle Jamie had died the exact day and hour. It was sad and shocking. They should have never parted the way they did… Oh, it's just life I guess. Anyway, as I said, we're looking for land up in Tennessee."

* * *

The candles had been blown out hours ago, and peaceful sleep was only disturbed by occasional snoring of those who reclined on their backs. Hannah tossed and turned, but a dry throat caused her to get up and go to the kitchen for a drink of water. Her bare feet, practiced to avoid the squeaks so as not to wake the babies, moved lightly across the floor. What remained in the fireplace was gray ash and a few lingering embers, and she thought it would be nice to start a fire, but shivering, she returned to bed. Snuggling against Jim, he warmed her with his body. Finally, exhausted, she fell asleep.

It was well after midnight, black as pitch in the house, when the family was awakened by what sounded like distant thunder, but the vibration continued rolling for many minutes. Loud and terrifying, it rumbled and horrified every occupant, throwing them out of bed. All were thrashing around bumping into one another, and their babies, sitting in the midst of it all, were crying, unable to stand or find solace from their parents.

Fumbling in the dark with the floorboards undulating, Hannah and Jim snatched up the children and took them outside, guarding them from the chimney's falling stones. The trees rippled with a heave, and then the earth stood still. It was eerily quiet until the entire chimney fell with a loud crash, taking out the wall with it. There was a wailing of fear in the settlement combined with terrified cackles, grunts, and whinnying in the yards and cattle bellowing in the byres. Panic rattled all living things, none knowing where to go or what to do. No one could breathe in the thick air.

When Hiram ran outside, he grabbed Hannah's shawl and quilts to wrap the babies in against the cold and cover Hannah. The adults stood there in their nightshirts, holding the children, trembling with fear.

A few hours later, a choking sun rose in a dirty sky, and the devastation became painfully apparent. While most of the cabin was still firm on its foundation, the chimney and wall were destroyed. Jim and Sol covered their noses and mouths with their kerchiefs and carefully surveyed the outside. It was surprising that no cracks were apparent, and the chinking still clung to the big logs.

Sol coughed. "You do good work, Jim. I'm stunned that it wasn't damaged more."

Jim started inside the dwelling. "Got to go back for clothes for the children before—"

"No! Don't go!" Sol yelled just as another shock hit them.

The ground rose up, and rock and debris cascaded over Jim and sent him sprawling. He coughed violently, tears flushing bits of dirt from his eyes, and red blood trickled from a scalp wound thanks to a sharp-edged rock.

The earth buckled and heaved again. They lost the use of their legs in the withering, frightening shaking. Before another hour was over, Sol and Hiram hitched up their rig, said their goodbyes, and hurried north toward Bedford County, Tennessee worried about their own family.

Mack, disheveled and covered with dirt, was the first to arrive at the Kimsey farm. "You look like you survived except for that wall and the cut on your head." He gestured toward his friend.

Jim only grunted. "How'd you fare?"

"Lost it all. The family's good, but the cabin's off its foundation. I'll have to rebuild. I think there's enough salvageable to redo it though. Jacob and Lizzie are okay. They lost their chimney, but Nancy and English lost everything too." Mack looked beaten.

"We will begin again, my friend. Do not worry." Jim sighed.

The initial quake was December 16, 1811, but the aftershocks continued for the next two months through February 7, 1812. When the *Nashville Review* was back up and running, settlers read about the horror of "The Missouri devastation at New Madrid" that had been witnessed firsthand in Alabama. The earthquakes were felt all the way to Washington, DC.

The Kimsey, McCracken, Simpson, and English families covered their wagons again with canvas and lived out of them until the earth settled and they could rebuild their broken homes.

* * *

By summer, most in the settlement had rebuilt and resumed planting. The earth quieted, with only an occasional quiver to remind them how lucky they were to be alive. Cotton, tobacco, and corn grew again, causing money to flow from buyers shipping down the Mississippi River. Business picked up, and fields of cotton stretched for miles.

Huntsville grew as Jim figured it would. With Athens on the west and New Market on the east, it didn't take long for the fertile land of the Tennessee River Valley to grow substantially in the next years. It was a land rush stirred by the demand for more cotton and more profits for the farmers and speculators.

The families reaped the fruit of their labors and applied for loans at Farmers and Merchants Bank, chartered in 1817, to purchase more land. Mack's eldest sons, John and William, bought land west in Limestone County and produced hundreds of acres of the finest cotton. But by 1818, the bottom fell out, trade dried up, prices fell, folks defaulted on their loans, and the city of Huntsville sold four hundred thousand acres out from under its farmers to the federal government to defray its loans. Banks failed across the country. Farmers could buy their farms back, but the price was outrageous, and no one could afford to do so. The Panic was in full swing in 1820, and the farmers were griped as hell over the tax bills they received.

Chapter 42

A State of Panic

1819

THE MEN IN the settlement came together in Mack's cabin to discuss the seriousness of their state of affairs. "We could buy slaves if we had the capital," his son John suggested.

Jim stood to talk. "That practice is loathsome and not something we would do. We have always relied on our own strength to farm our lands."

Even though he heard himself say it, Jim wasn't sure anymore, looking around at his friends and family. Slavery was a bone of contention among the settlers as many of them had brought their workforce with them when they migrated to Madison County. The 160 acres he had inherited from his father, Jamie, in 1805 was a hell of a lot of land to work. He was still young enough to bear the burden on his own, but his children were very little and he relied on others to help him plant—and especially harvest. Mack's oldest children were working alongside their father, but some were marrying and setting up their own farms.

Jim's glance fell on his dearest friend, and while he hated admitting it, Mack's health wasn't that good. Both he and Mollie were in their sixties, and his youngest was, at twelve, as hardworking as the rest.

Mack's health had grown worse with the loss of his land. He coughed more, was short of breath often, and wanted to give up even when Jim encouraged him. Mollie did what she could for her husband, and John took on more of the responsibility.

It pained Jim to say this in front of them all, "I think we should leave this place," but he said it. There was a sudden chill in the hearts of the farmers who may have thought it, but no one wanted to concede they were defeated. The panic was out in the open.

In the morning, Jim walked the entire perimeter of his farm. Dew sparkled on his cotton and tobacco plants. He stopped and picked off a bug chomping away on a delicious breakfast leaf and started to crush it between his fingers. *What for?* he asked himself and let it go to its repast. It was all for naught anyway as the plants would die in the fields because he couldn't sell his crop.

They had to leave.

Jim did not want to be a debtor, and he had to give in to failure as there was no Uncle Benjamin to bail him out like Ben had done for his father, Jamie. Hard work and prudent economy always got them through, but this time they would not overcome his loss of hope.

The sun rose higher as he walked, and he could smell it: what he had worked for, what his father worked for, his Uncle Benjamin, and their father before them—from Scotland to Alabama, all totaled seventy-three years for his family and untold years of farming before that. Where would he go next? It was all he knew.

Hannah was waiting for him when he came in. As he sat exhausted at the table, she walked over and kissed him in a way that was more than welcoming. "I've something for you," she said with a gleam in her eye.

"I'm hungry, wife, but not for that."

"How about some biscuits and sausage gravy instead?"

"Sounds good. Is that all you've got for me?"

"What more do you want? We already have six children and another on the way."

"How 'bout scrambled eggs?" His broad smile lifted their spirits from the grim destiny before them. He pulled her to him, rested his head on her pregnant belly, and felt the energetic kick of his unborn child. Despite their troubles, Jim was supremely happy and grateful for his life with Hannah.

* * *

Jim and Hannah walked away from their farm in Alabama, getting only pennies on the dollar from the sale to a speculator. They sold the cow, horse, and some furniture for a little money and combined it with what they had saved for this "rainy day." Every bit of their life was packed into the wagon.

On a clear afternoon, Jim unlocked the break, flicked the reins, took his family, and went with their related families—Simpson, English, and the McCrackens—to find a new home where there was good land. However, it was decided that Mack and Mollie would move with their son John and his family, and so at the junction of the north road toward Flat Creek and the Indian trail northwest into Giles County, Tennessee, the McCrackens parted company with the Kimseys.

This very moment was the most dreaded of their lives, and they were deeply disturbed by the turn of affairs. Jim's Pa, Jamie, had met Mack at Yorktown during the Southern Campaign in 1781. When by chance they met again in 1792, the families traveled many miles together and shared their investment of hard work and sweat, successes and failures, loves and tragedies, and solemnized events with laughter and tears. Memories would linger, but there were no words that could salve the inexorable separation of these friends.

Hannah was overwhelmed with sorrow. Bitter in her mouth were her goodbyes to her parents and her brothers and sisters—the worst pain she had ever suffered in her life. It would be a very long time before her wounds would heal.

Would she ever see her family again?

* * *

The beauty of Bedford County, especially the Flat Creek area—a tributary of the Duck River in the Tennessee country—was not lost on Jim. It was glorious land, heavily timbered with green rolling hills stretching for miles. Solomon and his family, with Hiram, stayed along the river on land belonging to his grandsons who had traveled with them all the way from North Carolina. Sol told Jim that when he rolled in, the Lord told him to stay in the area—that they would meet up again and that their lives would change forever.

It was a grand reunion. Jim began to see they still had a lifeline of support, so they stayed and prayed for guidance in their decision to move on. The answer came with word sweeping Tennessee, Kentucky, Virginia, and North and South Carolina, that the territory west of the Mississippi River and north of the Missouri River was opening to settlement. The Baptists were intruding on French and Spanish Romanism, gathering converts, and in 1816 had founded a church. They were followed by Presbyterians and others with rumors that statehood was in the wind.

Despite Jim's lingering sadness at the loss of their friends, he was itching to build a new farm, and this desire made him happy with the thought of pushing farther west into unknown territory.

"What do you think, Hannah? There are Baptists there."

"I don't mind, dear heart, but our newest addition is about to be born." Her pains were coming in quick succession, and Jim's sister Lizzie was by her side.

A hastily built tent was put up, fires were started, and water was boiled. The labor was intense and long, and Hannah's screams grated on the men's nerves. Some went off to hunt, and others rearranged wagon contents. The women prepared food, and suddenly there was the thin wail of a newborn. Jim and Hannah's seventh child was named Edna.

"Another girl!" cried thirteen-year-old Sam. "Nuts!"

"Nuts!" repeated seven-year-old Johnny. "I don't want another sister, Pa. Can't you take it back?"

"No, son. That's not the way it works." Jim gushed as he held the new pride and joy of his family in his arms, rocking her gently. He sat on the wagon's tailgate and was besieged by an outpouring of motherly affection from his four daughters. Three-year-old Achsah[35] Jane crawled up next to her daddy to see better and to touch the new baby. It looked like her own doll, but it was different—it moved.

There was a lull in the drive to move on while Hannah recovered and the child grew in strength. During that time, the families again discussed the issues around moving on or staying put. There was nothing at all wrong with their beautiful surroundings, and many would have to make that decision, but Jim wasn't satisfied with staying where they were.

There was something else. It was early August, and Jim longed to follow the sun. "Who wants to walk with me?"

Hannah was nursing Edna in the wagon. The older children were busy playing a game, and the two youngest were sound asleep in the grass on the warm summer evening.

Jim's second son volunteered. "I'll go, Pa." Young Johnny took his father's hand, and they headed off toward a likely hill to hike. It was reminiscent of the old days when he walked with his own father, Jamie. How he loved the intimacy.

It was a good walk up to the heights, and the boy was getting tired. Jim picked him up and put the youngster on his shoulders. When they reached the top, the view was something Jim had never envisioned. He reeled as if intoxicated and nearly fell, almost dropping his son.

"That's where we're supposed to be, Johnny," he said, pointing.

"Where, Pa? I don't see anything but a bunch of old hills off in the distance."

"Yes, boy, I know. But there we must go."

---

[35] Achsah (ak'-sa): 1 Chronicles 2—"She also bore Shaaph, the father of Madmannah, Sheva, the father of Machbenah, and the father of Gibea. Achsah was Caleb's daughter."

Joshua 16—"Caleb said, 'To the man who attacks Kiriath-sepher and captures it, I will give my daughter Achsah in marriage.'"

Chapter 43

Rivers to Their New Home

FIFTY-SIX MILES FROM Flat Creek to Nashville. It won't take long, Jim said, and suddenly it was time to go. He placed his broad-brimmed hat on his head. Hannah tied the strings of her bonnet under her chin and cradled Edna in her arms. He flicked the reins lightly on the backside of the mules, and they forged ahead.

Hannah tried hard not to cry, but her efforts were in vain when she looked behind the canvas of the big wagon to see family and friends waving. She held up her hand to say goodbye for the last time, and tears washed her face. So many left behind, especially her own family. "See how they cling like baby possums to their mama," Jim had said when he first saw Hannah and her brothers and sisters in that wagon so long ago. And now their wagon was filled with "baby possums."

The white canvas whipped gently in the summer breeze as the long line of worn wood-covered wagons bucked and rattled over wilderness and rivers, trailed past scattered farms, and drove through small settlements and growing towns. Blue-black sky was above them, a hot sun burned their faces, and trail dust lodged in their nostrils. After the bitter loss of their farm, the Kimseys were traveling on with hope for a new and exciting future. They were heartened by Isaiah 30:23, 25—"Then shall he give the rain of thy seed, that thou shalt sow the ground withal; and bread of the increase of the earth...

And there shall be upon every high mountain and upon every high hill, rivers and streams of waters."

Reaching Nashville, they descended a bluff to the water's edge and saw the broad Cumberland River flowing past the city, its fort, and 3,300 residents spread out along its banks.

Jim smiled as he watched Hannah's delight at seeing the large bustling waterfront. Steamboat whistles and shrill cries of men declared their navigational scraps while positioning their crafts along the river. Jim, acting as unofficial captain of the train, bought passage for the next day on the new *General Jackson* and other riverboats that could take the rest of their wagons. They waited in a queue stretching through town. Jim walked the wagon train, giving each head of family their boarding ticket and warning them to be vigilant of vagabonds.

"Our destination is St. Louis, and it will take many days and the difficult navigation of three rivers," he told his fellow teamsters. Sharing his enthusiasm for future success, he said, "I also overheard the captain talking to a wealthy fur trader about trips to New Orleans and the profitable trade in other goods along the river. Keep a good watch, my brothers and friends. Good night."

The dawn was purpling up the sky when Hannah awoke, and Jim's brightly burning fire greeted her as she crawled out of the tent after nursing Edna. This was the day the family would begin the next chapter of their lives. In a few hours, the sun would be at their backs, pushing them in the direction they should go. For now, she washed her face and hands, made the porridge as all the other frontier women were doing at this hour, and corralled the children for their breakfast.

Heat rose with the sun, and they were ready to board the large boat. Hannah tied her straw hat under her chin. The ferryman roughly grabbed the reins of the mules and pulled—they balked at the strange hands. Jim took command of the reins, and Hannah, giving baby Edna to Mahala, stepped down from the wagon. The animals' nostrils flared as they maneuvered the boarding plank, and they were reluctant to step onto the unstable deck. Looking up into their brown trusting eyes, Hannah whispered, "Don't be afraid," and with firm hands upon their bridles, she took them on board. The rig settled on the steamboat, and it accepted the weight. Jim locked the wagon's brake, and stepped forward to join Hannah. The mules were unhitched and penned on the front deck of the boat.

For their reward, Jim offered them apples and Hannah patted their necks. She wondered about the new home they would all create. Jim said it was on the Missouri River, the very river that Meriwether Lewis and William Clark had—sixteen years earlier—navigated in an attempt to find a water route to the Pacific. Jim had told Hannah in all seriousness that someday he would like to see that ocean they called the Pacific, but for now, "it will take many days to get where we're going."

Long low blasts of the steamboat whistle pierced the blue sky as white clouds of steam thickened the air above the boat. It backed away and turned into midstream. The mules started, Hannah soothed them, and the boat left the muddy riverbank of Nashville behind.

That night, torches lit the deck area, and Jim stayed with his rig and mules, and around midnight, Samuel joined him. "Anything happening, Father?"

"Nothing, just smooth sailing. We're traveling pretty fast. How's your mother and the babies?"

"They are all asleep. Why don't you join them?"

"Think I will. Be back in a few hours."

Next morning, a bright sun lit the sky as Samuel and Jim stood at the railing watching the docking of the boat. Heavy ropes were thrown to men onshore who tied the big steamer to sturdy trees, and the boarding plank was lowered. Jim met the captain at the bow.

"Good morning, sir. May I ask how far we've come and where we are?"

"We made excellent speed overnight going downstream. We're in Paducah, Hickman County,[36] Kentucky, Mr. Kimsey—on the Ohio River. We're here to pick up some passengers and mail. Where are you from?"

---

[36] Now McCracken County, founded in 1825, from Hickman County and was named for Captain Virgil McCracken of Woodford County, Kentucky, who was killed in the Battle of Frenchtown in southeastern Michigan during the War of 1812 (https://en.wikipedia.org/wiki/McCracken_County,_Kentucky).

"Originally Henry County, Virginia, but lately of Huntsville, Alabama."

"Oh…bad situation that—bank failure and the panic and all. Hope it didn't strike you hard, sir."

"We're survivors, Captain." The whistle blast interrupted their talk. Jim walked away, thinking, *My goodness. We're on the Ohio River!*

* * *

Several days later, they reached Cape Girardeau, Missouri, having come down the Ohio and onto the Mississippi River. The steamboat stopped again for passengers, mail, water for the boiler, and wood for stoking. From there, the trip northward up the Mississippi would be against the current going north, but the paddle wheels would help them make good time. Jim and Hannah watched the big wheels turning, swishing, and splashing the river's water. Her body tingled with excitement as they followed the twists and turns of the wide Mississippi. They had crossed rivers before with their own challenges, but this was different. It was said that this river went all the way south to Louisiana and in the north—she didn't know, but it cut the United States in half. In half! After what they had seen of America, she was in awe of the notion that there were hundreds, maybe thousands of miles to the west of them—"all the way to the Pacific Northwest coast at the Columbia River," the captain said. It whetted Jim's appetite all the more and was irresistible to him.

It took many days for all the wagons to gather at the shore at St. Louis, but all made it safely and were accounted for: Jim's sister Lizzie and Mr. Simpson; Jim's brothers Littleberry and Samuel with his wife, Penny, and their children; and Benjamin's son Solomon with his wife, Mattie, and their family.

* * *

Missouri

As the long train of wagons made their way west to the Franklin Land Office in Howard County, Jim's mind reviewed his life and those who had preceded him. The green hills of Scotland had spawned a war that killed a proud people's spirit. But a questionable fortune of indenture to the American colonies had presented the Kimseys with a new life and a long line of generations of farmers where miles of rows of crops stretched west from Maryland and now forward headlong into Missouri. The men who survived the journey—Benjamin, Jamie, Charles, and Alex Kimsey née MacKenzie—told the tale to their offspring over their campfires for years, and Jim would do the same with his family.

That first evening as the blue time was about to descend, Jim, his son John F., and Sol stood on a bluff, looking westerly along the great Missouri.

Sol put his arm over Jim's shoulders and said, "You know, cousin, my father told me once when I was being obstinate at sixteen and wanting to join the war effort, 'We arose from the ashes of our homeland, and we will arise from whatever will come. You may go if it is your heart's desire.' I think he's here with us now. He would be happy to see how far we've come."

Jim smiled.

The End

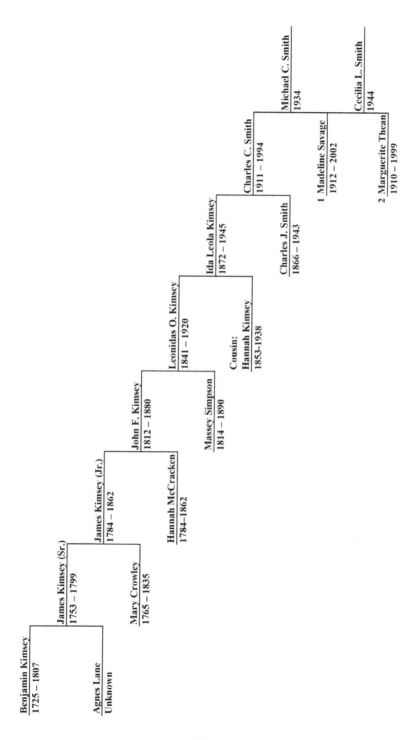

Benjamin Kimsey
1725 – 1807

James Kimsey (Sr.)
1753 – 1799

Agnes Lane
Unknown

James Kimsey (Jr.)
1784 – 1862

Mary Crowley
1765 – 1835

John F. Kimsey
1812 – 1880

Hannah McCracken
1784–1862

Leonidas O. Kimsey
1841 – 1920

Massey Simpson
1814 – 1890

Ida Leola Kimsey
1872 – 1945

Cousin:
Hannah Kimsey
1853-1938

Charles C. Smith
1911 – 1994

Charles J. Smith
1866 – 1943

Michael C. Smith
1934

Cecilia L. Smith
1944

1 Madeline Savage
1912 – 2002

2 Marguerite Thean
1910 – 1999

Agnes Lane B: 1727 Wales
(Aggie)
M: 1744

Benjamin (Ben) Kimsey
B: 1725 D: 1805

Robert MacKenzie
B: 1700 D: 1746

M: 1720

Mary MacKenzie
B: 1705 D: 1746

Alexander MacKenzie
B: 1729

Charles MacKenzie
B: 1731

Duncan MacKenzie
B: 1737 D: 1746

Jamie Kimsey
B: 1740 D: 1805

M: Sept. 1761

Mary Crowley
B: 1743 – Wales

Aggie	Ian B: Jan. 1, 1746
Ben Kimsey	Benjamin Jr. B: Feb. 1, 1748 (Benjie)
	David B: 1755
	Solomon (Sol) B: 1756 **
	Twins Hiram B: 1756
	William B: 1757
	Polly B: 1759
	Humphrey B. 1766
Jamie Kimsey	Sarah B: 1761 D. 1761
Mary	Samuel Crowley B: 1762
	Littleberry B: 1768 (Berry)
	Eleanor B: 1771 (Ellie)
	Elizabeth B: 1773 * (Lizzie)
	James Jr. B: 1785 *** (Junior/Jim)

**Solomon B: 1756
      (Sol)
M: 1775   **Solomon Jr.**
      Joanna Ruth Kimsey

Martha Baley
      (Mattie)

*Elizabeth Kimsey (Biggerstaff)
      (Lizzie)
M: 1805

James Simpson
      (Jacob)

      Samuel B: 1806

      Mehalah B: 1808

***James Jr. Kimsey **Hilah B: 1810**
      (Jim)
      John F B: 1812
M: June 1805

      Huldah B: 1814

Hannah McCracken **Achsah Jane B: 1816**

      Edna B: 1819

The McCrackens

	John B: 1779
	Jane B: 1781
	Hannah B: 1784
James	Nancy B: 1786
B: 1754 D: 1924	
(Mack)	Lettice B: 1790
Mary Smith	William B: 1793
(Mollie)	
B: 1758	Jeremiah B: 1801
	Nimrod B: 1803
	Anson B: 1806

Nancy McCracken B: 1786

M: 1805

James English B: 1787
(Mr. English)

James Kimsey Jr. 1784–1862
Birth 30 MAY 1784 • Henry Co, VA
Death 1862 • Dixie, Polk Co, OR

Mother or Daughter?
Hannah McCracken Kimsey or daughter Hilah Kimsey
as identified in the Polk County, OR Historical Society
collections. Compare both portraits taken circa 1860s
seemingly with the same dress and in the same studio setting.

Left to Right:
Cecilia Smith Johansen (author), Marguerite
Thean Smith (my mother),
Charles Clark Smith (my father and Michael's father),
Elizabeth Klatt Smith (my sister-in-law),
Madeline Smith Beyer (my brother's mother),
Michael Clark Smith (my brother),
Arthur Beyer (my brother's step-father)
April 1961

At our home in Los Angeles, Nellie Fay Kimsey, her nephew
Charles Clark Smith, and Sandy. Taken in the late 1950s

Dad and Mike 1992
Charles Clark Smith and Michael Clark Smith

Charles Clark and Marguerite Ann Smith, my Mom and Dad
March 1974 at his retirement from Southern
California Gas Company

About the Author

AFTER THE DEATH of her husband, Charles Kanewa, in Los Angeles, 2003, Cecilia met his cousin a year later at a Hawaii Marines reunion in Las Vegas. She fell in love with the handsome, virile cowboy, and after four months, she took a leap of faith and moved to Hawaii to marry Bernard Johansen and live in the lush up-country of Waimea on the Big Island. After his death, she continued to live in Hawaii for fourteen years, and there she published her first novel, *The Canoe*

Maker's Son. She has published stories and poetry in *North Hawaii News, Freida Magazine,* and contributed her husbands' stories to *Hali'a Aloha no Kalapana* (*Fond Memories of Kalapana*). She is a cofounder of Hawaii Writers Guild and has published an excerpt of her new novel in their first ever online magazine, *Latitudes.*

Back in her home state of California, Cecilia finished her new novel, *Kimsey Rise: A Family of Farmers.* She tells the saga of the progenitor of the family Kimsey, Benjamin, his brothers and their lives as Scottish warriors, prisoners, indentured servants, and freed men to endure in the colonies of America. They lived the dream of abundant land, preservation and increase of their families, and freedom to profess their religious faith. These freedoms were won with hard work and prudent economy.

About the Artist

Gray Artus

GRAY ARTUS IS an up and coming self-taught artist and an Asheville native. He currently continues the corporate work week but longs to be painting every minute of those long forty hours.

In 2011, he created a series of photo composites that really sparked his creative energy. His photographic artwork is conceptual and created with a message in mind—some easily understood, and others evoking thoughts of one's own life experiences of love, loneliness, desires, and fears.

In 2013, he painted his first acrylic, which began his journey to becoming an artist. Just a few short years ago, in 2016, he tried his first watercolor. That same year presented the opportunity to try oils, when a friend offered him a freebie set of Grumbacher oil paints, which quickly became his favorite medium.

Gray states that "each piece of his art is personal, a part of his soul and connected to him in some way." Many times, he's awakened with an idea or a visual that he just can't get out of his head until it's on canvas.

A modern expressionist painter, his style incorporates the looseness of an expressionist, reflecting the joys of the painting process, yet exhibits just enough realism to bring it to life! In between commissions, his current work is a series of North Carolina landscapes in oils. His progress can be found on his blog, and many can be seen in person at the Woolworth Walk in Downtown Asheville.